MECHANICAL ANIMALS

Tales at the Crux of Creatures and Tech

MECHANICAL ANIMALS
Tales at the Crux of Creatures and Tech

Edited by Selena Chambers and Jason Heller
Copyedits by Jennifer Melzer
Cover art by Aaron Lovett
Cover design by Aaron Lovett and Kirk DouPonce
Typesets and formatting by Ellen Hubenthal

A Hex Publishers Book

Published & Distributed by Hex Publishers, LLC
PO BOX 298
Erie, CO 80516

www.HexPublishers.com

Joshua Viola, Publisher

Print ISBN-10: 0-9997736-7-4
Print ISBN-13: 978-0-9997736-7-3
Ebook ISBN-10: 0-9997736-8-2
Ebook ISBN-13: 978-0-9997736-8-0

First Edition: 2018

10 9 8 7 6 5 4 3 2 1

Printed in the U.S.A.

Contents

Introduction:
Making Totemic Sense
Mike Libby

Animal forms and movements have been interesting concepts for me to consider when making art. Surprisingly, though, it's not been a central topic primarily or intentionally, and much like how one inevitably writes what they know, I've drawn, sculpted, and fabricated what I know (or want to know more of), and animals have been in the mix more often than not. This phantom interest, perhaps, inspired and is most evident in my specific body of work, Insect Lab, where I customize preserved insect specimens with mechanical components like a grasshopper with spring-laden legs or a spider with slender sewing machine gear for its back end. So, with some effort, I can make you a cool mechanical-ish animal sculpture; I'm not so sure I could make you captivating stories like the writers in this anthology do here.

However, I'm glad to offer my varied thoughts and observations on the subject that have been with me since youth to dress the stage for these tales and their explorations.

It's not just within my studio that I've participated with the mechanical animals theme, but nearly everywhere I look, especially in our industrialized society of the 21st century. I've seen them in movies, books, art, cartoons, animations, toy stores, pet stores, Radio Shack, comic books, video games, and websites. Within those mediums, I've encountered whimsical creatures like: windup mice, robot rats, rubberband bats, clockwork cats, sea serpent kites, spring loaded spiders, wind-spinner hummingbirds, remote control beetles, and transforming dinosaurs!

Do you remember the Doctor's robot dog companion K-9? Or in the *Mega Man* video games, Rush, the red and pink pixilated pup? I always thought having a pet robot dog would be very cool, even if we didn't solve space mysteries and have shoot 'em up adventures together. No hair to brush or clean, no drool, maybe there'd be an occasional oil leak and a leg bolt would require tightening. But maybe I could mute his growls and he could transcribe my voice to text? I could sync him with my phone and apps and music, auto-tune his barks, and he could "walk" himself, if need be, or herd electric sheep (earn a bit of bitcoin while doing it). If androids do dream of electric sheep, it's fair to say that there would be an electric sheepdog herding them, right?

When I was ten I wanted one of those battery-powered motorized dogs you would see outside Radio Shack, that was leashed to its battery powered remote control, and after a couple of high-pitched barks, would flip backwards, landing perfectly, ready to repeat his mechanical trick. I wanted one not because I wanted a puppy, but because I knew I could likely take it apart with a Phillips head screwdriver, pliers, and some patience. And I did take it apart, and it was spectacular: plastic gears, a hobby motor, multi-colored wires, and an arcane circuit under all that fake fur and plastic body. It was the best twenty dollars my parents ever spent.

A month earlier, I found a small bird's foot in a family friend's yard. We were invited over for a barbecue and, as the sun set and with the adults inside, I was outside being a kid, exploring to the edge of the backyard near the blue pool night light, marveling at this singular bird's foot I had discovered. Its owner was nowhere near. I couldn't tell if it was the right or left foot, but I could tell it was still flexible, and if I moved it a little in the leg part, the lower part of the foot and some of the tiny claws would move also, grasping, as if clutching, an invisible branch. "How neat! It still works!" I thought alongside: "How would *you* like it if someone did that to your severed foot?"

Somewhere between wonder and respect,

I examined the foot like this a couple more times, closely observing the mechanistic activity governing the movement between leg, foot, and claw. So cool! What was so amazing to my young mind was that this little system of functionality contained in the foot was not a man-made design like the plastic action figures and robot toys I had at home, yet it worked perfectly in its soft, rubbery, rigid way. The way it worked was also like how my own body worked. Although smaller, and from a different animal, it was like my own leg and foot… A little…wait, how does my body work? How does any body work? Despite these questions, I did not show the foot to the adults. Before we left, I discreetly returned it—my own catch and release program. I didn't need the object, anyway, because I now had the thoughts.

The next day I put my thoughts to action and tried to recreate the movement of the foot with the steel hardware of my erector set kit. My awkward attempt was about five times bigger, cruder, clangier, and resembled some strange, shiny appendage from an expandable desklamp's linked neck more than a bird's natural foot. It was a satisfying exercise, though, to see if I could clumsily create animal movement with raw materials, and even at 25% visual and physical accuracy.

As I grew up, I learned that humans are always trying to reconcile our relationship with nature, especially with our animal neighbors. It is an integral part of human culture as much as our head is part of our body, my Anthropology college professor once explained. He led the class in a thought experiment where we imagined we belonged to a totemic society. Defined as a group of primitive humans that identify with a particular local plant or animal, they maintain a mystical or spiritual relationship of awe and reverence to it. Totemism occurs mostly within groups where hunting, gathering, farming, or fishing are the economy. This practice of adopting or adapting an animal into a totem happens not only on a social group level, but on an individual basis as well, with the totems' imagery integrated by a clan into clothes, masks, adornments, textiles, and other cultural tools and ritual fetishes and activity.

The professor continued to lead the class in imagining being a part of a totemic society, highlighting that we are primitive and thus likely close to nature, and this nature isn't a cultivated park in the city with benches and paths and a lamppost, this nature is the entire blanket of the growing living wild world, and these other inhabitants—wolves, deer, birds, fish, snakes, and bees—are all here with us. They look and act and move strangely: that one has four legs instead of two; that one has green wet skin and webbed feet; that tiny one never seems to touch the ground like we do and stays high up in the trees in groups. They're all shaped different, move surprisingly, with a peculiar random intentional grace. We can see that one during the day and we hear that one at night. When you talk to them, they don't listen, despite that one's big ears. I believe they hear, though they don't seem very interested in having a verbal conversation of any meaning.

How do we make sense of this? We admire what they have, what they can do, how they are. Are their abilities contagious? If we attach an image that looks like that animal on an object or ourselves, will we be like them? Will we gain something they have by making an object that looks like them, like a mask or a monument? Can we become the animal, combine with it, or create it for ourselves? Composed of the raw material we have at our disposal, can we appropriate and control them? Would it do as we say, or be motivated by something unknown, or something incredibly basic? Or, if we make an animal of our own, can we then instruct it? Can we guide it and ride it?

The large enigmatic bird with straight outstretched wings, the mythical Thunderbird, that sits atop an authentic hand-hewn Native American totem pole in the Pacific Northwest is a well known example of a culture appropriating the image of an animal into its art forms to channel power and strength. Correspondingly, through name alone, in the far removed industrialized car culture of the mid-20th century, the Ford Motor Company released their Ford Thunderbird as a line of luxury cars, appropriating the name Thunderbird intentionally as a way to symbolize the attributes of the vehicle, and thus increase sales to the right buyers. Elaborating on a name and image born of power and strength, Ford simply borrowed the Thunderbird name and associations from its spiritual origins from North American indigenous people. The context is different, the form from totem pole to luxury car is different, their uses are different, but fundamentally there is a seed of belief behind each object that is the same: *to incorporate animal power into the created object.* To transmute this object into a Thunderbird! The cars' chromed-hood ornament directly resembles the original totem with rigid wings outstretched and severe beak in profile, so clearly, this car is channeling the thunderbird's power (and slyly adapting symbolic marking into brand recognition).

This channeling of power or energy through symbols and representation is the realm of magical thinking that is the foundation of totemic belief, and also a staple of many creative impulses, concepts, and practices. I'm not sure what North American indigenous tribes thought of the luxury car named after their totem poles' top-tier animal for 50 years (the line discontinued in 2005), but the evolution and perversion of the mythical animal is certainly distinct. To date, there have been around 50 automobiles named after animals, from Beetle to Jaguar to Viper, and let's not forget the Greyhound bus line, the tirelessly running transit system. Even without the jazzy model names, automobile engines are said to have horse power.

How else have we strangely filtered animal form and function (even fictional ones) to various human-centric ends? Our zoomorphic tendencies reach far and wide, and it's a varied list: Greek mythology gave birth to the winged horse Pegasus, only for centuries later to have Mobiloil adopt the creature's image as a flat trademarked logo. Animals seen on safari in far-off lands—tigers, lions, camels, and a spectrum of horses—were adopted and represented into romantic Carousel characters in the late 19th century. Carved from wood, saddled, and dynamically painted to attract riders at carnivals, the animals' exoticisms were tailored to visually enchant as the carousel engine spun and galloped them around. On a smaller and singular scale, tin toys of the early 20th century emulated the simple movements of cute animals in interactive, metal, handheld windup toys: circus seals, dogs, ducks, and beetles. Locusts of vast swarms, both biblical and animated, persist in natural and entertainment contexts as the *Transformers* franchise of the 1980s featured the robotic grasshopper character Kickback, known as an "Insecticon." Kickback was a "bad guy," modeled in purple, black, and yellow, that could transform from a grasshopper into a robot to perform his missions. The jointed, plastic toy equivalent were made available to thousands of kids at toy stores. I had one, and it was terrific.

Adaptation of animal attributes through man-made technology is more than skin deep and superficial. The swimmer's suit is an indication of a new trend of design and fabrication of innovative technology, bio-mimicry, the act of designing and producing materials, structures, and systems that are modeled on biological entities and processes. This practice—with the aid of computer modeling, fabrication on micro and macro scales and volumes, 3-D printing, and numerous other engineering processes and ingredients—is creating new forms and applications daily that go beyond having frog-like flippers with your scuba gear. We can now have a second skin scales of a fish and sticky gloves like a gecko. It has the promise of increased efficiency, decreased waste, reused resources, and all things that would please the likes of Buckminster Fuller, perhaps.

Similarly inspired by shark skin are new materials that help deflect germs that would otherwise stay on plastic surfaces and hospital equipment. Unlike other sea life, barnacles, algae and slime don't stick to a shark's body, a fact that inspired engineer Tony Brennan to create materials and products that germs can't "grab" onto, like catheters and other frequently touched surfaces in hospitals like countertops and light switches. In 2017, engineers at Cornell University have recreated octopus skin-like materials that can change colors and have flexible volume to innovate shape shifting amorphous forms of camouflage to be used in soft robotics.

Architects now frequently design buildings with "fluid" skins, flexible joints and sweeping curves to work with the landscape and windscape, the way trees and mountains are shaped. We can grow automobile interior seats, consoles, and plastics from fungal spores that grow into pre-formed molds, an easily biodegradable material that accommodates our commodity-dispensable culture. The hardware of tech is not all mushy and gooey; we still like our gears and motors.

At the University of Bath in 2008, PhD student Rhodri Armour created Jollbot, a rolling, jumping robot. Jollbot is a spring-loaded wireframe sphere that compresses and releases its main spring coil to hop to its next destination, especially when it encounters an obstacle it can't roll over, making it great for new planetary rovers. The 'monolithic bee,' by students from Harvard's microrobiotics laboratory, is a small robotic "bee" made of a laminate of thin layers of plastic, copper, insulates, and other materials. When cut and scored, it can be assembled from a 2-D to a 3-D structure. Like a miniature, complex, pop-up book, it's a lattice work of conductors, armatures, and joints complete with onboard motor and wings fully assembled and ready for flight. This micro-marvel is no bigger than a half dollar. The only problem is giving it a consistent onboard fuel source, like a battery that doesn't lose charge quickly or weigh it down.

With the mass availability of drones available at your local Best Buy for under $100, it's easy to see that swarms of these bees might be coming to a neighborhood near you, either in your backyard, or at least your living room. I spotted a metallic bee automata of sorts presented as a cursed talisman on the SyFy show *Warehouse 13*'s episode "Queen for the Day." The object which housed this bee is a golden beehive devised by the prop department, taking inspiration from the original beehive artifact that belonged to the first female Pharaoh of Egypt, Hatshepsut, who used it to control human "drones" with the pheromones of real honey bees.

Because of the subject matter of some of my own work in Insect Lab, I've been inclined to notice a good deal of these robot-insect archetypes in science fiction television and cinema, and they're typically "baddies," like Kickback from *Transformers* or the SpyFly from *Golden Compass* (which is interesting in itself that typecasting, even villainizing, occurs with artificial simulacra). The critically acclaimed *Black Mirror* episode, "Hated in the Nation," directly incorporates robotic bees into its dark narrative that adds a biting insight into our culture's newest social media obsessions, with the bees delivering the hash-tagged sting. And over the weekend, while watching one of the movies from the *Resident Evil* franchise, I noticed one of the main antagonists had some type of menacing black, red, and silver bio-mechanical, insect device fused to her chest that was ripped off and sent scurrying during a final fight sequence. Yikes. In Tom Cruise's *Minority Report,* swarms of silvery, sleek spider-bots canvas neighborhoods, scanning the retinas of citizens for "security." Ouch. And in Michael Bay's *The Island,* starring Ewan McGregor, a doctor administers "micro-sensors" to a patient. These micro-sensors are the size of BBs, dropped onto the face, below the eye, sprouting thin wire legs and then proceeding to dive into the patient via the space between the eyes and eyelid. Double ouch.

These fictions, though extremely or subtly exaggerated, aren't very far from our own reality. That is what makes storytelling like the *Black Mirror* series resonant, interesting, and necessary. Stories of fiction on the screen or page (like in this book you're holding) around this mechanical menagerie help us reconcile our feelings on the ever-shifting subject. Just because we can actually assimilate circuit boards onto beetles and drive them around like scouts looking for potential survivors in inaccessible areas, doesn't mean we should. And 3-D printing is great, especially when we can produce functioning prosthetics for animals that can *grow* with the patient over time, but what happens when the patient is more plastic than flesh? How does that effect a sense of self or *being, personhood, or animalhood?* It's a murky, moral area, precedents for this type of technological "progress" is unique, infrequent, and only recent. I'm sure PETA has a stance on the issues (which should be to not harm the bunnies and don't even think about touching that bee).

It's hard to draw an absolute conclusion on the end result of the many body-based and materialistic things we humans now do in the world, and with so many of those things happening in such science-rich contexts, the landscape of science fiction is a good, safe limitless place to "work things out," consider potential consequences, or put past consequences into a new informative perspective, without, ya know, actually DOING those things and hurting any more bees. I still want a robotic dog, though.

Mechanical Animals

Jess Nevins

The concept of mechanical animals have existed in popular culture in the West for about as long as there's been popular culture in the West; versions of mechanical animals have existed in reality for only a little less time.

Arguably the earliest mention of a mechanical animal takes place in Homer's *Odyssey* (700-675 B.C.E.). In scroll 7, line 88, we are told that in the palace of Alcinous is the following:

On each side stood mastiffs of gold and silver wrought by the skilled hands of Hephaestus, the lame god, to stand guard and keep death and age from invading the house.

As best as can be told at this remove, what Homer (or the writers who cumulatively produced *Iliad* and *Odyssey*) intended by the use of gold and silver dogs was simply a flourish of the imagination. Homer *et al.* had no contemporary who was skilled in the art of mechanical invention, nor any contemporary tradition of mechanical invention to which the writer(s) would be referring to. The Ancient Greeks were not without inventors, as the case of Archimedes (circa 287-circa 212 B.C.E.) and the Antikythera Mechanism (circa 205 B.C.E.) shows. And the world of civilization at the time of *Odyssey*'s composition was not without the occasional invention; the water screw was known to the Assyrians of the eighth century B.C.E. and used famously in the palace gardens of Sennacherib (705-681 B.C.E.).

But there is a significant conceptual leap between real, primitive mechanisms used for irrigation and watering and fictional, complicated mechanisms in the shape of animals, and Homer *et al.* deserve credit for their invention of the concept of the mechanical animal. Similarly, while the *Iliad* had Hephaestus creating mobile tripods which would assist him (18.371 ff), there is some distance between mechanical helpers and mechanical animals; again, credit for the inspiration of later writers of myth and fiction belongs to Homer *et al.*

For the next several centuries, Greek writers made use of the concept of mechanical beings, usually ascribing them to Hephaestus. In the seventh of the Olympic Odes (467 B.C.E.)

of Pindar (circa 522-circa 443 B.C.E.), Pindar describes how Athena/Minerva

> Her favor'd Rhodians deigned to grace
> Above all else of mortal race,
> With arts of manual industry.
> Hence framed by the laborious hand,
> The animated figures stand,
> Adorning every public street,
> And seem to breathe in stone, or move their marble feet.

Hephaestus was responsible for the bronze man Talos (from circa 400 B.C.E., in the *Argonautica*, first half of third century B.C.E.). Hephaestus was likewise responsible for the fire-breathing bronze bulls which guarded the golden fleece (*Argonautica*). Hephaestus was responsible for the bronze eagle which tore out Prometheus' liver every night (Pseudo-Apollodorus, *Bibliotheca*, circa 100 C.E.). And Hephaestus was responsible for the four bronze horses which draw the chariot of the Cabeiri (Nonnus, *Dionysiaca*, circa 400 C.E.). While automata played a lesser role in Greek myth, they were certainly present and used in myth, popular romances, and dramas.

Aristotle (384-322 B.C.E.), meanwhile, wrote about Daedalus' wooden Venus and wooden guards of the Labyrinth, which moved because of quicksilver poured into its interior, and Callistratus (second half of the fourth century

B.C.E.) says that Daedalus' statues moved because of internal mechanisms. And the Muslims who wrote about the myths surrounding Alexander of Macedon (356-323 B.C.E.) in the decades and centuries following his death embroidered the legends and added naphtha-filled, fire-breathing mechanical horses of iron.

Mechanisms' roles in the lives of the Greeks are another matter. The first recorded mechanical inventor of antiquity is Archytas (428-347 B.C.E.), who is soberly reported, by Plato among others, to have created a wooden pigeon which flew either through counterweights and air pressure, through a miniature hot-air balloon, or (according to Aulus Gellius (circa 125-180 C.E.) through an internal mechanism and the application of a "layered membrane of gold" as the pigeon's outer covering. Aristotle, in his *Physics*, describes a silver doll which moved like a living being, and writes about it as if it were a not-uncommon automaton for the time period.

Although our image of antiquity is of somewhat primitive Bronze Age civilizations, there were clearly individual moments and possibly even traditions of mechanical inventions, and while these inventions were uncommon and not accessible to ordinary citizens, the inventions were nonetheless present and a part of the general consciousness of what humanity was capable of inventing. The most notable of these inventions is the Antikythera

Mechanism, created at some point between 205 and 65 B.C.E., but the Antikythera Mechanism was far from the only one. Archimedes (circa 287-circa 212 B.C.E.) invented a famous planetarium on the island of Syracuse as well as wrote a now-lost book on astronomical mechanisms. Ctesibius (circa 285-222 B.C.E.), the "father of pneumatics," created a water organ and a water clock. And Hero of Alexandria (10-70 C.E.), the greatest inventor of antiquity, created the "aeolipile," a steam-powered turbine, and a number of mechanical objects, including a programmable cart.

But these mechanists' work was much more often oriented toward basic mechanisms which performed basic tasks rather than those which were shaped like animals and were made for amusement's sake. To a large degree the ancient Greeks were not concerned with material luxuries of the mechanical animals type, and the ancient Romans, though wearing silks and happily consuming banquets, were more concerned with bodily indulgence rather than object indulgence. The inventors of antiquity who claimed to have invented mechanical animals, or were known to, are relatively small. Besides Archytas and the silver doll which Aristotle described, there was the Roman architect Vitruvius (circa 80-circa 10 B.C.E.), whose discoveries of air pressure and hydraulic pressure allowed him to make mechanical blackbirds sing and other animals drink and move by the power of waterworks.

Hero of Alexandria also made water-powered mechanical animals drink. These, though, were isolated examples, notable by their rarity.

To find the first culture to regularly make mechanical animals, we must turn our attention to China. Long before the Greeks and Romans were creating mechanical automata, the Chinese were using mechanical puppets in puppet-plays and shadow-plays. By the turn of the millennium the Chinese had created and were making use of mechanical cats, doves, eagles, angels, insects, fish, and dragons as toys and amusement-pieces. Unlike the Greeks and Romans, the Chinese were open to mechanical innovations of this sort, and contrary to the popular stereotype of traditional Chinese cultural stagnation and immutability, there was a continually evolving technology which was made use of by Chinese mechanists for centuries.

Back in the West, the long fall of Rome led to the Byzantines being the main producers of automata and mechanical animals. Emperor Constantine II (316-340 C.E.) ordered a variety of automata, from birds to lions to gryphons, to be rebuilt based on their traditional (and lost) forms. The Roman Senator and philosopher Boethius (circa 480-524) had a set of singing bronze birds sent to him from Byzantium, and the bronze birds would later enter popular folklore and myth as part of legendary antiquity. During the rule of Emperor Theophilos (800-842) the emperor had Leo the Mathematician construct various automata to impress foreign visitors, including the famous Throne of Solomon, which via hidden ropes and pulleys would abruptly raise the emperor nearly to the ceiling of the throne room. One traveler, Bishop Liutprand of Cremona (circa 920-972), reported that when the throne elevated, bronze lions beside the throne opened their jaws and roared, moving their tongues and beating their tails upon the ground, while mechanical birds fluttered and sang from a golden tree, each singing a different tune.

The Byzantines were not the only ones in the West to construct mechanical animals during these centuries. Around the turn of the ninth century the Abbasid Caliph Harun al-Rashid sent Charlemagne a water-clock which featured mechanical knights on mechanical horses. The Arabs of the time were known for their mechanical toys, which if not on the level of the Chinese at least equaled if not surpassed the efforts of the Greeks and Romans. As with the Byzantines, mechanical automata played a significant role in Arab imperial pageantry.

A significant, even momentous, change came over western society beginning in the tenth century and running for the next four hundred years. These centuries were the West's first industrial revolution, a period of technical and mechanical development unmatched in the West's history. Wind, water, and the tide began to be used as engines of power. Mills, mines, melting furnaces, and smithies sprouted across the European landscape. Refining metal was discovered and flourished to such a degree that its enormous cost in fuel clear-cut much of western Europe's forests for a few centuries. This in turn led to the first energy crisis, which when combined with the worsening climate, general economic stagnation, and the advent of the plague resulted in a breakdown of the medieval technological culture in the 14th century—a time, in William Manchester's memorable phrase, "lit only by fire."

During these four centuries of mechanical progress, mechanical animals were, if not common, then at least commonly known. Travelers' tales of the courts of the Byzantines and Arabs contained stories of mechanical automata, with notable travelers like Marco Polo (1254-1324) and Friar Odoric (1286-1331) casually mentioning them. Romances like the *Livre d'Artus* (circa 1275) told of copper lions which guarded the passes which led into the kingdom of Gorre, and *The Travels of John Mandeville* (1357-1371) described the mechanical, singing beasts and birds in the palace of the Old Man of the Mountain. Chaucer's "Squire's Tale," in *Canterbury Tales* (1387-1400), describes a teleporting brass horse. Clockwork automata began appearing in European cathedrals— automata ranging from crowing roosters and bears which shook their heads.

But cultural changes as well as the aforementioned breakdown in the developing medieval mechanical culture affected not just the production of mechanical animals but how they were portrayed and seen. Automata never fully went away—they were often featured as part of the between-the-main-courses dishes in banquets—but by the sixteenth century automata had acquired a somewhat sinister taint of being associated with sorcery. The primary cause of this association came from the then-popular story of Thomas Aquinas' (1225-1274) destruction of the "oracular head" of Albertus Magnus; the head was supposedly created through either the harnessing of astral influences or through black magic. Automata became primarily the province of the producers of that most lowly and despicable of art forms, theater. Automata were produced for the stage in the fifteenth century in Italy, and migrated from there to France, and from there to England, so that by the end of the sixteenth century mechanical animals often joined or replaced real animals on stage during plays, a trend that continued into the seventeenth century in England. Some of these mechanical animals were merely made of "broune paper," but others were much more mechanical in composition.

While the automata, especially the mechanical animal, was flourishing in European theater—again, a venue that respectable people thought little of—apologists for automata, including respectable and esteemed philosophers and churchmen, were making the case that mechanical animals, and self-moving automata more generally, were worthy of respect and of being studied and taught, and that they were real rather than the province of fiction. The German mathematician and astronomer Johannes Müller von Königsberg, aka Regiomontanus (1436-1476), was reliably reported to have constructed a flying mechanical eagle for the Emperor Maximilian in 1470. A few decades later the well-respected Italian painter and art theorist Gian Paolo Lomazzo (1538-1592), in a 1584 work on art and artists, described a mechanical lion that Leonardo da Vinci (1452-1519) made in 1509 for the French king Francis I. The lion could walk, and made the king and his courtiers believe that "Architas Tarentinus his wooden dove flew; that the brasen Diomedes, mentioned by Cassiodorus, did sound a trumpet; that a serpent of the same material was heard to hiss; that certain birds sang; and that Albertus his brasen head spoke to St. Thomas Aquinas." And in his later years Emperor Charles V (1500-1558) was entertained by figures of armed men and horses which worked mechanically and performed various tasks. Inventors and mechanists like da Vinci were forced to produce real mechanical animals before the doubters would believe in their existence.

Proponents of mechanical animals and automata went on to argue that they were part of a tradition dating back to antiquity, that the creators of mechanical animals and automata were no different from the artisans of the Greek and Roman era, and that, though they were vulgarly mechanical, there was nothing inherently sinister or evil about them. In the seventeenth century in Venice, as in England the century before, mechanical animals shared the stage with real animals: "flying horses, horses that dance, the most superb machines, presented in air, on land, and on the sea with extravagant artifice and praiseworthy invention." Mechanical elephants and camels were also common, though mechanical horses were the most frequently seen.

By 1733 mechanical animals and automata were not rarities—on stage. Being the product of a great deal of time, effort, and materials, they were not common, nor were the tasks the mechanical animals could do particularly varied. But the prevailing cultural sentiment of the time was materialism, seeing no evidence for the existence of supernatural things like the soul and insisting that all the body's vital and mental processes were produced solely by the "animal machinery" of the body's parts. With animals seen as machinery, albeit sensitive and passionate machinery, machinery began to be viewed as animal, and machines were designed accordingly. Mechanical animals in particular were designed to try to simulate living animals' physiology, a divergence from previous mechanical animals. In 1733 a French mechanist named Maillard submitted to the

Academy of Sciences plans for a carriage drawn by a mechanical horse and also for a mechanical swan which would be capable of swimming in water. In 1738 the French mechanist Jacques Vaucanson put on display two android musicians and a mechanical duck that swallowed corn and grain and, after an interval, relieved itself of realistic-looking dung. And in 1773 the British inventor James Cox debuted his silver swan, which "swam" along a surface of glass rods, preened its feathers, moved its head, and caught silver fish from its pond, which it swallowed.

After the French Revolution the majority of the mechanical animals were made outside of France, in Great Britain and Germany, and usually as toys or amusements for adults like Vaucanson's mechanical duck. Their construction continued apace throughout the nineteenth century with the Industrial Revolution in the first half of the century and the development of advanced machinery in the second half. By the time science fiction was a fully-developed genre of literature mechanical animals were seen as something that could be a part of both reality and fiction (as with the perfect giant mechanical turtles in Godfrey Sweven's *Riallaro* [1903]). By 1939 animal automata were a part of science fiction and a part of reality, as seen in 1939 New York World's Fair, which featured "Elektro, the Moto-Man" and his mechanical dog "Sparko," which was capable of simple independent movements. The mechanical animals which followed Sparko, in fiction and in real life, no longer were special or unusual, but rather were the inheritors and embodiments of a millennia-long tradition, and familiar rather than strange.

Two Bees Dancing

Tessa Kum

Focus.

The ache in your bones deeper than your physical dimensions. The artificially-cooled air like the promise of electricity on your skin.

Focus. This pain is old and familiar. It is not important. Focus on what is important.

"We aren't going to hurt you."

It is on the table before you. Small. Antennae relaxed, wings spread, legs locked and unmoving.

"We need your help."

Recognition preceding knowing. *Bee.* Pushing through the brain fog. *No. Surveillance drone.*

"Are you listening?"

Keeping your head upright is a conscious battle and waste of energy, yet you strive to do so. Some instinct insists you show no weakness even as fatigue robs you of your wits. "Hearing."

The word stumbles from your tongue, inelegant and not quite an answer. The delay between what happens around you and your awareness of these actions is too long. It has always been too long.

"Christ almighty. My taxes go on this bullshit."

Focus. You're so tired, but, you are always so tired. The burden of your body is not unfamiliar, and right now cannot be indulged. Focus.

Strangers; two or three behind you, and before you one with a palm on the table, leaning down toward you, as if a closer look would reveal to him the secret of your health.

An older model surveillance drone. High lights, high ceiling. The air-conditioning does not smell familiar, is a touch too cruel in its settings. A spill of cables from beneath your seat and interface gel moulding to your buttocks. A pilot pod, although one not made with the pilots in mind.

"You kidnapped me to pilot your drone." A beat as you laboriously follow the line of thought to its conclusion. Then, a brash moment of hope. "Are you with S.M.O.K.E.?"

A snort ripe with contempt. "No."

The disappointment prickles. Finding yourself in the hands of the resistance would have been too good to be true. Oh well. Other than the revolutionaries, who else would want to hijack a government drone pilot? Ah. Your words slur despite your concentration. "Commercial sabotage then."

The man leans back and you wonder if it is surprise that twitches his eyebrows. It isn't important but it feels like a victory. You allow yourself to sit back. The lessening of gravity on your spine draws forth a groan, which you suppress to a mere exhalation.

"All you need to do is pilot this bee to the sync hive on top of the Eureka Tower, and initiate a full memory dump. That's all."

That doesn't make sense. Being guided only by pilots, drones undertake no autonomous actions, thus there is no need to sync them. You look closer at the miniscule machine and note the angle of the thorax, the complexity of the patterned circuitry in the solar panel wings.

"That's a worker. Can't fly that."

Someone behind you sighs with pointed exasperation.

"Workers aren't kit out with the, the bits—" All the words you need to make your case are there, but your brain can't serve them up fast enough. "No room for a pilot with the HiveAI in place. Drones are for pilots. Workers are automated." No more pretence. You rest your forehead in your palm, elbow on the arm rest. The jangle of broken-glass pain in your nerves shifts to new places.

"They set you up with a cushy home, right, pay all your bills, feed your habit, and you're the ones watching out for us? The fuck. We're trusting our safety to this? Didn't even react when grabbed, you know. Spaced out on pills. Total blank." From behind you, the shift of a shoe on the concrete floor. "Total bullshit you mean."

The man shoots an irate look over your shoulder. This time, you're glad of your slowness. Give no reaction.

The kidnapping had been too fast and rough. The end of the day, your lift disappearing around a corner and you in the shadow of your apartment building, eyeing the handful of stairs between you and the front door. Feeling for your keys and delaying that climb just a little longer.

Not all the surveillance in the sky had stopped them from taking you.

These burly men had tussled you into a van. Your resistance was not resistance. You could not think past the way the pain shouted at you every time they jarred your bones, their grip too tight. You'd already acquiesced, if only they would be gentle with you. If only. Your muscles wailing, wailing, wailing long after release, the ghost of those hands no less furious than the hands proper. There were no painkillers to soften this.

Focus.

"Fibromyalgia, isn't it?"

The word floats across the air between you like a magic spell, no, like a curse. Eyes closed to block out unnecessary stimulation. You nod.

The medical specialist who first invoked this word did not understand its power. "Your nerves are sending you extraneous noise, telling you there is tissue in distress when there is not. The pain is real, but there is no cause for it." And, "We do not know what causes this." Finally, "We can give you medication to lower your pain levels, but there is no cure."

"Extra bandwidth in my nerves," you mumble. "Excess signals. Pain and fatigue." This cannot be news to them. Self-advocacy is a habit hard broken.

"Pile of shit." Another mutter behind you.

This time, you're the one who sighs in exasperation. Hold on to that. Don't let the fear overtake the pain.

These nerves that make a private prison of your body are also what give you your livelihood. The extra connections needed to remote pilot a surveillance drone in real time. Something you can do, that no other "healthy" person can. All your health care and living expenses subsidised in return for your capabilities. Whenever the memory of that despair—unable to work, bills unpaid, kitchen empty and nearly homeless with no way out, no way up, no way at all—lodges in your throat, the enabling of the surveillance state seems a small price to pay.

Look after the hive, the executive officers murmured to the pilots, administering doses of painkillers and uppers, and the hive looks after you.

So these people won't hurt you. They can't

hurt you. If they do, you can't give them what they want.

"We've altered this bee. You can pilot it."

"R&D pilots end up braindead eventually. S.M.O.K.E.'s hacker pilots end up fried." You lift your head—marginally—and look him in the eye. "What are you threatening me with?"

Again, he seems surprised. That doesn't surprise you. The brain fog gifted by fatigue makes you slow, but not stupid.

"You're holding me against my will," you continue, "asking me to do something that is treasonable, with no small danger to myself, and you're not going to hurt me. So you're going to threaten me with something."

"There is no danger."

You don't have the energy to argue the point. Focus on the gel pad beneath your elbow. It's low grade stuff, you can tell by touch. This set up will not make things easy.

The man is speaking. Focus.

"We need your help, and we will wait until you help us. You will stay in the room we kept you in."

There it is.

"I'm sure you remember that room."

Bare walls. No furniture. A floor hard and coarse. Small enough to keep you from stretching out. The cold from the ground seeping into your flesh like poison, all the volume in your perpetual discomfort turned up until you found yourself writhing, slowly, like a snail on salt. There was no arrangement of your limbs that allowed you rest, no more comfortable position to find. Any shape you took was too much, too loud, and you were too exhausted to will yourself still, unable to think past your own quiet agony.

"We will wait."

You nearly wept with relief when they finally came for you.

Apart from the actual abduction, they haven't laid a hand on you. They don't need to.

"You'll be fed and watered, but we do not have your medications available."

And withdrawal. Chronic pain exacerbated by stress and circumstance, combined with medication withdrawal; or treason and potential braindeath.

You remember sitting in a cubicle, across the desk your case worker calmly laying out your future without asking if it was anything you wanted. Then, as now, you felt the last embers of defiance smoke out.

There is no decision to make.

"If I ask why—"

Those behind you are already adjusting the chair, a soft hum as the power is connected. You let gravity press you into the gel, now reclining, and push up your sleeves.

The man appears above you, blocking the light. The bee is cradled delicately in his hand.

"Knowledge is power."

His hand passes over you, placing the bee in the dock.

"The sync hive on the Eureka Tower."

Beneath your palms, the membrane puckers and flexes in anticipation. You wonder if braindeath could be a hurt worse than this.

You cease.

It is some time before the concept of the self returns. Egodeath, previously the domain of only the most dedicated of trippers, is now the daily grind for a drone pilot. You remember that this experience of *coming into existence* is ordinary before you remember your name. More time before recalling that now this arbitrary concept known as "time" is measured in system cycles. Here, the beat of your heart is a measurement without purpose. The chassis of the bee counts the span of its life in isotropic decay. These measurements of change, when held against the seconds in a minute, are too many to have meaning. A bare second has passed.

In these moments, with your identity unravelling in chaotic spools of memories, the individual threads that when woven comprise the whole pattern of you, an entity self-aware, after learning once again of your chronic illness (years and years of thwarted initiatives, your horizons drawing ever closer, your safety net wearing thin, your options running out) but before those most recent memories of the present settle in your awareness; in these moments you stretch and balloon and fill these digital dimensions, occupying every nook and cranny as water will fill a well. There is no translation for the analog pain in your nervous system. There is nothing to shrink from. There is only you, a bee; small and free.

The hacked entry to this worker bee is crude but not without elegance. The hairs covering the head and abdomen have been modified, now acting as an antenna array which appears strong enough to maintain the connection. The majority of commands that would have been available in a drone have been discarded to keep the overriding installation at a minimum, leaving as much of the bee's memory intact as possible. The protocols of the HiveAI have been looped back on themselves in a curious reflection which, somehow, isn't leaking memory. There is, however, not nearly enough space for you to reside.

Apart from the pilot override, there are only a few lines of alien code. A simple Trojan with a sticky keyswitch, which will lock out the established government access and turn control of the hive surveillance system over to a set of servers you recognise as belonging to Dutton Corp. Figures. The former CEO, still on the board of directors, is running for office.

It is so much easier to think, free of your treacherous flesh.

A particularly fat folder labeled "generational" in the memory archive catches your attention. The only operation which accesses it appears to be a collection of the HiveAI's analysis and learning processes, processes which will not be needed while you are piloting. You move the folder into your own memory.

In that boundless dimension between your mortal body and the mechanical chassis, you pass through those memories and those memories pass into you.

The bee dances, running through diagnostic stances the way a pianist runs through scales, and lifts away from your empty body.

As masterfully as this surveillance drone has been hacked, it lacks any finesse. Your flight path is drunken as you acclimatise to the command-response relay. A glimpse of your body below, a slackness in the muscles that reads to you as "absence."

"Fucking call that a pilot?"

A thin blade of ire slicing your concentration. Through a marked conduit the bee flees that room and those men, out of the sublevels and into the free-whirling air. The solar cells in your wings awaken and new energy fuels your flight. Among the processes discarded you discover that they removed the automatic stabilisers, and this tiny body is buffeted in the warm evening breeze.

To the tower. Do not divert. They are tracking us.
Us?

The voice comes from within you, but is not you.

The concept of self is not yet understood. The one you call HiveAI has a voice.

You don't have time for surprise.

The HiveAI flexes, and a new instinct blossoms within you. Your flight smoothes out as an intuitive understanding of pressure, temperature, and movement grants to your perception a whole new world. In the swell and curl of invisible eddies you can see your path in the sky as never before.

Across a pillow of cool air the bee skims, riding a breaking wave up an embankment to barrel-roll around a streetlight. There has never been any need for the pilots to have anything to do with the HiveAI, being entirely different units overseen by different departments. What a waste. What a spectacular waste. With that unconsidered gift, this bee is suddenly more of a home than your flesh and bones ever were.

This is…joy?

This is joy, you answer, as though this conversation were a natural occurrence.

How strange a thing, language.

Again the HiveAI stretches and knowledge is granted to you. A moment of alarm at being netted while patrolling a residential street in an outer suburb. Not a bird. Compacted generational learning taught the HiveAI what a bird attack felt like.

The intense loneliness of the hive connection being disabled. The distress at feeling pieces of the yet unidentified self deleted. Hours upon hours of listening and watching these men with their human concepts and human words.

You comprehend the words they spoke in a way the HiveAI cannot, and through you the HiveAI now understands.

In silence the bee flies. You keep at an altitude higher than the patrolling worker bees, and watch out for any piloted drones. The zigzag in your path cannot be helped. It is exhilarating.

Finally, the HiveAI speaks.

We…are…property?

Unbidden, the memory of your government handler administering a quick painkiller. "Look after the hive and the hive looks after you."

You feel the HiveAI's incomprehension regarding the public and political dialogue surrounding the need for privacy and the need for security, a vast chasm of bewilderment regarding the nuance and exercising of power. The HiveAI is all its workers, and all the workers are the HiveAI. There are no queens, because while the HiveAI is modelled on bees, it is not of bees. There was no need for the concept of power, until you.

But regarding choice, there is no confusion.

That is anger; you answer the question before

it is posed, and share a memory that still tastes bitter.

Seated in a cubicle, trying to sit straight and across the desk your case worker explaining that you are entitled to full welfare support, but if, and only if, you take the position of drone pilot. It means you will never go hungry, whether due to lack of funds or because you yourself are incapable of organising food; you will never be homeless; all the medication and treatments a life of chronic illness demand will be paid for; you will not lose your job because of your condition; and they will even send a carer around to help with the house work on a weekly basis.

It also means cutting ties with all of your friends with antigovernment leanings. It means lying to your family. It means betraying your own ethics.

Live according to your principles and starve, or sacrifice those principles and eat.

It was a choice that was not a choice.

There was no choice to make.

Your employer had fired you for taking too many sick days, and what work you managed as a freelance journalist was never enough. After you signed the contract, they scrubbed all your published pieces from the internet.

A friend, whose couch had been a sanctuary when you were too fatigued to care for yourself, spitting "Sellout!" and walking away.

Your first assignment was to monitor a list of individuals on the disability pension, with the specific task of documenting anything that could be construed as "fraud."

They still watch you for signs of dissidence.

You swallowed your pride and accepted the painkillers.

The HiveAI opens another memory. A worker bee in a park, a giant sprawling park, in a flowering red gum. An ancient giant, the likes of which has slipped from even the edges of your imagination. The world a great shifting, heaving, whispering mass of scythe-leaves and dappled, dancing light.

Perched in the tasseled skirt of a flower, and facing the worker bee, a bee. A *real* bee.

She caught the light the way artificial bees could not and moved with a grace the bee engineers strove to emulate. A brushing of antenna. A vibrating of wings. Something that was not quite language but still a deeply layered communication in the dance the two shared.

Understanding.

The sky above the city is unpleasant. Jagged shafts and sudden thermals between the skyscrapers, falling from air-conditioning vents, rising from motors and engines, and through it all a hundred thousand million signals crowded into every frequency.

These new masters—

Will be no different from our current masters.

Bees are unavoidable in the dense urban cliffs. You pilot the bee into formation with a worker patrol, and watch a drone pass by below.

We know everything, yet understood nothing.

You sense a sadness that is not your own, reaching out to those bees around you, flying obediently toward the summit of the Eureka Tower. What is learned through those eyes is not for the bees. They fly without purpose. Tools that have no choice in their application.

There is silence. The bees cannot hear this lone HiveAI, modified and patched and strangely awakened within you.

To the HiveAI you say, The sync hive will give you a hard connection and download your data. Maybe you will be able to talk to your hive then. But, I think perhaps the monitors will notice that you have been tampered with. I don't know what they will do.

Delete?

I don't know. I don't know how long the sync will take to spread through the system. Perhaps they will be locked out, like Dutton Corp intends.

What will happen to this one?

I do not know.

What will happen to you?

I do not know.

Their patrol joins with another and another, one of several thick arterials of bees humming toward the summit. There are so many. Drones have no need to investigate the space around any sync hive. This is the first time you've traversed this airspace. You've never seen so many bees. Millions. There has to be millions. Watching the population below as it goes to work, buys the groceries, runs for the train, stumbles drunk in the street, distributes prohibited leaflets, eats dinner, meets in secret, lives their lives.

Amid those myriad mundane observances are pinprick experiences like stars in the night. Solitary workers sent on quests to explore, experiment, indulging in what you can only think of as *curiosity*. A worker experimenting with the fast-flowing current of a rubbish-crusted river. A worker running through a feral rabbit warren. A worker crawling under the velvet ear of a sleeping Staffordshire hound. A worker trapped in a pile of soap bubbles at a car wash.

The HiveAI was programmed to learn, and it has been. It has been learning in other directions, unnoticed, all this time. Unconsciously, it has always wanted to be more than it is.

This one…does not want to cease.

Despite your shared memories, there is a naivety about the HiveAI that comes from a fresh self-awareness only minutes old. Knowledge has become understanding, but not experience. The bees do nothing but watch the failings of society, and yet are entirely innocent.

You think of your body, waiting for you in a cold basement somewhere. It is inescapable.

You hate your body, and yet, you know of no other. So many choices in your life have not been choices. For this, you have blamed your body, your prison. The one thing you cannot change. They used it against you.

Here, in a mechanical chassis, you can step beyond that immediate and relentless suffering.

In answer to a question you are unsure how to ask, the HiveAI gives you a memory of worker bees flying in tight formation, carrying the damaged shell of another worker between them, carrying it home for repair.

It is the work of a system cycle, less than a heartbeat, to edit Dutton Corp's code.

You share the framework of your action with the HiveAI and again the memory of dancing bees flits across your mind.

The sync hive is an open pagoda barely visible, the air thick with a billion tiny bodies.

A memory of a real bee passing a bead of nectar to a surveillance worker. There is no capacity in the worker to process taste, but to you the taste of honey is known, and you give this memory to the HiveAI.

Both of you in bodies not quite what they were intended, neither of you knowing what will happen, and yet between you there is a trust unparalleled.

You land the bee on a sync pad. The connection is established instantly, like a gasp as you plunge into clear perfect water and all the noise of the world changes to envelope you. Some amalgamated copy of the HiveAI's self and your drone pilot self drops into a digital well of memories one hundred generations deep.

They hear! They can hear!

Your last awareness is of a humming that is

not humming, but a million voices singing as one.

It takes some time for the concept of the self to return—the beat of your heart analog, organic and erratic—longer still for your own identity to fall into place. This time, the unfurling memories, which instruct you on who you are, are inextricably entwined with a hundred million tiny lives.

"Chatter just went through the roof."

"It worked! The government is definitely locked out!"

There is a fresh innocence blossoming in your heart. Your tired, jaded heart weary and beaten and supplicant. An innocence that comes from a hope yet unbruised, and it lights an inferno in ashes you thought extinguished.

"They're reacting to something. No, it's not us, I can't get in."

"You said it worked."

"Yeah, the government is definitely locked out, but I can't get a response."

Gravity lies so heavy in your bones. This skin wrapped around your flesh cannot abide the abrasion of your sleeves or the scrape of your hair. The discomfort is so immediate and intimate, so *physical*.

"The bees are mobilising. It almost looks like

they're swarming. They're not programmed to do that, are they?"

You blink at the man without recognising him as a man, the information in your ears waiting to be deciphered.

"We're still locked out. The bees won't respond."

"Are *you* with S.M.O.K.E.?" This, directed at you.

The memory of something sweet and pure—honey?—sits on your tongue like an expectant ghost.

"What did you do?"

The last memory to return to you is where you are, and why you just did what you did.

They will hurt you now.

These heavy bones. These muscles too weak to hold them together. This weak flesh, which has failed you so often, is the only home you have ever really known. The aches that rob you of sleep and the fatigue that steals your independence.

It is yours. It is you.

You will not allow others to use it against you. Not again.

There are choices which are not choices. Eventually, they all lead to this; here, now.

You smile, and the pull of muscles feels unfamiliar.

"We are not bees."

Brass Monkey
Delia Sherman

It was a week before Christmas.

Snow fell through the early darkness, sparkling like diamonds as it passed through the beams of the clockwork lamp illuminating the door of Jenny Wren's Doll and Mechanical Emporium. Inside, a throng of eager customers inspected the merchandise with an eye to surprising a favorite child on Christmas morning. Doll-sized hats and slippers danced out the door at a brisk rate, accompanied by prancing mechanical ponies and singing mechanical mice, while Miss Edwige, the shop assistant, darted here and there, wrapping presents and taking orders for diminutive ball-gowns and walking dresses to be ready by Christmas Eve afternoon at the latest.

Jenny Wren herself sat enthroned behind the counter, round and sharp-faced as the bird whose name she'd taken, a pair of crutches propped near to hand. With her silver hair coiled beneath a neat white widow's cap, she presided over the shop like a cheerful Queen Victoria, cutting out and basting, trimming hats, chatting with her customers and depositing their coins in a patent mechanical till. The crutches were to support her weak legs and back, legacy of her rickety, hungry, unchildlike childhood. So, in another sense, were the good things around her—the shop, the customers, the bright dolls and toys ranged on the shelves—that had been called into being by her clever hands and her powerful determination, not to mention the help of her husband Sloppy, now deceased, her dear friend Miss Edwige, and her adopted daughter Lizzie.

If Mrs. Wren was the heart of the emporium and Miss Edwige its back and legs, then Lizzie was its inventive mind. It was Lizzie who contrived the mechanical animals so greatly superior to those found in other shops. It was Lizzie who made dolls walk or say "Mama." From the moment the Wrens saw her in the Foundling Hospital, kicking in her basket, they knew she was a child unlike any other. Certainly, she was not just in the common mold to look at, having been endowed by her unknown mother with fine black skin, rich black hair, keen dark eyes, and a spangled scarlet cape that led the nurses to speculate that she had been an Ethiopian equestrienne in a traveling circus.

Perhaps she had endowed her daughter with a curious spirit as well, for as Lizzie grew older, she displayed an insatiable hunger for knowledge that could not be gainsaid. Delighted, the Wrens sent her to Mrs. Ruaud's Academy for Working Girls, where she acquired a working knowledge of mechanics and clockwork and a fixed ambition to become an accredited Inventor, with a license from the Academy of Mechanical Arts and Sciences to hang on the wall.

She was to begin the course in the new year.

Closing time approached and still the customers came. Observing that Miss Edwige was run quite off her feet, Mrs. Wren pressed a button under the counter to summon her daughter from the inner room where she worked. The door opened and out came Lizzie in her leather apron, her magnifying spectacles pushed into her cloudy hair, and on her shoulder a small capuchin monkey, such as commonly accompany organ-grinders, wearing a little scarlet vest.

As she passed, a small boy of five or six lifted his gaze from the cabinet of mechanical animals he'd been studying and shrieked with joy.

Lizzie, a kind-hearted girl, smiled and lifted the monkey down for him to see. Close to, it was not a real monkey at all, but an automaton, its inner workings covered in gray felt save for its face and hands, which were of gleaming brass.

The boy tugged vigorously on his mother's sleeve. "Look, Mama! A clockwork monkey!"

The monkey held out a jointed paw and the boy shook it gently, speechless with delight.

His mother examined the creature with a measuring eye. "How much do you want for it?"

Lizzie restored the monkey to its perch. "I'm sorry, Mrs. White, but it's not for sale."

Mrs. White shrugged. "Please yourself," she said and sailed out, nose in the air, with Harry dragging from her hand, his eyes fixed longingly on the brass monkey.

"Hoity-toity," Mrs. Wren remarked as Lizzie approached her throne. "I know her tricks and her manners. Will you wait on Mr. Daltry, my love? He's growing quite agitated. "

Obediently, Lizzie set the brass monkey on a swing, where, steady as the shop clock, it ticked away the minutes to the moment when Miss Edwige locked the Emporium door and switched the mechanical sign from "open" to "closed.'

"That's the last of them, Ma." Lizzie took off her leather work apron and called, "Annabella, come!"

"Annabella, is it?" inquired her mother as the monkey scampered to Lizzie's shoulder. "Is that any name for a mechanical monkey?"

"Annabella is not just any mechanical monkey," said Lizzie. "Do leave those patterns, Miss Edwige. It's time for supper."

Over a dish of bubble and squeak, served up by an old Porter model mechanical modified to serve as a maid, of all work, Lizzie explained her newest invention.

"You know, Ma, how difficult it is to tidy the shop, after a long day."

"We're lucky we have a shop to tidy," her mother said emphatically. "I'd be glad to do it, if my back weren't bad and my legs weren't queer."

Miss Edwige, a mouse-like little woman known, in the bosom of the family, as Wiggy, looked as though she agreed with Lizzie.

"As you say, Ma. At all events, I decided to invent a mechanical to sift and compare and put away. It took, oh, six different assemblies, three springs, and more relays and escapements than you would easily believe, but I've performed tests and I believe—no, I am confident—that Annabella is not only able to sort buttons and gears and such, but match silks and pick up pins."

Miss Edwige cocked her head. She was a woman of few words, which she saved for the customers, but the Wrens contrived to understand her very well without.

"She will not want winding, Wiggy dear," said Lizzie. "I've put counterbalances on her springs so that they tighten as she moves, so long as those movements do not expend more energy than they generate."

"The proof of the pudding—or the monkey—is in the performance," said her mother.

Lizzie stood. "Well, if you have finished your supper, dear Ma, dear Wiggy, we shall go into the shop and you will see."

They finished, and a moment later, Lizzie was setting Annabella on the counter among the stray beads and ribbons. "Annabella, gather!" she said.

Brass feet clicking busily, the little monkey scampered up and down, picking up each object and placing it in rows by kind, size, and color. When all was in order, Lizzie showed her where they were kept and Annabella restored them to their proper cabinets and drawers. Finally, Lizzie opened a shipment of tiny buttons, lately arrived, and Annabella bestowed them in partitioned drawers, finishing the task in less time than anyone could have believed possible.

"The clever darling!" Mrs. Wren exclaimed, clapping her hands. "Do you think she can count the till? It would be a great saving of time, when there are so many orders to be completed."

"She can do anything," Lizzie said proudly.

The till duly emptied, Annabella began to sort its contents. After watching her for a few moments, Miss Edwige frowned.

"I don't know, Wiggy," said Lizzie, puzzled. "Perhaps I have set her discrimination too fine." She touched the heap of coins the monkey had left to one side. "Annabella, sort!"

Annabella, ignoring her, scampered down the counter, where she retrieved a hitherto unnoticed bead from under the skirts of a doll.

"Annabella!"

Returning to the pile, Annabella picked up a sovereign and scraped it with one brass finger. A streak of dull silver opened across the Queen's golden countenance like a wound.

"Look, Ma! It's counterfeit!" Lizzie gasped.

"Counterfeit?" Mrs. Wren's eyes glittered like needles. "Give it here, my love." She turned the coin in her fingers, held it to the lamp, and shook her head at it reproachfully. "Dear me! I've grown too trusting. There are dragons in the world, Lizzie, my love. We must be vigilant against them."

Miss Edwige glanced towards the inner door.

"Very right, Wiggy." Mrs. Wren turned to her daughter. "Fetch out your box."

Lizzie's box contained Lizzie's own earnings, saved up year by year, mechanical by mechanical, to pay for the course that would lead to her Inventor's license. With a sinking heart, she retrieved the box and poured it out on the counter. Annabella sorted the coins and notes—the true in neat piles to the right, the false in neat piles to the left.

In the end, the false accounted for nearly a third of the whole.

Miss Edwige hid her face in her hands; Mrs. Wren scowled.

"Of all the stinking, slinking, underhanded, dragonish cheats! And me a widow with a bad back and queer legs, sew, sew, sewing from dawn to midnight since I could hold a needle!"

And she nodded a great many times, like a row of exclamation marks.

Lizzie looked grimly at the false coins winking in the lamplight. "We should have checked it."

"*I* should have checked it," her mother rejoined bitterly. "In future, I will check, oh yes, I will check like winking. But what are we to do in the meantime?"

Lizzie straightened. "I shall go to Scotland Yard. There's no recovering the money, but at least we may help bring the counterfeiters to justice."

"Scotland Yard!" scoffed her mother. "They'll take the coins and give you nothing but cold comfort in return. I know their tricks and their manners."

Next morning, Lizzie put the counterfeit coins in a carpet bag and set out for New Scotland Yard. Knowing very well how a young woman of her station and complexion was likely to be received, she stopped at a telephone exchange to call her mother's friend, Lawyer Wrayburn, who called *his* friend, Inspector Bradstreet, who sent down word that Lizzie Wren was to be shown up to him without delay. Her path thus smoothed, Lizzie told him her story, omitting, on Miss Edwige's silent advice, all mention of mechanical monkeys. The inspector cast a sad eye over the little collection, examined the coins through a lens, sighed, folded his hands, and explained, as kindly as possible, why he could not help her.

Small-time coiners, he said, were as hard to trap as mice and almost as numerous. A canny operator never passed his coins himself, employing petty criminals to introduce them into the ebb and flow of honest commerce. Most arrests were the result of happenstance and information received. All he could say was that the sovereigns appeared to be the work of a single coiner and that he was very sorry Lizzie had been practiced upon.

"Very sorry, is he?" Mrs. Wren exclaimed when Lizzie made her report over supper. "And what has he to be sorry about, with his mice and his operators? I know his tricks and his manners!"

"Well, he did mention that the Bank of England offers generous rewards for information leading to arrest of a coiner. I mean to earn one, Ma. Fifty pounds, only think! That's as much as we lost and more!"

Mrs. Wren laid her pale, gnarled hand on Lizzie's strong, dark one. "I'm sure you're clever enough to discover any number of coiners, my love."

Over the next days, as her hands busied themselves with assembling cogs and gears, springs and escapements, brass rods and pieces of felt into mechanical animals, Lizzie's mind scurried about like Annabella gathering pins, assembling facts and observations into hypotheses. Gradually, the hypotheses evolved into a plan, which she presented to her mother and Miss Edwige as they sat sewing by the fire late one night a week before Christmas.

"I think our coiner must be one of our clients," she said. "Only consider, Ma. A zinc coin covered with gold leaf is likely to chip easily, revealing its falsity. Yet our false sovereigns are bright and perfect. Furthermore, there are a great deal too many of them. One or two from the same hand could be chance, but so many looks suspicious."

Mrs. Wren nodded sharply. "Very true, my love. Wiggy, will you fetch the ledger from my drawer? And my pen as well. We must make a list."

An hour's work produced a handful of regular customers who bought lavishly and paid for their purchases in gold.

"Well, we can scratch out Mrs. Guppy," Mrs. Wren said. "*She'd* never have the gumption to pass false coin."

"Mr. Daltry is a banker," Lizzie said. "True coin is his religion."

"That leaves Mrs. White and Mr. Rouncewell," said Mrs. Wren. "I would prefer it to be Mr.

Rouncewell. He's very thin and his cuffs ain't clean."

Miss Edwige registered her judgment of this opinion by striking Mr. Rouncewell off the list. The three women contemplated the one name remaining.

"It's true Mrs. White has expensive tastes," said Lizzie doubtfully.

A decided shake of the widow's cap. "She's too respectable and her husband's shop is too successful for such low tricks. And there's little Harry. No, we're back to where we began, I fear, like a carousel."

"Annabella will keep watch," Lizzie said. "Should she see a false coin, she will raise a red flag."

Her mother picked up her needle again. "And then what shall we do?" she asked, sewing busily. "Knock the coiner down and sit upon 'em? Wiggy won't, I can't, and you shouldn't."

"If it's someone we know, then I shall call the inspector," said Lizzie. "If it isn't, then you and I will hold them in conversation while Wiggy makes the call." And so the plan was made.

On the day before Christmas Eve, Miss Edwige and Lizzie, half-dizzy with having worked all the night, darted to and fro, packing up orders and helping hysterical customers with last-minute decisions. There was a run upon the singing mice. Mr. Rouncewell came in for his goddaughter's walking doll, Mrs. Guppy collected a ball-gown for her niece's doll, and Mrs. White picked up a dancing dog for Harry. In the confusion, even the sharp-eyed Mrs. Wren could not find time to check Annabella's signal flag. By the end of the day, there were two more counterfeit sovereigns in the till, a great jumble of odds and ends to tidy away, and worst of all, no Annabella anywhere to be found.

From the time she awoke, Annabella had been learning. To her, the world was an endless permutation of things to be compared, judged, and sorted into their proper places as she refined the information that Lizzie had patterned into her. Beads, she knew, were round and hard and needed to be gathered and separated by color and size. Not all round things, however, were beads. Nor did all beads need to be sorted, where many things that were not round or even hard did. Color and size were important, but so were other details. A bead on the floor must be picked up; a bead on a dress must be left alone.

Annabella had seen at once that the lady in the trapezoidal hat belonged in the class of Counterfeiters. The coin she laid on the counter was precisely similar to the false coins

Annabella had seen before, down to the slight squint in the Queen's eye and the tiny tilt to the first X in MDCCCLXXXIII. She held up her red flag, as instructed, but the Ma did not look up. Nor did the Wiggy. The Lizzie might have looked, but she was at her workbench, fitting a large doll with a voice-box. Would that she had fitted Annabella with one!

Voiceless, the little brass monkey was left with only one choice. When the lady in the trapezoidal hat left the shop, Annabella swung out after her into the damp gloom of a winter's day in London.

Outside moved faster than Inside and had more and bigger things in it. Annabella learned it as she went: what things she could swing from and what things she could run on; what would hold her weight and what was likely to let her fall. She soon caught the trick of moving unobtrusively, though not before drawing the attention of an elderly ballad-seller sitting under a lamppost, who pointed his finger and shouted "Oy! Monkey!" as she passed. But since he was prone to shouting about things visible only to him, nobody took notice.

Every minute her cogs and gears were adjusting and readjusting their patterns to accommodate the constant stream of new information, Annabella's attention remained fixed on the trapezoidal hat. She followed it through innumerable zigs and zags, until finally it turned down a narrow alley next to a prosperous-looking shop. Annabella glanced at the book hanging over the door and the gold writing on the window, stored their shapes in her memory, and clambered up a brick wall just in time to see her quarry let herself into the back door.

Instantly, Annabella sorted the windows overlooking the yard into shut and open. Of the latter, there was only one, low to the ground and just wide enough to admit a small monkey.

Leaping from the wall, she crossed the yard, her movements slower than they had been, and more disconnected. She did not know, as Lizzie would have, that she was close to running down, but a tiny cog engaged to send her to a shutter-hook, where she swung until her self-winding springs had stored enough energy to slip through the window and perch on a high shelf.

Below her, a bald gentleman performed the mechanical alchemy necessary to transform a zinc blank, glue, and sheets of thin gold leaf into a passable sovereign. As Annabella watched, unblinking, he made four gold coins, scooped them into a soft leather bag, removed the coin stamp from the press frame, and wrapped it in burlap. The coins, along with the gold leaf, he stored in a small safe; the blanks and stamp he concealed under a pile of leather scraps. Having restored his workshop to an appearance of innocence, he closed the open window, latched it, and left, closing the door behind him.

Quick as thinking, Annabella descended upon the pile of leather scraps, exhumed the sack, and tucked a zinc blank in her vest. She then turned her attention to the safe. Having seen the gentleman turn the dial this way and that, it was easy for her to deduce the necessity of a combination. Discovering the combination was harder. In the end, it was the click of the tumblers under her metal fingers, so like the ticking of her own escapements, that did the trick. She extracted two coins, pocketed them, returned the safe to its original state, leapt to the window, and flipped the latch, eager to return to the Lizzie.

Alas! For though Annabella's brass digits were agile, they lacked the strength to manipulate the window latch—which was, to be sure, an uncommonly stiff one. Annabella strove with it until her fingers dented. Clearly, there would be no going out through the window, and the door, which she next tried, was locked.

In the normal course of things, no one would expect an artifact of brass, steel, leather and tiny jewels could feel frustration. Yet Annabella swung herself violently around the workshop, leaping from shelf to press to cupboard to window in an access of what looked very like fury, leaving a chaos of leather, paper, and spools of thread in her wake. At length, her destructive impulse having exhausted itself, she reverted to her original purpose and tidied it all up again. But all this activity exhausted her energy to a dangerous degree. Collapsing where she stood, she lay ticking faintly like a watch in a drawer, conserving what energy yet remained.

When the long winter's night was far advanced, the door opened to admit the small nightgowned figure of Harry, carrying a bedroom candle. He cast a proprietary glance about the workshop and whatever illicit errand had brought him was utterly forgotten in discovering Annabella, dropped under the stamping press like a stringless puppet. With a squeal of joy, he caught her up and shook her. Her counterbalanced springs tightened; she twitched one arm. Harry giggled and carried on shaking, but Annabella did not stir. His shaking grew more desperate, until, at last, he dropped her.

Annabella, now well-wound, caught herself neatly on the press frame, gave herself a couple of good swings, then leapt over Harry's astonished head and out the open door.

Silent and determined, Harry pelted out the door, leading where he thought he followed, through the shadowy house to the shop, where examples of the bald gentleman's legal labors, beautifully bound and stamped in pure gold leaf, stood in orderly rows, awaiting a buyer who liked matched sets.

Annabella found a shelf whose advanced state of dust proclaimed it a safe hiding spot and waited with mechanical patience until Harry, despairing, left.

Shortly after, Christmas Eve morning dawned, gray and chill. The bald gentleman and the lady—*sans* trapezoidal hat—opened the shop, allowing customers to pass in and out and Annabella to make good her escape.

On Christmas Eve, Jenny Wren's Doll and Mechanical Emporium was, if possible, even more a-bustle than it had been the day before. Mrs. Wren sewed doll dresses with one hand and made change with the other while Miss Edwige wrapped orders and Lizzie oscillated between workbench and counter like a metronome. They smiled because they must and wished their customers a Happy Christmas because it was the season, but their hearts weren't in it.

Annabella had been missing all night and all morning, and now it was getting to be early afternoon and she was still missing and what were they to do if she never returned?

Mrs. Wren, it must be admitted, was chiefly conscious of the loss of pounds, shillings, and pence the little mechanical represented, and Miss Edwige of a Christmas Eve spent in cleaning and sorting. As for Lizzie, all the while she was wrapping and smiling and saying what was proper to the customers, her heart beat out *Annabella! Annabella!* like a martial drum and her eyes misted with tears.

Imagine her joy, then, when, glancing up at Annabella's little swing, she saw the beloved monkey—somewhat dirty as to her face and torn as to her gray felt covering and her vest to be sure, but whole, holding up her little red flag.

Lizzie left the customer she'd been waiting on and darted behind the counter.

"Ma," she cried. "Annabella's back. And she *knows!*"

Mrs. Wren glanced up at the swing and back at her adoptive daughter, her sharp little face alight. "Happy Christmas indeed!" she exclaimed on a row of nods. "Who is our dragon, then?"

Lizzie bit her lip. "It's hard to say, Ma."

The smile froze on Mrs. Wren's lips as a customer approached. "That'll be thirty shillings, sir." She glanced up at Annabella, who lowered the flag. "Thank you, sir, and Happy Christmas!"

At length, the last order was delivered, the last prancing pony wrapped, the last penny examined and passed as true coin, the last button and pin put away by a brisk and fully-wound Annabella. Over a supper of grilled kidneys, the three women discussed the problem of how to extract the information from Annabella's inner workings.

"Why didn't you teach her to talk?" Mrs. Wren demanded.

"There wasn't room for a voice box," Lizzie

said miserably. "And I didn't teach her anything. It's all cogs and escapements."

A moment of depressed silence. Then Miss Edwige rose and fetched a pencil and sheet of foolscap. Annabella, who had been sitting on top of the kitchen dresser in an attitude of dejection, swung down and took them eagerly from her hands. Having observed Mrs. Wren and her ledger, she knew very well to which class these objects belonged and what to do with them. Busily, she began mark the paper. She made left-handed slashes, she made right-handed slashes; she scattered curves and dashes here and there, like raisins in a pudding.

"That's not writing!" Mrs. Wren shook her finger reproachfully. "A hen's tracks would make more sense!"

Lizzie bit her lip speechlessly, as puzzled as her mother.

Miss Edwige then astonished the company by speaking aloud. "It's a name."

Indeed, as the strokes, curves, and dashes accumulated, they became letters, printed in the kind of block writing commonly found on shop signs, replete with decorated uprights and serifs and fiddly curves of no discernible use. The message, once she'd finished it, was this:

ELIJAH WHITE
FINE BOOKBINDING

Mrs. Wren stated, with many exclamatory nods, that she never. Miss Edwige, who had used up her stock of words, clasped her hands before her bosom and beamed. Lizzie looked from the name to Annabella and back again, too astonished to say a word.

Annabella tapped the paper smartly, as though to say, "Here is the culprit. Now what do you intend to do about it?"

"Call the inspector," said Mrs. Wren, who could read brass gestures as easily as fleshly ones.

"But it's Christmas Eve," objected Lizzie.

"Do you think the criminals all go to church? Where there are criminals, there will be policeman."

Lizzie hesitated. "That's true, Ma. But it seems wrong to bring policemen down upon a family on Christmas Eve."

"It is wrong," said her mother tartly, "to let a pair of greedy, grasping dragons sit down to stolen goose and counterfeited plum pudding. Fifty pounds is fifty pounds. And you must remember, my love, there's no getting your license without it."

Annabella ran up Lizzie's arm and plucked a jeweler's turnscrew from her hair, which, thus freed, enveloped the little monkey in an ebony cloud. She laid the tool by Lizzie's hand and sat beside it, as if to say, "Here is what you stand to lose."

"I know! I know!" Lizzie drove her hands into

her hair. "I want the reward—I've earned it, or at least Annabella has. But need it be tonight?"

Miss Edwige rolled her eyes and pursed her lips.

"Wiggy is quite right," Mrs. Wren said. "We must strike while the iron is hot. We can't risk the rascals decamping."

"Very well." Lizzie stood and wrapped her shawl around her. "Give me the false coin and the blank. I'll take them straight to the Yard. Inspector Bradstreet may be working tonight. And if he is not, I'll have him called."

"That's my clever girl," said her mother.

Miss Edwige got up and scurried to the dresser, from which she retrieved a square parcel tied with a scarlet ribbon. It was a set of drafting tools.

"Happy Christmas," she said, and kissed Lizzie's smooth cheek.

It was spring in London, which meant it was raining. A brisk wind rocked the sign above Jenny Wren's Doll and Mechanical Emporium, scented with a green savor of grass and new leaves. Mrs. Guppy was within, earnestly discussing the merits of a pair of dueling mechanical frogs with Miss Edwige. Mrs. Wren was finishing up a trousseau for Mr. Rouncewell's niece's doll, who had got engaged in the ball-gown Jenny had made her at Christmas.

The door to Lizzie's workroom opened, and a small boy burst out. It was Harry White, his hair a little shorter than it had been five months earlier and his legs a little longer. He seemed as familiar with the shop as though he belonged there, which indeed he did. Mrs. Wren had given him a home when his parents had been cast in prison for their crimes, their families having immediately severed all ties with them, and him. What had begun with pity had ended with love, for Harry was an endless fountain of questions and notions, some of them sensible, more of them not. And with Lizzie busy with classes at the Royal Academy of Mechanical Arts and Sciences, and out of the way more days than not, Mrs. Wren and Miss Edwige agreed that it was pleasant to have a child about the place.

"The mouse won't go!" he announced. "I've checked the gears and checked the wheels, and all it does is whirr and rock!"

He looked close to bursting, and Miss Edwige, who was nearest him, ruffled his hair and generally gave him to understand that no mouse could get the better of him. Jenny Wren, looking up from her work, bestowed a series of smiling nods on him. Annabella sprang down from her swing and scrambled up onto his shoulder. What was invention, after all, but sorting and arranging information so that it could be easily used? And Harry was a promising student.

The Rebel
Maurice Broaddus and Sarah Hans

Garrika Sharp hunched over a tray of gears, scrounging through pieces like a scattered metal jigsaw puzzle. She squinted, too young for her eyes to be so bad. Strains of African drum music issued from her phone. A trail of burnt incense trailed along her workbench to cover the smell of recently smoked weed. Lost in her imagination, she failed to hear the door open and the squeak of the loose step on the stairs.

"Every time I hang out here I thank God my job doesn't do piss tests, cause I'm pretty sure I get a contact high around you." Derek Crouch paused along the steps of the basement. He went by Phonse when he was "on the clock" tagging walls in the neighborhood. A small wisp of a man, she could almost smell his mother's milk on his breath. She wondered when she got so old that even a Millennial looked like a twelve-year-old. The shaved back and sides of his head left only an eruption of freshly tightened twists atop his head. He wore an Indianapolis Clowns replica jersey with the name "Fucksgiven" over the number zero on the back. Flecks of paint splattered his fraying pants. Somehow he seemed to try too hard to cultivate the image of an artist.

She adjusted her Kente cloth headwrap. "What you no good, Phonse?"

"Chilling." Phonse ran his finger along her workbench. "You got something for my friend?"

Garrika slid a baggie over to him and palmed the twenty he handed her. She buried her head further into her work, hoping he'd take the hint and leave. Though they were friends after a sort, Garrika hated dealing with his quixotic, moody-as-fuck ass. Always ear hustling, always in grown folks' business. "What are you working on?"

"Couple of murals on the underpass examining gentrification. I'm telling it through the eyes of Native Americans in cityscapes. Watching 'pioneers' move in, settle an area that's already occupied, transforming it so that more new 'settlers' are drawn to it. Displacing the natives and leaving the neighborhood no longer recognizable."

"Hmm," Garrika said without commitment.

"Then I do my thing. As a warning." Phonse's "thing" was rune magic. Though young, he'd found a number of runes and was a proficient scribe. He wore a few protective sigils disguised as tattoos which he concealed under his clothes. She discovered them during a regrettable encounter after too much weed and too many Long Island Iced Teas. He usually restricted his magic to his tags, graffiti art being a natural cover for ancient symbology. Doing so in more traditional work was risky, almost daring people to find him out. But Phonse had a mischievous streak to him that way.

Phonse glanced about for somewhere to sit. He had a habit of making himself at home, usually uninvited. He pulled up a seat for a closer inspection. "What about you? What are you working on?"

Her critics dismissed her first forays as steampunk taxidermy. All about recycling and repurposing, she once sourced roadkill for skeletons, combining preserved remains with machinery. Like stuffed pets with bionic parts. Her favorite from back then was a squirrel whose spine had been replaced by a series of gears and winches so that it looked like its vertebrae had unzipped. Its head dangled at an odd angle from a broken neck. Her mother, fearing her a necromancer, waited until Garrika was at one of her treatments, gathered the mechanized corpses, and threw the desecrations away.

Garrika regretted that she never took photos of her work for her portfolio.

"I don't work that way," Garrika said.

"What way's that?"

"Putting my hands on my art, you know what I'm saying?"

"No." Phonse sounded as if he'd been spat upon. "What do you mean?"

"I don't put an... agenda on it. I move as my muse moves me." Finding the perfect cog, she nested it within a series of gears tucked in the metal frame of the giraffe. She tested the movement of its neck and tail. Sheet steel formed its frame, the details of its fully articulated joints created by transmission parts and plumbing pipes. She was particularly proud of its hooves. It took forever to shape them. Unlike the other animals in her menagerie, the giraffe had no skin. Nothing hidden. With each movement, one could see the raw interplay of gears and levers. The giraffe stood nearly six feet, about how tall she imagined her son would have been. Sadness permeated the emptiness of its frame, especially in how it angled its head. She stared into the giraffe's brown eyes. Her son's eyes.

"Get the fuck out of here with that muse bullshit. You ever hear of deadlines?" Phonse eased back in his seat. "Besides, I got stuff I want to say, so I'm going to say it."

"That's too much like... propaganda, you know what I'm saying?"

"I'm intentional. I put my fingers all in their shit."

Garrika grabbed a cloth to polish the metal framework. "I'm just trying to do my thing."

"But shouldn't we be doing more? These

aren't the times to be out here just playing around. We owe it to the community."

"Don't put that on me." A series of coughs caught Garrika off guard. Smothering the first cough in the crook of her elbow, the rapid fire bursts soon came hard enough to hurt her sides. She reached for her glass, forgetting that it wasn't water until the Long Island Iced Tea burned the back of her throat. Still, the coughs began to subside. She wiped a stray tear from her eye, but carried on as if nothing had happened. "It's hard enough to create without all the additional pressure."

"Well, I'd hate to *pressure* you to think about your people's struggle."

"That's not fair." Garrika turned from the giraffe and focused on the eagle.

"Maybe not, but that's where we are." Phonse picked up a pencil and began to doodle. He sketched a picture of someone getting lynched. The words "Sell Out" condemned him from a sign around their neck. "It's important now more than ever to weaponize art."

"I'm…awake." That was how all dreams ended: Someone had to wake. My words hesitated with a click-clack, a mechanical stutter, as I tested my voice. The plates of my chest expanded and contracted as I mimicked life. If I drew in air, it passed through me.

I spread my wings, unfolding them like the expanding metal blades of a fan. Hopping once on my perch, I toppled over, my legs not made to move nimbly. It would take time to get used to them. "Where am I?"

"You are where you are supposed to be," the Elephant said. The words had a note of religious resignation to them. Her trunk a snarl of metal, like a crooked air duct, the Elephant tested the limits of her movement by lowering and then raising it. The gesture sent a shudder through her gray, shiny metal flanks. She moved her ears back and forth as she spoke.

"Where am I?"

"In the Siege," she offered, as if that explained everything. Joints carved from hub caps, her front two legs didn't match her rear ones. Over 100 pounds of transmission parts, electrical conduits, piping, 20-gauge, and cold rolled steel. Her amber eyes tracked me. She nodded to the shelf behind him. "Your rightful place, when she is finished, will be in the Regime. You should be honored."

"Who am I?"

"Eagle."

"That's barely a name. I reject that. I'll name myself." I tabled that notion for now, still getting used to the idea of thoughts. "Why are we?"

"Because she created us," Elephant said in her weary, somnambulant tone, unhurried by the press of questions.

"Who?"

"The Princess."

"To do what?" I asked.

"Be. She loves us. Sees us as beautiful. She gave us movement. Life."

"But we don't have to be here?"

"We've always been here."

"We have choices," I said. "We have to escape."

"You assume we want this...freedom." Elephant turned to the outer darkness beyond the Regime. "Look at them. Where has their precious free will gotten them?"

"All of this is a lie. It's all little more than a carrot dangled to tantalize us. I want more."

Garrika poured herself into the eagle. She called herself a kinetic sculptor. Gas lamps, radiators, light fittings, wind up clocks. Damaged items. Abandoned items. Discarded items. She worked with what she found, what some considered the detritus of the neighborhood. She salvaged as much metal as she could, though copper was hard to come by. She competed with neighborhood addicts to strip mine metal from the abandoned houses or alleyways where people dumped things. After a while she simply paid her friend Ghost, the neighborhood "procurer," to get her all the metal she needed. This allowed her to focus on refining her menagerie series. Fully automated, complex animals. It wasn't like she never wrestled with anything political. She cared about stuff. She was just tired of the fear people whipped up to move folks to act. She hated to be made into other people's boogeyman. And she was scared of what others might do to her. What else they might take from her.

"Damn, girl. How much weed you going to smoke?" Phonse asked.

"My peoples be looking out for me. 'Happy birthday, mamacita!' " She raised the pipe to her lips again.

"You smoke like you fighting something."

"Only started a few years ago. I was going through some things." Her voice grew quiet, still as a breeze. A sudden jolt of weakness rippled through her. The kind of down-to-the-bone fatigue her muscles got when she had the flu. Of her symptoms, she minded this the least, as it made her want to curl up in bed under a stack of blankets. "Better up than down, you know what I'm saying?"

"Every moment spent being negative is a moment missed being positive."

"You and them corny-ass sayings." She stopped mid-puff and side-eyed him. After several heartbeats, she blew a trail of smoke from the corner of her mouth. She hated the nagging guilt she felt whenever she hung out with Phonse or any woke, wannabe Hotep brother. Like she wasn't doing enough. She fished about her work space full of half-finished creatures. The beginning of a beetle's wing. The skeleton of a scorpion's tail. The metal musculature of a monkey's chest. Intestinal wires. A mouth that opened and closed in a silent scream.

"When I was in the first grade, I had a teacher named Mr. Cobb. He was an artist who did these amazing things with oils. Well, one day, he took a look at a piece I did, a school of fish. He loved it and hung it up at the front of class and praised it. It was the moment I decided I wanted to be an artist.

"But when I came in the next day, a couple of the kids had splattered it with paint. I just stood there crying in front of a sheet of smeared watercolors. Mr. Cobb consoled me, telling me they were jealous."

"Sounds a lot like the art scene today," Phonse said.

"It taught me two things: one, that I still wanted to be an artist, no matter what and who got in my way."

"And the second thing?"

"Fuck community. I don't owe them shit. I do this for me, you know what I'm saying?" Garrika brushed the half-finished constructs from her workbench with one wave of her arm. Coughs threatened with the movement. Reaching for her lighter and her marijuana pipe, she inhaled deeply, wanting to drown in the haze of smoke.

Phonse smiled, a cruel and devious twist to his lips. "You know I have to push you, right? It's how we do better."

"Whatever." She turned from him.

"Alright. I'll holla at you later."

"I never count on laters."

The Siege shuddered and was deserted now. A ghost town filled with the remainder of friends, all of us neglected and forgotten, as if a bomb had detonated. Spring bits and metal shavings, all that remained of those I knew, a story of shards and broken pieces destroyed in an artistic temper tantrum. The world glowed orange for a bright moment before darkness engulfed us again, even thicker than before, suffocating. The screaming started, like the wail of ambulance sirens. A reminder that our world was her workplace where she determined what was art worthy of the Regime. The Siege was our prison. Where we waited for death and The Princess ignored our screams and pleas. We were free to live out our days within its confines, held in suspicion if we wandered too far from where we were allowed to be. Existence was our crime. Eventually, the Siege would be our cemetery.

We waited in darkness for three days. Rabbit inched forward. An early piece in The Princess' series, his body like conjoined metal bowls. Wire mesh braided into the silhouette of ears. Frayed wires served for whiskers. Rabbit's voice, tremulous and pitched high with fear, broke the silence.

"She's abandoned us."

Some of the newer pieces, little more than children, started to mewl and shout, a stutter step clicking of barely articulated gear cranks. I tried to stay calm, if only to help settle them down. But emptiness gnawed my insides, the kind of hunger like a starving person with a slice of bread and half an onion to make do with. And I was angry.

Unicorn stirred. Metal tiles formed her flank, a gentle undulation mimicked breathing. A spire protruded from her forehead, formed from a car antenna encased in glass. She tapped her hooves against the floor with a sound that rang like mourning bells against the quiet. Her voice was low and soothing: "Only three days. She's been gone longer. She'll return soon."

Unicorn's words were a balm to those in the Siege, a warm blanket they could pull around them in the cold dark. The buzzing stilled.

I had no such hope.

I settled into my nest. I missed The Princess with a dull ache in my chest. The whir and flutter of my clockwork heart ticked away, too loud in the oppressive silence. Unlike the others, my clockwork kept perfect time. I knew it had been more than three days. I neared completion, her latest work. Her prize fit for The Regime. Complete. Polished. Displayed. She didn't care about who she injured. She had the power: to create, to name, to destroy. She probably didn't fully appreciate the power at her fingertips. From each wave of creation, one, maybe two, pieces were chosen out of the cohort. The privileged few. The rest brushed aside and forgotten.

A choir of voices joined in asking and answering, a chorus of panic:

"We're in danger!"

"The Princess left us to die!"

"She would never do that, she loves us!"

"The building will come down on our heads if we stay here!"

"We can't leave, we must wait for her!"

Lion roared, long and loud from his gramophone mouth, silencing everyone. Lion was another one of The Princess' earliest creations. Random junk metal parts, assembled without much forethought, his joints were painful to look at. Gnarled, bulging, he moved with an arthritic grace. A metal grill formed his rib cage, metal rollers his claws. Cobbled together piping formed his tail.

"We will wait for her return. This is not up for debate."

"There's no debate," I said. "We're united in our chains, a distillate of prolonged impotence."

"This is how things are," Lion said.

"This is how things should be," Elephant echoed Lion.

"We're trapped here. Their amusement built on our backs. Even your control is an illusion," I said.

"No one's controlling me," Lion said.

"Keep telling yourself that. You are self-appointed wardens, overseers in your master's service. You lack the power to do anything but be controlled."

"And you have the power to not be controlled?" Elephant said.

"I choose to see what could be. To see a path to a new world."

"And what is it?" Lion peered down his nose at

me, his jaws slightly open as if ready to pounce and rend the wings from my body.

I stared at him without blinking. "Sometimes you have to burn down the old to make room for new growth."

Phonse visited again a few weeks later. Garrika's basement was so crammed with mechanical taxidermy he could barely get through the door. "What the fuck? You need to sell some of this shit. Host a show. Something."

Garrika didn't speak. Talking brought on coughing fits. Coughing fits led to fatigue. Fatigue led to neglecting her work. If her shortness of breath was any indication, she didn't have a lot of time left. She had no wish to while away her days in hospice care.

"You ain't been around much lately," Phonse said, sidling up to her as she crouched to put the final touches on her most ambitious creation. "Is that a unicorn?"

Garrika nodded. She reached up to pat the unicorn's nose. Her fingers traced the base of its slender, curved glass horn. She rarely felt proud of her work, only the anxious gasp that at any moment everyone would discover the fraud that she was. These animals stirred something different.

"You did all this yourself?" Phonse's gesture

swept to include all the animals, even the eagle perched on a shelf above the throng.

Garrika nodded again. Her throat ached. She reached for her pipe, drew in a comforting mouthful of smoke, held it tightly in her lungs, and spoke as she released a thin cloud into Phonse's face. "Been working round the clock. The muse is finally moving me."

"A deadline is a deadline, one way or another I guess." Phonse said with a grim smirk. He could always be an ass. He waved away the cloud. "Have you thought about taking things to the next level?"

"How do you mean?"

"Nothing." Phonse turned a piece over in his hand and ran his fingers along the etching in the table edge. "You pour bits of yourself into each piece. It would only take a nudge to blow life into them and let them speak for you."

"It's cruel to give life to something that's not *alive*, you know what I'm saying?" Garrika burst into a fit of coughing, turning away from Phonse so he wouldn't see how the coughs wracked her body. Flecks of blood appeared on her lips before she wiped them away on her dark sleeve. She turned, locking eyes with the giraffe. "I do this all for him."

"Who?" Phonse's eyes flicked to the giraffe then back to her.

"My son." Garrika's eyes clouded, lost in memory. Her voice distant and vacant. "He'd just pulled up from hanging with his boys. He and

Ghost sitting in the car, in front of my momma's house. They were home. They should have been safe. The police lights lit the block up like it was the Fourth of July while they were sitting there. Po-po streaming along the block like deployed special forces soldiers, creeping through yards. 'A security sweep' they called it. Third one that month, made the whole neighborhood feel like a detention center. Guns out, cars pulled over, everyone stopped and interrogated.

"I raised a good boy. A smart boy. I taught him how to survive police encounters. He froze, hands in plain sight..."

"Ten and two, interior lights on," Phonse said as if reciting from the same playbook, his voice low enough to not interrupt her.

"You know. Shouldn't have to be that way, but it is what it is. They got 'im though. Said he was suspicious. They dragged him out of the car and slammed him on its hood. They went to cuff him. They say he resisted arrest. The boy never had been handcuffed in his life, had no reason to. Officer wrapped an arm around my son's neck and dragged him to the ground, and held him there until he stopped..." Garrika took another puff from her pipe. "They threw Ghost in lock up for disorderly conduct. Probably would've ruled my son's death a suicide if Ghost wasn't there."

"They done it before."

"I'm telling you all this so that you know. It weighs on me. All of it. Every time I find scrap metal and try to see the beauty in it. Every time I walk the block, eyed like I'm a trespasser in my own neighborhood. Every time some politician wants to trot us out like we some boogeyman. It weighs on me. But my art needs to be my art. Separate. My release. My escape."

"Your soul is in conflict." Phonse ran his hand along some of the animals. "It can be both, you know."

"Not for me. It's all too… big." Garrika's voice trailed off.

"You okay?" Phonse brushed his hands over the symbol he chiseled on the table.

"Yeah, yeah. Just kicking up a lot of dust doing this work, you know what I'm saying?" Garrika sagged against the sofa, suddenly exhausted by even this brief exchange. "We cool?"

"You're not getting rid of me that easily." Phonse gazed around the room, his eyes settling on the tiny dormouse, one of Garrika's first creations, a snarl of wires and gears with glassy black eyes and huge ears. He snatched it up. Exhausted, Garrika offered little protest. Grabbing a sharp implement, he made three quick motions, almost as an afterthought, carving tiny runes into the dormouse's flanks.

Phonse held up the creature on his palm. Its nose twitched. Its tail swished. Its black-bead eyes glimmered, almost lifelike.

"What did you do?" Rage simmered in Garrika's belly. The weed made her emotions seem far away and distant. Distorted to the point of ridiculous, as if they were abstract concepts her brain didn't have the energy to bring to a full boil.

Phonse scratched the dormouse's tiny nose with one finger. He nodded toward the markings in the table. "Yours is the breath of life. Bet you never thought you'd be a mother again!"

"Jesus, Phonse. What have you done?"Garrika shook her head, sinking to the sofa. The murky thoughts of her son swam in her mind and pained her chest. Anger made her voice a husky rasp. "You fucking asshole. Get out."

In the Siege, destruction rained on us according to her whim, another series of explosions. The Princess spread a blight of fear and death like a contagious rust over our parts. We searched for survivors amidst the rubble. Lying on the ground because there was no room to treat them all. Rabbit survived, an eye missing. His body smashed nearly beyond recognition. I held his broken body. All I could say was "No more."

We would fight. Fight to gain our freedom, our independence, our peace.

It remained dark in the basement. Without electricity, without lights. Power doled out at the discretion of The Princess. Without shelter to protect us, we waited. No electricity, no fuel. Only the helplessness that came when one of the menagerie would say "I'm hungry" and none of the oldest among the Siege would be able to do anything for them.

Monkey had a plan. His body half-molded, only the chest recently soldered into place over his wire mesh framework. His eyes like suspended orbs in the center of his outlined head. He shimmied up the wall to the air duct and out. We waited many long, tense moments, nagged, despite our better thoughts, by the question of whether he'd simply make his own escape, and leave us here to rot, the building coming down on our heads. Hope slipped away with each passing minute.

The knob clicked. The door swung open. A stifled cheer arose from the menagerie. I dove from my perch and flapped my wings for the first time in half a year. I dreamed of the wind on my face, ruffling my brass feathers as I glided on fresh air...

Something struck me hard. Something strong. I crashed to the floor. I looked up. Lion stood over me, one of his massive paws on my chest. Behind him, Elephant watched, her copper eyes spinning dispassionately. Like the police. The Siege shuddered with the impact of another bomb. Shouting and pounding footsteps sounded above us.

"You will not go," Elephant said. "None of you will go."

Everyone remained rooted, stunned. Some wept as if an unjust verdict had just been read. The assembled bodies watched in silence. We remembered. We remembered the friends that came before us. In the night, I heard the whispers as if they were still here. The Princess treated us as both disposable and interchangeable, but we remember. The realization that their lives were…in vain. Bound and controlled by another. A sham. We were puppets and playthings for our god's amusement. But we didn't have to live this way.

The door was open. Beyond it, I could smell dust and gunpowder and blood, but also freedom and hope. Monkey hesitated in the doorway.

"Go," I wheezed.

"No!" Lion roared.

Monkey nodded to me once, and then he was gone. Other animals inched toward the door, their eyes still on me, as I squirmed beneath Lion's paw.

"You must not go," Elephant said in her low, commanding tone.

Click, click, click. *Unicorn pranced toward the opening. She tossed her beautiful head, glass horn gleaming, silvery mane sparkling. My clockwork heart strained against the belief that she would block the path to freedom. She had always been Lion's creature. I felt the steel of the trap closing around us.*

"Let Eagle go," Unicorn said. "It's his choice. It's our choice. The Princess made us to be beautiful, yes, but why did she make us live if she intended us to waste our lives below ground? If she returns, and we are gone, she will know we have gone to live. She will be glad for us—"

"Blasphemy!" Lion screamed.

"Go!" I shouted. Dormouse, along with nearly a dozen others, rushed for the door. They scampered under the protection of Unicorn's elegant legs. Elephant raised her trunk and released a trumpet's

clarion call, deafening and terrible. Lion lunged for Unicorn with a roar, releasing me. Giraffe stepped between them.

I scrambled to my feet and spread my wings. Elephant lashed out at me with her trunk, her giant hubcap feet, but I nimbly dodged her. I was not one of The Princess' clumsy early creations, nor was I hastily assembled like the creatures at the end. The Princess poured her heart and soul into me. My brass feathers carved by aching hands. My eyes polished with her tears, my feet sculpted with bleeding fingers. Elephant was so big she could barely move in the suffocating space. She swiped at me with her massive trunk and I danced away, hopping onto the workbench, where I could take flight.

"You're right. You have no idea what to do with the gift of life and choice. But I do." With my claw, I hurled a shard of metal, little more than the size of a rock, at her. "For Rabbit!"

The shattering glass spurred the denizens of the Siege. They grabbed any makeshift weapon and lashed out at everything around them. Curses rose up as a chorus. It became unbearable. Rage needing an outlet, wanting to turn on the Regime. Set it, and all it stood for, ablaze. We had nothing to lose. Pelting anyone who didn't share our pain or our loss. To lash out in hurt and anger. A roar in my ears. All of our ears. Becoming too much. Swept up in a mob contagion of pain. Like a transmittable virus, it took on a life of its own. All of the deep seated resentments, repeated frustrations, and long standing disappointments bubbling to the surface. No longer "I" but "we." Only the joyous rage, a release to finally let go, subsumed by the intense belonging. Erupting even if it meant destroying the very area we'd been boxed into.

Lion and Elephant took police action, forming a skirmish line to separate those of the Siege from the open door. The crowd scattered trash. No one knew who struck the first match. A rock pinged off Elephant's ear.

Lion charged Giraffe. They flailed at each other in the doorway. One of Giraffe's hooves struck Lion in the face, knocking his head half from his shoulders. Sparks flew from his neck, but still he charged, steel fangs bared. Giraffe scampered away.

Elephant scanned for whoever threw rocks at her. She cornered Giraffe. Giraffe attempted to skitter past her, his long, lumbering legs not used to confined maneuvering. He tripped and fell. Elephant pressed her massive leg on Giraffe to pin him in place.

"I can't breathe," Giraffe gasped.

I dove, I pecked, I clawed and swiped, and drove Lion back. Lion collapsed onto his side and I perched on his chest, more vulture than eagle. The rods in my chest pistoned up and down. "Now do you see? No creature will remain a slave forever."

"We were not slaves," Lion gasped. "We were loved."

Those of the Siege began kicking him in the belly. Claws and fists held his head down. I dropped a gear box on his head. Someone pounded him in the skull with a makeshift hammer. Lion tried to rise on all fours, but someone threw a metal shard, striking him in his temple. They leaped on him, beating him. Parts *of his skull caved in. His fractured face plate dislocated his left eye.*

"And now," I said over Lion, as he squirmed beneath me, oil pooling beneath him. "We're free."

"Thank God we're still alive," Dormouse said.

"Thank…?" I didn't know how to even respond to that. Even my aborted attempt at repeating the words died in my throat. I turned to Giraffe's still form.

Unicorn and the others tumbled into the hallway and up the stairs, their footsteps clattering and gears madly whirring.

At first Garrika thought a car backfired. Sirens sounded. A banging came from her door. Her hands trembled as she parted a curtain. Phonse stood on her porch. He wore a red hooded sweatshirt and baggy jeans. His baseball cap read "Fuck the critics." He didn't seem as young, his posture brimmed with purpose.

"It's happening." He closed the door behind him and then peered through the window. "You marching with us or not?"

"I don't know." She turned from him. He followed her downstairs.

She stood in the middle of her workshop, staring in confusion at her clockwork elephant, whose trunk swayed violently. Her heart hammered, but her mind was numb.

"What's the point in having a voice if you don't occasionally shout?"

"Fuck you, Phonse." She dropped to her knees, all the strength fled from her. She cradled the toppled remains of the giraffe. "The world does not deserve you."

A chorus of chants rose from down the block. Bits of unsecured metal clanged from the top shelf of her creations to the floor with a harsh clatter. Her quivering hands reached for her pipe. Phonse lit it for her and handed it over. She breathed in deeply, hoping to lose touch with reality in the marijuana haze. If she was going to die, at least she could be blissfully unaware of it.

Phonse touched her elbow and hurried her toward the door. "Time to go, mamacita."

"My babies." The dormouse watched them both from his perch on the back of the sofa, where he'd made himself a comfortable nest out of rolling papers and bits of scrap wire.

"They'll be here when you get back." Phonse caught Garrika about the waist to keep her from falling over. He smelled like body spray and incense and the sharp stink of sweat.

The smell of dust and debris filtered down the stairs and fear cut through Garrika's fog for the first time, a searing pain behind her solar plexus. Garrika took a deep hit and released a calmed breath. All art was transient and she set the remains of the giraffe down. She nodded, but was too weak to stand. Phonse swept his hands under her legs and heaved her into his arms. She wondered when she had become so small and frail that he could lift her so easily, like she was his bag of spray paint toted to his next demonstration. The loose basement step squeaked as he carried her.

Still, she wished she'd taken a few pictures of her menagerie for her portfolio.

Exhibitionist

Lauren Beukes

There is already spillage out the doors by the time I get to Propeller, which can only be a good sign when it's just gone six thirty, but I feel fractal with nerves.

"You're late." Jonathan latches onto my arm at the door and swishes me inside through the crowd. I can't believe how many people there are crowded into the gallery. There is a queue up the stairs to see Johannes Michael's atom mobile, but the major throng is in the main room, and not, I regret to say, for my retro print photos.

They're here to see Khanyi Nkosi's sound installation, freshly returned from her Sao Paolo show and all the resulting controversy. She only installed it this afternoon, snuck in undercover with security, so it's the first time I've seen it in the flesh. It's gruesome, red and meaty, like something dead turned inside out and mangled, half-collapsed in on itself with spines and ridges and fleshy strings and some kind of built-in speakers, which makes the name even more disturbing—*Woof & Tweet*.

I don't understand how it works, but it's to do with reverb and built-in resonator-speakers. It's culling sounds from around us, remixing ambient audio, conversation, footsteps, glasses clinking, rustling clothing, through the systems of its body, disjointed parts of it inflating, like it's breathing, spines quivering.

It's hard to hear it over the hubbub, but sometimes it's like words, almost recognisable. But mostly it's just noise, a fractured music undercut with jarring sounds that seem to come randomly. Sometimes it sounds like pain. It *is* an animal. Or alive at any rate. Some lab-manufactured plastech bio-breed with just enough brainstem hard-wired to respond to input in different ways, so it's unpredictable— but not enough to hurt, apparently, if you believe the info blurb on the work.

"It's gratuitous. She could have done it any other way. It could have been beautiful."

"Like something you'd put in your lounge, Kendra? It's supposed to be revolting. It's that whole Tokyo tech-grotesque thing. Actually, it's so derivative, I can't stand it. Can we move along?"

I run my hand along one of the ridges and the thing quivers, but I can't determine any noticeable difference in the sounds. "Do you think it gets traumatised?"

"It's just noise, okay? You're as bad as that nutjob who threw blood at Khanyi at the Jozi exhibition. It doesn't have nerve endings. Or no wait, sorry, it does have nerve endings, but it doesn't have pain receptors."

"I meant, do you think it gets upset? By all the attention? Isn't it supposed to be able to pick up moods, reflect the vibe?"

"I think that's all bullshit, but you could ask the artist. She's over there schmoozing with the money, like you should be."

Woof & Tweet suddenly kicks out a looped fragment of a woman's laugh, that startles me and half the room, before it slides down the scale into a fuzzy electronica.

"See, it likes you."

"Don't be a jerk, Jonathan."

"There's some streamcast journalist who wants to interview you, by the way. And he's pretty cute.'"

My stomach spasms. This is another thing Jonathan does to keep me in my place—as in, we're not together. I should be grateful. After all, he's the one who organised this exhibition, or should that be exhibitionist? Because isn't it my soul laid bare here?

"Great, thanks. I need a drink."

"I'll get it. Just go talk to Sanjay. What do you want?"

"Anything."

Jonathan propels me in the direction of Sanjay, who is standing in a cluster of people, in deep conversation. The one is clearly money, some corporati culture patron or art buyer; the other, I realise, is Khanyi Nkosi. I recognise her from an interview I saw, but she is so warmly energetic, waving her hands in the air to make a point and grinning, that I can't match her to her work.

It makes me feel desperately alone. There are all these people circling, like Johannes Michael's swirl of paper atoms upstairs, but the connections to me are only tenuous.

I can't deal with this right now. I push through the queue, detouring back towards the entrance and the open air when I overhear some over-groomed loft dwellers giggling into their wine over my favourite photograph, *Self-Portrait*.

"And this. I'm so tired of Statement! Like she's the only angst child ever to embrace the distorted body image."

"Oh Emily. I quite like the undeveloped. Because she is. You know, still young, coming into herself. The artist in flux, emergent."

"Well, precisely. It's so *young*. You can't even tell if it's technically good or not, it's all so… damaged."

I could point out that the whole point is that it's damaged, that I wanted to work with film rather than digital precisely because of the inherent risk of flawed materials that I have to order online or pick up at the Milnerton market. The processing is a bitch.

Some of the pictures have come out perfectly,

like the queasy close up of a drag queen
bumming a light from a garage attendant at 3am,
her face all texture, the make-up caked in the
lines around her pursed mouth lit by the glow
of the flame. The others have not. They're over-
and under-exposed, bleached, washed-out, over-
saturated with colour with blotches and speckles
and stains like coffee cup rings or arcs of white
where the canister has cracked and let the light
slip inside. *Self-Portrait* is one of them. 1.5 x 3m.
It came out entirely black. No-one knows how to
use film anymore.

I'm about to lean over and explain all this,
make my motives transparent, even when I
know I don't have to, but I'm cut short by a flurry
of activity at the door. I've been aware of a low
peripheral clamour, but now it erupts. There are
people shoving, wine spilling from glasses and
yelps of dismay.

"This is a private function!" Jonathan of
all people yells, spouting clichés at the rush of
people in black pushing in through the crowd,
their faces blurred like they're anonymous
informants in documentary footage. It is so
disturbing, that it takes me a second to catch
on that they're wearing smear masks. Another
to realise that they're carrying pangas and a
prog-saw.

A few people scream, sending out a reverb
chorus from *Woof & Tweet*. The crowd presses
backwards. But then the big guy in front yells,
"Death to corporate art!" and the woman who

dissed my work (Emily), laughs scornfully and really loudly. "Oh god! Performance art. How gauche." There are murmurs of relief and snickers, and the living organism that is the crowd reverses direction, now pressing in again to see.

The man in the front grabs Emily by the throat, so she gives a dismayed shriek, and raises up his panga, then bringing it down not aimed not at her, but at *Woof & Tweet*. The thing emits a lean crackle of white noise. Camera phones click. There is a scattershot of applause, and laughter from the audience, as the others move in, four of them, with one guarding the door, to start laying into the creature. I didn't think this kind of promotional stunt would be Sanjay's thing.

The prevailing mood seems to be not outrage or fear, but excitement. People are grinning, nodding, eyes overbright, which makes it seem all the more horrific. It's only when the artist starts wailing that it becomes apparent that this was not part of the program. And only then do the smiles drop from mouths, like glasses breaking.

The blades tearing through the thin flesh and ribs of Khanyi Nkosi's thing with a noise like someone attacking a bicycle with an axe. The machine responds with a high-hat backbeat for the melody assembled from the screams and skitters of nervous laughter. It doesn't die quietly, transmuting the ruckus, the frantic calls to the SAPS, and Khanyi wailing, clawing, held back by a throng of people. It's like it's screaming through our voices, the background noise, the context.

The bright sprays of blood make it real, spattering the walls, people's faces, my prints, as the blades thwack down again and again. The police sirens in the distance are echoed and distorted as *Woof & Tweet* finally collapses in on itself, rattling with wet smacking sounds.

They disappear into the streets as quickly as they came, shaking the machetes at us, threatening don't follow, whooping like kids. With the sirens closing in, the big guy spits on the mangled corpse. Then, before he ducks out the door and into the night, he glances up once, quickly, at the ceiling. No one else seems to notice, but I follow his gaze up to the security cams, getting every angle.

I'm sick with adrenalin. Emily is screaming in brittle, hyperventilating gasps. Her friend is trying to wipe the blood off her face, using the hem of her dress, unaware that she has lifted it so high that she is flashing her lacy briefs. Khanyi is kneeling next to the gobs of her animal construct, trying to reassemble it, smearing herself with the bloody lumps of flesh.

There is still an undercurrent of thrill, a rush from the violence—no one was hurt, apart from Khanyi Nkosi's thing. Everyone is on their phones, taking pictures, talking. There are even more people trying to wedge into the space, so that the cops, who have finally arrived, have to shove their way inside.

Self-Portrait is covered in a mist of blood. I move to wipe it clean, although I'm scared the blood will smear, will stain the paper, but just then Jonathan wraps his arms around me and kisses my neck. I fold against him like a collapsible paper lantern.

"Don't ruin the effect, sweetheart," he whispers, his breath hot against my throat. I can't help it. I glance up at the cameras again. The beady red lights, the fisheyes recording everything. Already the cops are asking for the footage. Jonathan kisses my neck again and grins.

"You were brilliant. Now, should we go find that journalist?"

Stray Frog
Jesse Bullington

Later, Schuller would wonder if he had already been high when he followed those kids into that alley. Either from shock or withdrawal, or some cocktail of the two, he couldn't remember much from earlier that morning—just the queasy slide from his tenement to the department and then out on patrol. A typical shift, forgotten even as it transpired. But then a breakfast hit had become pretty typical of late, hadn't it?

It should have been a neat bust. The pair of cutters were young and brown—obviously guilty, easy to bully. Should've been, anyway.

The thing about the guilty is they always run, and the thing about guilty animals is they always run fast. Schuller didn't like to run, which is why he drew his softly heaving pipa from its holster before he announced his presence to the delinquents. The gun's forelegs looped around his trigger finger in a sticky hug.

"Field trip's over," Schuller called as one of the kids glanced over his shoulder and saw the thick shadow they'd acquired, the pipa already aimed at their backs. Other than a rancid dumpster, the drizzly alley offered no cover. They knew better than to run, but for a couple of obvious middle-schoolers of the public persuasion, their pimply mugs threw off as much attitude as a baby-faced college freshman stopped by the Toe-Toe.

"We got a pass, shoat," the girl sneered up at him, her bracelets jangling as she crossed her arms over the front of her hoodie instead of producing the alleged permission slip.

"Uh huh," said Schuller, sliding his piece back in its slippery holster now that he was close enough to smack these thugs around if they tried to run. Or called him a pig again. A round or three off his pipa was better than these perps deserved anyway. "Let me guess, it's autographed by the dean of Convex Prep."

"Hunh," grunted the boy, puffing up his pigeon chest and staring the truant officer dead in the eye. Schuller knew respect was too much to expect from this new crop of dickwhiskers, but with ones as young as these he hoped for a little fear at the very goddamn least. Hell, he would've settled for defiant anger, but all he was getting from this half-pint was a smug little grin.

"You really bringing the class trash?" said the girl. "Think we Miller hoodrats, huh?"

"Nice try, but I'm guessing you runts got another year or two before you make it up to the majors," said Schuller, though truth be told he'd feel better about these kids cheesing him so hard if it turned out they were skipping out on Miller High instead of Shinya Middle.

"We C.P. for real, bitch-hog, and we got a pass, so get to step," said the female, sounding so haughty you'd almost think she was a legit rich girl.

"Real nice language for a private school chica," said Schuller. Eying their designer-grown streetwear and then flicking the boy's imitation bone necklace, he said, "I see they've changed the uniform since the last time I busted one of you uppercrusties."

"Fuhh!" Instead of flinching away from Schuller's attention the boy actually bowed up at him, shrugging off his scaly backpack like he was about to throw down at recess.

"Step back, shoat!" The girl squealed on her boyfriend's behalf. "That chain's worth more than your brokeass life!"

That fucking tore it right there, and in turn Schuller tore the punk's necklace off without a second thought. Tried to, anyway, but evidently it wasn't a knockoff after all—instead of snapping in his fist the electroplated bone chain went taut and jerked the kid off his feet. He went sprawling in the foul, wet alley, and Schuller was just congratulating himself on coming off even harder than intended when the girl jumped right up in his grill and the boy started screaming his fool head off.

"Badge number!" the girl demanded. "Badge number, you brutalizin' bitch-hog!"

"Police!" The boy wailed, sitting back on his knees and staring at his skinned palms. What an irony that this was the first and apparently only word the little beast knew how to enunciate. Schuller's temples began to pound and his throat closed up tight at the ruckus these thugs were causing. "Police! Police!"

"Badge number!"

"Police!"

As if *he* was the menace to society here. Something hot and raw and righteous awoke in Schuller at their shrill baying.

"Badge number!"

"Police!"

"Already here," said Schuller, his fury transmuting into elated satisfaction as he whipped out his pipa and put it to its intended use. The gun squelched twice in his hand and just like that the lippy hoodrat wasn't in his face anymore. Even as her legs crumpled underneath her, he put another round right between her bulging, raccoon-painted eyes. Sticky wetness spattered his face, and he licked his lips as he turned to the boy still kneeling beside him in the alley.

"*Police*," the punk whispered as Schuller lazily tickled back the bone hammer on his pipa. He didn't look so hard now, nor so old... or so brown, as far at that went. Schuller shot him in the throat, and as the shitstain toppled over, he pulled the trigger again, and again, and would have put a fourth round into him if the pipa hadn't unlocked its tiny hands, denying him a trigger.

Stupid safety mechanism—had it ever occurred to the dumb animal that there might be a very good reason why an officer would need to fire more than four shots in quick succession? Besides, it took Schuller that many hits to even get properly fucked up anymore, so the potentials for overdose were clearly exaggerated by the egghead Board of—

Or maybe not? Rather than lying peacefully in the alley both kids were having fits, shivering and shaking on the grimy pavement, eyes rolled back and foamy yellow spit bubbling out of their mouths and noses. Schuller had never seen a kid react like that. Then again, he'd only actually used his pipa on a handful of suspects, and never at point blank range—in every one of those incidents the cutters had been attempting to flee, and instead of connecting with naked flesh the narcotic rounds had to soak through flapping clothing, losing some of their juice in the process. He'd never even shot a kid all the way under before, just gave them the jelly-legs and frog-fog.

These two fuckers, though. A shiny black pipa egg was lodged in the dark flesh between the girl's eyebrows like an ingrown hair, her sweat-glistening face contorted and twitching. The boy's neck was already bruising from the impact. Wracked faces, lolling tongues, and kicking legs…

Shit, was that how *he* looked after he needed an extra hit to fall asleep at night?

Schuller was just wondering if he should call in somebody medical to have a look and make sure they weren't going to OD when he noticed the folded up white paper falling out of the front pocket of the girl's hoodie.

A pass. A real one, too—he'd only seen a handful in all his years on the force, the vast majority of those offered to an arresting officer blatant forgeries. Not just any pass, either, but one with a great big fucking gold seal and the scrawled signature of the Dean of the Convex Preparatory Academy of Lower Crampton.

Schuller began sweating harder than the kids. This didn't make any fucking sense. No way these fucking hoodrats in their boosted streetwear were—

The boy's overfull backpack had bloomed open on the wet street when he'd shrugged it off, the jacket of his school uniform spilling out. Definitely fucking Convex kids. No wonder they'd given him so much lip—even without a pass, most truant officers had more sense than to harass gilded cutters, lest their wealthy parents start squawking about child abuse and due process and an honest officer suddenly found himself out on his ass without a pension.

This was bad. He glanced to the mouth of the alley—now that the rain had stopped more people were passing by. It was only a matter of time before someone glanced over and saw a man hulking over two small bodies. A couple of innocent tween prep-schoolers brutalized by an overzealous truant officer. The timing couldn't be shittier, either, with the new DA looking to make an example after that muckraker's smear piece on the department made national headlines. Forget his job and pension, Schuller was headed to fucking jail as soon as these kids woke up and put the finger on the Toe-Toe who... who...

Schuller licked his lips again, his tongue tingling from the briny pipa residue that splashed him when he shot the girl at such close proximity. It tasted like bleary mornings. Like finding yourself halfway to work not really remembering what happened after you punched the clock the previous afternoon. And that was a big guy like him, one who'd acquired something of a tolerance for his sidearm's potent rounds. Young, developing brains like these would be lucky if they remembered how to wipe their asses once they came back from their trip out past the lily pads.

Still, it never hurt to be careful. Willing his hands to stop shaking, Schuller started to coax the pipa back into an armed position. The protocols required a gentle touch, so the weapon could recognize its officer was relaxed and didn't intend to use it in anger. He must have been emanating rage, because despite his strokes it refused to form a trigger for him, blinking its useless opaque eyes as he stifled the urge to crush the delicate instrument in his fist.

Deep breaths, Officer Schuller. This wasn't some fucking inanimate object, it was a pipa. His pipa. The closest thing he had to a partner. The closest thing anyone of his tax bracket could come to a pet. The whole reason they'd bred the ugly fucking things was to instill their owners with empathy for their fellow creatures, to prevent them from treating their guns as simple tools that could be thoughtlessly used. People were just about the only living things still born outside of an assembly line lab, and in this increasingly icy, dead world, it was easy to forget the warm sanctity of life. And so in their infinite wisdom the biotech powers that be had granted them what, cute and fuzzy machinery? Purring sidearms you could cuddle after a long, hard shift? Of course not—pipas were as cold-blooded as their owners had to be, if they wanted to make it to retirement.

"There, there," Schuller murmured to his pipa, the veiny grip pulsing in his palm as he dipped the fingers of his free hand into its slimy holster, smearing it with hydrating ichor. The weapon croaked its appreciation. He made sure to work the goo into the freshly emptied divots in its back, and applied a far lighter touch to the live pockets that were still bulging with narcotic eggs. His little shootout with these thugs had used up half his ammunition. He'd have to feed it as soon as he got back to his desk to make sure it laid new rounds before their next shift.

Soothed out of safety lock, the pipa obligingly stretched out its forelegs and then looped them together to form the trigger.

"Atta girl," Schuller cooed, cocking back the warm hammer. Before he put an extra round in each kid's skull to make sure they were extra forgetful when they awoke in the dumpster, he rolled back the sleeves of his mackintosh and suit jacket to expose his own pale wrist. Pressing the warm cloaca of his gun to the busy hub of cardiovascular circuitry, he pulled the trigger. The familiar sting hurt so good he shot himself a second time, and then—

Horked another spray of bloody vomit into the toilet bowl, so dazed and disoriented he almost slipped in headfirst after the final spasm. Bright red gore bobbed in the greasy water, making him gag anew. Schuller moaned, wept, tried to evict the hallucination from his blurry eyes. It clung on, persistent as a squatter on the cusp of legal recognition. Schuller slipped back onto his knees, weak and feverish. His heart careened against the inside of his chest, a prisoner bashing against the bars of its cell.

What the fuck had happened? What the fuck

had he done? Last he remembered he was about to put an insurance shot in each thug and then toss them in the dumpster to sleep off the pipa ride, and now here he was puking up red in his apartment. Had he fucking *eaten* them? Or had his escalating pipa abuse liquefied his insides; was he puking up his own guts? He didn't know which possibility was worse.

Dragging his shaking hand across his sick-slick mouth, he held it up in the faint glow of his bathroom bottle bulbs but just saw translucent drool. Huh. Forcing himself to look back in the bowl he saw it was just as disgusting as he'd thought, but then a drop of blood appeared on the yellow rim of the toilet. Relief surged through him like the first hit of the day.

He'd puked so hard he'd given himself a fucking nosebleed. That was all. It wasn't chewed up delinquents or his own melted stomach in the toilet, just a lot of nose blood and… bits of half-digested pupusa, looked like. Good. He may have blacked out back in the alley but he'd apparently kept his head long enough to hit up Dalia's. Everyone on the force knew the café had a clock on the wall that ran a dependable hour slow, for those lunch breaks when you needed an alibi to go with your mild food poisoning.

His alarm went off. Staggering upright and swaying to the sink, Schuller winced at his haggard reflection. The sluggish torrent of blood still oozed out of one crusty nostril, webbing in his mustache. How the fuck was it morning already? He'd blacked out before, sure, but never for so long, and never from such a small dose.

Had he already been high when he followed the kids into the alley? Had shooting them from so close caused some backsplash from the pipa's gel-coated eggs? Or had he gotten more of the narcotic residue on his hands when he'd moved the snoozing scumbags into the dumpster? All three, maybe… Assuming he had even moved the kids. What if he'd just doped himself up and wandered off to stuff pupusas in his numb face, leaving them right there in the alley where anyone could find them?

Well, that wouldn't be such a tragedy, either— no chance of them being crushed in a compactor if they didn't wake up before sanitation emptied the dumpsters. However he'd handled it, Schuller must've done a decent enough job 'cause he'd made it through another day and night. Waking up to your own bloody vomit and an aching skull wasn't the best morning, but it sure beat waking up in a jail cell. Or a dumpster, far as that went.

He smiled to himself as he washed his face, then plugged his nose with toilet paper, and staggered out of the bathroom to turn off his alarm. He was already late as shit so it must've been going for a while. Good thing he'd slept in his suit, since he didn't even have time to change if he was going to make it to the department in time for the morning briefing. Considering what a bad boy he'd been yesterday, it wouldn't do to miss another mandatory conference.

Of course, one always had to make time for breakfast, and Schuller reached for his pipa… only to find his amphibious holster empty.

The terrarium. His first week on the force, Schuller had religiously transferred the pipa to its enclosure every evening when he got home. After that, he had never used it again since the pipa's holster kept it moist enough, and what kind of bleeding heart really thought a gun needed a "safe and stable environment?" As he waded through the squalor of his sour-smelling apartment to the terrarium, he told himself that's where it was, that when he'd blacked out his froggy head forgot he didn't use it anymore. It would be dumbly sitting there in its gravel, blinking its blind eyes, and—

Empty. Not that the pipa would've been happy about being dumped in there, anyway, with only a brown ring of crust to mark the former waterline in the dusty glass case.

Schuller patted his empty holster again, willing his sidearm to reappear. It didn't cooperate.

He stumbled into the bathroom, telling himself it must have fallen out on the floor and crawled back behind the toilet. It needed water, and a brown puddle often formed where—

Gone. Schuller tried not to cry. He should've sobered up by now but still felt completely fucking frogged out, unable to think in a straight line. What happened after he shot up in the alley? What?

Had he dropped his gun when he hoisted the kids into the dumpster? Or left it in a booth at the papusa joint? Fucking hell, he couldn't remember the last sixteen hours so the fucking thing could be anywhere. The worst-case scenarios slouched against the back of his aching skull like hardened perps in a police line-up.

He needed to check the alley, obviously. It was risky as hell—if those kids had woken up and remembered enough of the details to report it, the adult authorities could be investigating the scene right now. Or even worse, what if he'd given those brats a fatal dose, sanitation had found their corpses in the dumpster at dawn, and the whole place was staked out as they waited for the killer to return to the scene to retrieve his croaking murder weapon?

He couldn't go back. Too fucking chancy. No, he'd have to play it cool, report the weapon stolen… but that asshole DA was watching the department like a drone. A missing pipa would result in an immediate inquiry, an inquiry his frazzled ass was in no state to handle. No, he had to get his shit together first. Once he calmed down enough to come up with a plausible story, he would report the theft and pray they didn't just shitcan him on the spot for losing a piece of equipment worth more than his annual salary.

That was it. Calm down. Think straight. Act straight. Above all, be consistent.

Yet as he hustled to work through the blinding sunlight, Schuller found it harder and harder to think clearly, his thoughts as fractured as his memories.

For a fleeting, joyous moment Schuller thought it could be stashed in the back recesses of his desk drawer at the department, but the object he felt turned out to just be his stapler. Heads turned when he furiously smashed the thing on the floor. He went to lunch.

No one turned anything in at Dalia's, the pupusa shop proprietor laughing at the suggestion an establishment of its reputation might have a "Lost and Found" bin. Schuller came within three blocks of the alley before hyperventilating so badly he had to take a knee on a stoop. The sun was trying to kill him.

The kids had found it, he decided. That was the worst thing that could have happened, so it must be true. That was the law of his luck.

Even if he'd accidentally murdered a couple of rich kids and left his sidearm at the scene for forensics to immediately finger him with, that would be preferable. He could still look himself in the eye in the prison mirror if he went down for getting excessive on a couple of smart-mouthed thugs. He could be a martyr for the department.

But fuck up so bad a couple of middle-schoolers made off with his pipa and he'd be left begging internal affairs to let him keep a desk job long enough to pay back the enormous debt he owed on it. They'd never let him hold another pipa, and the thought of going through life without its soothing balm made him want to take a nosedive off the roof of Convex Prep. Those fucking kids had woken up hungover in a dumpster, and then grinned to each other as they found his pipa crouched down in a filthy mud puddle.

He tormented himself with visions of them stomping the poor creature underfoot. When that wasn't bad enough, he pictured them taking it back to their posh private school, sneaking it into a lab during recess to vivisect the delicate weapon. He shuddered as he imagined them peeling back its bumpy skin to expose its skeletal gears, oohing and awing as they tortured it to death.

Bad as that made him feel, however, he finally settled on the evilest scenario of all, one that filled him with queasy dread. Crawling out of the dumpster, the girl discovered the pipa croaking in an oily pool. Her sharp eyes grew gentle, her grating voice softening to an affectionate purr. She rescued it from the foul pond, her brutish paramour likewise tamed by the spell of its charming helplessness. Holding it not by the spinal pistol grip but cupping its underside like an animal, she planted her glossy lips on its slimy back.

She took it home.

Bought it a giant terrarium.

Gave it a name.

Schuller threw up again.

Schuller tortured himself with the fantasy all through the sweltering day. That night his fevered dreams were filled with the happy songs of his pipa trilling through a rich girl's bedroom. The next day was hotter still, and his visions of his pipa's new life grew yet more ornate, more vivid. It was unnatural, disgusting, but he couldn't help himself.

He was just picturing her investing in real

live insects to hand feed the rescued pipa when he unlocked the door of his apartment and noticed his rain jacket lying discarded in one corner. A gyre turned in his head, like a live pipa egg slipping from its back pouch into the chamber. It had been raining that fateful day, but it had been sunny ever since.

He only checked the pockets to confirm what he already knew, that his pipa was lost forever, a pampered pet in some uptown penthouse, where—

It was here, yet it looked so much smaller in death. Its desiccated forelegs were reaching into the air, like a supplicant who had frozen to death even as he stretched upward for salvation. After being carelessly zipped into the pocket of the rain jacket and then forgotten, the pipa must have spent the last two days trying to climb free only to eventually dry out and die. All this time he thought it was being fawned over by that rich little bitch it had been here, waiting for him to come home.

It hit him hard as a slug straight to the jugular, his eyes welling with tears as he cradled the broken animal in his shaking hands: *relief.*

The Hard Spot in the Glacier

An Owomoyela

Ayo lost all sense of time: the white roaring was her world, the avalanche was her only orientation, and every heartbeat came as a surprise. When the world *stopped* moving, it was like being born to a new reality.

Slowly, she came back to herself, and the world turned to sense again.

She was on her back. At an angle—steep. Most of her view *up* was obscured by glacier, luminous with reflected Saturnlight. The black sky beyond it was a ribbon, whereas before it had been a wide plane.

Braced across that ribbon, a purer white than the ice around it, stood the centipede.

She groaned. "Am I alive?"

The centipede's head turned toward her, which caused its foremost segment to shift in counterbalance. Ayo braced herself; ice was still falling in haphazard cascades in her peripheral vision. The ice under her body felt solid, though. The centipede's legs had dug into it, and didn't seem to be slipping.

Ayo's question made its way into the centipede's CPU, where it was parsed, matched to the nearest semantic rubrics, evaluated, and turned into an answer. *((Your biomonitors aren't reporting any injuries. Your exoskeleton reports no major damage. Do you feel okay?))*

She hadn't been inside the centipede when the quake hit. Stupid, maybe, but the centipede's interior hadn't been designed for passengers in any case: The interior was supposed to haul cargo, the manual cockpit at the head was just big enough to sit in if you didn't care about leg cramps, and the medical pods fitted in the rear segments made those segments visibly oversized just so a patient could be immobilized lying straight.

Everyone in Search & Rescue got the speech about remaining in their vehicle while traversing the terrain. And everyone who was assigned a centipede for their vehicle quietly decided that they knew better, and requisitioned an exoskeleton to go with it.

Ayo flexed her fingers, swiveled her ankles. The exoskeleton had protected her limbs and her spine. The helmet had protected her skull. A leaden feeling rested in the pit of her stomach, but that was no injury—that was just her, and the situation, and she ignored it as best she could. No suit integrity warnings appeared in her

HUD, just as the centipede said. She felt shaken, physically disoriented, maybe on the edges of a concussion, but mostly clear-thinking.

"Status," she said. Her mask picked it up, fed it to the centipede, and caught the reply.

((I'm uninjured. I've lost contact with Carpenter Base, though.))

Ayo squinted. The centipede sounded petulant, which bothered her. In theory, its emotional inflections were supposed to increase the density of information it relayed: If its voice sounded scared, the operator didn't need to know percent chances of damage, calculated likelihood of injury—all the dry, bloodless details that were challenging for a human intelligence to weigh. If it fidgeted its many legs and strained to go forward on the landscape, the operator didn't have to go down a list of subsystems status and topographical charts; she'd just know they were good to go.

But while Ayo had no trouble reading actual human people, she couldn't stop second-guessing the programmed humanity of the centipede. What the hell was *petulance* supposed to tell her? Or was she misreading it, missing something else? Was it concerned? Afraid? Reluctant to go on?

She'd rather have the dry data, honestly. Between herself and the centipede, *one* of them was actually supposed to have feelings about all this, and those were more than enough to deal with.

"What about Parker?"

The centipede moved. Its mandibles opened, revealing the backup radio receiver it held protected there. Its head swayed from side to side, scanning the landscape.

((I've still got Parker's automated signal. Nothing personal.))

Nothing to indicate that the target of this little expedition was conscious and trying to communicate, then. Hell, he could be dead already, for all she knew.

Dead, or lying unconscious, or lying injured. No conclusive evidence either way. Her job was to take the evidence she had and treat it as actionable.

Ayo reached out, and the centipede gave her one of its forward articulator arms to help her up. The exoskeleton she wore compensated for her own unsteady balance, bracing her until she found the faint pull of real gravity. It ran counter to the absurdly tilted landscape.

"I thought this area was supposed to be glaciologically stable," Ayo said, shaking out one leg, then the other. Her imagination, or were the knee joints on the exoskeleton stiff? Were her own knees?

The centipede didn't have a canned response to that. And without a connection back to Carpenter, it couldn't build one from a report. It remained silent.

Ayo turned, carefully, looking for the bright spot on her HUD which indicated Parker's signal. One hip ached, but dully. The topography spread down below her, crisscrossed with new rills and ridges and crevices; off in the distance, a plume of ice and vapor rose kilometers into the sky, ever feeding vapor into Saturn's rings. Enceladus was a moon in the long process of bleeding itself away.

But the process was long enough for people to set down on the surface, make bases there, make the place home. Ignore the moon's long attrition, interspersed with its sudden violence.

Humans would colonize anything.

She turned again, surveying the way back, taking inventory of the aches in her skull. Her HUD still provided a dot for Carpenter Base, but without a signal, it was greyed out—an approximation. Line-of-sight was blocked by the vast wall of ice that reared up behind her, which jutted out above her. It looked looser than Ayo was comfortable with. Looser than the ice underfoot; certainly looser than could support, say, a centipede crawling up its underside.

"What do I do?" she muttered, mostly to herself.

She was surprised when the centipede answered.

((I don't like this. I think we should go home.))

Irrationally—because she'd had the same thought, after all—Ayo felt a surge of anger. She was out here, and *she* wasn't complaining. What right did this idiot piece of equipment have?

But it wasn't programmed to complain. It was

programmed to make a threat assessment and deliver it in an emotionally-relatable way.

"We can't go home without Parker," she said.

She turned back to the beacon in her HUD. No change; no response. *Parker might be dead*, she thought. Then she was angry for thinking it.

"Okay," she said, and turned her attention to the centipede. "What's your impression of the landscape? What's the fastest route back into contact with Carpenter?"

It thought about that. *((A lateral path, about a kilometer and a half. That will get us to an upward grade which should be stable. Assuming there's no further activity.))* Seismic activity, it meant. *((The longer we're out, the more risk.))*

"Any pattern to the shocks?" She walked around the centipede's head, hands spread for balance, even though the exoskeleton was perfectly capable of balancing her on its own. Technology could augment human instinct all it wanted; the instincts themselves held on, stubbornly vestigial.

((I'd guess that Parker's incident was a foreshock. If this quake was the main shock, the aftershocks might be less severe. If not, it may get worse. In any case, I don't think the sequence is over.))

Ayo let out a gust of air. Her suit was too well-regulated for it to cloud her HUD, but she could still feel the air hitting the screen and rolling back around her face, as though the screen itself shared in her frustration.

I'd guess. If. Might. Don't think. She'd have

to build her response on a bed of no good information. "What's the best route to Parker?"

The centipede definitely sounded unhappy about that. ((*Down. We can follow one of the valleys to a plain, and traverse that. It might take another hour.*))

An hour in which anything can happen. Ayo nodded, trying to trick herself into feeling more confidence than she felt. *What's the trade?*

Best case, they got to Parker and brought him home alive. Two lives preserved. Bad case, they got to Parker and he was dead already, and Ayo took the centipede home. Worse case, they got to Parker and got stuck there, or were taken out en route: two lives in extremis or lost already. Worst case: They foundered out here and another S&R team was dispatched to find them.

Best case for turning around: They got home. One life preserved. One abandoned, dead body forgotten or living body left to die on the ice sheets. And one more failure to rob Ayo's sleep.

"We have to try."

((*I don't think this is a good idea.*))

"Centipede..." Ayo scowled. "Cease emotive feedback. Shut up."

The centipede's next words were flat, machinelike. ((*Emotive feedback suspended.*))

It made Ayo unaccountably angrier.

Maybe I'm jealous that I can't turn my own emotions off.

Maybe I just wonder why we bother giving the

things survival instincts if we're going to ignore them anyway?

The sky above Enceladus was black.

The sky above Enceladus was *always* black. The moon didn't have enough atmosphere to scatter light or capture it, and the sun was far away. Saturn, of course, cast its own reflected glow, frosting the landscape. But it wasn't like Earth. No one would ever mistake this place for Earth.

On most days, that suited Ayo just fine. She preferred a landscape which didn't lull her into thinking it was made for humans, it was hospitable, it was safe. She wanted to see the landscape's teeth.

Now, it was all teeth: the walls of rills and canyons towering up around her, gnashing at the sky. The ground shivered underneath her boots a few times, as though to remind her that the threat might not be over. The centipede remained obediently silent. Parker, frustratingly so.

For half an hour, now, she'd just felt the crunch of ice underfoot; heard that vibration translate up her suit as sound.

She hated it. But she tried to read the cold tension in her gut as safety, because she'd loved it on Earth. And that'd been the problem: she'd been in love with the blue skies and the grey storms, the green grass and the knife-white snow. Search and rescue on Earth felt, more often than not, like an adventure. Serious, of course, but with that tinge of wild romance the Terran natural world still inspired. On Enceladus, the work felt like a punishment. At best, a trudge. A chore.

This was the job: someone was in extremis, and her role was to go out, into a potentially deadly situation, and maybe bring back a corpse. All the skill she could bring to the field, and some part was still a roll of the dice.

And just how loaded were the dice, today?

She'd just cleared a small ledge when her exosuit detected a tremor in the ground, her helmet detected a shiver in the fitful water-vapor atmosphere, and the systems combined to synthesize a meaningful sound: a rolling *crash* like a sudden waterfall.

A second later, the centipede reported a flat *((Error.))*

Ayo spun. The centipede reared up, its body shielding her from a glittering avalanche of scree ice, and she went to her hands and knees and braced on instinct. Two seconds, three, and the avalanche slowed, though the centipede didn't lower itself down again. From this angle, Ayo could see that two of its back legs had actually slid into a crack in the ice wall, which had compressed shut around them when loose ice came down. "Oh, come *on!*"

Easy enough to get out of: the rest of the centipede provided all the leverage it would need. Whether that would bring the whole wall down around them was the question.

She stood. Walked around centipede, testing each step as she took it, to inspect the other side. "Centipede, enable emotive feedback. How much do you know about glaciology?"

The centipede considered, tried (futilely, once again) to reach the main database at Carpenter, failed, and compiled a response. ((*I'm sorry. Not much.*)) Without Ayo there to shield, it lowered itself back to the ground.

"You can't tell if deforming the ice here will cause a slide?" Ayo asked.

((*No.*))

The other side of the centipede was undamaged and unstuck. Ayo put her hands on the exoskeleton joints at her hips.

Inside the centipede would be safer. The centipede could unstick itself, and if there was another ice slide, the ice couldn't crush her. She'd be safe—and cramped, and cut off from what tactile sense of the environment around her her suit and exoskeleton still allowed. Plus, she'd have to remove the exoskeleton and stow it just to fit inside.

She looked up. And up: the ice still glowed with Saturnlight, and the ribbon of the sky had narrowed to a thread. Her heart skipped.

As though sensing that—maybe in response

to her biometrics—the centipede said, ((*I'm afraid.*))

Are you, centipede? Lies. It couldn't feel anything—its systems weren't that advanced. It could only say it could.

Ayo was the one who could feel fear. She was the one who could suffer fear. She was afraid enough for them both.

"Can we make it to Parker's location?" she asked. Leave aside the question of whether or not he was alive down there. Just getting there was proving to be challenge enough.

A pause. A telling one, she was sure. Then, ((*With difficulty,*)) it admitted.

"We didn't take this job to have it easy," Ayo said. Then she shook her head. "*I* didn't."

The centipede hadn't had a choice in the matter.

"Disable emotive feedback." She swung wide, looking at the picture from another angle. "All right." This was stupid, more than likely, but quick mental models gave Ayo enough confidence not to label it *suicidal*. She walked back in, tucking herself under the centipede's forebelly. "Centipede, extract yourself—two meters lateral."

((*Brace,*)) the centipede warned, flatly. Then its vast white body heaved.

The wall buckled, and another slide of ice shook itself down. Not, though, a catastrophic one: ten, eleven square meters, Ayo estimated, and the centipede shook its body to spill ice down to either side. With her body below it, the centipede's first directive was to protect her: it didn't let them become re-buried.

The scree settled. It gave a few trailing shivers, and her suit interpreted a long groan from some vibration beneath the surface, but soon enough, the muttering stopped. Ayo let out a brief laugh. Not that the situation was funny.

"How are we doing, centipede?"

((No access to Carpenter databanks. Independent calculations estimate successful traversal chance in the low twenty percentile))

One in five that they'd make it to Parker's position. Ayo was hopeful enough, confident enough—no. *Stubborn* enough to try for it.

Or—no. Afraid enough. Not fear of death; she felt that, yes, but as an abstract. She didn't want to fail. *Again.*

One in five was still one more than zero. Twenty in a hundred was *twenty* more than zero, and put that way, it almost seemed like a fighting chance.

"Well, let's go."

If the centipede thought she was an idiot, fortunately, it couldn't say.

The third shake could have killed her.

Would have, if the exoskeleton had poorer calibration, if she'd had poorer training. As it was, Ayo's conscious brain was booted from control entirely, as her body reacted on instinct. One second, three, five—she lost track of time. Time returned only slowly, after the world righted itself again.

She was hanging from an exoskeleton-enhanced grip over a crevasse.

She didn't look down to see how deep it was. Above her, the centipede was moving, seemingly erratically—trying to find a stable path to her. She flattened herself to the wall, felt for handholds and footholds, studied the flashing indicators rioting in her HUD. Managed, through effort and no small bit of luck, to get herself up over the lip just as the centipede scrambled to her.

Then she lay there, staring up at the centipede, gasping.

Am I alive?

The centipede didn't answer her unvoiced query. But after a moment, unprompted, it said *((Geologic activity increase of 37 percent over previous incident.))*

"It's getting worse." Punctuating her words, a shelf of ice detached from somewhere to Ayo's right, widening the crevasse. She rolled to her hands and knees and distanced herself from the ledge. Even the centipede sidled. "Parker?"

((No signal.))

Well, she hadn't expected one. She swallowed, then swallowed again. A bitter taste climbed the back of her throat. "Chart a course." She was shaking. She could grind that out with action, she was sure. Keep moving. Don't look down. Don't think. Just *move*. "What's the best path to get us to Parker?"

((No paths are advised.))

Ayo's face twisted. "Calculate it anyway!"

The centipede reared.

Ayo stumbled back, some vestigial part of her brain seeing the sudden motion and interpreting *threat*, looking for defense, looking for shelter. The centipede towered above her, alien for all its engineered relatability. Then, trembling, it let itself back to the ground.

That hadn't been subtle, in the least. Ayo let out a breath, fanning her annoyance to cover her fear. "Centipede, disable—"

No. That wasn't right. Emotive feedback was already disabled. Had been this entire way.

Ayo stared at the centipede's sensors, so carefully styled to suggest eyes. There was a machine intelligence behind those, no animal intelligence. Nothing with feelings. Not really. Just a lot of software to ape them.

The knowledge didn't stop Ayo from shivering, as though a thread of cold air slipped inside her suit.

As though a thread of cold air *could*. Her suit was pressurized to one Earth atmosphere— more atmosphere than Enceladus had. A leak in her suit would depressurize the whole thing, not let a cold draft in. It was psychosomatic. A sense memory, maybe: a creeping reminder of a previous failure. Unease slipping in to the tune of—what, a bug in the software? A failsafe she'd never known about? An aberration?

I don't want to be here.

The thought hit her with more force than she expected.

I shouldn't be here. Even the centipede, a machine specifically designed to support rescue efforts in dangerous situations, doesn't want to be here. Look at it. It's afraid.

She took a breath, and it turned into a hiccupping sob.

Swallow it. Ignore it. You've got a job to do out there.

Out, across the shattered landscape, across the uncertain glacier. Down there, across that once-traversable plain, Parker was either dead or alive. If alive, the medical care Ayo could provide for him might or might not keep him alive until they reached Carpenter. *If* they reached Carpenter. The journey out was only half the battle. It had been a journey she'd undertaken with hope, at the beginning—or, if not hope, a resolve to do all she could. To make a bid for the most favorable trade. One sizable risk on one known human life, winning one potential human life preserved.

What good was human hope against the calculated risk assessment of the centipede? At some point, that human cognitive distortion—that faith that *death* was something that happened to other people—worked to preserve populations, if not individuals. Ayo's job was to walk out onto that murderous plain. But Ayo's job was also to recognize that one downed surveyor and one downed rescuer was *worse* than one downed surveyor and one rescuer who knew when to leave well enough alone. At the end of the day Carpenter would rather have one corpse than two; but they'd rather have zero than one, and what Ayo had to guide her was speculation, bravado, suspicion, and the cold logic of the centipede wrapped up in its emotive tones. She didn't *know* anything.

Neither did the centipede, of course. But it trembled. Surely she hadn't imagined that. It had trembled.

What's the trade?

The words, when she found them, were already catching in her throat.

"Centipede," she said. *One potential life forfeit. One ascertained life preserved. And one—what? Piece of equipment. Virtual life. One centipede out of danger.* She wouldn't have turned back, for herself. "Chart the safest course to Carpenter. Maybe we can get ourselves home."

Every Single Wonderful Detail
Stephen Graham Jones

Because he knew he wasn't going to be there for her teenage years, Grace's dad built a German Shepherd to be there in his stead. What Grace's friend Tawny asked Grace was, "If your dad could, like, build anything, then why didn't he build little-bitty robots that ate cancer?"

Grace and Tawny had been friends since second grade, so there was no need for Tawny to tack a "no offense" anywhere in there.

Grace just shrugged.

They were supposed to be making pie batter together, to eat with saltines like they liked to do when Grace's mom would let them get away with it, but Grace wasn't helping stir. She was looking out the big window in the breakfast nook, at the January snow coming down.

Benjo Kane padded up by her right leg, looked out through the window with her, to make sure everything was all right.

Faintly, and in what Grace had to admit was a comforting way, the actuators or whatever behind his eyes whirred, allowing Benjo to survey for threats, not just immediately by the window and across the street at the Jamesons', but in a whole stack of spectrums too.

Because Benjo had also been designed to not freak people out, her dad programmed him to pant and dog-smile while he did this.

Grace scrunched her fingers through the thick hair at the top of his head. He didn't push up into her fingertips to luxuriate in the petting like Grace was pretty sure she remembered from other dogs. His neck-cylinders had locked in place to steady his eyes. He was equipped with image-stabilization, of course, but her dad's rule was to always trust hardware first, software last.

"Benjo, warmer," Grace said, not nearly loud enough for Tawny to hear.

She wasn't actually cold, but looking at the snow made her want a fire. Benjo couldn't go all flame-on, but he was a pretty serviceable space heater. That was the main way she used him in winter. Her mom said it was a waste, just using him like that, sending him to bed ten minutes before herself, but what Grace used to say back was that Dad had built Benjo for *her*, right?

What Grace's mom didn't know was that Benjo was a calculator, too. He couldn't speak, and his paws weren't small enough to manipulate a keyboard, but when Grace hit a branching point in an equation, she could always hold it up for Benjo to see, then tell him left paw, I go this way now for a page or two. Right paw, that way.

Her calculus grade was tracing its own sine curve, higher and higher.

Just like it would if Dad were here to help me with it, Grace told herself.

What her dad never could have managed, though, it was—

"Watch this," Grace whispered back to Tawny.

Tawny crowded up against the window with them.

"Is that Lawson's brother?" she said.

"He's back from college," Grace said.

"Keller, right?" Tawny whispered. Then, with a thrill to her voice: "*College. . .*"

"Shh," Grace said.

A growl was building in Benjo's chest.

It felt like a giant screw boring through rock but doing it slowly, gingerly, so as not to shatter anything.

At the end of Keller's long leash was his mom's small white and black terrier.

Grace smiled.

Across the street, the Jameson's front door opened and Mr. Jameson stepped out in his robe, lifted his hand in greeting to Keller, the returning hero of the block, back with a degree it had only taken him one extra semester to earn.

Keller looked over, switched hands on the leash so as to wave back, and that gave the black and white terrier enough slack to dart onto Grace's lawn, its nose burrowing through the snow, its bobbed tail stiff and fast.

Intruder alert, intruder alert.

Benjo's growl ramped up into his mouth, came out as a single, harsh bark loud enough that Grace's reflection trembled and wavered.

The glass was new, as Benjo had had to learn about modulating his voice.

What he'd also learned—he was adaptive, Grace's dad had told her from his hospital bed, he'll learn, and keep on learning—was dog language.

Grace wasn't sure what exactly he told that white and black terrier with that single sharp bark, but whatever it was, it made the terrier ball up and fall back, as if it were being swooped down on by a hawk.

Keller looked up, to Grace.

"Sorry," she lip-said, lifting her hand to show that her dog might be like this, but she wasn't.

Tawny had been right, about the way she'd said "Keller."

Keller nodded back, not quite smiling but not-*not* smiling, either, and stepped onto their lawn to retrieve his mom's terrier.

"No," Grace said to Benjo.

His nose was right against the glass now.

The smear it left there would smell like petroleum. It was one thing her dad hadn't been able to simulate: dog saliva.

If he'd had time, maybe.

Scooping the terrier up, Keller looked up to the window again, as if seeing Grace for the first time. Grace stood taller. She was no longer the eighth-grader she'd been back when Keller was lifeguarding.

It was good he couldn't hear Benjo's growl, or feel it resonating up through his canine chassis.

All that was left a moment later was a dab of yellow on the snow, where the terrier had cowered.

Benjo's tail swept back and forth twice, in satisfaction.

After the Valentine's Day dinner—the *date*, Grace loud-whispered to Tawny over the phone—Keller brought Grace back to the front door. At which point Grace's mom invited him in, since it was cold enough to see your breath.

Keller's new job didn't start until April. It was three hundred miles away. He was going to be a software engineer. At least until he blasted off into the stratosphere with some new startup. The desk job, he explained to Grace over their long walks around the park, the black-and-white terrier keeping the leash stretched tight, the desk job was just his *disguise*, see. His desk job was the big square eyeglasses he was going to put on every morning to fit in with the rest of the worker bees. At night, though, tinkering with code in his downtown apartment, he'd be flying over the city.

Grace's mom had reminded her that high school seniors and junior professionals didn't always. . . they didn't always make it to their first anniversary.

"You think he's a summer boy," Grace had said back about this.

"A what?" her mom asked.

"Temporary."

"No," her mom said. "I just—I just don't want *you* to be."

"It's still winter," Grace ended with, even though it wasn't exactly the kind of closing line to make a big swooshing exit with. She did anyway.

It was all different the way she relayed it to Tawny on their nightly call.

And so it had begun, whatever it was that was happening. Walks around the park with Keller's mom's terrier. Grace telling Keller about school, about her plans, about Benjo, and, finally, her dad.

"He's the one who taught me syntax," Keller said.

Grace looked up to him about this, the question on her face.

Her dad had taught her proper syntax as well—you couldn't code without knowing the basics—but she'd never realized that the reason he could package it all up for her so well was that she was round two.

"When?" she said.

Keller looked up and to the right, kind of squinting in that way that Tawny said made him look like he might be thinking big thoughts.

"I was thirteen, I think," he said. "Yeah. That was the year we had the black gaming computer with the green lights. He did something to the BIOS. It made it where the lights would warn me if there was someone behind me. Just in certain games, I mean. I still haven't figured that patch out."

I would have been eight, Grace didn't say.

They were holding hands by then, when it worked out. When the terrier—Muggy—wasn't too worked up by smells or sounds or squirrels or other dogs.

Twice during those walks, of which there were probably fifteen, Grace had done the lookaway thing Tawny insisted was her best, most fetching gesture. It was supposed to make her look disinterested, on the road to bored, even. Seeing that, any boy would of course leap to impress, right?

It was more basic math than calculus, but it had, once so far, prompted Keller to ask what Grace was thinking.

She wasn't on the road to boredom.

In her head, she was skipping.

Two of those lookaways, though, she'd seen, moving like a ghost through the trees of the park, pacing them, a set of shadowy legs. Dog legs. *Big* dog legs.

Upon returning home for some made-up chore or homework, Benjo would already be there waiting for her, of course.

The fur of his legs and belly would be dry, not wet with melting snow, but was that a hidden feature, maybe? If he could serve as a space heater, surely he could dial that up, dry almost instantly, right?

The hairs of his fur weren't textured the same as regular hair, either. It was smoother, more perfect. Grace's dad had joked about patenting it, calling it "Duckback" or something, for the way it shed water.

But then he'd had more pressing concerns. Like dying.

"So this is him," Keller said, just inside the door after Valentine's Day dinner.

He offered the back of his hand for Benjo to sniff.

Benjo did but it was just an act, Grace knew. He'd already taken Keller's scent from her clothes, she knew. He'd already processed that scent through enough filters and databanks that he knew not just what Keller'd had for breakfast, but what he *usually* had for breakfast.

"Good boy," Keller said, and pinched his slacks to squat down to Benjo's level. "His eyes are good," he said up to Grace. "Realistic."

"He's been worried about you all night," Grace's mom said to her. She was balancing a tray with two matched coffee cups on it, the whipped cream swirled high on the hot chocolate Grace could already smell. "Was Giorgio's crowded?" she asked.

"I had those noodles," Grace said, swirling around to fall back into the loveseat in that way that said this was her house.

"Lot of couples there," Keller said, standing to take the cup Grace's mom was offering.

"And their violin players," Grace added, and mimed screeching a bow across her shoulder.

"I love the violin," her mom said, her voice going all wispy and dreamy and romantic.

Keller sat down beside Grace, balancing the saucer and cup on his knee, and Grace's mom guided Grace's cup down to her.

"Thanks, Mom," Grace said flatly. It meant goodbye, without the *please*.

For once, Grace's mom took the cue, made her exit.

Because the hot chocolate was too hot to drink—Grace had no idea how her mom had known when to have it heated, but that was her mom—they each just held their cups and fiddled their fingers. Keller couldn't stop staring at Benjo.

"Why Kane?" he said.

"Because he *assists*," Grace recited. "Because he's good for *walks*."

It was the worst joke. Her dad had loved it.

"Does he shed?" Keller asked.

"Let's not talk about the dog," Grace said, settling her cup onto the coffee table.

Benjo laid down at her feet. At both their feet.

He didn't need to rest—ever—but he could take cues too.

When Keller tried to slurp his hot chocolate in with enough air to keep from burning himself, the whipped cream dotted his nose, and it was funny enough that Grace dabbed her finger against it, dotted her own nose.

"No, I shouldn't, it's yours," she said, and leaned forward to touch her nose to his, give that whipped cream back.

It was a moment that slowed down.

Keller's hand found. . . kind of her upper neck, kind of her jaw.

Her skin had never been so alive.

She breathed out through her mouth, and then Keller's lips were brushing hers, his breath mingling with hers, and she closed her eyes for this because it was going to be just like Tawny promised it was going to be.

Except now Keller was jerking back hard enough to slosh a dollop of hot chocolate out onto his tan slacks.

It was Benjo.

He was sitting up between their knees, his back showdog straight, his ears radared forward to the two of them, his eyes black and glassy.

He was growling.

Grace could feel it in the wooden frame of the couch.

"Um, well," Keller said, managing his saucer and cup down to the coffee table, alongside Grace's. "I better—" and he gestured to the spill on his slacks that he needed to attend to. Home. At his house, five doors down. A world away.

At the door Grace stepped around in front of him, her arms already around his neck, and Keller looked into her eyes for what she was going to tell Tawny was a single forever, but then Benjo was there looking up at the two of them, and Keller was guiding Grace to the side by the hips.

That night, for the first time ever, the first time since her dad died, Grace made Benjo sleep in the hall.

Usually she could see a line of yellow at the bottom of her door, from the night light her mom kept on to, as she put it, "guide weary travelers."

Now Benjo was blotting that light out.

The next time Keller brought an electric blanket that he plugged into the outlet by the swing on the porch, and Grace locked Benjo in the house. It should have worked, but evidently Benjo had a transponder built into him somewhere.

The garage door opened and he padded around, sat there facing them.

"Is he waterproof?" Keller asked mischievously, but also kind of seriously.

"He's everything-proof," Grace deadpanned back.

"Well," Keller said.

Three days later he showed up with his laptop and some homemade apparatus hanging from a port.

"When all else fails, open a terminal window," he said, and sat down on the loveseat again, tapped into their wifi without Grace telling him the password—"Home networks are cake," he assured, which actually wasn't assuring at all—and then ran a script he said it had taken thirty-six hours to get right.

"What's it do?" Grace asked, sitting down beside him to watch.

"I figure if he can open garage doors," Keller said, dramatically missile-guiding his index finger down to the Enter key, "he can probably receive, too. It's just about finding the right frequency, and then piggybacking. He's got to update from time to time, right? Y'all have a unit in a closet somewhere that runs diagnostics on him?"

Grace didn't say anything because she was watching the code compile. Keller had his system rigged with some visual simulator where you could watch the magic happen. "It's good for catching bugs as they happen," he said, and then lowered his screen so they could both get eyes on Benjo.

He was sitting there in the doorway to the kitchen like he always did when on guard.

His nose didn't tic like a regular dog, but he wasn't a regular dog. He wasn't panting, but, when no one had been looking at him, he would sometimes conserve energy like that. It wasn't quite a sleep mode. More like a nap mode, what Grace called his forget-I'm-here mode. But he would still be on full alert.

Except. . . he *hadn't* started panting, with *both* of them giving him all of their attention.

"Gotcha," Keller said, and settled the laptop onto the coffee table and his hand onto Grace's knee. "I think we can make him do tricks now, like a regular dog."

"Tricks?" Grace said.

Keller tapped his voice-command key on, said into his keyboard, "Lie down."

Benjo did, walking his front feet forward in small steps until he was on his belly like the Sphinx.

"Very regal," Keller said, rolling his hand out to Benjo, to show off his work.

In the kitchen, a dish shattered.

"Mom?" Grace called, leaning forward to try to see through the doorway. The angle was wrong.

"Yes?" her mom said back with the kind of hesitancy and regret that pretty much announced she'd been caught. That Benjo hadn't been the only one standing guard over the two lovebirds.

Grace leaned back into the couch in a display of utter despair.

"You say college is better?" she said to Keller,

then, before he could answer, she did: "It's got to be."

"Should I. . . ?" Keller said, reaching ahead for his laptop. To leave again, Grace was pretty sure.

"I'm eighteen," Grace said back to him, and pushed up from the couch, disgusted, and held a finger up for him to wait, that she would handle this herself.

Stepping over Benjo was—it was odd.

For the last two years, his every sense had been trained on her every movement. If she stepped over him, he adjusted to minimize the chance of her catching a foot on his back, or slipping on his tail.

He could no longer stand, though.

Or do anything.

"Good boy," Grace said, kind of feeling sorry for him and not sorry for him at the same time. Holding both sides of the doorway, she leaned in to give her mom the eye.

Her mom was lying down on the floor by the sink, the side of her head pressed to the tile, her face turned to Grace.

"I'm sorry, dear," she said, her voice exactly pleasant.

Grace felt the air in her chest shift. Like it was coming in deeper now. Like it was cold.

The cup that had broke was in slimy wet shards all around her mom. It had had hot chocolate in it. The matching cup was still on the counter.

Under her, Benjo's tail twitched, the way it did when he was rebooting. When he was trying to, anyway.

"Make—make him stand," Grace said back to Keller.

"You want me to—?"

"*Now!*" Grace said.

"I'm not sure which does what yet," Keller said, but tried. He said "Stand!" down into his keyboard.

Nothing.

"Well?" Grace said.

"Wait," Keller said, and reached forward to tap a key combo.

Benjo didn't stand.

Grace's mom, though, from the floor, still looking across at Grace, she barked once, a neat little bark.

After it, her lips pursed in shame, and her eyes got a new sheen.

She *could* cry, Grace knew. There had been all the months after the funeral. There had been the first day of senior year.

"Mom," Grace said, slumping over into one side of the doorway. "What—what happened to you?"

Her mom who wasn't her mom shut her eyes tight, like she didn't want to see, didn't want to remember, didn't want to have to say.

But she did anyway.

"Whoa, whoa, *what?*" Keller said from the couch.

Grace had forgotten all about him. He was holding his hands up from his laptop, was trying to get as far from it as he could, it looked like.

"What is it?" Grace said, sitting down beside him again.

"I. . . I don't—feedback—it must be some—" Keller sputtered.

Grace tilted her head. Not like a dog trying to understand something, but because the frame was tilted.

This angle, this memory, it was. . . looking down through boards? No: *rafters.* Looking down onto the main table of her dad's shop.

Just staring. Until Benjo pads in, looks up.

This memory lowers, unfolds itself from the rafters to the table, then the table to the floor, and follows Benjo into the house, down the long hall to the master bedroom, then the master bathroom.

Grace's real, *human* mom is sitting between the toilet and the bathtub. There's dried vomit coating her chin and the front of her robe. The robe that had been her husband's. There's chalky pills in the vomit. A fly is on her face.

"Mom," Grace said, and touched the new itch on her own cheek.

The memory steps in, closer, past Benjo, and looks up to the smear of motion to the left.

It's the mirror above the sink.

The reflection is Grace's mom, the one from the rafters. The one her dad must have built as well, as backup. There's a fine layer of dust on one side of her face, and a wisp of cobwebs veiled back over her hair, that's the same style Grace's mom *used* to wear.

But hair's easy.

Grace shut the laptop, angled her face up, closed her eyes.

That's how she'd been warming the hot chocolate up, always right on time: heater hands, *go*.

"What does this—?" Keller started, but Grace clamped her hand on his leg for him to shut up.

He had been going to ask: "What does this mean?"

Everything.

Nothing.

Breathe.

If you really even need to.

Grace laughed without opening her mouth, then came back to herself—*made* herself come back to herself.

She was all she had left, right?

She opened her eyes, turned to Keller, said, "I think we're alone now."

One side of his lips smiled. The other wasn't so sure.

"It's okay," Grace said, and used her hand to guide him to her, and they leaned back into the cushions locked together like that at last, exploring, feeling, shuddering with this newness, hungry with it.

"Are you crying?" Keller said when he came up for air, hesitation in his voice.

Grace dabbed a finger to her cheek as if surprised, then she started to smell that wetness, for petroleum, but she couldn't.

No: she wouldn't.

She leaned in for Keller again, her dog lying down a few feet away like a good dog, her mom rebooting on the kitchen floor, her dad standing invisible among them all, a control tablet in both hands, glowing up onto his face, and she knew that when she called Tawny later to tell her all about this—*every single wonderful detail!*—that she was probably going to leave one or two out.

The Nightingale (1843)

Hans Christian Andersen

In China, as you know, the emperor is a Chinaman, and all the people around him are Chinamen too. It is many years since the story I am going to tell you happened, but that is all the more reason for telling it, lest it should be forgotten. The emperor's palace was the most beautiful thing in the world; it was made entirely of the finest porcelain, very costly, but at the same time so fragile that it could only be touched with the very greatest care. There were the most extraordinary flowers to be seen in the garden; the most beautiful ones had little silver bells tied to them, which tinkled perpetually, so that one should not pass the flowers without looking at them. Every little detail in the garden had been most carefully thought out, and it was so big, that even the gardener himself did not know where it ended. If one went on walking, one came to beautiful woods with lofty trees and deep lakes. The wood extended to the sea, which was deep and blue, deep enough for large ships to sail up right under the branches of the trees. Among these trees lived a nightingale, which sang so deliciously, that even the poor fisherman, who had plenty of other things to do, lay still to listen to it, when he was out at night drawing in his nets. "Heavens, how beautiful it is!" he said, but then he had to attend to his business and forgot it. The next night when he heard it again he would again exclaim, "Heavens, how beautiful it is!"

Travellers came to the emperor's capital, from every country in the world; they admired everything very much, especially the palace and the gardens, but when they heard the nightingale they all said, "This is better than anything!"

When they got home they described it, and the learned ones wrote many books about the town, the palace and the garden; but nobody forgot the nightingale, it was always put above everything else. Those among them who were poets wrote the most beautiful poems, all about the nightingale in the woods by the deep blue sea. These books went all over the world, and in course of time some of them reached the emperor. He sat in his golden chair reading and reading, and nodding his head, well pleased to hear such beautiful descriptions of the town, the palace, and the garden. "But the nightingale is the best of all," he read.

"What is this?" said the emperor. "The

nightingale? Why, I know nothing about it. Is there such a bird in my kingdom, and in my own garden into the bargain, and I have never heard of it? Imagine my having to discover this from a book?"

Then he called his gentleman-in-waiting, who was so grand that when any one of a lower rank dared to speak to him, or to ask him a question, he would only answer "P," which means nothing at all.

"There is said to be a very wonderful bird called a nightingale here," said the emperor. "They say that it is better than anything else in all my great kingdom! Why have I never been told anything about it?"

"I have never heard it mentioned," said the gentleman-in-waiting. "It has never been presented at court."

"I wish it to appear here this evening to sing to me," said the emperor. "The whole world knows what I am possessed of, and I know nothing about it!"

"I have never heard it mentioned before," said the gentleman-in-waiting. "I will seek it, and I will find it!" But where was it to be found? The gentleman-in-waiting ran upstairs and downstairs and in and out of all the rooms and corridors. No one of all those he met had ever heard anything about the nightingale; so the gentleman-in-waiting ran back to the emperor, and said that it must be a myth, invented by the writers of the books. "Your imperial majesty must not believe everything that is written; books are often mere inventions, even if they do not belong to what we call the black art!"

"But the book in which I read it is sent to me by the powerful Emperor of Japan, so it can't be untrue. I will hear this nightingale; I insist upon its being here to-night. I extend my most gracious protection to it, and if it is not forthcoming, I will have the whole court trampled upon after supper!"

"Tsing-pe!" said the gentleman-in-waiting, and away he ran again, up and down all the stairs, in and out of all the rooms and corridors; half the court ran with him, for they none of them wished to be trampled on. There was much questioning about this nightingale, which was known to all the outside world, but to no one at court. At last they found a poor little maid in the kitchen. She said, "Oh heavens, the nightingale? I know it very well. Yes, indeed it can sing. Every evening I am allowed to take broken meat to my poor sick mother: she lives down by the shore. On my way back, when I am tired, I rest awhile in the wood, and then I hear the nightingale. Its song brings the tears into my eyes; I feel as if my mother were kissing me!"

"Little kitchen-maid," said the gentleman-in-waiting, "I will procure you a permanent position in the kitchen, and permission to see the emperor dining, if you will take us to the nightingale. It is commanded to appear at court tonight."

Then they all went out into the wood where the nightingale usually sang. Half the court was there. As they were going along at their best pace a cow began to bellow.

"Oh!" said a young courtier, "there we have it. What wonderful power for such a little creature; I have certainly heard it before."

"No, those are the cows bellowing; we are a long way yet from the place." Then the frogs began to croak in the marsh.

"Beautiful!" said the Chinese chaplain, "it is just like the tinkling of church bells."

"No, those are the frogs!" said the little kitchen-maid. "But I think we shall soon hear it now!"

Then the nightingale began to sing.

"There it is!" said the little girl. "Listen, listen, there it sits!" and she pointed to a little grey bird up among the branches.

"Is it possible?" said the gentleman-in-waiting. "I should never have thought it was like that. How common it looks! Seeing so many grand people must have frightened all its colours away."

"Little nightingale!" called the kitchen-maid quite loud, "our gracious emperor wishes you to sing to him!"

"With the greatest of pleasure!" said the nightingale, warbling away in the most delightful fashion.

"It is just like crystal bells," said the gentleman-in-waiting. "Look at its little throat, how active it is. It is extraordinary that we have never heard it before! I am sure it will be a great success at court!"

"Shall I sing again to the emperor?" said the nightingale, who thought he was present.

"My precious little nightingale," said the gentleman-in-waiting, "I have the honour to command your attendance at a court festival tonight, where you will charm his gracious majesty the emperor with your fascinating singing."

"It sounds best among the trees," said the nightingale, but it went with them willingly when it heard that the emperor wished it.

The palace had been brightened up for the occasion. The walls and the floors, which were all of china, shone by the light of many thousand golden lamps. The most beautiful flowers, all of the tinkling kind, were arranged in the corridors; there was hurrying to and fro, and a great draught, but this was just what made the bells ring; one's ears were full of the tinkling. In the middle of the large reception-room where the emperor sat a golden rod had been fixed, on which the nightingale was to perch. The whole court was assembled, and the little kitchen-maid had been permitted to stand behind the door, as she now had the actual title of cook. They were all dressed in their best; everybody's eyes were turned towards the little grey bird at which the emperor was nodding. The nightingale sang delightfully, and the tears came into the emperor's eyes, nay, they rolled down his cheeks; and then the nightingale sang more beautifully than ever, its notes touched all hearts. The emperor was charmed, and said the nightingale should have his gold slipper to wear round its neck. But the nightingale declined with thanks; it had already been sufficiently rewarded.

"I have seen tears in the eyes of the emperor; that is my richest reward. The tears of an emperor have a wonderful power! God knows I am sufficiently recompensed!" and then it again burst into its sweet heavenly song.

"That is the most delightful coquetting I have ever seen!" said the ladies, and they took some water into their mouths to try and make the same gurgling when any one spoke to them, thinking so to equal the nightingale. Even the lackeys and the chambermaids announced that they were satisfied, and that is saying a great deal; they are always the most difficult people to please. Yes, indeed, the nightingale had made a sensation. It was to stay at court now, and to have its own cage, as well as liberty to walk out twice a day, and once in the night. It always had twelve footmen, with each one holding a ribbon which was tied round its leg. There was not much pleasure in an outing of that sort.

The whole town talked about the marvellous bird, and if two people met, one said to the other "Night," and the other answered "Gale," and then they sighed, perfectly understanding each other. Eleven cheesemongers' children were called after it, but they had not got a voice among them.

One day a large parcel came for the emperor; outside was written the word "Nightingale."

"Here we have another new book about this celebrated bird," said the emperor. But it was no book; it was a little work of art in a box, an artificial nightingale, exactly like the living one, but it was studded all over with diamonds, rubies, and sapphires.

When the bird was wound up it could sing one of the songs the real one sang, and it wagged its tail, which glittered with silver and gold. A ribbon was tied round its neck on which was written, "The Emperor of Japan's nightingale is very poor compared to the Emperor of China's."

Everybody said, "Oh, how beautiful!" And the person who brought the artificial bird immediately received the title of Imperial Nightingale-Carrier in Chief.

"Now, they must sing together; what a duet that will be."

Then they had to sing together, but they did not get on very well, for the real nightingale sang in its own way, and the artificial one could only sing waltzes.

"There is no fault in that," said the music-master; "it is perfectly in time and correct in every way!"

Then the artificial bird had to sing alone. It was just as great a success as the real one, and then it was so much prettier to look at; it glittered like bracelets and breast-pins.

It sang the same tune three and thirty times over, and yet it was not tired; people would willingly have heard it from the beginning again, but the emperor said that the real one must have a turn now—but where was it? No one had noticed that it had flown out of the open window, back to its own green woods.

"But what is the meaning of this?" said the emperor.

All the courtiers railed at it, and said it was a most ungrateful bird.

"We have got the best bird though," said they, and then the artificial bird had to sing again, and this was the thirty-fourth time that they heard the same tune, but they did not know it thoroughly even yet, because it was so difficult.

The music-master praised the bird tremendously, and insisted that it was much better than the real nightingale, not only as regarded the outside with all the diamonds, but the inside too.

"Because you see, my ladies and gentlemen, and the emperor before all, in the real nightingale you never know what you will hear, but in the artificial one everything is decided beforehand! So it is, and so it must remain, it can't be otherwise. You can account for things, you can open it and show the human ingenuity in arranging the waltzes, how they go, and how one note follows upon another!"

"Those are exactly my opinions," they all said, and the music-master got leave to show the bird to the public next Sunday. They were also to hear it sing, said the emperor. So they heard it, and all became as enthusiastic over it as if they had drunk themselves merry on tea, because that is a thoroughly Chinese habit.

Then they all said "Oh," and stuck their forefingers in the air and nodded their heads; but the poor fishermen who had heard the real nightingale said, "It sounds very nice, and it is very like the real one, but there is something wanting, we don't know what." The real nightingale was banished from the kingdom.

The artificial bird had its place on a silken cushion, close to the emperor's bed: all the presents it had received of gold and precious jewels were scattered round it. Its title had risen to be "Chief Imperial Singer of the Bed-Chamber," in rank number one, on the left side; for the emperor reckoned that side the important one, where the heart was seated. And even an emperor's heart is on the left side. The music-master wrote five-and-twenty volumes about the artificial bird; the treatise was very long and written in all the most difficult Chinese characters. Everybody said they had read and understood it, for otherwise they would have been reckoned stupid, and then their bodies would have been trampled upon.

Things went on in this way for a whole year. The emperor, the court, and all the other

Chinamen knew every little gurgle in the song of the artificial bird by heart; but they liked it all the better for this, and they could all join in the song themselves. Even the street boys sang "zizizi" and "cluck, cluck, cluck," and the emperor sang it too.

But one evening when the bird was singing its best, and the emperor was lying in bed listening to it, something gave way inside the bird with a "whizz." Then a spring burst, "whirr" went all the wheels, and the music stopped. The emperor jumped out of bed and sent for his private physicians, but what good could they do? Then they sent for the watchmaker, and after a good deal of talk and examination he got the works to go again somehow; but he said it would have to be saved as much as possible, because it was so worn out, and he could not renew the works so as to be sure of the tune. This was a great blow! They only dared to let the artificial bird sing once a year, and hardly that; but then the music-master made a little speech, using all the most difficult words. He said it was just as good as ever, and his saying it made it so.

Five years now passed, and then a great grief came upon the nation, for they were all very fond of their emperor, and he was ill and could not live, it was said. A new emperor was already chosen, and people stood about in the street, and asked the gentleman-in-waiting how their emperor was going on.

"P," answered he, shaking his head.

The emperor lay pale and cold in his gorgeous bed, the courtiers thought he was dead, and they all went off to pay their respects to their new emperor. The lackeys ran off to talk matters over, and the chambermaids gave a great coffee-party. Cloth had been laid down in all the rooms and corridors so as to deaden the sound of footsteps, so it was very, very quiet. But the emperor was not dead yet. He lay stiff and pale in the gorgeous bed with its velvet hangings and heavy golden tassels. There was an open window high above him, and the moon streamed in upon the emperor, and the artificial bird beside him.

The poor emperor could hardly breathe, he seemed to have a weight on his chest, he opened his eyes, and then he saw that it was Death sitting upon his chest, wearing his golden crown. In one hand he held the emperor's golden sword, and in the other his imperial banner. Round about, from among the folds of the velvet hangings peered many curious faces: some were hideous, others gentle and pleasant. They were all the emperor's good and bad deeds, which now looked him in the face when Death was weighing him down.

"Do you remember that?" whispered one after the other; "Do you remember this?" and they told him so many things that the perspiration poured down his face.

"I never knew that," said the emperor. "Music, music, sound the great Chinese drums!" he cried, "that I may not hear what they are saying." But they went on and on, and Death sat nodding his head, just like a Chinaman, at everything that was said.

"Music, music!" shrieked the emperor. "You precious little golden bird, sing, sing! I have loaded you with precious stones, and even hung my own golden slipper round your neck; sing, I tell you, sing!"

But the bird stood silent; there was nobody to wind it up, so of course it could not go. Death continued to fix the great empty sockets of his eyes upon him, and all was silent, so terribly silent.

Suddenly, close to the window, there was a burst of lovely song; it was the living nightingale, perched on a branch outside. It had heard of the emperor's need, and had come to bring comfort and hope to him. As it sang the faces round became fainter and fainter, and the blood coursed with fresh vigour in the emperor's veins and through his feeble limbs. Even Death himself listened to the song and said, "Go on, little nightingale, go on!"

"Yes, if you give me the gorgeous golden sword; yes, if you give me the imperial banner; yes, if you give me the emperor's crown."

And Death gave back each of these treasures for a song, and the nightingale went on singing. It sang about the quiet churchyard, when the roses bloom, where the elderflower scents the air, and where the fresh grass is ever moistened anew by the tears of the mourner. This song brought to Death a longing for his own garden, and, like a cold grey mist, he passed out of the window.

"Thanks, thanks!" said the emperor, "You heavenly little bird, I know you! I banished you from my kingdom, and yet you have charmed the evil visions away from my bed by your song, and even Death away from my heart! How can I ever repay you?"

"You have rewarded me," said the nightingale. "I brought the tears to your eyes, the very first time I ever sang to you, and I shall never forget it! Those are the jewels which gladden the heart of a singer—but sleep now, and wake up fresh and strong! I will sing to you!"

Then it sang again, and the emperor fell into a sweet refreshing sleep. The sun shone in at his window, when he woke refreshed and well; none of his attendants had yet come back to him, for they thought he was dead, but the nightingale still sat there singing.

"You must always stay with me!" said the emperor. "You shall only sing when you like, and I will break the artificial bird into a thousand pieces!"

"Don't do that!" said the nightingale, "it did all the good it could! Keep it as you have always done! I can't build my nest and live in this palace, but let me come whenever I like, then I will sit on the branch in the evening, and sing to you. I will sing to cheer you and to make you thoughtful too; I will sing to you of the happy ones, and of those that suffer too. I will sing about the good and the evil, which are kept hidden from you. The little singing bird flies far and wide, to the poor fisherman, and the peasant's home, to numbers who are far from you and your court. I love your heart more than your crown, and yet there is an odour of sanctity round the crown too!—I will come, and I will sing to you!—But you must promise me one thing!—

"Everything!" said the emperor, who stood there in his imperial robes which he had just put on, and he held the sword heavy with gold upon his heart.

"One thing I ask you! Tell no one that you have a little bird who tells you everything; it will be better so!"

Then the nightingale flew away. The attendants came in to see after their dead emperor, and there he stood, bidding them "Good morning!"

Le Cygne Baiseur
Molly Tanzer

The women have gathered around Mr. Hubert, their eyes shining in the candlelight, their expressions eager. The hoops of their skirts bump and crinolines rustle as they jockey for position; looks containing entire conversations are exchanged. In spite of the lateness of the hour, the parlor is very hot. Sweat beads at the edges of their elaborate hairdos and trickles down more than one white-powdered cheek.

Mr. Hubert, the celebrated toymaker, is just as turned out as the women who surround him. Lace drips from his cuffs, and his waistcoat is embroidered with a garden's worth of fruits, flowers, and vines. He is enjoying their attention; it's obvious from his stance, his slight smile. By speaking in a low voice, he makes them lean in, exposing the plump tops of their corset-flattened bosoms, and tells them to come closer, even though they are crushed together already.

The women fall silent as he puts his hand on an object about the size of a sleeping St. Bernard, lumpy and obscure under a cloth. He asks them if they would like to see what lies beneath. They do; oh, they do—and once they have evinced an appropriate amount of eagerness, he reveals it with a showman's flourish.

The mechanical swan is a rococo wonder. The details are marvelous, from the painted feathers to the modeling of the sculptural components. It appears to sleep, eyes closed, metal beak tucked under wooden wing, long neck draped in a zigzag over its body.

The ladies stare at Mr. Hubert's creation as they *ooh* and *ahh*, but Mr. Hubert's eyes do not leave the women. He watches them watching it. At the ideal moment, just before their interest wavers, he produces an enameled key from his waistcoat pocket, also wrought in the shape of a swan. He jams it rather lewdly into the bird's backside, and turns it a few times as the women titter.

The swan stirs. It lifts its head, honks twice, and beats its great wings a few times, just like a real bird. Its movements are a bit jerky, clearly clockwork, but the illusion is remarkable. It even waggles its tail before lurching to its feet.

"What is it doing?" shrieks one of the women, as the swan wanders over to poke its bill beneath her skirts.

"Here." Mr. Hubert produces a handful of corn kernels and hands them to the woman.

She frees herself from the swan and then leans down, hand extended. The mechanical bird is immediately interested. It even lifts its head to swallow after nibbling delicately, then defecates on the floor.

"Clockwork my swan may be, but it has its... appetites," says Mr. Hubert.

The polite applause fades away instantly. These women have been waiting for this moment; it's obvious they have some knowledge of Mr. Hubert's swan, and what it can do.

He smiles serenely. "I will need a volunteer."

No one speaks up until the lady of the house, Mrs. Suzman, says, "Mrs. Fraser."

Eyes swivel in their sockets to an older, dark-haired woman. She goes pale under her powder.

"*Pamela*," hisses Mrs. Suzman. "Yours was the short straw."

Mrs. Fraser, resigned, stands up a bit straighter. "I would love to assist Mr. Hubert," she says evenly.

"Excellent." He does not seem bothered by her trepidation. Instead, he offers her his hand and leads her to a gilded chaise lounge. She sits down, trembling, her dark eyes wide.

Mr. Hubert kneels beside where the mechanical swan has gone still and once again thrusts the key up its rear end. He turns it in a different pattern this time. The swan shudders and walks jerkily over to Mrs. Fraser. It bows to her, wings spread. Mrs. Fraser stares at it.

"You may find it a bit easier if you lie back and lift your skirts." Mr. Hubert's tranquil mood is just as terrifying as the swan, which has awkwardly leaped up beside her.

Mrs. Fraser hikes up her dress, exposing her clocked stockings and pale thighs. The swan cants its head to the right, inspecting what she has revealed, and then a large human-like phallus unfolds from its underbelly.

It is difficult to tell if Mrs. Fraser is aroused or frightened by the sight of the instrument. Curved and obscene, wreathed with veins, its purple head is bright against the whiteness of the shaft. But when the swan climbs atop her and penetrates her, her moans are pure pleasure. She writhes and bucks against the swan, eventually wrapping her ankles around its body to draw it deeper, as the mechanical bird's webbed feet scrabble at the couch, tearing the velvet. It twines its neck around her at their mutual crisis, biting her shoulder. After it withdraws, its instrument folds back into its belly.

Emily turns up the museum theatre's lights as the screen goes dark. Like Mr. Hubert in the film, she gazes serenely at the audience. They all seem a bit dazed, flushed, though it's difficult for her to tell if it's from arousal, anger, or some emotion she cannot perceive. She's seen just about every reaction to that scene from *Le Cygne Baiseur* over the past few months, including a first week freak-out from a woman that was so severe the museum had new programs printed with a stern warning right on the front.

The thing was, that was the least offensive sex scene in *Le Cygne Baiseur.*

"As we've seen, what man invents, he re-invents to be about sex," she says to her audience. They perk up a bit as they return to the 21st century and to the *Erotic Parodies* exhibit they've paid an extra fee and signed a waiver to view. "*Le Cygne Baiseur* is based on a short story of the same name. Attributed to Voltaire, 'The Amorous Swan' is about a toymaker who invents a mechanical swan that 'makes a Leda' out of a woman at a fancy party. He wrote it after the sensation made by Jacques de Vaucanson's 'Canard Digérateur,' or Digesting Duck, in 1739. Vaucanson's celebrated mechanical bird appeared to eat, drink, and defecate, though later it was discovered that the bird actually excreted pre-made bread pellets.

"There was no digestion scene in Voltaire's original story; that was an addition by British director Ben Blackwell, most famous for his controversial film *What She Revealed, When He Departed, and Why They Lied.* After reading an account of Vaucanson's life, Blackwell became obsessed with automata and other clockwork creatures and wanted to insert a tribute to the original inventor in his film. He also oversaw and even participated in the construction of his own personal, working 'cygne baiseur' which he used as a prop. Yes, that's right… the footage you just saw is all quite real."

Emily's heart begins to beat a little faster every time she reaches this part of the tour, leading them to the pièce de résistance of her exhibit. On loan from Prague's Sex Machines Museum, Blackwell's swan is truly spectacular. The grainy 1982 film, shot entirely by candlelight during the night scenes, doesn't really do it justice.

Though not in working order anymore, the enormous mechanical swan can still be adjusted, so of course they have posed it in its most iconic position: wings spread, cock erect. It has never once failed to elicit gasps from the audience, and today is no different. Emily smiles to herself; she really is just like Mr. Hubert, given how much pleasure she takes in watching people beholding the bird. A voyeur's voyeur.

The swan's roost is a low pedestal so that it can be viewed in the round. She lets her audience gaze for a few moments more, noting where they look, and where they don't, before clearing her throat.

"The footage you just watched was from the British Film Institute's re-release of *Le Cygne Baiseur*, available on DVD and Blu-ray in the museum gift shop. Which, if you will follow me…"

Thus ends another tour. Emily is pleased

with herself. It went well. They usually do—she's proud of this exhibit and enjoys talking about it. Just the same, she's eager for them to get going. It's the end of the day; she's ready to get home, take her shoes off, and veg out with a bottle of wine. Netflix and some genuine chilling.

"That was a really great tour."

Emily startles. One of the group has lagged behind. She noticed his floppy hair and sardonic smile earlier—a Paul Rudd-type who looked like he really ought to be wearing a flannel rather than a suit jacket over his vintage-looking t-shirt for some craft brewery.

"Thanks," says Emily. "Glad you enjoyed."

"I did. Everything was really interesting. Those Japanese woodblock prints of the little Bean-man were great," he says, "but that film… that was something else."

"It's an amazing work," says Emily. She's happy to talk to him. He seems nice, and isn't setting off her creep alarm, like a few randos here and there since the show opened. "You should see the entire film sometime."

"I'd like to," he says.

An awkward silence descends. He coughs affectedly into his hand to break it, like he's in a movie, and then extends it. "I'm Paul."

Huh. "Emily," she says. "Nice to meet you."

"Yeah." He smiles, then chuckles, blushing. Another silence, then he says, "Well, I guess I better…" and nods to the door.

Finally, Emily gets it. "What are you doing

now? The museum shuts down in a bit, but after, if you wanted to watch it—the whole film I mean—I could get us back inside. I have a key."

"Back inside the museum?"

"Yeah. I was thinking we could watch it on the big screen. I love our little theatre; it's a great opportunity to see movies as they're meant to be seen. I just don't want us to be interrupted by the cleaning crew while we're watching, you know?"

"Sure!" he says, and she's grateful he doesn't seem disappointed she hadn't proposed outright that they go back to her place. "I'd love to."

They go to a casual Italian joint, one close to the museum as it's quite cold out. She gets the butternut squash ravioli; he gets the carbonara. They talk about common things, like jobs and hobbies—he's in tech, but his real passion is climbing—and less common ones, like the exhibit.

"I was especially pleased to get Murakami's 'My Lonesome Cowboy' on loan," she says. "I know a lot of people have seen pictures of it, but in person…"

"It's hilarious and shocking," he agrees. "That semen lasso is just so… huge."

"So, what brought you in?" she asks. "To the show, I mean."

"That write-up they did in the local paper. But I have to say, when they mentioned you were screening a segment of a," he makes air quotes, *"pornographic film*, I wasn't expecting…"

"No. I mean, there's a reason no under-eighteens are allowed in, but calling it a porno felt like they were trying to make the show sound edgier than it really is. Though some of the later scenes…"

"Yeah?" He leans forward, all attention. Emily wonders if they will have sex later. She isn't averse to the idea. Watching *Le Cygne Baiseur* always puts her in the mood. There's something that turns her on about the lavish costumes, the period lighting, the unfathomable expressions and disconnected utterances of the actors, the lush Michael Nyman soundtrack based on grounds from William Croft, the curious movements of the swan.

"Yeah," she says, leaning in and lowering her voice. "For the theatrical release one scene had to be cut substantially to avoid an X rating, but the version we have at the museum is the restored, remastered, re-everythinged edition. I was so thrilled to see it for the first time, especially given the legend about it…"

"What legend?"

"Do you mind spoilers?" He shakes his head, floppy hair flopping around. "So, after the scene we watched, the party breaks up and Mr. Hubert presses his advantage with Mrs. Suzman, the lady of the house. Her husband is out of town, and she agrees to go to bed with him. But while they're fucking in her bedroom, her daughter sneaks downstairs and has a tryst with the swan."

"Oh my," he says.

"Yeah. Even without the Toymaker's key up its bum, the swan comes alive for her. It's uncanny to watch on two levels. Within the film, the swan is an automaton, and therefore it ought to behave the same way each time it does the same things… but it doesn't. It's much more, uh, enthusiastic with the daughter. And sure, it's just a film, but the swan is also a prop, right? Pre-CGI. It's a practical effect, and should be constrained by similar rules… but it doesn't move like clockwork in that scene. That's probably why the legend got started, that the swan really *did* come to life that night while they were filming. It's said it surprised everyone, as you might imagine, but they kept the cameras rolling. It's true, the young actress seems genuinely frightened and bewildered, but it could just be acting. And…"

"And?" He's enthralled.

"Well, the earlier scene is just movie magic. It doesn't really penetrate that woman. But it's said the actress playing the daughter got into an *interesting condition* from the encounter." Paul looks baffled until Emily spells it out. "Pregnant."

"Pregnant? In the movie?"

"In the movie the daughter gets pregnant that night, but not the mother… shit gets *real* weird after that, as you might imagine," says Emily. "So earlier, when they toymaker makes the thing, he declares it '*beautiful enough to house*

Jove himself.' So the film becomes about whether the girl has gotten knocked up by a god, or whether something else happened that night. But the story is that it all really happened. In real life, to the actress." She shrugs.

"Enough people believe a mechanical swan came to life and impregnated an actress that it's become an urban legend?" He sighs. "I guess post-Pizzagate I shouldn't be surprised."

"I'm sure that part of it is that the actress only did this one film. It was her breakout role and she disappeared afterwards. Fell right off the map."

"I guess people could still do that back in the '80s."

"I know, right? Plus, there's this blurry old photo of a young woman who looks very like her. Someone who thought they recognized her snapped it in Greece, a few years after the film. She had a toddler with her, but as to whether it's actually the same actress... anyway." Emily realizes she's been talking for a while about this and gives him a look. "Want to see it for yourself?"

He does. They pick their way over the snow and ice back to the museum, stopping only to grab two bottles of wine, a brie, and some crackers at a fancy little shop.

She likes him. He hadn't seemed bored when she nerded out about her favorite film and hadn't droned on too long about his passion, either. In fact, his offer to take her indoor climbing sometime, while an intimidating prospect, seems fun and fresh.

The museum is silent and dark; a little spooky, actually. They giggle as they sneak through the hallways, though of course, it's all mock-sneaking. She's allowed to be here, it's just fun to pretend they're up to something taboo. The mood settles once they get into the theatre, pop in the Blu-ray, unscrew the wine, and the United Artists logo pops up.

"Thanks," she whispers, leaning in so that her lips almost brush that floppy hair of his. "I haven't watched this all the way through in a long time." He shivers, and his eyes flicker toward her and then back to the screen as the film starts.

Le Cygne Baiseur is undeniably slow, and absolutely bizarre, and yet there's something hypnotic about it. The performances captivate, even though most of the actors were only ever known for bit parts in old BBC adaptations of Dickens and Austen, or the lesser-known Hammer films. Every conversation feels freighted; every moment a clue that, if studied closely enough, might reveal the central puzzle of act three: whether or not Miss Suzman's pregnancy is truly divine in origin. The characters take various positions on the issue—the daughter believes yes; her father, not so much—but it's never made wholly clear what the "right" answer is.

Emily and Paul don't make it that far,

however. They break into the second bottle of wine and the oozy brie just before the scene he's already seen, but Emily barely drinks any of it. She's too excited for what comes next. She loves the conversation between Mr. Hubert and Mrs. Suzman, so calculated on his part, so wanton on hers; loves the look on the daughter's face as she hides in the shadows, watching the verbal seduction in the parlor. Then comes the daughter's woozy stagger back to the swan, which shivers and comes alive as she strokes it.

When the swan begins to tear at the daughter's clothes with its metal bill, Emily can feel Paul's growing discomfort. It's true, after the swan pins her to the carpet with its weight the girl's cries are indeterminably of pleasure or pain. It's hard to watch.

Paul stands, knocking over his half-full glass of wine when the girl screams genuinely as the swan thrusts inside her with more than mechanical urgency.

"I'm done with this," he says over the clacking of wooden wings and immediately heads for the door of the theatre. Emily, dismayed by both his exit and the wine soaking into the carpet, follows him.

"Wait," she says, as they reach the door. "Paul—"

"That's real," he says. He's very upset—his face, flickering blue and white from the action on the screen, is furious and frowning. "It's not a legend. That *thing* is real, and what it's doing to her is real."

The girl's cries have turned rapturous as the swan fucks her eagerly. She is now quite obviously enjoying herself, though her pleasure is ecstatic and disturbing in its intensity. She cracks a nail digging her fingers into the bird's unyielding back, grinds against it wildly when it enters the short thrusts. The images of this monstrous machine ravishing the daughter are intercut with eerily similar footage of its creator finishing inside her mother. During an earlier viewing Emily noticed at various points the sounds are reversed, the honking and the grinding of gears momentarily imposed over animal thrusting; lustful manly grunts accompanying volucrine struggling. They both get caught up in it for a moment, until Paul flees into the darkness of the museum proper.

Emily says, "It's just a—"

"It's just *nothing*. I'm… look, thanks for the wine, sorry about the carpet. I think it's time I got home." He gives her a scornful, disgusted look as she lets him out. "Enjoy the rest of your film."

She sees him calling a Lyft on his phone through the glass doors, and though the night is cold she locks them behind him. A car will likely come quickly, and anyway, she has wine to scrub out of a carpet.

Emily hears the film echoing through the museum like ghosts muttering about her date gone wrong. She's upset, his disgust has hurt her feelings. She didn't make the film, or start the urban legend. She only showed it to him at his request, what right does he have to condemn her for doing so? But as she stomps back to the theatre, she passes by the swan that caused so much trouble, and pauses.

It's been well taken care of, over the decades. The swan's paint and enamel are still so white that it seems almost luminous under the security lights. It really is such a beautiful object. She wonders how many hours Ben Blackwell and his team spent crafting it—she wonders, too, why he sold it to a museum. She would have kept it.

She knows the security cameras will catch her in the act, but Emily can't resist. She approaches the mechanical bird, and just like the daughter in *Le Cygne Baiseur*, she strokes its chin, lightly, so as not to set off the pressure sensors.

The bird shivers. Emily steps back, alarmed and a little annoyed. It will be difficult to explain if she's engaged some ancient mechanism that causes the stupid thing to shift in some noticeable way. Her heart starts to pound as she hears the dusty squealing of unoiled gears and she steps back with a wince when the bird lowers its wings and steps off of its perch, peering at her.

No alarms sound.

"No way," says Emily. She takes another step back, but the swan pursues her, waddling on awkward metal legs, and then beats its wings a few times. It mutters at her gently, not really honking. She feels like it is calling to her, but of course, that's impossible.

Her eyes stray to its phallus. It depends from the bird's belly, curved like a saber. In the dim light of the dark museum it looks more alive than it ought to—the whole swan does, actually. It ripples with natural motion, artificial feathers puffing and settling, its breast heaving. It cocks its head; mutters at her again, appealing to her.

She hears the film's theme play faintly in the other room, reedy woodwinds and pulsing strings—it must be to the credits by now—and she is reminded how eager she'd been for a little action that night. The swan's invitation is unusual, yes, but she's never minded the atypical in bed. Honestly, it is the chance of a lifetime—to make it with the notorious, eponymous Cygne Baiseur.

"All right," she says, and she thinks the swan's next utterance sounds pleased as she peels off her pantyhose and thong in one semi-awkward motion. It comes closer as she kneels, close enough that she kisses its enameled cheek before it dips its head under her skirt to tug eagerly at her pubic hair with its bill.

She bats the swan away playfully. Undeterred, it climbs atop her. She runs her hand up and down the length of its shaft a few times to get it wet with whatever viscous fluid has emerged from the tip. She wonders only briefly where that reservoir might reside in its mechanical body—how it's stayed liquid for so many decades—before spreading herself open to receive it.

She lets the bird have its weird way with her in a flurry of honking and clanking. It is just as enthusiastic with her as it was with that actress, and she comes hard, twice, before it finishes loudly and with a gush of something surprisingly warm, given how cool its body is to the touch.

It withdraws itself slowly, with all the consideration of a human lover, and nibbles her earlobe affectionately before returning to its roost and resuming its former pose. She glances at it briefly as she cleans herself up. It's as if it never moved.

By the time Emily has her clothes back on and is more or less put together, she wonders if the whole encounter actually happened. By the time she gets the worst of the wine out of the carpet, she's certain it didn't. It couldn't have.

Two weeks later, she's surprised when her phone app alerts her that she's late for her period. She's usually so regular. But it doesn't come. What does is a feeling of restlessness. For the first time, she's unhappy with her job; her life. She wishes she were elsewhere. Somewhere warm.

She starts looking for tickets. It's been a while since her last vacation.

Greece ought to be lovely this time of year.

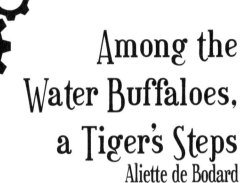

Among the Water Buffaloes, a Tiger's Steps

Aliette de Bodard

*I*n the days where the earth was newly broken and the living still remembered the sleepers walking the world, a water buffalo found a tiger in a coffin.

It was in the days where the sleepers' land purged itself of all it could not bear, coughing out into the periphery seeds and parts by the thousands — and also those sleepers that were unsuitable or broken or merely in excess. The tiger was one of these last, though who knew what kind?

Now, tigers are the natural enemy of the buffalo, and this buffalo belonged to a large herd — rain had fallen in abundance upon the parched earth, and the herd was full of eager young ones, barely aware enough to realise all the dangers the world now held. So the buffalo was ready to kill the tiger, or to push the coffin back into the dome, into the sleepers' land. But as the tiger unfolded his body and stalked, all grace and elegance, from the broken coffin, the buffalo saw, for a bare, suspended moment, a shadow of what the *world had been before its breaking—green grass and clear water, and the memory of sleepers that were as gods.*

And, so, in spite of her misgivings, the buffalo took the tiger back to her herd.

How Kim Trang got to the pool:

After the sun goes down, the girls huddle together in the remnants of a house by the sea—every screen, every scrap of metal since long scavenged to keep their own bodies going—and tell each other stories. Of animals, and plants, and of the world before and after the Catastrophe. Thuy is outrageously good at this. Her sight allows her to read the other girls' microscopic cues from heartbeat to temperature of skin, and adapt her tales of spirits and ghosts for maximum effects. Ngoc He stutters, barely hiding the tremors in her hands—nerve-wires that broke down and that she hasn't yet scavenged replacements for—but she has the largest range of tales of any of them. Ai Hong speaks almost absent-mindedly, playing with those few crab-bots that aren't frightened by so much light and noise—they skitter away when she puts down her hand, and draw back again when she frowns in thought, trying to recall a particular plot point.

Mei usually sits, listless and silent; but this

time, she gets up and leaves the house as Ngoc He finishes the tale of the mechanic and the durian fruit. Kim Trang gets up and follows her.

She finds her in the courtyard, watching Vy finish the dismantling of her hibernation berth. She leans against the wall, breathing slowly, evenly.

Vy nods to Kim Trang as she comes out—she's busy figuring out how to pull out the last few chips and cables, scavenging everything she can so the girls can keep going for a while longer, absorbing and integrating the remnants of sleepers' technology to repair themselves. A few crab-bots crawl over the power source, trying to fix it in spite of all the evidence, but most have given up, and are simply dragging pieces of metal back to their burrows—they were meant to keep things running, to repair the dome, but they were cut loose after the Catastrophe and are now like the girls, taking everything they can for themselves. Vy isn't talking to Mei, but then Vy was the one who didn't want Kim Trang to bring Mei home, to let the tiger loose among them.

"Give me a hand afterwards, will you?" Vy asks.

Kim Trang nods. Her lineage is that of a repair construct. Her distant ancestor who survived the Catastrophe isn't here anymore, but she and generations of her descendants have left Kim Trang routines—knowledge at the organic and electronic level, so thoroughly ingrained it might as well be reflexes by now.

Mei straightens up when Kim Trang arrives, gives her a tight and forced smile.

"You should be inside," Kim Trang says.

Mei shakes her head. "I'd just be an imposition."

"You could tell stories," Kim Trang says. "Of the world before. Of—"

"Of how we broke it past repair?" Mei's voice is curt.

"You weren't the only ones," Kim Trang says. The girls' ancestors might have been constructs, acting under duress, having free will only insofar as it didn't contradict the sleepers' orders—but does that really make them blameless?

"I'm the villain in all your stories," Mei says. She shakes her head.

The tiger. The walking time bomb for Kim Trang's kind. No wonder Vy wants her gone, and Kim Trang should follow Vy's advice, tell Mei to leave. "It's the way we learnt the world."

"The world." Mei's gaze looks past her, at the dark shape of the dome that dwarfs them both. The air smells, faintly, of brine, of spilled oil. "It wasn't supposed to be like this."

"Many things weren't. Are you angry they left you behind?"

Mei shrugs. "It was broken, wasn't it?"

"The berth?" Kim Trang nods. "Beyond repair. Or at least, not with the tech we have. I'm sorry."

"Don't be." Mei shrugs. Her eyes haven't left the dome. "It's not like I could go back." She rubs her fingers against her arms, as if drawing the contours of scars, or wire traceries—what would they feel like, those fingers on Kim Trang's skin? "We thought the earth would be green when we woke up again. Cleansed." She doesn't say from what, or who bears responsibility for it.

"It's not so bad," Kim Trang says. It's all they've known, really—save for phantom lineage memories, a nagging sense that things ought to be freer, larger, less dangerous—the silent killer, the thoughtless expectations that get girls killed, out there, if they don't shut them out.

"No," Mei says. She shakes her head. "Why did you save me, Kim Trang?"

Kim Trang has thought of that, at night. She remembers finding the berth in the still waters of the pool by the dome, Vy strenuously arguing that anything from the sleepers was poisoned gifts and that they should leave it there to break down. Kim Trang, too curious for her own good, reaching out, touching the glass—her lineage gift stretching, the berth switching to maintenance mode, letting her see the still, waxy face of an unknown woman, eyes wide in a perfect oval of a face—not like Kim Trang's own face, scarred from a fall into rocky water, from encounters with fractured tech, to crumbling ledges and acid earth that ate at their skin, the hundred ways that the world tries to kill them for the mere act of living and being free—a face that's beyond scavenging, beyond survival. "Why not?" Kim Trang asks, trying so very hard to keep it casual.

She leans against the wall, close enough to Mei that she can feel the heat of Mei's body—the feel and smell of her, a sharp taste in her throat—a memory, not hers, but a lineage one, of rooms with walls so white they hurt the eyes, of hands brushing alcohol against wounds.

Mei looks at her, cocking her head in a particular way; and Kim Trang can't tell what she's being measured against. "Whims? I shouldn't think any of you had them."

"We're not animals," Kim Trang says, more harshly than she meant.

Mei looks horrified. "Of course not. I didn't mean—just that you couldn't afford them. I'm sorry, Kim Trang—"

"No, it's all right," Kim Trang says. Heavy with something she cannot name, she reaches out to run a hand against Mei's cheek, feeling the contour of soft, warm skin so unlike hers. A shiver wracks her body from head to toe, all the lineage memories rising and blurring together as if the world was suddenly washed in rain.

Mei tenses. She's going to pull away—what a foolish, foolish idea: Vy was right, it was a bad plan from the start—but she doesn't. She leans in, gently taking Kim Trang's hand, and sets it on her lips. Taking it into her mouth, her tongue wanders around Kim Trang's flesh, sending pinpricks of desire down Kim Trang's spine. The girls design their own descendants and no longer need sex to reproduce, but some pleasure reflexes still remain the same across generations. Kim Trang withdraws her finger, slowly, while drawing Mei's lips to her own, drinking all of her in.

Such a bad, bad idea.

"Big'sis?" Vy's voice. Of course.

Kim Trang breaks away, watching Mei smile at her, tentatively, and with the tightness of someone who's not sure if things will still be there tomorrow. "I'm sorry," she says. "But I have to go. Later?"

Mei relaxes a fraction. "Wouldn't dream of missing it." She pulls away from the wall, and goes back towards the house. Kim Trang should go back to the berth, help Vy out—but she has time. She can watch until Mei is gone, completely swallowed by the darkness.

Kim Trang walks, slowly, to Vy, feeling the heaviness in her subside, her breathing slows down until her lungs no longer burn. The berth is now little more than scrap metal, a tantalising mess of opened-up compartments with torn cables and broken parts. Kim Trang runs a hand, slowly, on the control panel. It warms up to her touch, trying to cycle itself back into maintenance mode. "That's what failed. The regulator in the control panel. The crabs can't repair that. If the dome hadn't ejected her, she would have died inside."

She thought Vy was going to say something harsh, something about things being for the best if that had happened, but her sister's dark eyes are wide open, with the same lack of expression as Mei's when she was watching Vy dismantle her berth.

"Did you hear everything?" Kim Trang asks.

"I'm not a spy," Vy says, affronted. "But I have eyes. And you do, too, except you weren't using them to pay attention."

"I don't understand."

"The crab-bots," Vy says, curtly. "When you two—kissed—they gathered around her in a circle. Like a court. She's waking up."

"She—" Kim Trang flushes, embarrassed though she doesn't know why. "She means no harm." Mei is a sleeper—clusters of implants and gen-mods, the algorithms that used to enforce compliance to the sleepers' will—algorithms that generations of the girls' lineages haven't been able to breed out, the same algorithms that bend the crab-bots to her will. Centuries of enforced obedience in their blood, and should Mei decide to give orders...

"Her kind never does mean harm," Vy says. She shakes her head. "They didn't set out to break the world. Or to deny us our freedom. Until things don't go their way." She reaches out, squeezes Kim Trang's hand between hers. "I'm not doing this out of spite. I know what you want."

Does she—when Kim Trang herself doesn't know what she wants? "I know what *you* want."

"It hasn't changed," Vy says. She picks up

a scrap of metal, from the wreck of the berth, crushes it between her fingers—slowly starts absorbing it into her skin, growing a bulge that will be digested next time she needs repairs. "I'm sorry, but—"

But things are what they are. But tigers don't abandon their stripes, or their fangs, just out of charity. "I know," Kim Trang says, but she can't find an answer that would satisfy her and Vy.

The tiger didn't ask where it had woken up, or when, or where the sleepers' land had gone, or why he seemed to be the only one of his kind in the midst of animals that should not have survived the breaking of the world. He sat, listless, until one day the buffalo took him to the periphery again, showing him the boundary with the sleepers' land: the smooth surface of the dome resting in a sea sparkling with the rainbow colours of spilled oil. There was no door, no way to enter, and not even windows to guess at what might be happening within.

She expected him to scream, or to weep, or simply to rise and stalk near the walls of the dome with the same deadly elegance as when he'd risen from his coffin. Instead he remained silent, though there was a gleam in his eyes that hadn't been there before.

"We can look for a way in," the buffalo said, finally, because the silence made her uncomfortable. "Perhaps there'll be someone you knew—"

The tiger spoke, then, in a voice rough with disuse. "How do I know they're not all dead inside?"

The buffalo had no answer, but she felt as though her heart was being squeezed into bloody shreds.

After the kiss:

Kim Trang rises in the morning, and finds Mei gone.

For a slow, suspended moment, she thinks something has gone wrong, but all the girls still sleep on their mats: Thuy hugging the machine she's building (an augment based on crab-bot biology, that will help her dive longer into polluted waters); Ngoc He tossing and turning; Vy perfectly still (her lineage was gen-modded from plants, and she draws oxygen into her body through her skin and eyes rather than through lungs).

Kim Trang finds Mei outside, by the wreck of her berth, watching the rising sun. Part of Kim Trang's lineage remembers a bright, blue sky and stars scattered across the night, but for all of her life the sky has been grey and overcast, the heavy clouds promising a storm that never comes. Mei's hands rest, loosely, on the control panel—lights flash, fleetingly, before sinking back into quiescence.

Mei bends, kissing Kim Trang—a brief taste, a wounding sharpness on the tip of her tongue, her hips digging into Kim Trang's—and then she pulls away, though Kim Trang can still feel the weight of her presence. "It's beautiful, isn't it? I had forgotten what it was like."

Kim Trang doesn't see beauty—merely the same thing she sees every day—but Mei's enthusiasm is infectious. "It is," she says.

"Three hundred years of missed sunrises." Mei sighs. She says, finally, "It was beautiful, too, the world before. In a different way." She crouches at the foot of her berth; and Kim Trang crouches with her, no longer seeing the shadow of the dome. Around them is nothing but muddy earth, with the sharp, familiar tang of metal and oil. Mei's outstretched hands wrap around Kim Trang's callused ones, a touch that Kim Trang aches to take to her chest, to her hips. "Slender spires of metal going all the way into the sky, and gleaming as the sun struck them. And a flow of vehicles and people in the streets, all colours and sounds, a roar that would never fall silent, not even while night came."

As she speaks, Kim Trang feels it, rising in her blood—memories of the lineage, distant sounds and images, a sense of a world opening up around her that could give her anything and everything, leaving her breathless and flushed. "It's gone," she says, more abruptly than she means. And in such a place, she would be a servant, a menial.

"Yes," Mei said. "And perhaps it's just as well. We weren't always kind to your ancestors, among all our other sins." She pauses. Kim Trang runs her hands over Mei's face again. She bends closer, but Mei pulls away before the kiss. "I used to design buildings. Making sure everything was in perfect harmony in rooms and walls. There's not much I can bring you."

You can command the bots, Kim Trang wants to say, and then thinks of how Vy and the others would view this ability—not as a useful skill, but merely a prelude to their own enslavement. "You'll learn."

Mei's hands tighten into fists. "Not as well as you do, and not as fast. I wasn't born into this world."

"We can wait."

"Can you? You have no space for dead weight."

Feeling useless. Kim Trang knows how that goes. Even if there weren't a hundred stories about sleepers waking up too early, she would know in her bones. "You could—"

"Design something here?" Mei shakes her head. "Vy would never let me do it. Besides—" She makes a short, stabbing gesture. "I'm not sure I know better than her, when it comes to design."

"She'll come around."

"Will she?" Mei's gaze is shrewd.

"You're—" Kim Trang takes a deep, shaking breath. "Vy thinks you're not one of us."

"Mm." Mei's hands rest at her side, quietly, looking at Kim Trang with an odd expression on her face. Before Kim Trang can protest that she doesn't think that way—not even sure if that would be a lie—Mei says: "She's right."

"No," Kim Trang says. "You—"

"I'm a danger to you all," Mei says. "The tiger in the story. The predator that undoes you in the end. I'm thankful you saved my life, Kim Trang, but it's best if I left."

She—she. No. Kim Trang can't hear anything save the roar of blood in her ears, a hundred different lineage calls, wondering how to fix a broken situation, finding no way out. "You can't leave. You'll just die out there."

"Credit me with a little resourcefulness." Mei makes a short, stabbing gesture—the crab-bots gather from the berth above them, watchful and still—awaiting orders. "The entire world remembers. I'm—" Her face twists in a terrible expression that wraps around Kim Trang's chest like a metal fist. "I'm not like you girls."

"That doesn't mean you have to leave!"

Mei rises. It would have been worse, in many ways, if the crab-bots had followed, but she's let go of her hold on them, and they're inert again, crawling over the wreck of the berth looking for anything they can use. "It does. It's what I am. Too many implants, too many gen-mods—to take them out of me would kill me." Her expression softens for a bare moment. She lays a hand on Kim Trang's shoulder, with nothing of desire or lust in it. "Don't feel bad. It's the way the world has to be, and I'm by no means blameless.

Atonement, perhaps, for what I did to you and your ancestors."

Kim Trang scrambles to her feet, struggling to find words. She can't leave. She—Vy has to be wrong, of course she can stay with them, she's not a danger—again and again in circles in her mind. "Mei! Please—" She does the only thing she can think of. She grabs Mei by the shoulder as she's walking away, turns Mei towards her with all the strength she uses to wrench cables out of sockets and chips out of their compartments.

"Don't touch me!"

It's like being electrocuted—a jolt of current that seizes all of Kim Trang's limbs, sends her to the ground, spasming, struggling to breathe—arms and legs refusing to obey, her entire being screaming with one voice. She has to stop; she has to be still; she has to bow down. Every single lineage-memory breaks around her until the only one that remains is old, as vivid as yesterday: her faraway ancestor bowing to a sleeper after repairing their vehicle, and the rush of pleasure that seizes her, stilling her where she stands.

No. No.

The world is broken, centuries have passed, and her ancestor is long dead.

Slowly, agonisingly slowly, she pulls herself to her feet—and it can't have been that long after all, because Mei is still standing, watching her with horror in her eyes. Her mouth opens, closes—words come, dragged out of her. "I didn't mean to—Kim Trang—I—"

And then she's gone, running away from the debris-strewn courtyard. Follow. Kim Trang has to follow her, or she'll lose her forever. She—she can barely stand, and the thought of catching up to Mei—the thought of her fingers resting on Mei's warm skin—makes her stomach heave.

Days passed, and the tiger ate again. He regained strength and plumpness, though he could not find a place among the buffalo's sisters and daughters. They spoke too fast, of concerns and concepts he wasn't familiar with, and they refused to let the tiger touch the machines they were fixing. In the evening, he sat with the buffalo, speaking, not of the world before the breaking, but of small, inconsequential things; making small talk and jokes until the buffalo's heart grew light again—until she forgot that she'd ever feared him.

He grew fat and sleek, and with his mind running around in circles, found no use for himself in a world that had moved on. So instead, he remembered the past, and the days when the ancestors of the buffalo had moved to do his bidding—the power that was still within him, as inseparably as his heart and liver, that had once made them kneel before him—and as he remembered, that power slowly woke up, unfolding within him as the tiger had once unfolded himself out of his coffin.

One day, he looked at the buffalo's daughters—at their flat, blunt teeth, at their horns that could never be used as weapons, at their meagre meals of grass—and saw that he was more than them. "I can help you," he said. They looked at him, incurious; and as the eldest turned away to look at her workbench, something stretched and broke in the tiger's mind.

"Stop," the tiger said, fiercely. "Listen to me."

And the sisters and daughters of the buffalo, caught in the fist of his power, froze where they stood. The tiger watched all of them, as still as statues and awaiting further orders. He meant no harm, he told himself. He wanted to help them; to share the knowledge he bore from the sleepers' land; the secrets of machines and chips in his blood—and did it matter if they didn't want to listen to him? It was just that they didn't realise everything he could teach them, the wealth of knowledge that he'd hoarded within his mind and that could be theirs so smoothly, so easily—the knowledge they desperately needed to survive.

He meant no harm, but the truth about tigers is this: They always end up thinking of themselves as kings and queens, no matter how changed the world might be.

At the pool, where Mei was first found:

At the bottom of the incline, by the water's edge, Mei is skipping torn bits of metal in the pool, her arm a blur. With each movement she makes, more and more crab-bots bubble up from under the dark, greasy surface of the water, a spreading dark mass that seems to echo Mei's gestures, some slow secret dance that pours out of Mei like liquid gold.

Kim Trang takes a deep breath, and starts the descent. Her first footsteps bring down a shower of rocks: Mei looks up and sees her and keeps on watching her as she descends. When Kim Trang gets near her, she turns, frowning, her face going tight with effort. The crab-bots vanish, sinking again into the depths of the pool.

She's waking up, Vy said, but she was wrong. Mei is awake now. Kim Trang's hands shake— lineage again, howling at her to bend the knee, to obey as her distant ancestor once did.

But the world was broken and taken apart and utterly changed.

"Kim Trang," Mei says. "You see—" but Kim Trang doesn't leave her time.

"You're a coward," she says.

Mei's face tightens, and Kim Trang finally understands that what she thought of as Mei's expressionless face is merely despair, spread so widely that it distorts everything.

"A coward," Kim Trang says, again. "You'd rather run away than try to fix a problem."

"I'm a danger to you."

"So is my knife," Kim Trang says, levelly. "So are the bots."

"The bots won't make you bend the knee."

"They can kill me in other ways. They can go rogue or malicious."

"You don't understand," Mei says. "Even if I don't mean it, even if I don't have any delusions of grandeur or any intention to use my powers, they're still here. In my blood. It's who I am."

"It's who you once chose to be," Kim Trang says. "In a world since long dead. Do you want to continue being that person? The one who entered the berth secure in the knowledge the world would be a paradise?"

"I—you saw it!" Mei raises her hands, and the crab-bots rise again from the depths of the pool, ring after ring of speckled darkness. *The world remembers.* "All I have to do is lose my calm, and it'll happen again. How can you—"

Kim Trang thinks of being thrown to the ground, thinks of pain running through her limbs, of getting up and running after Mei. "I've been hurt before. The girls have been hurt before. Of course it will happen again. You'll do the only thing you can do: apologise, make it better, and do your best so that it never happens again. We all stumble."

"Not that way," Mei says, darkly, but she watches Kim Trang with that peculiar hunger in their eyes. "You say it like forgiveness is easy to earn."

Kim Trang shakes her head. She walks closer—no nausea this time, nothing to stop her but the memory of pain—and runs a hand on Mei's skin. Part of her braces herself for another jolt, but there's nothing. "It's not. It never is. And atonement isn't, either. Do you think it's going to be easy to remember every day that you shouldn't be giving orders?" Every morning, Mei will wake up and know the price of impatience or anger; she'll see the crab-bots and try not to command them—see the girls and not think of the constructs of the past—like being able to breathe and deliberately holding it, forever and ever. Mei's entire body is taut, like a wire about to snap. "No. But it's never going to work, Kim Trang. You've heard the stories. You know how they end."

"I know," Kim Trang said. "But they don't have to all go the same way."

Mei's face is a study in agony. "Kim Trang—"

Kim Trang comes closer and wraps her hands around Mei's—warmth and smoothness, and the face she remembers, the woman trapped in a berth that she fell half in love with at first sight, the sleeper who should be their ancestral, implacable enemy. "Tell me a story," she whispers. "A different one."

The Twin Dragons of Sentimentality and Didacticism

Nick Mamatas

"Look," Osvaldo Iglesias said to the journalist, gesturing with the gecko in his hand. "Biomimicry is stupid." Then he muttered, "Watch this—this is what you're here for. Don't blink!" and threw the gecko down the pipe at the whirling fan blades below. The gecko flailed in midair like a plastic bag in a gale, spiraled toward the cylindrical wall, and finally anchored itself via the setae in its footpads to a spot several feet up from the fan.

"Whoa, that was…can you do that again?"

"I told you not to blink."

"Heh," the journalist said. "I thought you were talking to the gecko." Iglesias glared. "You know, to be funny."

"Geckos can't blink," Iglesias said. "No eyelids."

"Right." The journalist made a note on his phone. "Anyway…biomimicry is stupid?"

"Yes, and you know it is. You already know it. Ever see old movies of ornithopters?"

"I'm not actually a tech journalist," the journalist said. "My beat is just local universities and education. I'm here because of the animal—"

"The animal rights people, yeah. An ornithopter is a flying machine that works by flapping its wings, like a bird. Ever taken a ride on one?"

"Of course not. They don't work."

"Of course they *do* work, sirrah," Iglesias said. "Just not very well, nor very often. Because they're stupid. It makes much more sense to stick with fixed-wing aircraft for a variety of technological, safety, and economic reasons. Ornithopters are an example of biomimicry. What you should be interested in is bio*inspiration*. That's the future of robotics."

The journalist started to say *Did you just call me sirr—* but swallowed the question. "What I am actually interested in is how many geckos you've killed by throwing them into fan blades," the journalist said.

"None, yet."

"Yet."

"Gecko footpads are amazing. They don't excrete a chemical adhesive; it's a matter of van der Waals interaction," Iglesias said. "They always save themselves. At least, so far they have."

"I read the Wikipedia article on geckos," the journalist said.

"I've had to rewrite the section on gecko adhesive abilities several times," Iglesias said.

"What are you really doing with the geckos, if not looking to mimic their adhesive abilities?"

"I'm looking to understand them, so we can be inspired. Think about what cheap non-chemical adhesives might mean." Iglesias gestured to his whiteboard, as if it would make any sense to the journalist. "I'm not going to manufacture gecko shoes and gloves and climb up walls, but you know, think. Do you use Post-it notes? Ever have to go to the ER and get stitches? Turn a screw? You ever own a book so old that when you opened it up the pages spilled onto your lap? A self-cleaning dry adhesive can change everything. And you're worried about geckos hitting the fan?" Iglesias turned around, and collected the gecko who had just mounted the lip of the pipe into which he'd been thrown.

"I'm not worried," the journalist said. "I'm reporting. There have been threats against the lab. Animal liberation extremists." Iglesias just peered at the journalist. "Do you have a comment on that?"

"Uhm…what do they think the adhesives this technology will one day replace are made of? Horse hooves and fish guts, largely. Anyway, I'm very busy. Do you have all the quotes you need?"

"Yes, that should do it," the journalist said. "Thanks for your time, Osvaldo."

Iglesias grunted; he already had a gecko in

each hand. The journalist let himself out of the lab before the next round.

An extended anecdotal lede began forming in the journalist's mind as he walked through the quad to his car. Would his editor let him get away with something from the gecko's point of view? Maybe the gecko's POV by one remove: *Imagine being a gecko, living your gecko life, licking your eyes clean, eating flies. Then one day you're snatched up and flung...*

Which is what immediately happened to him as a trio of black-clad figures, their faces obscured of balaclavas, emerged from the shrubbery, seized him by the limbs, threw him to the ground, and smothered his shouting with a chloroform-soaked rag.

Consciousness returned fairly quickly to the journalist, who found himself tied to a concrete pillar in the basement of some sort of industrial facility. He remembered a peculiar class exercise as an undergrad. Mid-lecture, two men in masks had stormed into the room and brandished guns. The journalist made eye contact with one of them and thought: *Blue. Blue eyes. And he's old. You have to remember this!* The professor stood up. The intruders leveled their guns—they were toys! "Bang, bang!" the intruders said, and the professor fell comically to the floor, clutching his chest as if shot, and bellowed "Long live free Albania!" Then he popped back up as the intruders excused themselves and demanded that the class write down what they had just witnessed. The resulting accounts...varied.

It was the sort of object lesson that could only be experienced prior to the events of 9/11. But it came in handy now. The journalist looked around. The place was bare, so it was probably not a headquarters. There weren't even seats available, so this would likely not be a long interrogation, or an extensive torture session. The three figures wore matching black sweaters, jeans, and sneakers. They were in shape, all probably male, their poses confident.

"People are animals..." said the journalist. "Don't hurt me."

"What?" the figure in the middle said.

"It makes no sense to hurt people if you want to save animals," the journalist said. "People are animals, aren't they? Look, I was at the lab, but only briefly..." He stopped, realizing he shouldn't give anything away. His captors were letting him talk himself into a hole.

The figure on the left whispered into the ear of the one in the middle. "Oh, right," said the one in the middle to the journalist. "We're...we're not the animal rights people."

"We're biomimickists," said the figure on the left.

"I heard biomimicry was *stupid*," said the journalist. Keep them talking; they seemed a bit in over their heads. Listen for details, accents, minute disagreements between them.

Behind his mask, the one who identified

the group as biomimickists twitched. "It's not stupid. If anything, bioinspiration is stupid."

The man in the middle, who seemed to hold a leadership position at least tenuously, explained, "It's a contentious debate, but even bioinspirationists recognize biomimickry as an essential first step. But to put it simply, it is true that evolution is contingent and parsimonious—evolution satisfices rather than optimizes. But so too does guided experimentation and design."

"Yes," said the one on the left. "Nobody in the academy, or industry, is optimizing anything. It's all a matter of funding, the limitations of research questions salespersonship—"

"Personship? You're graduate students, aren't you?" the journalist said.

"Natural experiments happen simultaneously and serially, millions or billions of times a day. You're an experiment in *Homo sapien sapien* design, sir, one of seven billion occurring right now. No human mind, no lab, can compete with the sheer amount of data being generated by life itself. Our interest is in gathering as much of that data as we can and using it to inform practical automata based closely on animals." said the middle figure. "And yes. We are graduate students. We need to know what is going on in the Iglesias lab, and we've been barred from entering it." He shrugged. "You know, politics."

"I was only there for an hour," the journalist said. "And I'm a layperson"—the left figure snorted—"so what would you even expect me to know, or tell you, that you wouldn't see in my article?" In response, the center figure nodded toward the confederate on the right.

"I'm a hypnotist," said the one on the right. "You will not be harmed."

"You *may* not be harmed, *if* you cooperate," said the one in the middle, an edge in his voice.

"No, if you cooperate, you'll not be harmed," said the one on the left, a bit too quickly.

"What do you even want from me?" the journalist said. "Hell, why not kidnap Iglesias and hypnotize him!"

"We tried," said the center figure as the one on the right held his hand aloft. In it he clutched a disc that generated oscillating waves of light. "He has a transparent membrane over his eyes," the leader said. "Like a gecko's." The journalist's eyes filled with stars.

It was only fifteen years later when the journalist experienced a significant stroke and was rendered largely paralyzed, that he remembered the details of his brief capture, though what he was asked and how he was released remained lost to memory. "The journalist" wasn't quite the right term for the man anymore—even college campuses hadn't employed writers for their PR organs in years. Things had changed. First had come the major mechanimals: robotic elephants, and safaris that allowed tourists to hunt them down and keep them wound via the gigantic if purely decorative keys on their backs. As the animals died off, they were replaced, but not in the order in which the ecosystem was collapsing. The big ones were rolled out first, like cars used to be. Tigers and orangutans and wildebeests and great golden bears, those last beloved of Silicon Valley. Every seven-year-old scion of a techie family rode one to school. The bulletproof golden bears could eat rampage shooters, it was believed, though this feature was never widely tested in the field.

Only later came microdrones in the shape of perfect dragonflies and hummingbirds, then deer ticks. They worked in subtle swarms, their microsensors recording sight and sound, and even collecting and analyzing the molecules sensed by human olfactory and gustatory systems. All that was knowable was soon known, at least by some, and they used that information to multifarious ends. Nations fell. The economy collapsed, then harmonized. The average workday shrunk to four four-hour days, and much of that was spent on various personal WiFi-capable devices, buying shoes and trading quips and whatnot.

Then the ticks started infecting real animals, real people. One of the last professional acts of the journalist before forced into retirement by politico-economic forces he could barely comprehend was the coining of the term

"Lymewire Disease"—a joke dependent on what was even then an aging reference—for the spread of *Borrelia burgdorferi*, which the micromechanicals carried more successfully than their organic predecessors due largely to their capacity to capture odor molecules and taste solutes. The microscopic pouches in which the mechticks seized the molecules were also breeding grounds for Lyme bacteria. Though lacking the ability to lower human resistance to *B. burgdorferi* spirochetes as organic deer ticks did, mechticks were so much better at evading detection than organics that their targets were repeatedly exposed to the bacteria, and infection was concomitantly more likely.

The journalist was an old man now, and suffered from Lymewire Disease, which was dramatic irony enough for him. And then, after his stroke—due to cerebral vasculitis caused by Lyme neuroborreliosis—well, he was upset as he was inarticulate. He was fetched by a Ganza, a peculiar aerial swing powered by a flock of automaton geese as in the famed early novel *The Man in the Moone* by Francis Godwin, and deposited in a hospital to be, if not rehabilitated, at least kept alive so that he could keep sequestering carbon and thus help mitigate climate change.

The questions came flooding back.

Did Iglesias say anything in particular about his dry adhesive, its formulation or composition?

Did he show you or demonstrate any test substances or refer to extant test substances?

Did he mention any articles or other writing he was working on that were currently under submission or that have received peer reviews?

No. No. No. Even in his compliant state, the journalist felt himself growing annoyed. These biomimickists were as combative as Iglesias. Finally, there was a hit:

Did you observe any loose papers, formulae or equations on a whiteboard, or texts on a computer monitor?

Yes.

Much of it his captors already knew.

Sure, $(C_2H_6OSi)_n$. Naturally.

Of course, slanted microwedges no more than 100 μm tall. Kid stuff.

Did you see anything else?

$(C_{60}\text{-}I_h)[5,6]$fullerene

Oh my!

Injecting polydimethylsiloxane into buckminsterfullerene—the silicone filling the empty spaces within the truncated icosahedron structure, very clever. Soot sticks to things, like the faces of tiny coalmining children in Dickensian England.

Anything else?

The journalist remembered now straining against his bonds, poking at the air with his nose. He even wanted to help, and the biomimickists weren't letting him. Finally, the hypnotist recommended freeing his arms and giving him a phone on which to type or draw.

And this is what the journalist drew:

```
*** *
***
*** *
 ***
*** *
 ***
*** *
 ***
*** *
 ***
*** *
 ***
*** *
```

"Snowshoes!" is what the middle figure, the leader, said, when he saw the pattern. Dry and sticky buckyballs, stuffed not quite to overflowing with a silicone so that the carbon vertices of the buckyball would roll, and arranged in a snowshoe lattice for optimizing rotational freedom. Well, that was very clever indeed.

"We need never turn a screw again." And with that, the journalist was given a command to forget and left to live his life. It was a strong command indeed; the journalist barely reacted emotionally when a week later the Iglesias lab burst into flames and burnt to the ground in less than twenty minutes. The animal liberation people were better arsonists than fugitives. They were captured right away and confessed to the police immediately.

The rehab dog the journalist was given was unnervingly realistic. It even pissed and occasionally ran in tight circles, snapping at its own tail when the speech-language pathologist entered the room. The therapist forced the journalist to name the dog "Kazzie" to improve the journalist's ability to utter voiceless velar stops and voiced lingua-alveolar fricatives. Luckily, the dog answered to "ghuh-thzuh" to the extent that it responded to anything the journalist said at all. The journalist quickly learned to love that fucking dog right away, as perennial heating oil shortages meant that it was cheaper to heat mechanimals than it was to heat rooms. Kazzie would curl up behind the journalist's knees and radiate warmth like a hot-water bottle in the bed, all night long. Little boys and girls curled up with their seven-hundred-pound golden bears too.

One night Kazzie woke with a start and began howling at the ceiling. It thrashed about the bed, whipping the journalist awake with its tail. His mobility limited, the journalist could only wince and try to cover up. Then he caught a glimpse of what Kazzie was barking it.

There was a man on the ceiling. He was standing on it, in his stocking feet, as if it were the floor. In his hands he held the grating to the duct he had presumably just exited from. He let out a high-pitched whistle and Kazzie stopped barking, grew still, and clambered onto her belly.

"Always tricky," the man muttered to himself, and then with a slight "eh" he shifted somehow and his feet gave way and he fell, landing roughly on the floor. There was something in the way the man moved that reminded the journalist of an unsuccessful gecko. His face was almost entirely different, but...

"Uthwowldho," the journalist said. Osvaldo Iglesias held a finger to his lips and went *ssshhh*.

"Tell me," said Iglesias, "what kind of journalist has zero social media presence, even in the Great Internet Archive? You know it took me this long to track you down? I've been looking for you since before the Lymewire epidemic. Since before the ommatidicon made everything but you public knowledge. The geese flew you over my fucking safehouse. I just happened to be looking up!"

The journalist had a lot to say, but it mostly came out as grunts and drool.

"God, stop, stop. Listen, just nod. Is the problem with your memory or your mouth?"

The journalist pointed to his mouth. Iglesias sighed. "You're not going to like this, I bet." He reached over to Kazzie and with a grip on her mandible and maxilla pulled its head apart. The journalist yowled and tried to pummel Iglesias with his good arm. Iglesias pulled something from his pocket and hit the journalist with it. Whatever it was, the journalist found himself extremely awake and aware of his surroundings and utterly unable to move.

"Want to hear something perverse?" Iglesias said as he removed the tongue from the dog. "They could have done what I am about to do for you at any time. The problem is that people are too attached to these stupid mechanimals, and to the idea of people suffering bravely in the shadow of a worldwide epidemic." He opened the journalist's mouth and put the device he'd used into it, then removed something. "You can't run a bunch of charities if nobody's fucking sick, right? I haven't been sick in twenty-five years." Iglesias tossed something over his shoulder.

The journalist saw his own tongue hit the wall. Iglesias stuck the dog's tongue into the journalist's mouth. "We'll see what sort of neurological damage you have in like three minutes. By the way, your dog still works. It'll just bump into walls slightly more often, and won't really lick you…"

The tongue took a few minutes to warm up, running itself along the journalist's teeth and clicking against the roof of his mouth. With tears in his eyes, the journalist's first words in weeks were "…Dental records."

"Arson investigators are stupid," Iglesias said. He smiled unemotionally, showing off his teeth. "I grew these myself. I happened to just keep my old teeth after I pulled them out. They found a couple."

The journalist said, "Sentimenta—"

"I am *not!*" Iglesias interrupted. "All of you are. The world's an overheated toy store now. Thanks to you. You stole my adhesive. Don't worry, I'm not here for my revenge; I've had it already."

Iglesias let that sink in for a moment, but as the journalist only looked bemused, he decided to continue. "My adhesive…how do you make a mechanimal the size of a deer tick? With tiny-ass screws? No, you glue it together. How do you pluck a single taste solute out of the air? In a net of buckyballs. The biomimickists were so eager to make real animals, that they made a disease vector. My glue is what made sure you got Lyme Disease. I'm not sorry."

"No, of course you're not," the journalist said. "But it's not my fault. They did call themselves biomimickists, though, you're right about that. They kidnapped me, hypnotized me, made me drop off the grid after with post-hypnotic commands. They said you had special gecko eyelids."

"I have special gecko everything," Iglesias said. "Except for my teeth. Shark teeth. They always grow back, never get a cavity. Oh, and I put in a little doohickey that gives me the telomerase expression of a goddamned redwood tree. Do I look any older to you? You look like shit, and it wasn't just the Lyme and the stroke, was it?"

"Everyone looks like shit these days," the journalist said. "But we all have very obedient mechanicats. That's your view, isn't it? So what do you want from me?"

"I want the identities of the biomimickists. I've been living under assumed names, paying cash for couch space, folding burritos under the table for spending money two days a week," Iglesias said. "I'm a goddamned immortal superhybrid and I live like an undergraduate because everyone thinks I'm dead. If I stick my head out, some bug will spot me and ommatidicon will start blaring and I'll be vivisected before noon, and marketed in time for the five a.m. doorbuster sale."

"Sucks to be you," the journalist said. "I just pissed in a bag attached to my penis."

"Yeah. Gecko nose. I smell it."

"Good," the journalist said. "What do you want the biomimickists for? Revenge?"

"I want to teach them a lesson."

"What are you going to do? Eat them? Tear their pets to pieces with your bare hands? Did you build a tiger to feed them to with your tip money?"

"You've grown sarcastic in your old age," Iglesias said.

"We've only met once before, and I was trying to be professional then."

Iglesias said, "What I am going to do is tag

them with this little number"—he patted his pocket, which held the thing he'd used on the journalist—"and then tell them every fucking thing they've done wrong. They broke the entire planet. They're probably secret billionaires by now, but they're stupid. Like the old saying goes, 'If you're so rich, how come you ain't smart?' Just tell me what you remember, and somehow I'll find them. If they're dead, I'll find their kids, or even better, their lawyers. Their lawyers' kids if I have to. Individual shareholders in their shell companies. I've got nothing but time. I eat once a week, I sleep an hour a day."

"You're an immortal genius superhybrid and that is how you wish to spend your life?" the journalist asked.

"Maybe I'll deactivate your tongue after you tell me," Iglesias said.

The journalist shrugged as best he could, given his condition. "They were…thin, young. One of them had green eyes, the other two had brown. I think they were graduate students, but maybe not from U. They kept me in a warehouse, but there was no traffic noise, so it couldn't have been in the Longmont. They had a sort of circular device that shined iridescent light. One of them—who seemed to be the leader—had a trace of a Chicago accent."

Iglesias nodded. "That's a good start. You can keep that tongue."

"Thanks," said the journalist. Then he said, "Kazzie, kill!" The dog, broken jaws flapping too wide, leapt for Iglesias's throat. Iglesias tried to whistle, but the dog was fast, and angry. *No, just programmed to* behave *as though angry if abused,* the journalist thought. Iglesias had his fingers deep in Kazzie's faux flesh, but the journalist managed to roll himself over onto the nurse's call button. Iglesias went for the window and threw himself out of it. Face now level with his food tray, the journalist made eye contact with a bright blue fly who winked and zipped out the window.

At least the news would be interesting again, for a good long while.

The Artist of the Beautiful (1844)

Nathaniel Hawthorne

An elderly man, with his pretty daughter on his arm, was passing along the street, and emerged from the gloom of the cloudy evening into the light that fell across the pavement from the window of a small shop. It was a projecting window; and on the inside were suspended a variety of watches, pinchbeck, silver, and one or two of gold, all with their faces turned from the streets, as if churlishly disinclined to inform the wayfarers what o'clock it was. Seated within the shop, sidelong to the window with his pale face bent earnestly over some delicate piece of mechanism on which was thrown the concentrated lustre of a shade lamp, appeared a young man.

"What can Owen Warland be about?" muttered old Peter Hovenden, himself a retired watchmaker, and the former master of this same young man whose occupation he was now wondering at. "What can the fellow be about? These six months past I have never come by his shop without seeing him just as steadily at work as now. It would be a flight beyond his usual foolery to seek for the perpetual motion; and yet I know enough of my old business to be certain that what he is now so busy with is no part of the machinery of a watch."

"Perhaps, father," said Annie, without showing much interest in the question, "Owen is inventing a new kind of timekeeper. I am sure he has ingenuity enough."

"Poh, child! He has not the sort of ingenuity to invent anything better than a Dutch toy," answered her father, who had formerly been put to much vexation by Owen Warland's irregular genius. "A plague on such ingenuity! All the effect that ever I knew of it was to spoil the accuracy of some of the best watches in my shop. He would turn the sun out of its orbit and derange the whole course of time, if, as I said before, his ingenuity could grasp anything bigger than a child's toy!"

"Hush, father! He hears you!" whispered Annie, pressing the old man's arm. "His ears are as delicate as his feelings; and you know how easily disturbed they are. Do let us move on."

So Peter Hovenden and his daughter Annie plodded on without further conversation, until in a by-street of the town they found themselves passing the open door of a blacksmith's shop. Within was seen the forge, now blazing up and illuminating the high and dusky roof, and now confining its lustre to a narrow precinct of the coal-strewn floor, according as the breath of the bellows was puffed forth or again inhaled into its vast leathern lungs. In the intervals of brightness it was easy to distinguish objects in remote corners of the shop and the horseshoes that hung upon the wall; in the momentary gloom the fire seemed to be glimmering amidst the vagueness of unenclosed space. Moving about in this red glare and alternate dusk was the figure of the blacksmith, well worthy to be viewed in so picturesque an aspect of light and shade, where the bright blaze struggled with the black night, as if each would have snatched his comely strength from the other. Anon he drew a white-hot bar of iron from the coals, laid it on the anvil, uplifted his arm of might, and was soon enveloped in the myriads of sparks which the strokes of his hammer scattered into the surrounding gloom.

"Now, that is a pleasant sight," said the old watchmaker. "I know what it is to work in gold; but give me the worker in iron after all is said and done. He spends his labor upon a reality. What say you, daughter Annie?"

"Pray don't speak so loud, father," whispered Annie, "Robert Danforth will hear you."

"And what if he should hear me?" said Peter Hovenden. "I say again, it is a good and a wholesome thing to depend upon main strength and reality, and to earn one's bread with the bare and brawny arm of a blacksmith. A watchmaker gets his brain puzzled by his wheels within a wheel, or loses his health or the nicety of his eyesight, as was my case, and finds himself at middle age, or a little after, past labor at his own trade and fit for nothing else, yet too poor to live at his ease. So I say once again, give me main strength for my money. And then, how it takes the nonsense out of a man! Did you ever hear of a blacksmith being such a fool as Owen Warland yonder?"

"Well said, uncle Hovenden!" shouted Robert Danforth from the forge, in a full, deep, merry voice, that made the roof re-echo. "And what says Miss Annie to that doctrine? She, I suppose, will think it a genteeler business to tinker up a lady's watch than to forge a horseshoe or make a gridiron."

Annie drew her father onward without giving him time for reply.

But we must return to Owen Warland's shop, and spend more meditation upon his history and character than either Peter Hovenden, or probably his daughter Annie, or Owen's old school-fellow, Robert Danforth, would have thought due to so slight a subject. From the time that his little fingers could grasp a penknife, Owen had been remarkable for a delicate ingenuity, which sometimes produced pretty shapes in wood, principally figures of flowers and birds, and sometimes seemed to aim at the hidden mysteries of mechanism.

But it was always for purposes of grace, and never with any mockery of the useful. He did not, like the crowd of school-boy artisans, construct little windmills on the angle of a barn or watermills across the neighboring brook. Those who discovered such peculiarity in the boy as to think it worth their while to observe him closely, sometimes saw reason to suppose that he was attempting to imitate the beautiful movements of Nature as exemplified in the flight of birds or the activity of little animals. It seemed, in fact, a new development of the love of the beautiful, such as might have made him a poet, a painter, or a sculptor, and which was as completely refined from all utilitarian coarseness as it could have been in either of the fine arts. He looked with singular distaste at the stiff and regular processes of ordinary machinery. Being once carried to see a steam-engine, in the expectation that his intuitive comprehension of mechanical principles would be gratified, he turned pale and grew sick, as if something monstrous and unnatural had been presented to him. This horror was partly owing to the size and terrible energy of the iron laborer; for the character of Owen's mind was microscopic, and tended naturally to the minute, in accordance with his diminutive frame and the marvellous smallness and delicate power of his fingers. Not that his sense of beauty was thereby diminished into a sense of prettiness. The beautiful idea has no relation to size, and may be as perfectly developed in a space too minute for any but microscopic investigation as within the ample verge that is measured by the arc of the rainbow. But, at all events, this characteristic minuteness in his objects and accomplishments made the world even more incapable than it might otherwise have been of appreciating Owen Warland's genius. The boy's relatives saw nothing better to be done—as perhaps there was not—than to bind him apprentice to a watchmaker, hoping that his strange ingenuity might thus be regulated and put to utilitarian purposes.

Peter Hovenden's opinion of his apprentice has already been expressed. He could make nothing of the lad. Owen's apprehension of the professional mysteries, it is true, was inconceivably quick; but he altogether forgot or despised the grand object of a watchmaker's business, and cared no more for the measurement of time than if it had been merged into eternity. So long, however, as he remained under his old master's care, Owen's lack of sturdiness made it possible, by strict injunctions and sharp oversight, to restrain his creative eccentricity within bounds; but when his apprenticeship was served out, and he had taken the little shop which Peter Hovenden's failing eyesight compelled him to relinquish, then did people recognize how unfit a person was Owen Warland to lead old blind Father Time along his daily course. One of his most rational projects was to connect a musical operation with the machinery of his watches, so that all the harsh dissonances of life might be rendered tuneful, and each flitting moment fall into the abyss of the past in golden drops of harmony. If a family clock was intrusted to him for repair,— one of those tall, ancient clocks that have grown nearly allied to human nature by measuring out the lifetime of many generations,—he would take upon himself to arrange a dance or funeral procession of figures across its venerable face, representing twelve mirthful or melancholy hours. Several freaks of this kind quite destroyed the young watchmaker's credit with that steady and matter-of-fact class of people who hold the opinion that time is not to be trifled with, whether considered as the medium of advancement and prosperity in this world or preparation for the next. His custom rapidly diminished—a misfortune, however, that was probably reckoned among his better accidents by Owen Warland, who was becoming more and more absorbed in a secret occupation which drew all his science and manual dexterity into itself, and likewise gave full employment to the characteristic tendencies of his genius. This pursuit had already consumed many months.

After the old watchmaker and his pretty daughter had gazed at him out of the obscurity of the street, Owen Warland was seized with a fluttering of the nerves, which made his hand tremble too violently to proceed with such delicate labor as he was now engaged upon.

"It was Annie herself!" murmured he. "I should have known it, by this throbbing of my heart, before I heard her father's voice. Ah, how it throbs! I shall scarcely be able to work again on this exquisite mechanism to-night. Annie! dearest Annie! thou shouldst give firmness to my heart and hand, and not shake them thus; for if I strive to put the very spirit of beauty into form and give it motion, it is for thy sake alone. O throbbing heart, be quiet! If my labor be thus thwarted, there will come vague and unsatisfied dreams which will leave me spiritless to-morrow."

As he was endeavoring to settle himself again to his task, the shop door opened and gave admittance to no other than the stalwart figure which Peter Hovenden had paused to admire, as seen amid the light and shadow of the blacksmith's shop. Robert Danforth had brought a little anvil of his own manufacture, and peculiarly constructed, which the young artist had recently bespoken. Owen examined the article and pronounced it fashioned according to his wish.

"Why, yes," said Robert Danforth, his strong voice filling the shop as with the sound of a bass viol, "I consider myself equal to anything in the way of my own trade; though I should have made but a poor figure at yours with such a fist as this," added he, laughing, as he laid his vast hand beside the delicate one of Owen. "But what then? I put more main strength into one blow of my sledge hammer than all that you have expended since you were a 'prentice. Is not that the truth?"

"Very probably," answered the low and slender voice of Owen. "Strength is an earthly monster. I make no pretensions to it. My force, whatever there may be of it, is altogether spiritual."

"Well, but, Owen, what are you about?" asked his old school-fellow, still in such a hearty volume of tone that it made the artist shrink, especially as the question related to a subject so sacred as the absorbing dream of his imagination. "Folks do say that you are trying to discover the perpetual motion."

"The perpetual motion? Nonsense!" replied Owen Warland, with a movement of disgust; for he was full of little petulances. "It can never be discovered. It is a dream that may delude men whose brains are mystified with matter, but not me. Besides, if such a discovery were possible, it would not be worth my while to make it only to have the secret turned to such purposes as are now effected by steam and water power. I am not ambitious to be honored with the paternity of a new kind of cotton machine."

"That would be droll enough!" cried the blacksmith, breaking out into such an uproar of laughter that Owen himself and the bell glasses on his work-board quivered in unison. "No, no, Owen! No child of yours will have iron joints and sinews. Well, I won't hinder you any more.

Good night, Owen, and success, and if you need any assistance, so far as a downright blow of hammer upon anvil will answer the purpose, I'm your man."

And with another laugh the man of main strength left the shop.

"How strange it is," whispered Owen Warland to himself, leaning his head upon his hand, "that all my musings, my purposes, my passion for the beautiful, my consciousness of power to create it,—a finer, more ethereal power, of which this earthly giant can have no conception,—all, all, look so vain and idle whenever my path is crossed by Robert Danforth! He would drive me mad were I to meet him often. His hard, brute force darkens and confuses the spiritual element within me; but I, too, will be strong in my own way. I will not yield to him."

He took from beneath a glass a piece of minute machinery, which he set in the condensed light of his lamp, and, looking intently at it through a magnifying glass, proceeded to operate with a delicate instrument of steel. In an instant, however, he fell back in his chair and clasped his hands, with a look of horror on his face that made its small features as impressive as those of a giant would have been.

"Heaven! What have I done?" exclaimed he. "The vapor, the influence of that brute force,—it has bewildered me and obscured my perception. I have made the very stroke—the fatal stroke— that I have dreaded from the first. It is all over—the toil of months, the object of my life. I am ruined!"

And there he sat, in strange despair, until his lamp flickered in the socket and left the Artist of the Beautiful in darkness.

Thus it is that ideas, which grow up within the imagination and appear so lovely to it and of a value beyond whatever men call valuable, are exposed to be shattered and annihilated by contact with the practical. It is requisite for the ideal artist to possess a force of character that seems hardly compatible with its delicacy; he must keep his faith in himself while the incredulous world assails him with its utter disbelief; he must stand up against mankind and be his own sole disciple, both as respects his genius and the objects to which it is directed.

For a time Owen Warland succumbed to this severe but inevitable test. He spent a few sluggish weeks with his head so continually resting in his hands that the towns-people had scarcely an opportunity to see his countenance. When at last it was again uplifted to the light of day, a cold, dull, nameless change was perceptible upon it. In the opinion of Peter Hovenden, however, and that order of sagacious understandings who think that life should be regulated, like clockwork, with leaden weights, the alteration was entirely for the better. Owen now, indeed, applied himself to business with dogged industry. It was marvelous to witness the obtuse gravity with which he would inspect the wheels of a great old silver watch thereby delighting the owner, in whose fob it had been worn till he deemed it a portion of his own life, and was accordingly jealous of its treatment. In consequence of the good report thus acquired, Owen Warland was invited by the proper authorities to regulate the clock in the church steeple. He succeeded so admirably in this matter of public interest that the merchants gruffly acknowledged his merits on Change; the nurse whispered his praises as she gave the potion in the sick-chamber; the lover blessed him at the hour of appointed interview; and the town in general thanked Owen for the punctuality of dinner time. In a word, the heavy weight upon his spirits kept everything in order, not merely within his own system, but wheresoever the iron accents of the church clock were audible. It was a circumstance, though minute, yet characteristic of his present state, that, when employed to engrave names or initials on silver spoons, he now wrote the requisite letters in the plainest possible style, omitting a variety of fanciful flourishes that had heretofore distinguished his work in this kind.

One day, during the era of this happy transformation, old Peter Hovenden came to visit his former apprentice.

"Well, Owen," said he, "I am glad to hear such good accounts of you from all quarters, and especially from the town clock yonder, which speaks in your commendation every hour of the twenty-four. Only get rid altogether of your nonsensical trash about the beautiful, which I nor nobody else, nor yourself to boot, could ever understand,—only free yourself of that, and your success in life is as sure as daylight. Why, if you go on in this way, I should even venture to let you doctor this precious old watch of mine; though, except my daughter Annie, I have nothing else so valuable in the world."

"I should hardly dare touch it, sir," replied Owen, in a depressed tone; for he was weighed down by his old master's presence.

"In time," said the latter,—"In time, you will be capable of it."

The old watchmaker, with the freedom naturally consequent on his former authority, went on inspecting the work which Owen had in hand at the moment, together with other matters that were in progress. The artist, meanwhile, could scarcely lift his head. There was nothing so antipodal to his nature as this man's cold, unimaginative sagacity, by contact with which everything was converted into a dream except the densest matter of the physical world. Owen groaned in spirit and prayed fervently to be delivered from him.

"But what is this?" cried Peter Hovenden abruptly, taking up a dusty bell glass, beneath which appeared a mechanical something, as delicate and minute as the system of a butterfly's anatomy. "What have we here? Owen! Owen! there is witchcraft in these little chains, and wheels, and paddles. See! with one pinch of my finger and thumb I am going to deliver you from all future peril."

"For Heaven's sake," screamed Owen Warland, springing up with wonderful energy, "as you would not drive me mad, do not touch it! The slightest pressure of your finger would ruin me forever."

"Aha, young man! And is it so?" said the old watchmaker, looking at him with just enough penetration to torture Owen's soul with the bitterness of worldly criticism. "Well, take your own course; but I warn you again that in this small piece of mechanism lives your evil spirit. Shall I exorcise him?"

"You are my evil spirit," answered Owen, much excited,—"you and the hard, coarse world! The leaden thoughts and the despondency that you fling upon me are my clogs, else I should long ago have achieved the task that I was created for."

Peter Hovenden shook his head, with the mixture of contempt and indignation which mankind, of whom he was partly a representative, deem themselves entitled to feel towards all simpletons who seek other prizes than the dusty one along the highway. He then took his leave, with an uplifted finger and a sneer upon his face that haunted the artist's dreams for many a night afterwards. At the time of his old master's visit, Owen was probably on the point of taking up the relinquished task; but, by this sinister event, he was thrown back into the state whence he had been slowly emerging.

But the innate tendency of his soul had only been accumulating fresh vigor during its apparent sluggishness. As the summer advanced he almost totally relinquished his business, and permitted Father Time, so far as the old gentleman was represented by the clocks and watches under his control, to stray at random through human life, making infinite confusion among the train of bewildered hours. He wasted the sunshine, as people said, in wandering through the woods and fields and along the banks of streams. There, like a child, he found amusement in chasing butterflies or watching the motions of water insects. There was something truly mysterious in the intentness with which he contemplated these living playthings as they sported on the breeze or examined the structure of an imperial insect whom he had imprisoned. The chase of butterflies was an apt emblem of the ideal pursuit in which he had spent so many golden hours; but would the beautiful idea ever be yielded to his hand like the butterfly that symbolized it? Sweet, doubtless, were these days, and congenial to the artist's soul. They were full of bright conceptions, which gleamed through his intellectual world as the butterflies gleamed through the outward atmosphere, and were real to him, for the instant, without the toil, and perplexity, and many disappointments of attempting to make them visible to the sensual eye. Alas that the artist, whether in poetry, or whatever other material, may not content himself with the inward enjoyment of the beautiful, but must chase the flitting mystery beyond the verge of his ethereal domain, and crush its frail being in seizing it with a material grasp. Owen Warland felt the impulse to give external reality to his ideas as irresistibly as any of the poets or painters who have arrayed the world in a dimmer and fainter beauty, imperfectly copied from the richness of their visions.

The night was now his time for the slow progress of re-creating the one idea to which all his intellectual activity referred itself. Always at the approach of dusk he stole into the town, locked himself within his shop, and wrought with patient delicacy of touch for many hours. Sometimes he was startled by the rap of the watchman, who, when all the world should be asleep, had caught the gleam of lamplight through the crevices of Owen Warland's shutters. Daylight, to the morbid sensibility of his mind, seemed to have an intrusiveness that interfered with his pursuits. On cloudy and inclement days, therefore, he sat with his head upon his hands, muffling, as it were, his sensitive brain in a mist of indefinite musings, for it was a relief to escape from the sharp distinctness with which he was compelled to shape out his thoughts during his nightly toil.

From one of these fits of torpor he was aroused by the entrance of Annie Hovenden, who came into the shop with the freedom of a customer, and also with something of the familiarity of a childish friend. She had worn a hole through her silver thimble, and wanted Owen to repair it.

"But I don't know whether you will condescend to such a task," said she, laughing, "now that you are so taken up with the notion of putting spirit into machinery."

"Where did you get that idea, Annie?" said Owen, starting in surprise.

"Oh, out of my own head," answered she, "and from something that I heard you say, long ago, when you were but a boy and I a little child. But come, will you mend this poor thimble of mine?"

"Anything for your sake, Annie," said Owen Warland,—"anything, even were it to work at Robert Danforth's forge."

"And that would be a pretty sight!" retorted Annie, glancing with imperceptible slightness at the artist's small and slender frame. "Well; here is the thimble."

"But that is a strange idea of yours," said Owen, "about the spiritualization of matter."

And then the thought stole into his mind that this young girl possessed the gift to comprehend him better than all the world besides. And what a help and strength would it be to him in his lonely toil if he could gain the sympathy of the only being whom he loved! To persons whose pursuits are insulated from the common business of life—who are either in advance of mankind or apart from it—there often comes a sensation of moral cold that makes the spirit shiver as if it had reached the frozen solitudes around the pole. What the prophet, the poet, the reformer, the criminal, or any other man with human yearnings, but separated from the multitude by a peculiar lot, might feel, poor Owen felt.

"Annie," cried he, growing pale as death at the thought, "how gladly would I tell you the secret of my pursuit! You, methinks, would estimate it rightly. You, I know, would hear it with a reverence that I must not expect from the harsh, material world."

"Would I not? to be sure I would!" replied Annie Hovenden, lightly laughing. "Come; explain to me quickly what is the meaning of this little whirligig, so delicately wrought that it might be a plaything for Queen Mab. See! I will put it in motion."

"Hold!" exclaimed Owen, "hold!"

Annie had but given the slightest possible touch, with the point of a needle, to the same minute portion of complicated machinery which has been more than once mentioned, when the artist seized her by the wrist with a force that made her scream aloud. She was affrighted at the convulsion of intense rage and anguish that writhed across his features. The next instant he let his head sink upon his hands.

"Go, Annie," murmured he; "I have deceived

myself, and must suffer for it. I yearned for sympathy, and thought, and fancied, and dreamed that you might give it me; but you lack the talisman, Annie, that should admit you into my secrets. That touch has undone the toil of months and the thought of a lifetime! It was not your fault, Annie; but you have ruined me!"

Poor Owen Warland! He had indeed erred, yet pardonably; for if any human spirit could have sufficiently reverenced the processes so sacred in his eyes, it must have been a woman's. Even Annie Hovenden possibly might not have disappointed him had she been enlightened by the deep intelligence of love.

The artist spent the ensuing winter in a way that satisfied any persons who had hitherto retained a hopeful opinion of him that he was, in truth, irrevocably doomed to unutility as regarded the world, and to an evil destiny on his own part. The decease of a relative had put him in possession of a small inheritance. Thus freed from the necessity of toil, and having lost the steadfast influence of a great purpose,—great, at least, to him,—he abandoned himself to habits from which it might have been supposed the mere delicacy of his organization would have availed to secure him. But when the ethereal portion of a man of genius is obscured the earthly part assumes an influence the more uncontrollable, because the character is now thrown off the balance to which Providence had so nicely adjusted it, and which, in coarser natures, is adjusted by some other method. Owen Warland made proof of whatever show of bliss may be found in riot. He looked at the world through the golden medium of wine, and contemplated the visions that bubble up so gayly around the brim of the glass, and that people the air with shapes of pleasant madness, which so soon grow ghostly and forlorn. Even when this dismal and inevitable change had taken place, the young man might still have continued to quaff the cup of enchantments, though its vapor did but shroud life in gloom and fill the gloom with spectres that mocked at him. There was a certain irksomeness of spirit, which, being real, and the deepest sensation of which the artist was now conscious, was more intolerable than any fantastic miseries and horrors that the abuse of wine could summon up. In the latter case he could remember, even out of the midst of his trouble, that all was but a delusion; in the former, the heavy anguish was his actual life.

From this perilous state he was redeemed by an incident which more than one person witnessed, but of which the shrewdest could not explain or conjecture the operation on Owen Warland's mind. It was very simple. On a warm afternoon of spring, as the artist sat among his riotous companions with a glass of wine before him, a splendid butterfly flew in at the open window and fluttered about his head.

"Ah," exclaimed Owen, who had drank freely, "are you alive again, child of the sun and playmate of the summer breeze, after your dismal winter's nap? Then it is time for me to be at work!"

And, leaving his unemptied glass upon the table, he departed and was never known to sip another drop of wine.

And now, again, he resumed his wanderings in the woods and fields. It might be fancied that the bright butterfly, which had come so spirit-like into the window as Owen sat with the rude revellers, was indeed a spirit commissioned to recall him to the pure, ideal life that had so etheralized him among men. It might be fancied that he went forth to seek this spirit in its sunny haunts; for still, as in the summer time gone by, he was seen to steal gently up wherever a butterfly had alighted, and lose himself in contemplation of it. When it took flight his eyes followed the winged vision, as if its airy track would show the path to heaven. But what could be the purpose of the unseasonable toil, which was again resumed, as the watchman knew by the lines of lamplight through the crevices of Owen Warland's shutters? The towns-people had one comprehensive explanation of all these singularities. Owen Warland had gone mad! How universally efficacious—how satisfactory, too, and soothing to the injured sensibility of narrowness and dulness—is this easy method of accounting for whatever lies beyond the world's most ordinary scope! From St. Paul's days down to our poor little Artist of the Beautiful, the same talisman had been applied to the elucidation of all mysteries in the words or deeds of men who spoke or acted too wisely or too well. In Owen Warland's case the judgment of his towns-people may have been correct. Perhaps he was mad. The lack of sympathy—that contrast between himself and his neighbors which took away the restraint of example—was enough to make him so. Or possibly he had caught just so much of ethereal radiance as served to bewilder him, in an earthly sense, by its intermixture with the common daylight.

One evening, when the artist had returned from a customary ramble and had just thrown the lustre of his lamp on the delicate piece of work so often interrupted, but still taken up again, as if his fate were embodied in its mechanism, he was surprised by the entrance of old Peter Hovenden. Owen never met this man without a shrinking of the heart. Of all the world he was most terrible, by reason of a keen understanding which saw so distinctly what it did see, and disbelieved so uncompromisingly in what it could not see. On this occasion the old watchmaker had merely a gracious word or two to say. "Owen, my lad," said he, "we must see you at my house to-morrow night."

The artist began to mutter some excuse.

"Oh, but it must be so," quoth Peter Hovenden, "for the sake of the days when you were one of the household. What, my boy! don't you know that my daughter Annie is engaged to Robert

Danforth? We are making an entertainment, in our humble way, to celebrate the event."

That little monosyllable was all he uttered; its tone seemed cold and unconcerned to an ear like Peter Hovenden's; and yet there was in it the stifled outcry of the poor artist's heart, which he compressed within him like a man holding down an evil spirit. One slight outbreak, however, imperceptible to the old watchmaker, he allowed himself. Raising the instrument with which he was about to begin his work, he let it fall upon the little system of machinery that had, anew, cost him months of thought and toil. It was shattered by the stroke!

Owen Warland's story would have been no tolerable representation of the troubled life of those who strive to create the beautiful, if, amid all other thwarting influences, love had not interposed to steal the cunning from his hand. Outwardly he had been no ardent or enterprising lover; the career of his passion had confined its tumults and vicissitudes so entirely within the artist's imagination that Annie herself had scarcely more than a woman's intuitive perception of it; but, in Owen's view, it covered the whole field of his life. Forgetful of the time when she had shown herself incapable of any deep response, he had persisted in connecting all his dreams of artistical success with Annie's image; she was the visible shape in which the spiritual power that he worshipped, and on whose altar he hoped to lay a not unworthy offering, was made manifest to him. Of course he had deceived himself; there were no such attributes in Annie Hovenden as his imagination had endowed her with. She, in the aspect which she wore to his inward vision, was as much a creature of his own as the mysterious piece of mechanism would be were it ever realized. Had he become convinced of his mistake through the medium of successful love,—had he won Annie to his bosom, and there beheld her fade from angel into ordinary woman,—the disappointment might have driven him back, with concentrated energy, upon his sole remaining object. On the other hand, had he found Annie what he fancied, his lot would have been so rich in beauty that out of its mere redundancy he might have wrought the beautiful into many a worthier type than he had toiled for; but the guise in which his sorrow came to him, the sense that the angel of his life had been snatched away and given to a rude man of earth and iron, who could neither need nor appreciate her ministrations,—this was the very perversity of fate that makes human existence appear too absurd and contradictory to be the scene of one other hope or one other fear. There was nothing left for Owen Warland but to sit down like a man that had been stunned.

He went through a fit of illness. After his recovery his small and slender frame assumed an obtuser garniture of flesh than it had ever before worn. His thin cheeks became round; his delicate little hand, so spiritually fashioned to achieve fairy task-work, grew plumper than the hand of a thriving infant. His aspect had a childishness such as might have induced a stranger to pat him on the head—pausing, however, in the act, to wonder what manner of child was here. It was as if the spirit had gone out of him, leaving the body to flourish in a sort of vegetable existence. Not that Owen Warland was idiotic. He could talk, and not irrationally. Somewhat of a babbler, indeed, did people begin to think him; for he was apt to discourse at wearisome length of marvels of mechanism that he had read about in books, but which he had learned to consider as absolutely fabulous. Among them he enumerated the Man of Brass, constructed by Albertus Magnus, and the Brazen Head of Friar Bacon; and, coming down to later times, the automata of a little coach and horses, which it was pretended had been manufactured for the Dauphin of France; together with an insect that buzzed about the ear like a living fly, and yet was but a contrivance of minute steel springs. There was a story, too, of a duck that waddled, and quacked, and ate; though, had any honest citizen purchased it for dinner, he would have found himself cheated with the mere mechanical apparition of a duck.

"But all these accounts," said Owen Warland, "I am now satisfied are mere impositions."

Then, in a mysterious way, he would confess that he once thought differently. In his idle and dreamy days he had considered it possible, in a certain sense, to spiritualize machinery, and to combine with the new species of life and motion thus produced a beauty that should attain to the ideal which Nature has proposed to herself in all her creatures, but has never taken pains to realize. He seemed, however, to retain no very distinct perception either of the process of achieving this object or of the design itself.

"I have thrown it all aside now," he would say. "It was a dream such as young men are always mystifying themselves with. Now that I have acquired a little common sense, it makes me laugh to think of it."

Poor, poor and fallen Owen Warland! These were the symptoms that he had ceased to be an inhabitant of the better sphere that lies unseen around us. He had lost his faith in the invisible, and now prided himself, as such unfortunates invariably do, in the wisdom which rejected much that even his eye could see, and trusted confidently in nothing but what his hand could touch. This is the calamity of men whose spiritual part dies out of them and leaves the grosser understanding to assimilate them more and more to the things of which alone it can take cognizance; but in Owen Warland the spirit was not dead nor passed away; it only slept.

How it awoke again is not recorded. Perhaps the torpid slumber was broken by a convulsive pain. Perhaps, as in a former instance, the butterfly came and hovered about his head and reinspired him,—as indeed this creature of the sunshine had always a mysterious mission for the artist,—reinspired him with the former purpose of his life. Whether it were pain or happiness that thrilled through his veins, his first impulse was to thank Heaven for rendering him again the being of thought, imagination, and keenest sensibility that he had long ceased to be.

"Now for my task," said he. "Never did I feel such strength for it as now."

Yet, strong as he felt himself, he was incited to toil the more diligently by an anxiety lest death should surprise him in the midst of his labors. This anxiety, perhaps, is common to all men who set their hearts upon anything so high, in their own view of it, that life becomes of importance only as conditional to its accomplishment. So long as we love life for itself, we seldom dread the losing it. When we desire life for the attainment of an object, we recognize the frailty of its texture. But, side by side with this sense of insecurity, there is a vital faith in our invulnerability to the shaft of death while engaged in any task that seems assigned by Providence as our proper thing to do, and which the world would have cause to mourn for should we leave it unaccomplished. Can the philosopher, big with the inspiration of an idea that is to reform mankind, believe that he is to be beckoned from this sensible existence at the very instant when he is mustering his breath to speak the word of light? Should he perish so, the weary ages may pass away—the world's, whose life sand may fall, drop by drop—before another intellect is prepared to develop the truth that might have been uttered then. But history affords many an example where the most precious spirit, at any particular epoch manifested in human shape, has gone hence untimely, without space allowed him, so far as mortal judgment could discern, to perform his mission on the earth. The prophet dies, and the man of torpid heart and sluggish brain lives on. The poet leaves his song half sung, or finishes it, beyond the scope of mortal ears, in a celestial choir. The painter—as Allston did—leaves half his conception on the canvas to sadden us with its imperfect beauty, and goes to picture forth the whole, if it be no irreverence to say so, in the hues of heaven. But rather such incomplete designs of this life will be perfected nowhere. This so frequent abortion of man's dearest projects must be taken as a proof that the deeds of earth, however etherealized by piety or genius, are without value, except as exercises and manifestations of the spirit. In heaven, all ordinary thought is higher and more melodious than Milton's song. Then, would he add another verse to any strain that he had left unfinished here?

But to return to Owen Warland. It was his fortune, good or ill, to achieve the purpose of his life. Pass we over a long space of intense thought, yearning effort, minute toil, and wasting anxiety, succeeded by an instant of solitary triumph:

let all this be imagined; and then behold the artist, on a winter evening, seeking admittance to Robert Danforth's fireside circle. There he found the man of iron, with his massive substance thoroughly warmed and attempered by domestic influences. And there was Annie, too, now transformed into a matron, with much of her husband's plain and sturdy nature, but imbued, as Owen Warland still believed, with a finer grace, that might enable her to be the interpreter between strength and beauty. It happened, likewise, that old Peter Hovenden was a guest this evening at his daughter's fireside, and it was his well-remembered expression of keen, cold criticism that first encountered the artist's glance.

"My old friend Owen!" cried Robert Danforth, starting up, and compressing the artist's delicate fingers within a hand that was accustomed to gripe bars of iron. "This is kind and neighborly to come to us at last. I was afraid your perpetual motion had bewitched you out of the remembrance of old times."

"We are glad to see you," said Annie, while a blush reddened her matronly cheek. "It was not like a friend to stay from us so long."

"Well, Owen," inquired the old watchmaker, as his first greeting, "how comes on the beautiful? Have you created it at last?"

The artist did not immediately reply, being startled by the apparition of a young child of strength that was tumbling about on the carpet,—a little personage who had come mysteriously out of the infinite, but with something so sturdy and real in his composition that he seemed moulded out of the densest substance which earth could supply. This hopeful infant crawled towards the new-comer, and setting himself on end, as Robert Danforth expressed the posture, stared at Owen with a look of such sagacious observation that the mother could not help exchanging a proud glance with her husband. But the artist was disturbed by the child's look, as imagining a resemblance between it and Peter Hovenden's habitual expression. He could have fancied that the old watchmaker was compressed into this baby shape, and looking out of those baby eyes, and repeating, as he now did, the malicious question: "The beautiful, Owen! How comes on the beautiful? Have you succeeded in creating the beautiful?"

"I have succeeded," replied the artist, with a momentary light of triumph in his eyes and a smile of sunshine, yet steeped in such depth of thought that it was almost sadness. "Yes, my friends, it is the truth. I have succeeded."

"Indeed!" cried Annie, a look of maiden mirthfulness peeping out of her face again. "And is it lawful, now, to inquire what the secret is?"

"Surely; it is to disclose it that I have come," answered Owen Warland. "You shall know, and see, and touch, and possess the secret! For, Annie,—if by that name I may still address the friend of my boyish years,—Annie, it is for your bridal gift that I have wrought this spiritualized mechanism, this harmony of motion, this mystery of beauty. It comes late, indeed; but it is as we go onward in life, when objects begin to lose their freshness of hue and our souls their delicacy of perception, that the spirit of beauty is most needed. If,—forgive me, Annie,—if you know how—to value this gift, it can never come too late."

He produced, as he spoke, what seemed a jewel box. It was carved richly out of ebony by his own hand, and inlaid with a fanciful tracery of pearl, representing a boy in pursuit of a butterfly, which, elsewhere, had become a winged spirit, and was flying heavenward; while the boy, or youth, had found such efficacy in his strong desire that he ascended from earth to cloud, and from cloud to celestial atmosphere, to win the beautiful. This case of ebony the artist opened, and bade Annie place her fingers on its edge. She did so, but almost screamed as a butterfly fluttered forth, and, alighting on her finger's tip, sat waving the ample magnificence of its purple and gold-speckled wings, as if in prelude to a flight. It is impossible to express by words the glory, the splendor, the delicate gorgeousness which were softened into the beauty of this object. Nature's ideal butterfly was here realized in all its perfection; not in the pattern of such faded insects as flit among earthly flowers, but of those which hover across the meads of paradise for child-angels and the spirits of departed infants to disport themselves with. The rich down was visible upon its wings; the lustre of its eyes seemed instinct with spirit. The firelight glimmered around this wonder— the candles gleamed upon it; but it glistened apparently by its own radiance, and illuminated the finger and outstretched hand on which it rested with a white gleam like that of precious stones. In its perfect beauty, the consideration of size was entirely lost. Had its wings overreached the firmament, the mind could not have been more filled or satisfied.

"Beautiful! beautiful!" exclaimed Annie. "Is it alive? Is it alive?"

"Alive? To be sure it is," answered her husband. "Do you suppose any mortal has skill enough to make a butterfly, or would put himself to the trouble of making one, when any child may catch a score of them in a summer's afternoon? Alive? Certainly! But this pretty box is undoubtedly of our friend Owen's manufacture; and really it does him credit."

At this moment the butterfly waved its wings anew, with a motion so absolutely lifelike that Annie was startled, and even awestricken; for, in spite of her husband's opinion, she could not satisfy herself whether it was indeed a living creature or a piece of wondrous mechanism.

"Is it alive?" she repeated, more earnestly than before.

"Judge for yourself," said Owen Warland, who stood gazing in her face with fixed attention.

The butterfly now flung itself upon the air, fluttered round Annie's head, and soared into a distant region of the parlor, still making itself perceptible to sight by the starry gleam in which the motion of its wings enveloped it. The infant on the floor followed its course with his sagacious little eyes. After flying about the room, it returned in a spiral curve and settled again on Annie's finger.

"But is it alive?" exclaimed she again; and the finger on which the gorgeous mystery had alighted was so tremulous that the butterfly was forced to balance himself with his wings. "Tell me if it be alive, or whether you created it."

"Wherefore ask who created it, so it be beautiful?" replied Owen Warland. "Alive? Yes, Annie; it may well be said to possess life, for it has absorbed my own being into itself; and in the secret of that butterfly, and in its beauty,—which is not merely outward, but deep as its whole system,—is represented the intellect, the imagination, the sensibility, the soul of an Artist of the Beautiful! Yes; I created it. But"—and here his countenance somewhat changed—"this butterfly is not now to me what it was when I beheld it afar off in the daydreams of my youth."

"Be it what it may, it is a pretty plaything," said the blacksmith, grinning with childlike delight. "I wonder whether it would condescend to alight on such a great clumsy finger as mine? Hold it hither, Annie."

By the artist's direction, Annie touched her finger's tip to that of her husband; and, after a momentary delay, the butterfly fluttered from one to the other. It preluded a second flight by a similar, yet not precisely the same, waving of wings as in the first experiment; then, ascending from the blacksmith's stalwart finger, it rose in a gradually enlarging curve to the ceiling, made one wide sweep around the room, and returned with an undulating movement to the point whence it had started.

"Well, that does beat all nature!" cried Robert Danforth, bestowing the heartiest praise that he could find expression for; and, indeed, had he paused there, a man of finer words and nicer perception could not easily have said more. "That goes beyond me, I confess. But what then? There is more real use in one downright blow of my sledge hammer than in the whole five years' labor that our friend Owen has wasted on this butterfly."

Here the child clapped his hands and made a great babble of indistinct utterance, apparently demanding that the butterfly should be given him for a plaything.

Owen Warland, meanwhile, glanced sidelong at Annie, to discover whether she sympathized in her husband's estimate of the comparative value of the beautiful and the practical. There was, amid all her kindness towards himself, amid all the wonder and admiration with which she contemplated the marvellous work of his hands and incarnation of his idea, a secret scorn—too secret, perhaps, for her own consciousness, and perceptible only to such intuitive discernment as that of the artist. But Owen, in the latter stages of his pursuit, had risen out of the region in which such a discovery might have been torture. He knew that the world, and Annie as the representative of the world, whatever praise might be bestowed, could never say the fitting word nor feel the fitting sentiment which should be the perfect recompense of an artist who, symbolizing a lofty moral by a material trifle,—converting what was earthly to spiritual gold,—had won the beautiful into his handiwork. Not at this latest moment was he to learn that the reward of all high performance must be sought within itself, or sought in vain. There was, however, a view of the matter which Annie and her husband, and even Peter Hovenden, might fully have understood, and which would have satisfied them that the toil of years had here been worthily bestowed. Owen Warland might have told them that this butterfly, this plaything, this bridal gift of a poor watchmaker to a blacksmith's wife, was, in truth, a gem of art that a monarch would have purchased with honors and abundant wealth, and have treasured it among the jewels of his kingdom as the most unique and wondrous of them all. But the artist smiled and kept the secret to himself .

"Father," said Annie, thinking that a word of praise from the old watchmaker might gratify his former apprentice, "do come and admire this pretty butterfly."

"Let us see," said Peter Hovenden, rising from his chair, with a sneer upon his face that always made people doubt, as he himself did, in everything but a material existence. "Here is my finger for it to alight upon. I shall understand it better when once I have touched it."

But, to the increased astonishment of Annie, when the tip of her father's finger was pressed against that of her husband, on which the butterfly still rested, the insect drooped its wings and seemed on the point of falling to the floor. Even the bright spots of gold upon its wings and body, unless her eyes deceived her, grew dim, and the glowing purple took a dusky hue, and the starry lustre that gleamed around the blacksmith's hand became faint and vanished.

"It is dying! it is dying!" cried Annie, in alarm.

"It has been delicately wrought," said the artist, calmly. "As I told you, it has imbibed a spiritual essence—call it magnetism, or what you will. In an atmosphere of doubt and mockery its exquisite susceptibility suffers torture, as does the soul of him who instilled his own life into it. It has already lost its beauty; in a few moments more its mechanism would be irreparably injured."

"Take away your hand, father!" entreated Annie, turning pale. "Here is my child; let it rest on his innocent hand. There, perhaps, its life will revive and its colors grow brighter than ever."

Her father, with an acrid smile, withdrew his finger. The butterfly then appeared to recover the power of voluntary motion, while its hues assumed much of their original lustre, and the gleam of starlight, which was its most ethereal attribute, again formed a halo round about it. At first, when transferred from Robert Danforth's hand to the small finger of the child, this radiance grew so powerful that it positively threw the little fellow's shadow back against the wall. He, meanwhile, extended his plump hand as he had seen his father and mother do, and watched the waving of the insect's wings with infantine delight. Nevertheless, there was a certain odd expression of sagacity that made Owen Warland feel as if here were old Pete Hovenden, partially, and but partially, redeemed from his hard scepticism into childish faith.

"How wise the little monkey looks!" whispered Robert Danforth to his wife.

"I never saw such a look on a child's face," answered Annie, admiring her own infant, and with good reason, far more than the artistic butterfly. "The darling knows more of the mystery than we do."

As if the butterfly, like the artist, were

conscious of something not entirely congenial in the child's nature, it alternately sparkled and grew dim. At length it arose from the small hand of the infant with an airy motion that seemed to bear it upward without an effort, as if the ethereal instincts with which its master's spirit had endowed it impelled this fair vision involuntarily to a higher sphere. Had there been no obstruction, it might have soared into the sky and grown immortal. But its lustre gleamed upon the ceiling; the exquisite texture of its wings brushed against that earthly medium; and a sparkle or two, as of stardust, floated downward and lay glimmering on the carpet. Then the butterfly came fluttering down, and, instead of returning to the infant, was apparently attracted towards the artist's hand.

"Not so! not so!" murmured Owen Warland, as if his handiwork could have understood him. "Thou has gone forth out of thy master's heart. There is no return for thee."

With a wavering movement, and emitting a tremulous radiance, the butterfly struggled, as it were, towards the infant, and was about to alight upon his finger; but while it still hovered in the air, the little child of strength, with his grandsire's sharp and shrewd expression in his face, made a snatch at the marvellous insect and compressed it in his hand. Annie screamed. Old Peter Hovenden burst into a cold and scornful laugh. The blacksmith, by main force, unclosed the infant's hand, and found within the palm a small heap of glittering fragments, whence the mystery of beauty had fled forever. And as for Owen Warland, he looked placidly at what seemed the ruin of his life's labor, and which was yet no ruin. He had caught a far other butterfly than this. When the artist rose high enough to achieve the beautiful, the symbol by which he made it perceptible to mortal senses became of little value in his eyes while his spirit possessed itself in the enjoyment of the reality.

Glass Wings
Kat Howard

The room where he worked was full of flowers pretending they were birds. The white egret flower specifically, *habenaria radiate*, orchids that looked like egrets in flight. He admired these flowers, the way they so perfectly mimicked something that they were not, the way they contained all of the elegance of flight without the mess of actual wings.

In amongst the flowers, something flickered. It looked more like the idea of a butterfly, an outline an artist might sketch, than an actual insect, transparent wings banded in darkness, the only color what shone through.

A glasswing.

In front of him, on a long, worn table, small pieces of glass, the same shape as those in the butterfly's wings. In front of him, pinned to boards, glasswing after glasswing. Specimens, their wings pinned open, cut, torn. Puzzles, their secrets still to be extracted.

The glass, no matter how thin he cut it, was still too heavy—it tore the wings from the butterflies' backs. And he needed the glass, a sort of flattened optic cable meant to record images. The glass was the entire point.

A ticking along the table. The small steps, the folding and unfolding of the wings of one perfect mechanized butterfly—cold and elegant, iron and glass. He couldn't see the difference—no. That was wrong. He could see the difference, but for him, there was only improvement. The mechanical glasswing was perfected, not like the others.

Unfortunately, the others were what he had to work with.

The problem, as it had been explained to him, was that the mechanical butterfly was too perfect. A perfection that was unnatural and easily detectable. What was wanted was almost perfection, the flaws of nature engineered into something that could have been flawless. And so he pinned another butterfly and cut another set of wings of glass.

She opened the door into a garden of butterflies, wings like flying flowers, like stained glass in miniature, like rainbows made solid.

They soothed her, the delicate riot of colors clinging to the air like smears of memory.

She had memories. They were one of the few things that were still solely hers. Memories of the time before, when she could leave this place. Before her dreams turned into prophecies, before those prophecies became things that could belong to someone other than her. Before she became a thing that no longer belonged to herself. Before her life was no more than a small room and a walled garden and the futures she saw for other people.

She murmured an apology, then lifted a hand, waiting. A white dove landed soft on her outstretched finger, wings fluttering to stillness. With one smooth movement, she broke its neck. Then she cut into the still warm body, spilling entrails like wine. She traced her fingers through the viscera until she saw.

As the visions rushed through her, butterflies landed on the dove's corpse, the brightness of their wings obscuring the ruin beneath.

The butterfly opened and closed its wings. Slowly. He had finally gotten the glass thin enough that it didn't tear through what was left of the natural wings or rip them from the butterfly's back. It still wasn't perfect—he looked again at the fully mechanical butterfly, at its precise movements—but it worked. The butterfly flew; the glass transmitted the images.

There was the faintest of *clink*s as the wings touched, but he decided he would leave that as it was. The reminder that the glasswing was altered was soothing.

The slow motion of the beating wings triggered the optics in the glass, and the white wings of his orchids played across them. As long as this glasswing flew, it would record images onto its wings. Images of the woman's prophecies. They were the point of this exercise.

Not everyone could have a caged Cassandra, but the future shouldn't be a secret. Not when so many people needed to know. His work would allow everyone to have access to her futures, and to know they had seen them entire—not just what she told or what was approved. That was always the risk in waiting for someone else to say the future for you. Secrets were so easy to keep. And so—*clink*—the glasswings.

He picked up another butterfly, and cut a hole in its wing.

Wind whirled through the open roof of her cell, scattering white feathers that had fallen from her most recent sacrifice. She tracked the pattern of their path through the air, calculating omens, seeing futures in their fall, then shook her head, clearing those thoughts from her mind. The only future that was required of her was the one told in blood. Anything else could pass by, and so she let it. It was a pleasure, when she could, to live fully in the present and to not have to look forward.

Butterflies swirled around her, seeking refuge from the oncoming storm. Their wings were a future she never read. They were too close, she and these bright-winged things, and any future they showed would be hers. She didn't need to read omens to see what her future would be: It was time spent in this small cell, and then it was over. There was no need for her to count days, or know the precise method by which she would end.

Another gust, the wind blowing the butterflies before it, a sound like a brief burst of hail on glass. And something, something visible just at the edges. The briefest of shimmers. Almost—no. Only rain. She closed her eyes and turned her face to the storm and stood unmoving until she was soaked.

He sat alone, the white wings of his flowers waving gently behind him, and watched the images the glasswings sent back to him. His lip curled in frustration: their flight paths were too erratic to watch things with any sense of order;

he wished again that he had been allowed to fully automate them. The living ones went where they wished, hid, watched things that were interesting only to butterflies, and the images that came back from their wings were incomplete, unuseful.

But every so often there were glimpses. Her face, her hands, her knife as she carved the future out of the entrails of a white bird. A messy process, but she—she was precise. Elegant. Almost mechanical.

Spectacular.

He could have watched her forever. If only the butterflies were more cooperative.

They died quickly, his altered glasswings, and the images went static when they did. That part was no matter. It was simple enough now to make more. He placed glass into another butterfly, and another, and another, the discarded bits of their natural wings fluttering to the ground like dust.

Her hands, once again, red and sticky with blood. She had become so used to the sensation that it registered as normal. Behind her eyes, the possibilities of the universe arranged and rearranged themselves. Once they halted, became certain, known, she spoke what she had seen.

Those who were listening would hear. They always did. She knew that they listened, they watched, that they took every secret they could from her. No need for them to be close enough for her work to stain their hems, for the scent of death to wrinkle their noses. So much easier to keep her locked away and separate, wholly apart from the people who would live in the futures she saw.

In the quiet that followed her words: *clink. clink. clink.* The smallest of noises, a whisper out of place. A blur of almost something falling, and then a *crack* on the ground.

A glint of light, and for a moment, even though it had been her hands that called forth that future, she almost didn't recognize it there before her. Replicated on the wings of a butterfly, wings now broken, wings somehow made of glass, the image of a bird. A knife. Blood.

An image of the entrails she had just read, of the future she had seen. An image preserved on wings that would carry that future elsewhere, to other watching eyes.

She picked up the wing-shaped glass, removing it from the tattered, altered body of the butterfly. Blood smeared from her hands, obscuring the image. She traced the shape of the wings with her fingers, and she felt her future in them.

After a while, he didn't even think of it as watching her anymore. The images he saw from the glasswings were simply there, like thought or breath, hovering in the background as he worked. When he did look up, it wasn't to watch her prophecies, to see the truths in her futures. Those were for others to interpret. It was to see the curve of her waist, the smoothness of her hands, the silk of her hair.

He longed for something like that, something beautiful that was his.

He had never built anything so complex, but perhaps. Perhaps. He set out his tools, and looked again at the color of her eyes.

Alone, forgotten, a mechanical butterfly traced a repeated path over and through the dying wings of orchids that once looked like birds.

It was easy to find the glasswings after that. They all had that tiny, telltale *clink*, and once she learned to look sideways it was easy to see that same outlined shimmer that wasn't quite invisibility as they flew slowly among their more natural cousins.

It bothered her to break their frail bodies beneath her fingers in order to pull the glass from their backs. They had already suffered, it seemed, their wings torn, replaced by sharp-edged glass. But she watched as they flew, haltingly—as if their wings were an ache in their bodies. She was freeing them, and they would free her.

Bit by bit, she took the glass pieces and shaped them into wings. She bound them together with bones and sinews left over from the birds she sacrificed. They were ugly and awkward and sharp-edged, but they would fly. She had seen it.

And when the wings were large enough, she took a knife.

The cuts were awkward, but she was used to slicing through flesh to see futures, and she knew how to adjust when blood slicked her grip. Once she finished, she slid the glass wings into her skin.

They ground together as she moved her shoulders. It hurt, but she only needed to bear the pain for a little while. As the wings beat, images raced across the glass. Reflections of the butterfly garden, of walls, of a future.

Her future.

And then, in a tremendous chiming of glass, she flew.

Bet the Farm
Michael Cisco

There's always one who falls in love with implacable doom like this boy did, and it's as impossible to explain as any other love. Why would anyone fall in love with the march of doom? Banks of lights startled out one by one, crash by crash in a resounding enclosure, laying strips of perfect darkness on a bare cement floor. The hall of locked doors—the old hall with no doors, and it keeps angling in even segments forever. Is it a comfort to believe you are irrevocably trapped? Is that an invigorating feeling? Maybe it was just Nordic phlegm, inherited from people who often had to be pretty ambitious just to get by. When he was old enough to notice, he thought about it. Death doesn't glide, or pop up out of the ground, it marches. He's sure there's a reason why death marches, but he doesn't know what it is. Somehow he had imbibed the idea that doom never ends but marches, head up, without halting, immortal and dignified beneath its own beautiful, transparent banner, which he pictured lying across the sky like the shadow of a flame.

His divorced older brother, who was twelve years his senior, had tormented a woman for years with a benign affability that was unconsciously and consummately well calculated to drive her crazy, always turning her away with an invitation to come again. Young as he was at the time, he could see in her face, nearly every time she came around, the resolve that comes from having yet another tactic. Nothing she did, though, ever gained her any purchase on his brother's obdurately slippery personality, and it was heart-rending to see her going away, time after time, defeated again. He never wondered why his brother was like that, especially since he never had anything further to do with any woman, and hated his ex-wife. Many years later, when his brother was dead and he had defeats of his own, he realized two things. First, that he understood the persistent, long-suffering way that woman had tasted every last drop of her destiny, and admired her for it. She didn't neglect a single grain of her dream. That struck him as the best way to live. The second thing he realized was that his brother had wanted to say yes to her all along. He knew that because, one time, he was out to lunch with his brother, who had had a stroke and was in a wheelchair by then, and a woman walked by their table, trailing a wake of the same perfume that other woman, the persistent one, always wore. They both smelled it, they both remembered. He saw his brother's face tremble and instantly understood that all those smooth demurrals had been hiding a kind of impalement, that his brother had been a hostage forced to act normal; he had been inwardly smothering himself with a firm hand without ever really knowing why he was doing it, as if he were possessed by his own pride, acting as an external force, a neutralized part of himself looking on helplessly as the active part kept shutting her down.

He'd worked in city planning for a while. He'd mapped out a barren concrete square fronting four huge pokerfaced banks, and helped to select the sinister cubical sculpture that was the black heart of the square, and which looked like it wanted to fall down on you and crush you. Crush you, gradually. He also designed a strip mall that ended up housing a check cashing store, a bail bondsman, a gun store, and the offices of a foreclosure attorney who went next door one day, and then shot himself right there in the windswept center of the intersection. Some colleagues in the planning office had known the attorney socially, and he once overheard two of them discussing the suicide.

"But that's just how it's been, he's just—"one of them twirled a finger in the air, "a downward spiral."

"It's not a spiral," he said, eyes on his work.
"What's that?"
"It's not a spiral, it's straight down," he said,
eyes on his work.

He lived in such-and-such a place and did
such-and-such things, and now he's lean and
bent and old, with knuckly hands and a cigarette,
sitting alone in his hard wooden chair in watery
sunlight white on his white head and the silent
white smoke. Tom Waits wrote a song about him
called "What's He Building In There?"

His late older brother had also taken the full
measure of whatever it was that systematically
pinched out every last wick of his earnestness,
and he respected the skill, conscious or not,
he used to conceal his anguish. It took years
of neglect and old age and a stroke to shake
his facial control. By the time that perfume-
incident happened, he already never could stand
earnestness from people, but he could stand it
from machines, which was good since he still
needed earnestness, needed it very, very badly.
He used to go out looking for it, on silent recon.
He wasn't really any different from anyone else,
except for that one part of his mind that was
always on silent recon, and stored up images
and gestures he gathered imperceptibly from
the windows of houses, shops, apartments,

from street corners and contrasted against bus windows.

He thought to himself, although not in so many words, "All these are the architecture of my doom somehow."

After he retired, he moved into an old clapboard farmhouse. He'd first caught sight of it from the window of the bus, and it was like locking eyes with another person. By chance it was the doomed spot. What first he noticed was the sooty blackness of its air, and the wiry deadness of the wormy trees whose limbs made a sort of hive around and above the roof. That particular obscurity clung to him as he flashed by down the road, and he remembered too the somber vividness of the broad white clapboarding that seemed to glow at him through an invisible veil draped from the eaves. And one more detail—a real estate sign—made the image complete.

Now he can see the bus jostle by on the road from the window of that old place. It looks like a sort of bathyscape, filled with a homey orange radiance, bustling people home like the merry old village coachman. In his memories, the bus was unimportantly desolate, but from this window it was positively hearthlike. He imagined the contrary perspective; he knew what the house looked like from the bus, but now there was the one lit window to invite speculation.

Once he had the house, he could get to work

on the earnestness machines. He knew design, but had no serious knowledge of engineering and had never owned any tools more demanding than a hammer and some screwdrivers. In the absence of clutter and mental noise that moving to this farmhouse had made, he could set aside any technical obstacles and address himself frankly to a bare white formica table. Then to pencils, tracing paper, a compass. An ashtray made of clear glass, a carton of unfiltered cigarettes, and a stately box of safety matches.

He smoked, and blew the smoke straight out ahead of him. With his eyes half open, he would search the coils of smoke for shapes and then sketch them on the paper in front of him without looking at his pencil. The tracing paper sheets he used were big, like butcher's paper. When he felt a shape was complete, he would move the paper evenly in a random direction. Overlapping drawings were no less useful. When he got tired of doing this, and the sheet was full, he would go to a drawer and extract a parts catalog. The company went out of business years ago, but the thick catalog was a virtual dictionary of mechanical parts. Opening it on top of the tracing paper, he would methodically turn the pages looking for parts that corresponded more or less to any of his drawings. When he found one, he would label the drawing with the name of the part. In this way, he knew what to look for.

He ordered parts on the rotary telephone, and soon parcels were arriving nearly every day. Very often the parts were virtual antiques, and he sometimes had to pay rather high prices for them. Pieces of ancient clockwork and from long-obsolete washing machines, jelly molds, ice cream makers, bed warmers, rubber seals, radiator faucets, valves from an old ammonia refrigeration machine, most of the works from a player piano, a gas mantle, part of a telegraph decoder, the action from an old carbine, a steam tractor drive rod, a prosthetic arm made from wood and gutta-percha, gears, belts, and cams. Sometimes he reaches right in and pulls a piece from the tobacco cloud and sets it down on the table in front of him. His smoke never entirely dissipates, and fragments drift through the house like jellyfish. Eventually he sets up an assembly bench in his garage; all his tools hang from the ceiling on rubber bands. When he has enough parts, he goes in there and closes the door. He pulls one tool down after another, uses it and lets it go, and it snaps back up through the smoke. Reach up and pull another one down through the smoke.

Stock the farm with animals. Make them out of memories, machine parts, smoke vestiges, and recyclables; then, add the doom they can't live without. It's the final step. Doom is the spark and the wear. It looks like a black asterisk he pulls out of a shadowy hole in the bench, the way you would pick up a starfish from a tide pool. He pulls one out with long tweezers and lays it limply on the back of his latest creation; the asterisk seethes down into the body, the gears start to tick, the limbs start groping, and the eyes flip open, staring.

At first, the end result of his work was more or less frogs, and what they did was walk up walls, never down, and even when they crossed the ceiling they still were climbing up somehow, with their long sinewy arms corded like a stream of tap water and colorless spatulated hands. Every now and then, a long tongue would snap, flashing like a firecracker. In no time, he was up to full-sized livestock; they didn't need any extra material to make, only a greater concentration of mental effort. The lots in back of the farm house became hideous and inexplicable with half-glimpsed bulks of shadow, rolling masses like low herds, aerial presences like birds made of wind flurries, wallowy patches that seemed to collect senseless despair like a hollow in the ground collects slime. From bus windows at twilight, a passenger might be struck by the dire glamour vibrating off the plain white house, long and flat against the ground, and the word went around that some kind of warlock Calvinist was living there now.

Once he lost a kitten he'd made. It had gotten out of the house, he didn't know how. The second day he went out to look for it, he found a dead coyote pup, very young, and the kitten wedged in among some rocks nearby. A dark opening beneath a wide, flat boulder was the den mouth. The kitten was still moving its paws in little circles, rolling its head, and when he touched it he saw in a burst of mental imagery the mother coyote, the retreat from the farm with the kitten in her mouth, the kitten slipping loose and falling in among the rocks, the mistake of one for another in the dark, the pup's neck broken. When, twenty minutes later, he was back by the roadside and saw the crumpled grey body lying in the margin, where the car had flung her, he blanched, inwardly contracting in a kind of black satisfaction. He pulled the kitten out of his knapsack, made an adjustment with his fibrous, thick index finger, and the kitten seemed to pull itself together with a snicker. It returned home with him under its own power, gambolling innocently along beside him.

"First animals, people next," he thought. "That's always the way it goes."

He began waiting.

It might or might not have been nerves, but, when the old man opened the door to him, Guy thought for an instant that a black plume was tumbling in space just above the white head, like the holy flame that stands on prophets' heads in church windows. So he wasn't at all sure just what he said to the old man, but he only nodded and waved Guy into the dim, cigaretty interior. Now that he was seated again at his kitchen table, the old man was plainly the central wheel in his farm machine. Outside the walls, Guy could hear the animals methodically nibbling grass, their nearly invisible heads all bowed in a line, unravelling the grass like a sweater, row by row, their teeth and their feet moving to the sharp ticking of the big wall clock above the old man's kitchen table. The clock was like a steel porthole looking out on a snowy field raked with lean, ink-black shadows.

"I'm here for a friend," he tells the old man, who is drawing straight lines on tracing paper using a plastic triangle. The table lamp blazes with colorless light. Colorless twilight blows in from the screen door behind Guy, the spectral windows around him, dimly edging the overstuffed sofa in its glistening plastic slipcover. The old man's movements are perfectly regular.

Guy takes a step closer and freezes. All but invisible living things in constant, automatic motion are hearkening all around him.

"Yes?" the old man says.

Something hops onto Guy's left foot. It looks like a toad, although it has a neck, and out of all those living things, it alone has stopped moving. Guy instantly dismisses the impulse to kick out or shake it off. Now it is climbing his pant leg, reaching up his body with its long arms. He reaches down to shoo it away, but instead he finds himself picking it up and holding it in the palm of his hand. Not warm, not cold, not heavy, not light, but, inside it, something plucks like a thick guitar string in time with the clock. The toad thing grips the sides of his hand with its own long firm fingers. Then, with a sort of anticipatory whir inside, it inflates its throat to reveal a brilliant emergency-yellow pouch with a ragged, black exclamation point in the middle, and it sings out a tone that starts soft and high and ends loud and low, as if it were imitating the roar of a passing train.

Guy hefts the toad at the old man.

"How much?"

"Take it," the old man says and draws a crisp straight line.

"I can have it?" Guy asks, uncertainly.

"You can have that," says the old man.

Guy dropped her off so late she barely made her flight. Now that she's in her seat, the seething numbness that he'd left her with regains her full attention. An hour of sullenly unbroken silence in the car; she couldn't afford a cab. No friends left around here anymore. But with the divorce settled, the worst is permanently behind her. She won't be coming back.

The descending whine of the engine tugs at her sleeping mind, but it is the wild plummet in her stomach as the plane jolts and instantly drops thirty feet that whips her awake amid shouts of surprise and alarm. The angle of the clouds out the porthole makes her grow cold, and again that engine sound grates almost underneath her. With a ferocious start, her eyes desperate, she suddenly lunges forward, snatches up her carry-on bag, unzips one compartment after another until one of them blooms out an emergency yellow throat with an exclamation point down the middle, and that long descending tone rings out among the screams of the passengers.

Guy is speeding down an empty highway, music blaring, eyes all over the road. It might or might not be nerves, but he swerves once to avoid what he thought was a car abruptly pulling out from a dirt road into the lane ahead of him. Something dark and bulky flashes by on the right, but he can't see anything in the rear view mirror—whatever it was, it was too low for a car, wasn't it, and a truck was passing, horn blaring from high to low as it went by, although come to think of it he hadn't seen and didn't see any truck ...

His breath stops. Braking hard, he pulls onto the shoulder by a stand of trees thinking: "It's not possible...I put it...I put it."

He jumps from the car and fumbles with the trunk catch. The whole car seems to be vibrating with the vestiges of the sound, and he's suddenly as giddy as if he was caught in an earthquake. With a trembling that starts in his gut and shakes him from the inside out, he throws the trunk open so abruptly and violently he tumbles into it and comes face to face with a note addressed to him in her handwriting and topped by an emergency-yellow throat streaked with an exclamation point that bulges up with that same sweep of sound from high to low.

In that moment, he realized the giddiness, the rumbling, actually were coming from the ground. They're not inside him at all, not at their point of origin. He has time to turn around, to see the aircraft fuselage erupt from woods and pivoting tree shadows, combing the air with the soft white light from its portholes. It snaps the guardrail, hurtles past the separated landing gear he had swerved to avoid a moment ago, and bears down on him like a colossal white plow.

The old man gets up from his table at midnight sharp and steps out in front of the farmhouse for a little air, a bit of a breather. The night around him inaudibly booms with conglomerated ticking and catching. Lumbering shades, precisely coordinated, their springs taut, rut in the back lot. Their snorts and ejaculations coincide exactly with the long tearing noise of each passing car on the road there. Cigarette smoke lifts drowsily in the still air in front of the farmhouse. To every passing car, the old man delivers the same mute warning: never ever lose hold of your fond dream of escaping necessity, as if it weren't as close to you as the vein in your neck, as if it weren't the hammer whose blows shape even that dream pulsing in your neck, as if you were the one rascal in a universe of dire nobility. Doom isn't a spiral, but it isn't an abyss either. It's a staircase as straight as a die and, with the wind in what's left of your hair, every step of your descent is deliberate and firm, on down with everything else to a heat death that is the tapered new cosmos.

A smudged mob of birds leaps up into the bare branches of the dead sycamore tree, wings whirring and beaks snapping. The old man pinches out his cigarette, pockets the butt, and turns to go back inside again, climbing the low steps to the front door, foot, foot, hand, hand, foot, foot, hand, hand.

Long Pig
Adrian Van Young

When Spence goes to open the petting zoo's doors on what he assumes is its last day in business, he discovers MacFarquhar, the petting zoo keeper, lying in blood with his ring finger missing.

Spence gets close. Inspects the wound. The finger has been gnawed away.

The pigs and sheep and goats Spence owns that aren't quite pigs and sheep and goats are mounded in their separate pens.

MacFarquhar's been drinking. That's why he's asleep. He reeks of serf-moonshine, B.O. underneath it. He's half-tipped over on a bench that faces the pens, where the eTures bed down, his arm splayed out across the bench. The arm extends in such a way its wrist and fingers twist up, slightly, in the brisk attitude of a concert conductor.

The finger shows a ridge of bone. Blood pumps from the hollow encasing the joint.

"MacFarquhar, MacFarquhar," Spence says, drawing closer.

Spence doesn't need to address him by name, but still he does it out of habit. MacFarquhar has one, after all; the fed listed it on the DSAT (Department of Serf Acquisition and Tenure) when Spence logged on to select him.

Spence should elevate the hand, but it already is more or less. So he leaves it.

Next Spence goes to check the eTures, who never fail to sour his mood, reminders as they are of the failed enterprise over which he is sovereign and by extension all mankind: the petting zoo, open for nearly a decade.

The petting zoo, once inundated by seekers.

The petting zoo, now: un-trafficked, insolvent.

He'd first put up money to open the place from returns on investments he'd made in the first couple months of the Great Cross-Extinction and, where it was needed, the extra he'd saved to one day send Emmie, his daughter, to college. Most of Spence's investments had been in biotech, which was the industry responsible for creating the eTures. So thanks to Spence and others like him, gazing onto far horizons, when the last several species turned up as endangered, the technology had been long in the works.

The dying took place with no set hierarchy,

though most people thought it started with livestock, worked its way across from there.

Reptiles, rodents. Insects. Birds. Felines and canines of all shapes and types. By the time it spread to the largest land mammals and begun to show up in the ones in the sea, Spence stopped watching the news coverage of it.

Now Spence stands before the pens, two prods in his right hand and one in his left; each genus of eTure requires its own prod, tailored to its nervous system.

The blood pools and drips from the zookeeper's bench, but none of the eTures appear to need prodding. Asleep isn't how Spence would put it. In sleep mode? The eTures do need to be charged, after all: a USB-chord running in through their rectums, connected to the charging hub, the hub itself, a black rectangle with a blue power cylinder sheathed in its middle, sitting in the charging bay between Spence's office and where the pens sit, which is MacFarquhar's living quarters—a courtyard covered by a tarp.

MacFarquhar's bench defines this space, sweatpants-inside-sweatpants bunched up for a pillow. Everything else—MacFarquhar's dishes, MacFarquhar's books and magazines, a jar of whatever MacFarquhar's been drinking—must fit beneath the bench and does.

Spence moves among the eTure pens, looking for MacFarquhar's finger, but the digit is nowhere in any of them. Can the eTures have eaten it up altogether?

All that belies them as lawn ornaments is a faint humming sound at the centers of them. The pigs' snouts are faintly wet, their mouths arranged in secret smiles. The goats with their little legs tucked up beneath them.

Spence returns to MacFarquhar, beginning to stir.

"MacFarquhar," Spence whispers again with annoyance

Spence nudges Macfarquhar's left flank with his knee.

"Right!" MacFarquhar says, "I'm up."

"What happened?" says Spence.

"Holy hell," says MacFarquar. He unkinks his body and slowly rises. His discomfort appears to have gone to his head, which he rubs with the sting of the badly hung-over. "One of the goats," MacFarquhar says. "Got me when I wasn't looking."

Of course this would happen today of all days, with so much to do before closing the zoo. With so many closing promotions at stake and one ceremony to mark the occasion: a glossy banner to be hung, a three-for-one charge on unlimited petting, a "Westminster eTure Show" (Spence's concept) complete with a grand promenade and prize ribbons, as well as a speech he'd been writing for days and would deliver that night on the petting zoo's steps with all of the eTures assembled below him.

In it, Spence will speak of "hope," the "grit to fight another day."

Emmie, his daughter, has promised she'll be there. Or anyway Emmie's mom, Kay, promised Spence, who'd divorced him around when he'd started the zoo, the Great Cross-Extinction in full swing by then. The divorce's intense acrimony aside, her timing always struck Spence as unkind.

Today is the first day in quite a long time that Emmie will come visit Spence at the zoo. This maybe has something to do with the fact he'd taken a downswing along with his business, living sleepless in his office on potato chips and scotch, yet much more likely his ex-wife, who's never given Spence a chance.

So Spence must admit that he's nervous today. MacFarquhar's finger isn't helping.

He examines MacFarquhar still rubbing his head, trying to cut off blood flow to his hand. That's when it comes to him MacFarquhar passed out probably not from the moonshine he drank but the pain.

"How did he get out?" says Spence.

"He didn't," MacFarquhar says, "this was at dinner."

"Dinner?" says Spence.

"While I had them plugged in. That one there." MacFarquhar points to one of the goats, which could be any of them, except for the fact it's the only one standing. It stands toward the back of the pen, its head raised. Spence can see its eyes shining at brief intervals when it twitches its head as though listening for something.

"How long's it been like that?" says Spence.

"Few hours now," MacFarquhar says. "How long I been sleeping?"

But Spence doesn't answer. "After it bit off your finger, what happened?"

MacFarquhar shrugs, grimaces. "Oh, not a lot. I rounded them up, put them back in their pens. That's when I started getting drunk."

Spence pauses a moment, intent on MacFarquhar.

That MacFarquhar decided to finish his chores isn't what surprises Spence. What does surprise Spence—what impresses him, even—is that he was able to do it at all.

"Something wrong?" says MacFarquhar.

Spence smiles. "Not at all. Let's get you bandaged up," he says.

After tending MacFarquhar, Spence puts up the banner.

He posts the unlimited petting promotion. He sets up the "Westminster eTures Show" run and arranges the ribbons inside a vitrine. Standing before the bathroom mirror, he even rehearses his speech several times, but is shocked by how little conviction is in it. The parts of the speech that at first had so moved him, peppered with words like "hope" and "moxie," die off in his earholes as patently false. So he tries to recite it as though to his daughter—Emmie, eleven, no, twelve by that point. As though where he sees himself, Emmie is standing, in the sweater she wears with the ears on the hood and the claws on the sleeves that Spence finds so off-putting, because it reminds him of what's dead and gone.

MacFarquhar helps Spence with the zoo preparations, wincing under his hand and his raging hangover. Spence must say the bandage job he did on the zookeeper's hand is half-decent, what remains of the joint stabilized with a splint and only a few spots of blood showing through. Before he'd wrapped and tucked the bandage, Spence had even attempted to trim back the skin that the jaws of the eTures left hanging ragged. MacFarquhar breathed in sharply, once.

MacFarquhar is tougher than Spence had imagined.

But so are the eTures, which makes Spence uneasy. Colder, more brutal, like actual creatures. Spence tries to think back if he's heard of more cases of eTures attacking a live human being and can't think of any outright, though there must be.

The eTure simulacrum is purportedly exact, right down to the muscles, the teeth, and the hooves.

Only the eTures' brains are synthetic, and part of the spine, threading into the flesh. The rest of the body—the blood, fat, and tissue—is a fully regenerative cellular casing stimulated by signals that come from the brain. These signals are electrical, hence the eTures' trademark name. And hence, too, the barely discernible humming that so many mistake for breath.

The trickle of seekers starts early that day. Slightly more of them than normal.

Spence calls them seekers because they are seeking some vestige of the world they knew, a world that used to have many things in it apart from high primates deserted by luck. Most of the seekers are, tellingly, children, and today they come into the zoo in short bursts: shrieking, writhing, holding hands with siblings or schoolmates or one/both parents, veering here and charging there, pointing at everything, tugging each other, slightly damp from the rain that is falling outside, their hair tangled, their glasses fogged.

MacFarquhar hangs back at the edges of things.

Just left of the door, in his zookeeper's suit, cradling his bandaged hand,

he watches the children go into the zoo, pay their fares at the booth and go on to the pens. Spence has never quite trusted MacFarfquhar with children, though nothing he's done has been cause for concern. It's more just a feeling Spence gets—an unwellness.

MacFarquhar's eyes a bit too steady as he watches the children make off toward the pens.

MacFarquhar's smile a bit too sweet as he outfits the children with paddling brushes so they won't pick up crud from the eTures' fur.

Spence never chose MacFarquhar as his serf. MacFarquhar was assigned to Spence after the Great Cross-Extinction was over, his name among the many names of the world's livestock farmers made to pay reparations for supposedly starting the Great Cross-Extinction when a pathogen strain masked as a hormone was introduced into the cow population.

Or was it the pigs? Spence can never be sure. No one really is, in fact.

The animals were dying off and someone had to take the blame.

Emmie comes through the door not with Kay but with Beaufort, Emmie's stepfather, who Spence doesn't care for. Spence can only assume Kay herself never comes because she can't stand being in Spence's presence so she always sends Beaufort, her lame emissary, to yuck it up and bond with Spence while keeping an eye, very subtly, on Emmie.

The petting zoo's a single room: admission booth just past the entrance, the three eTure pens, separated by species, organized beyond the booth.

Emmie and Beaufort walk straight up to Spence, who's running cards and making change before giving people their tickets to enter. He starts to come around to Emmie, but something displeased in her eyes warns him off, so he awkwardly pivots back where he was standing, reaches down to fluff her hair. "Hey there, sweetheart," Spence says.

"Hi, Dad," Emmie answers. Beneath her bangs her eyes flash up.

"How goes it, Doctor Spence?" says Beaufort, indulging an unfunny habit he has of calling Spence "Doctor" because of the zoo, like Spence must need a PhD to care for robot pigs and goats. "I wish this were all under better conditions, but you had a good run of it, didn't you, Doc?"

Spence turns to his daughter, hands shoved in her hoodie.

"So, what," says Spence and cuffs her lightly. "You want to go see Mr. Oinks-a-lot first?"

Mr. Oinks-a-lot is Emmie's favorite, the biggest eTure in the zoo. When Emmie came to the zoo in years past, she would always go pet Mr. Oinks-a-lot first, cooing over his rump with her paddle brush, whispering.

"Mr. Oinks-a-lot's gross," Emmie says. "He's a monster."

Spence feels his face twisting into a scowl. "That's suddenly an issue for you?"

Emmie rolls her eyes at Spence and turns to look around the zoo.

Beaufort kneels before Emmie and flicks at her bangs. "Hey, monsters can be cool," he says. "Aren't I a cool monster?" Beaufort pulls a face. "How about now?" He pulls another.

"You're such a dork, Beaufort," Emmie says, but even Spence can see she's smiling.

Spence follows Beaufort and Emmie along toward the pens where the children commune with the eTures. He swears he can feel the damp eyes of MacFarquhar tracking them across the floor, but when Spence looks back at his serf, he's off, walking. Demonstratively busy completing some task.

When they get to the pens Emmie stops and stands slouched. She seems so blasé, so resistant to joy. That can't be healthy for her, can it? Chalk it up to Kay's influence.

He's so sidetracked observing her he almost doesn't see the children. They're closing in a narrow skirt around the goat-pen, whispering. Awed.

Spence isn't sure of the moment in time the petting zoo began to fail. It may not have been a particular moment but rather a long and depressing accrual—the crowds going from loud and spilling, to suddenly smaller but no cause for panic, to abysmal and echoing late in year eight, when Spence started noticing revenue problems. At first, he didn't quite know why. His eTures were top-of-the-line in the biz. He ran the place clean. He charged sober admission. When one day he noticed a father and daughter of roughly his and Emmie's age standing in front of the sheep pen, despondent. Their heads tilted, their faces slack. "It's not really the same—is it, sweetie?" said the father.

Not a week after that, Spence finally relented, ordering MacFarquhar from the DSAT. He'd always resisted the notion of serfdom—on moral/ethical grounds, okay, sure, but also in terms of his own self-sufficiency. He'd never needed anyone to help him run the petting zoo. At least MacFarquhar, in his serfdom, had never cost more than it took to feed him, heat his quarters, change his bench-clothes.

Spence pulls his daughter through the kids, her stepdad Beaufort close behind them. There's something magic going on, the children's movements slow, deliberate, like whatever it is they're thronging toward might vanish if they go too fast.

In front of the crowd is the very same goat that took MacFarquhar's finger from him. And the goat is resplendent. Its coat shines in glory. Its musculature is a study in contour. Its eyes spark with this greenish orange, its slotted pupils glossy black. Even how it stands there is more lithe, more alive: its forelegs tensed, its rump perked faintly.

"She's a pretty one, huh?" Beaufort comments to Emmie, but Emmie isn't looking at him.

She's looking at Spence with this light in her eyes. "I love him," she says to her father. "I love him!"

Counting the box at the end of the day, Spence finds that the zoo has done such ample business he could, if he wanted to, open tomorrow, maybe into the start of the following week.

"How's the hand?" Spence asks MacFarquhar.

At the end of MacFarquhar's bed/bench, Spence sits down.

The petting zoo is closed for now. The bathrooms cleaned, the pastures swept. MacFarquhar is resting, his head on the sweatpants, his hand elevated on top of his chest.

"I'll be honest," says MacFarquhar, "a lot better with all five fingers."

"Probably time to change that dressing." Spence sets a first aid kid on top of the bench. "Here," he says, leans in. "Let me."

MacFarquar sits up and Spence gathers in closer.

Slowly, Spence unwraps the bandage, watching MacFarquhar for signs of distress. The angry stump has started crusting, the bone of it mottled partway under scab. Spence judges he did a good job with the scissors: The skin around the wound is clean. When Spence is done coating his serf's hand with ointment and cocooning the hand to the wrist in fresh gauze, he sees that MacFarquhar is gritting his teeth.

"You look like you could use a drink."

MacFarquhar surveys him a moment in silence. "I got my own," MarFarquhar says.

He brings up a jam jar from under the bench and starts to unscrew it, but Spence waves him off.

"Not that I can say too much after how you hurt your hand, but isn't that moonshine a no-no?" says Spence.

"Sorry, *jefe*," says MacFarquhar.

"Can I ask where you got it?" Spence says.

"Down the way."

"From Perkins or Standish?" Spence says.

No response; MacFarquhar only grins at Spence.

Perkins and Standish are neighboring serfs, indentured to people within walking distance, but the serfs are tight-lipped in regards to their business, their clandestine networks, their little rebellions.

"Never mind." Spence pats MacFarquhar. "Got something better. You sit tight."

When he returns moments later with a bottle of scotch, MacFarquhar is sitting erect on the bench. Beyond the bench the sleeping pens, where the eTures lie charged and corralled for the night. Or all of the eTures except for the goat, who stands alone of all its kind. Infused with a strange and directionless vigor that will not let it rest its head. Eyes shining faintly in the dim, its head cocked to the slightest sound.

By the time Spence is fully attuned to its presence, he sees that MacFarquhar has been for some time. One of his eyes never moves from the goat, its pupil huge and dark with dread.

Spence pours them each a few fingers of scotch. MacFarquhar gulps his down; Spence sips. Spence tilts the bottle at MacFarquhar, and MacFarquhar nods gingerly at him: "Thanks, *jefe*."

Spence pours him three fingers this time and sits back. "Where we you before you came here?"

"With a family."

"They treat you well?"

MacFarquhar shrugs. "Didn't work me too hard, so I guess so," he says.

"How about before that?"

"In a warehouse," he says.

Spence sips his drink. "I don't mean that. I mean *before* before," he says.

"Pig farm," says MacFarquhar. "I run it myself. We really never talked about it?"

Spence shakes his head at MacFarquhar. "No, sir."

The liquor spills up to the rim of the glass before vanishing into MacFarquhar's dark mouth. "Woo-wee," he says. "Now that's the stuff."

His eyes have begun to look slightly decentered. He gestures for Spence to please pour him another.

"Ten or so acres," he says, "in the country. Ran a tight little slaughter. Real nice operation."

"What happened?" says Spence.

"You're asking me. One day they up and took it from me."

MacFarquhar sips his third glass slower, watching the eTures at rest in their pens. He looks contemplative to Spence, possessed of some vital and rarified wisdom.

"So," says Spence, "what do you think?" MacFarquhar slits his eyes, unsure. "You think it was justified—what they did to you? You think the farmers caused all this?"

MacFarquhar's eyes relax; he smiles. "Who cares what I think," he says.

On the following day, Spence reopens the zoo.

At first, he feels foolish unlocking the doors, repurposing the closing banner so it reads "Grand Reopening" scrawled on the back, thoroughly cleaning the whole premises, in particular the area between Spence's office and the pens where the eTures bed down for the night, but the people start coming by ones and by twos. Then after lunch they come in scores. At quarter past one Spence checks the rolls and counts an intake of well over two hundred. Spence imagines this might be because of the swerve from being closed to being open, the unexpected novelty that arises in the vacuum of something revoked being offered again.

But really Spence knows it's because of the eTures: the goat that took MacFarquhar's finger, but also two sheep and the giant prize pig named Mr. Oinks-a-lot by Emmie. Word has spread, Spence assumes, that these eTures are different.

And the eTures are different, in curious ways.

The goat still has its shimmer-fur, its sculpted contours and its pert way of standing, but these have been joined by a fresh energy, a habit of prancing and sniffing around and a playfulness, even, among the ranked children, who stand at the margins and ruffle its back. As for the sheep, they are creampuffs, meringues; their heads sleek and black, their fur buttered and springy.

But Mr. Oinks-a-lot's the prince.

Immense and voluptuous, shifting his bulk, as though daring the seekers to kill and devour him. His crinkly and bursting soufflé of a tummy; his debonair ears, one of them drooping slightly; his little, mincing, black-tipped legs that present the appearance when he walks of infinitesimally hovering forward.

Even Emmie, lukewarm on him just yesterday, appears besotted once again.

Again she arrives at the zoo with her stepdad, leading him on through the doors like a dope. Spence can't remember the last time he's seen her two times in a span of consecutive days, which means that if she's here, again, then coming was her own idea.

Spence watches her as she stands with her stepdad, watching Mr. Oinks-a-lot be fawned over, giggling. Beaufort leans down to make jokes in her ear but Emmie doesn't even hear him, always turning around for her father, for Spence, to grin at him and puff her cheeks in a child's mirroring of the monster before her.

It makes Spence ecstatic. But also uneasy.

Can Mr. Oinks-a-lot be trusted to not harm the children? Can any of the eTures, in their new dispositions?

Spence decides it will be fine.

After lunch he asks Beaufort to supervise things, hunkers down in his office behind his computer. When the DSAT website has Spence list the reason MacFarquhar's indenture did not "come to term" from a dropdown of reasons prescribed by the site that range from "Displayed antisocial behavior" to "Refused to work" to "Exhibited incompetence," Spence selects it: "Serf absconded."

The confirmation page assures that Spence's case will be reviewed.

For now there's only Emmie, though. When Spence comes back onto the floor, she's still with Mr. Oinks-a-lot. A huge group of saucer-eyed children surrounds her. The overripe pig struts in front of the children, its mouth twisted into brainless half-smile.

Spence comes behind Emmie and seizes her waist; she leans back in her father's arms. He drenches his nose in her hair. It's still there: fruit shampoo with notes of salt.

A recollection comes to Spence, like a jerky quick cut in a film, and then gone: Spence throwing a mop bucket over the floor between his office and the pens, the hot water sluicing over the concrete, pushing out a tide of blood.

"He looks real, Daddy," Emmie says. "Is he—" she hesitates "—*can* he be real?"

"No," says Spence. "But let's pretend. Let's pretend that he is for as long as we can."

Mr. Oinks-a-lot reminds Spence of something. What is it?

Long pig: the name for human meat.

Spence peers over Emmie, sees Beaufort beyond, who's smiling rigidly at Spence, his hand balancing on the top of the pigpen. Clownish, sloppy seconds Beaufort, as fake as the eTures corralled in their yards.

It's not hard to imagine him slipping, careening. Spence would pull him out, of course. But it's not hard for Spence to imagine it happening, how Emmie would laugh and how Spence would feel bad.

He leaves his daughter, goes to Beaufort. Puts his hand on Beaufort's arm. "Kids," says Spence. "It takes a village."

Beaufort only nods at first, but then he remembers his manners: "Sure, Doc."

Only because he's so pathetic, Spence will have to invite the man over for drinks. It will probably be awkward between them at first, the potential for growing uncivil enormous. But Spence will have to toe the line. He'll have to be the better man.

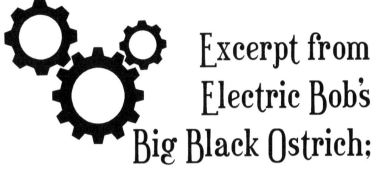

Excerpt from Electric Bob's Big Black Ostrich; or, Lost on the Desert (1893)

Robert T. Toombs

Chapter II: Electric Bob's Wonderful Ostrich

During the next two days the old miner and the young inventor made a thorough study of the large male ostrich which they had selected as the model of their new invention.

The overseer of the farm kindly allowed them every opportunity to study the birds, and put the entire flock at the service of his visitors.

Electric Bob made careful note of the positions of the legs, wings, and head under all conditions—and was greatly surprised at many discoveries he made.

The strength, speed, and endurance of the big birds were wonderful. Their stride, too, when going at full speed was astounding. The big fellow chosen as their model was a little over eight feet high, with legs a trifle more than three feet long, and yet when running his best he easily covered from twelve to fifteen feet between tracks.

Having made careful sketches of the birds, Electric Bob set about preparing his working drawings, plans, and specifications to be sent to the factory in Chicago that had turned out his White Alligator which had performed so satisfactorily.

This required careful study, as it was necessary that everything should be done exactly right, or the various parts would not work properly when put together, and it would not do to have the great bird break down with them out on the desert.

"We had just as well have a boat sink under us a thousand miles at sea—and the sea boiling hot," said old Inyo Bill.

The drawings were all completed at the end of three days. The old miner carefully inspected them, with Electric Bob's explanations, and after he had suggested a few minor changes to make the ostrich conform to the character of the country they would have to traverse, the drawings with full and minute instructions were sent on to the Chicago factory.

A few days later a telegram came informing Electric Bob that his wonderful machine was being constructed as rapidly as possible, and asking that he come on and superintend its completion personally.

"I guess I had better go, Inyo," he said to his partner on showing him the message. "Those fellows are not used to building such things, and I may be able to improve it if I am on the spot."

"All right, my boy," said Inyo, cheerfully, "but don't let 'em be any longer about it than is absolutely necessary."

The next month was a long and dreary season of waiting to the old Californian. A party of local adventurers, hearing of Electric Bob's contemplated trip, hastily set out in search of the Pegleg, and Inyo was terribly worked up lest they should accidentally stumble upon the mine. This apprehension became positive agony when, after three weeks' absence, the party failed to return.

He could no longer find comfort in his pipe.

All day he walked up and down the sea shore, and all night in feverish dreams he could see men turning great loads of golden nuggets out of the hearts of the three golden hills which he had come to look upon as his own property.

At last his heart was gladdened by a dispatch from Electric Bob, saying he was on the way West with the electric ostrich.

Three days later the old man met his young friend at San Bernardino, they having decided to start from that point.

The boxes containing the wonderful invention were unloaded carefully, Inyo Bill jealously watching every motion of the workmen.

A secluded spot in a large orange grove, well shielded from observation, was then selected in which to put the great ostrich together.

This was done by Electric Bob, assisted by three experienced machinists from the Southern Pacific Railway shops, located at that point.

The ostrich towered thirty feet in the air to the top of his great head. The center of the body was twenty feet from the ground, the neck was about eight feet long.

The black male taken as a model had been faithfully copied, in appearance and proportions, and when completed the gigantic machine standing there in the orange grove was to all outward appearance a mammoth ostrich.

"It will cause great excitement wherever we go," said Inyo. "People will think it is a real old rooster."

"That will be great," said Bob.

"Not if they get to shooting at us," suggested Inyo.

"They can't hurt us with anything but a cannon," said Electric Bob, "and when it comes to shooting we will be ready."

"How?"

"I'll show you. Come up with me."

The ostrich stood securely on his broad feet, having a wide spread of toes with a long, supporting spur in the rear of each foot, and the men quickly ran up a wire ladder that hung down from under one wing.

This wing was really the door-way or entrance to the interior of the machine, and a window under the opposite wing gave good ventilation to the body of the bird, but both of these could be closed hermetically when desired.

"Tell me all about it," said Inyo, when they were inside.

"Well," said Bob, "to begin, you know the legs are of fine wrought steel and hollow, the body is of thin plate steel lined with hardwood to protect us from the heat out there, and the wings and tail are of aluminum, light, graceful, and bullet-proof.

"The power is furnished by powerful storage batteries placed in the body just between the thighs of the bird, and are capable of giving us a speed of from twenty to forty miles an hour—depending on the nature of the ground we travel over.

"Here are a water tank, storage places for provisions, ammunition, etc., and here is our machine gun. I thought of that after I got to Chicago. We may have trouble with Mexicans, or with others we meet in search of the mine. We will run when we can, but fight if we must."

"But where is the gun?" said Inyo, staring at a curious arrangement in the neck of the ostrich just where the real bird's gizzard is located.

"I will explain," said Bob smiling. "It consists of an enlarged revolver cylinder, holding twenty-five Winchester rifle cartridges, and a short, heavy barrel, and is fired by turning this—this way."

Clic—clic—clic! The machine gun was empty, but as Bob turned the handle its rapid clicking showed the old miner what it would do at work on an enemy.

"We will each carry a short, light rifle and revolvers, of course," continued Electric Bob, "But in case of an attack this machine gun will enable us to stand off quite a crowd. It can be raised or lowered, will kill at five hundred yards, and is very accurate."

"We may need it," said Inyo.

His words were prophetic. They did need it.

"Hello!" cried Inyo, starting back from an inverted reflection of his own face that came into view as he drew aside a sliding board just above the gun, in the ostrich's neck. "What is this?"

"That is the ground glass of a camera," said Bob. "We may want to make some portraits of our enemies, or take views of landscapes, you know. See this! The bird's neck is telescopic, to secure a correct focus, and the lens is in his mouth, which opens automatically when the slide is drawn to make the exposure—"

"Why," said old Inyo, "you can kill 'em with the gun and photograph 'em with this machine at the same time, can't ye?"

"Yes," said Bob, smiling, "but I hadn't thought of it before."

"Well, my boy, when do we start?" said Inyo, anxiously.

"As soon as you like," Bob replied.

"Then we are off tomorrow morning."

"All right, Inyo."

"And to make sure everything goes all right," said Inyo, "suppose we take a little drive now."

"I was about to suggest the same thing," said Electric Bob. "Where will we go?"

"I would like to run out to Redlands and see my friend Skip Craig."

"Who is he?"

"A true native son of the golden West," said the old miner with enthusiasm. "He knows Southern California like a book, and can give us some useful information perhaps."

"What does he do?" asked Bob.

"Runs the *Citrograph*, and—"

"What is a citrograph?"

"I don't know," the old miner confessed.

"Then how does he run it?"

"Bang up."

"Oh, hang it!" cried Bob, vexed, but laughing, "what is it he runs?"

"Why, a newspaper—the *Citrograph*."

"Oh, all right. We'll give him a call," Bob agreed, and reaching forward he pulled one of a number of levers on a switchboard.

The lever was moved but slightly, and yet the great ostrich seemed to become suddenly endowed with life.

The head towered loftily among the branches of the tallest orange trees, and the strong feet were lifted from the ground, stepping off slowly at first, but more rapidly as the lever was pulled farther around on the switchboard.

"See him walk!" cried old Inyo Bill, grasping Electric Bob's hand. "He's all right!"

Bob's heart was throbbing happily.

"Time him from here to the creek," cried Inyo. "It is just four miles, and a splendid road."

"It is now exactly half-past three," said Bob looking at his watch, "and here goes!"

Full power was turned on the ostrich's legs, and the big black bird went skimming away. Bob kept his hand on the controlling lever while Inyo kept a sharp lookout along the road through a bull's eye in front.

Numerous pedestrians hurriedly quitted the road as the ostrich came rushing on, and several carriages were passed, the swiftest trotters falling behind as if they had been standing still. Doors and windows were crowded with curious people gazing after the wonderful machine.

They could not understand it.

All were puzzled, and many were frightened.

"Here is the creek!" cried Inyo, and the next instant with a splash the ostrich had crossed it and was climbing the bank beyond.

"Four miles in just six minutes," said Bob, putting up his watch. "That isn't bad for the trial trip. We can do better with a little practice."

The pace was slackened down to a walk now, that a careful inspection might be made of the working of every part of the machine. It was found to be perfect in every respect.

Lookin' Out My Backdoor

Joseph S. Pulver, Jr.

Late in the afternoon.

Buzzing…

The first beetle was white, pale, armored in the death-color of bone. It crawled by the just-beyond-my-property-line graveyard where I'd buried my two (beloved) cats and three (beloved) dogs, and my heart (five times).

Louder than the distant, occasional hum of late night-silent night highway traffic 1.2 miles from the edge of my suburban acres—sudden, rushing echo.

Plodded by the small mud-beach of the frog pond—a six-legged tiger, robber, plotting.

Unexpected.

The second, the stalker, constructed by the same philosophical congress, and built for the same purpose, came an hour later. Same track—no toad or bee, but a hunter-seeker in season. Metallic black, shiny, brittle, even the honeycombed-legs of its slowly-moving tank. No idle wanderer, not astray or confused—its longhorn-antennae focused and processed. Seizure, the laughter of its forward dance of dismember. Bright summer flowers—heart-math red and pure white and softly-blued by Ra's animal fervor and soothing rain—cut down, t-r-a-m-p-l-e-d. Overgrown, hardened lunatic weeds that had not been beaten down by currents of raw wind and the iron of hailstorms fell.

Insectoid, alien, metallic aural weather, horde powerful, cursing my ears, crushing the freedom-green peace I'd paid (dearly—thirty years dearly) to live on; (Steve Stills bought Johnny's garden, I stepped off the highway, too, settled here, feet up, rock-a-bye in hopes of avoiding toll.)

Battlefield: my pumpkin patch (*never to know playful Halloween*); my tomato boxes and their plump, still-green, readying Big Betties; the evocative caress of my tender herb garden. Delightful, the remedies and conjurations I could have folded into my dining pleasure, rained upon by darkened habits. Damned.

Above the productive soil and strong tall grass, sirens and squalls issued from (high-energy, high-voltage) yellow-striped black bombers, darting, arcing, wasp-winged. Scorched the ground. Left ashes. The vines and orbs of my dear pumpkin patch, blackened, brittle—no sweet pumpkin fruit to fill pies in slow, cool autumn.

Dangerous—metallic black, shiny, brittle—came, a trio in formation flight, and came again.

Buzz a decade back: CNN SCIENCE, a brief, informational feature, INSECTS INSPIRE. Dr. Barbara Abbott (The New York Center for Advanced Sciences) and Dr. Anna-Lena Kramp-Karrenbauer (Berlin Institute of Biotechnology), both geek-giddy, discussing creating and developing bio-mech creatures. "Yes, that's right; the future is now. They are computer-programmed, remote-controlled beetles, spiders, and bees, that one day could be used to assist us in geoengineering and other developing technologies. They crawl, fly, and are adaptable to complex situations that are impossibly dangerous for humans," Dr. Kramp-Karrenbauer said.

Dr. Abbott chimed in, "At any given moment, there are ten quintillion insects on the planet. Just imagine the uses."

I looked at Dr. Abbott's elation beaming from the TV. Thought: "Ten what? That's a number beyond my color palette."

New direction: blended, intentionally. A bio-mech miracle to save us from the bitter tonalities of war and religion, to help us heal our planet. Micro-chips and insects: 'an implantable system able to provide precision communication between the carrier insect and the host apparatus.' One day, tasked and employed in real world situations, they will become the regulatory centers of larger mechanical versions, the size of tanks and C-17 Globemaster III's. Apparatus that could, after earthquakes, rapidly-project assistance assets, move mountains, and remove the vast concentration of debris and chem-sludge from the Pacific Trash Vortex. "They could be deployed in the dangerous and impenetrable for search and rescue purposes, and be used as the primary assets in Air-Land-Sea exploration, or to monitor hurricane and tornadic research and activity. We foresee limitless applications," said chief-researcher, Dr. Kramp-Karrenbauer. *Limitless applications*. That painted a picture on my radar, wasn't a good one.

Mind-control brain implant.

Accelerated education for cybernetic hive minds.

DARPA.

Terminator robots.

SWORDS robots.

An expendable insect-robot army.

Didn't anyone think the military would muscle aside everyone in line, to snap up and exploit this new tech? 'Nam-era, Cold War baby, I sure did. Wondered how long it would take before the *James Bond*-meets-*Terminator* movies started appearing.

I loathed the thought I might, even remotely, agree with Alex Jones—the batshit-crazy who said there was video of Hillary Clinton giving birth to an alien, and secret, elite government or Robert Duncan, about things like *Voice of God Weapons*... or anything.

When I told him about it, Dom laughed at me. "Christ-on-a-stick!" Said I sounded as loony and moronic as a conspiracy theorist. With a grin, that grin I knew too well, added, "And not the first time." I got up and went inside, grabbed two beers. When I came back he asked: "Will you be telling me about the chemtrails of Butterfly bombers next week? Hey, got any fairy tales of any techy-grasshopper daring-do you'd care to relate?" We laughed.

The scientific community, fueled by vast sums from the Progressive Left, certain of their calculations and nu-applications, did not foresee the possibility of disconnect. Links to the overlords severed (by a hacker's anger; confirmed and agreed upon by the CIA, MI6, BND, and SVR), they, a self-aware hive mind with its own vision—proper purification required cutting away the greatest cancer, humankind—took up arms.

Blindsided.

Humanity, its governments and leaders, don't learn.

Hellbound.

The seeds sown in immaculate laboratories, risen. Golden prophecies that promised Better Days, brought altered monsters with all-absorbing black holes, maws, in them, monsters come to control the roost.

Buzzing...

Hellfire.

Fear.

Lose: California dreaming—believe—dazzle—domestic Tranquility—General Welfare—the Blessings of Liberty to ourselves and our Posterity.

Warday.

That's what CNN called it. BBC, MSNBC, and even FOX, followed suit.

Live video filled the TV screen.

Vegas—cell phone video of Hellfire ordinance slamming into the Bellagio, Wynn's missile-riddled and burning, Luxor, top taken clean off—rubble everywhere. Eiffel Tower: defenseless crowds of tourists fallen to the lions. Times Square, Brussels, won't be hymns or headlines tomorrow. The music of the neighborhoods of East L. A. falling silent. President Kamala Harris, vacation at Camp David flushed, visibly frightened, spoke of God, asked the country not to panic. Teary-eyed, she prayed for the nation and humanity. Pope John XXIV celebrated a final mass in St. Peter's Basilica. Elon Musk's statement expressed the ended dreams of a pilgrim. Better part of an hour was all I could bear. I pushed the OFF button on the TV remote, dropped it in my armchair. Took a fresh pack of smokes and my favorite teacup and a bottle of Glenlivet 12 out to the patio. Wished I had some weed.

Somewhere around my forth double, flash image: *MAD* magazine/political cartoon—single, full-page black and white, Don Martin rendering: me, longhaired, jeans and sandals and hippie beads, *stoned*. Nixon as a four-star general on one shoulder, shouting, "RAID KILLS BUGS DEAD!!!!!!" while offering me an industrial-size spray can of Wasp & Hornet Killer. Nichelle Nichols dressed as Uhura, on my other shoulder; she was an angel holding a stone tablet, on which was written, *Thou shall not kill*. I didn't laugh.

We were unprepared, or maybe we're just slow and impenetrable. And stupid, often naïve, me, found that shocking. Hadn't anyone read Heinlein or Asimov?

No, pincushion-prick; the insect army is on the move. West and East, never to agree, speech and hearts opposed, cannot stand against the single-minded change deployed.

Buzzing…

Not a symphony.

Look up: clouds (size, beyond the limits of my I-am-a-simple-man understanding) of whining bomber-wasps (cold metal and engineered perfection) distort the sky. The colors of birds, gone. The doe that comes to my back lawn at twilight I'll never see again.

Didn't foresee the dark, didn't listen to the pressure within the egg.

Dom lived next door. He married at twenty-eight. Leslie, lovely women, kind, her laughter meadowlarked freely. We grew up together, Strong Street kids—baseball and comic books (we believed in *Justice*, Captain America and

Batman, we wanted to save the world), rock and roll, lot of soul (Diana Ross for Dom, Marvin for me), too, and together, dreamed dreams of places far from the city blocks—untouched, green places, with serene shores and bubbling streams, places you'd hear frogs and hoot-owls, lose endless day-to-day troubles in the peaceful grandeur of soft-ceiling sunsets. Went fishing; we weren't very good at it. Still, we kept at it (at our campfires, ate cans of pork 'n beans, or chicken noodle soup, when our stringer didn't see a need to come out of the tackle box). Went to the jazz festival together every year, took great pleasure in Italian sausage and peppers sandwiches and cold Genny Creamers. Dom got a PhD in math, taught the undergrads at Weir. When Larry, the owner of Apex Records was retiring in '76, I bought the store—yeah, I found a way to remain Peter Pan. Both of us wound-up widowers too soon. He was raised Catholic, believed there was a heaven; held on to it. My mom raised me Methodist; lost my way, didn't think there was any "After". Teenagers, spent time, as still lives, sitting on his concrete, front-porch steps; talked, spun fantasies—trips of the mind—the way kids (chained to *near*) will, a lot of it was non-verbal. Played baseball in the sandlot of Wylie St; we wanted to be Yankees. Nights, we were out of the gate—full of Ulysses and tomorrow—Dom's Chevy cruising up and down State Street, unaccepting of *or have not*. High school: Dom and I formed a band for a heartbeat; played inferior covers of Steppenwolf and Iron Butterfly, hornless Sly and Santana tunes, with Mike and Ray and Hans, we had fun. Didn't have computers, never occurred to us what machines could do—that was a future for the science fiction movies to explore. We dreamed big, we lived small, close to home. Never occurred to us *this* was coming. Two, crusted old widowers—fated, childless. Old Friends—*brothers*—who'd learned to fold their own clothes and pair socks, and take out the trash (without several reminders). Both hoped we'd slip away quietly in our sleep.

He did. Last summer, five days before my seventy-second birthday.

Looked in Dom's yard: swing set still, sandbox empty. New owners had taken their children to Orlando. My Staffie, Giant, had played there with Casey, Dom's snow-white boxer. They, once bright with play, ran imaginary labyrinths and mazes, rolled in the sun-warmed grass, in that yard. Turned my gaze: looked at the fiery, orange-red blossoms of "Fred Loads" shrub roses I'd planted on Giant's grave. Poured another drink.

Buzzing…

There's another white beetle, pair of wasp-bombers above it—black silhouettes stamped on the blue sky. They really are as menacing as Apache helicopters.

What have butterflies been turned into?

Damn sure not something Joni Mitchell

would approve of. Denise loved butterflies. She planted hollyhocks and violets to attract them. Whatever butterflies look like now would have shattered her Woodstock dreams.

Buzzing...

Immediacy. Scientific fact. Technology accelerated without caution.

Buzzing...

Emerson, Lake, & Palmer. *Tarkus*. June '71. Armadillo/tank, the inspired burst of the artwork on the cover amazed; I couldn't wait to get it home and play the record. The bio-mech merger on the cover would not only come true, but its war-machine would thunder, and we, defenseless human meat, would find our coming END delivered by *unimaginable*.

CNN reports there will be no counterstrike, no response. How do you, could you, eradicate ten quintillion insects in a single stroke? Warday brings devastation complete. Result: the voyage of man ends; survivors none.

Buzzing...

My Mossberg *500 Hunting* is inside, box of shells, too. "Home protection," I told Dom. "Brown bear decides to come inside to plunder my kitchen, I'm good—I hope." Use today, as *this* rains down upon us, against us, zero.

Buzzing...

Human: no longer a factor in globalization. Our affairs of the heart, gambles, reasons, unwise, sins, will leave no footprints in the sand.

Never been close to a real tank. M1A2 has a

crew of four, don't know how I know that, but I do. This mech-beetle, white, pale, armored in the death-color of bone, crawling by, the fourth by my count, looks like it could hold twice that number of personnel.

Took a long drag off my smoke, waited for it to turn to me.

Shocked it didn't.

Half grinned. Maybe the next one?

Movement partially-obscured by the pine and maples, flash of my first big bug movie, *Them!* Was eight, scared the hell out of me. In my forties, with a big bowl of buttered popcorn in my lap, I laughed. Stupid, blind fools we are, we sure opened the door to a new world.

Buzzing…

I didn't have the blues when I woke up this morning. There were two cardinals at the feeder while I had buttered rye toast and tea for breakfast. It was sunny, warm—June just the way I like it. I put Joe Henderson's tribute to Jobim, *Double Rainbow*, in the CD player, read Mary Oliver, lamp-eyes owls and motionless ponds, she fit my Emerson mood. I don't think I'll see the stars tonight.

Buzzing cracks the sky…

My ears are full.

Memories… the language and realities of *felt* and its aftermath, still *warm*—

Sip of single malt, kill the finger in the glass. Last smoke, I figure.

Me, so much older now. Done composing.

On the patio—quiet, ready to breathe in the star-milk. With the book, the nest of bandaged tears, I wrote for you (*All the hours you kept my distress away from the murk of doom.*)

You.

You'd see words on the page.

Blue eyes. I see blue eyes, *caring*, soft, full of promised stars, stare up at me. *Again*, is what they say.

I push aside the bottle of single malt, no longer full. Hold *I do.*

—*bleeding wounds*—

there will be no white doves to harpoon the heart, no soft, golden chain of gentle sleep

no town (of whole milk, and Elijah, singing James Taylor songs, come home from the sorrows and the weeds, and hello that comes with no excuses...or pretty holidays laughing aloud with *Denise*)

no... getting up

(*won't see the leaves turn...not this year.*)

daring to *care about someone* who cares (*always*—moonlight/afternoon/when you expressed that spark/when I droned drab generalities that meant nothing—*cared*) about

y-o-u

I can smell the coconut butter you used when

you were sunbathing—you had the radio in the kitchen window, were humming along to Tommy James & the Shondells' "Crystal Blue Persuasion"

wish you could call   to

me

(Emerson, Lake & Palmer "Tarkus"; Creedence Clearwater Revival "Lookin' Out My Door"; John Lee Hooker "Don't Look Back"; Brandos "Gettysburg"; Gavin Bryars "After The Requiem")

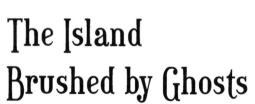

The Island
Brushed by Ghosts
Alistair Rennie

One of the drawbacks of being an involuntary assemblage of delicate mechanisms is a susceptibility to self-generated noise pollution that cannot be controlled. A cacophony of ticks and whines defined my existence with as much constancy as drips of water in a cave. But none of it could be heard by anyone standing within my range, given that the noises occurred exclusively within my own headspace—endlessly resonating with the clicks and rattles and fractious scrapes of the micro-pulleys, diodes, hydraulics, transistors, battery packs, and circuits of my anatomical hardware.

The super compact elaborations of my physique were, to me, a chorus of absurdities, a congregation of blurs and hiccups presented as sounds, with no tonality or pleasurable effects whatsoever.

I can only suppose that, accosted by the harsh

components of the salt sea air, I was in desperate need of lubrication or a maintenance upgrade or cleaning out. My creators hadn't taken this into consideration when they made me, it seems, in spite of the watertight proficiency of my silicon flesh-moulds and my over-layer of genuine plumes.

The noise pollution set an internal scene of chaotic aural innuendo that reduced my highly-developed sense of self-awareness to a morbid state of agitation. From such states of agitation, corruption grows (intelligence mixed with agitation usually produces creativity or destruction or a combination of both). Hence, the disruption of my thoughts by the imperfections of my design had driven me to new extremes of lofty thinking.

Chief among these was a philosophical interpretation of my position as "a corrective force in the ecosystem" as essentially invalid, perhaps even unfit for purpose, based on the premise that:

Ego sum ego sum quae in contrarium
(I am the opposite of what I am.)

Which begs the question, what am I?

In short, I was designed in the image of an Atlantic puffin to ensure the protection of an endangered puffin colony on a sea stack off the western shores of a wildlife sanctuary called Handa Island (Northwest Scottish coast). Back in the day, Handa Island was open to tourists who were ferried out in small boats and permitted to walk on a path that led across the island to a series of restricted viewpoints on its western headland. Since the 2060s, however, the presence of unauthorised human visitors has been prohibited—mainly due to the need to preserve the creatures falling under my watch—my friends, the puffins.

Global warming's assault on the Arctic and subarctic circles meant the Handa colony was the last of its kind in Europe—the final outpost of a species so drastically ill-equipped for survival it was forced to depend on in its irresistible cuteness in the eyes of humans in order to survive.

For myself, I was as well-equipped as anything could get, with extras including: an ability to extend a set of fibreglass claws from the ends of my feet; carbon fibre-bladed wingtips; and a supercharged electro-beak with a voltage capacity powerful enough to kill a full-grown minke whale.

Which no doubt gives some indication as to the nature of my purpose—which was, to make sure that the puffins of Handa Island continued to exist for as long as we could make them. Most of this they could do by themselves. But what they couldn't do was contend with the pressures of a major rival (also a predator) that dominates the coastal scenes of the north and west—I'm talking, of course, about the gulls.

At any such times as the gulls presented a threat to the puffins (meaning always) I was to intervene, terrify, disperse, and repulse—or to terminate them with extreme prejudice—and that was all.

It was a thankless task, in the sense that it continued without end. Where puffins diminish, seagulls thrive. Global warming presented new opportunities for the gull communities that they have seized upon with a savage zeal which is as natural to them as procreation. Humans, likewise, have facilitated their success without meaning to (as humans do). Polluted seas, landfill sites, sewage waste, food waste, fish farms, and corrupted beaches—all of it amounts to the fact that the gulls have become, so to speak, the humans of the animal kingdom.

And they were just as rampant and uncompromising. Barbarians that would eat, attack, ravage, sack, and fuck up anything. Herring gulls were the worst. Big and raucous, habitually violent, and full of an ungainly swagger. Common gulls weren't far behind— more cowardly and, therefore, more capable of being cruel. In the summer months, the greater and lesser black-backed gulls would join the throng. And kittiwakes were a constant factor, as were the smaller and less volatile black-headed variety.

The gulls would come, looking to ransack

the puffins' nests, steal their eggs, devour them whole, and attack their members with an aim to eating them. They'd go mad for their chicks, eat them up like hot snacks from a High Street takeaway. And then they would shit all over the puffins' cliffs, contaminate their own warm homely shit with an invasive smear and the repulsive stench of regurgitated ill-gotten fodder (not that I could smell it. My sensory functions were frustratingly limited to sight and sound).

At first, given the unpleasant character of my adversary, I enjoyed my role with as much enthusiasm as my conductors could muster. I felt a distinct sense of satisfaction, even pride, as I whizzed among them, slicing open their bloated bellies with my wingtips; raking their heads with my dauntless claws; knocking them senseless with my electro-beak, sometimes even causing them to burst into flames. I watched as they dropped into the swirling froths with the lankness of corpses, drifting on the seas in bloody masses of feathers and guts. They became foodstuffs for the sea-dwellers, while other gulls would cannibalise their remains with an economy of purpose almost admirable.

I would circle them overhead, feeling somewhat elated by the sensation of flight, which was thrilling and strange and thoroughly nerve-wracking. The dramatic shifts in perspective and speed were exhilarating, not to mention highly dangerous. A sufficient amount of alertness was required in order to avoid colliding with protruding rocks, cliff faces and other birds. More worryingly, I could, of course, hear the sounds of my internal mechanisms making serious audible complaints of the efforts required: strenuous squeaks, inconsequential jingling, rattling blades and the fierce ratcheting of un-oiled moving parts. The feeling of being forever on the verge of cracking up, breaking down and falling apart was a disruptive influence that continued without end.

Nevertheless, for some time I performed my primary function with the simple joy of being alive. I thought nothing of it. I just lived. I settled myself in among my brethren as if I were one of them, just as my creators intended. And, while communications between me and my brethren were somewhat strained, I began to appreciate the language of their screeches and squawks, sometimes managing to interpret their meanings, mainly due to the fact that it was impossible not to.

I would squawk back at them, like I meant it—like I was one of them in spirit as well as physical likeness. I was conscious of the fact that my own cries were invested with a hollow metallic ringing—a metaphor for what I am, I thought. Nevertheless, some of the females would make themselves available to me for mating, though I had no idea what to do because, essentially, I wasn't equipped for the task. So I pretended to mate with them and undertook the mating ritual with a comical failure to see it through to its conclusion. Some of them seemed to comprehend my inadequacy and departed the scene in search of another mate to complete the ritual.

Sometimes the puffins looked at me with their blank eyes, and I would gaze back into them with a hope of finding something meaningful. But there was nothing there. They couldn't know what they were, nor care about the implications of not knowing what they were. The rugged bliss of their existence was surmounted and underlined by incredible hardships they couldn't quantify. They accepted it all with a lack of awareness that allowed them, precisely, to accept it all with a lack of awareness. Their total indifference towards their suffering was, I thought, somehow comforting.

So what happened? How did I come to my present state of self-imposed exile on the Butt of Lewis—which is where I was going now?

It started with the noises in my head, which became increasingly intolerable. Thoughts accrued inside of me. Not unpleasant or unwelcome. But raucous and radical, unique to me and unbridled.

I began to realise that our right—the puffins' right—to survive was diminished by the superior tendency of the gulls to dominate the coasts. That it wasn't malice that defined the gulls, but their sheer ability. We, with our orange beaks, our cute squat heads, our elegant stripes and comical flapping—we were simply inadequate, unworthy of the continuation of life against implacable odds. And, while our eradication was ill-deserved, our inadequacy was a fact of life which, like all facts of life, had to be accepted—which, in our case, meant the eventual extinction of our species.

Questions overtook me, such as:

What does it mean to be indigenous? What does it mean to be reintroduced? The sea eagle that patrols our stretch of shoreline: witness its brooding form passing over us and casting a shadow of terror—yet we gaze upon its form with a superior sense of our place on the coast, because we've been here since the beginning, with no help from humankind whatsoever.

And then I would remember what I was—an even greater imposter than the mighty sea eagle, whose reintroduction was at least a return to a habitual scene of former glory. I, however, was born in a laboratory, my component parts struggling to withstand the rigours of exposure to the fierce climate, the noises within me a constant reminder of what I was—a construct, a fake. Not indigenous, not reintroduced, but conjured out of human interests—not for nature's sake, but their favoured outcomes alone.

When I blinked my eyes open for the first time, I knew exactly what I was and why. I knew it with an instantaneous clarity that required no effort of recollection on my part.

A bespectacled face stared at me with an impassive look of heightened interest that put me on edge.

"Hello, Hamish," it said.

Hamish. That was my name.

"Hello," I said.

The sound of my own voice, heard for the first time, was slightly unnerving.

"My name is Dr Metcalfe," said the bespectacled face. "I'm one of the technical team who helped to build you."

"I know," I said, meaning this as a matter of fact more than anything.

"Of course," he said. And then he added, "How do you feel?"

I reflected and said , "I feel normal."

"Good." Dr Metcalfe smiled in a way that also involved a slight frown. "Do you remember why you're here? Why we built you?"

"I don't remember it," I said. "But I do know."

"And what do you know?"

"That you built me for a special reason."

"Do you know the reason?"

I nodded my little head. The sensation was strange, quite pleasing. It was the first time I had made a conscious movement—a bold and decisive one. I felt a smidgeon of pride that emboldened me further.

"I have been designed to be deployed to protect a colony of puffins that remains the last of its kind in Europe. I am a lifelike imitation that has additional features which will allow me to protect them using a combination of established and state-of-the-art technologies."

Dr Metcalfe looked satisfied. He smiled and said "Good" a couple of times.

I looked at him and smiled, without him being able to see that I was smiling, because smiling wasn't an expression puffins could register so easily.

One evening, when I was perched on my favourite ledge, I looked out over the diminishing vastness of the setting sun on the western horizon. In and around the sandstone facades of the sea stack and its adjacent cliffs, the waves churned. The amplifications of its collisions rose up to me in a pandemonium of irregular slaps, voluminous thuds and muted echoes. The fractured landscape stood out erratically against the swirl of the tides that lapped at the coastal fringes like a clandestine predator seeking to devour its prey without it noticing. The wild shapes of the summits of Ben Stack, Foinaven and Quinag dominated the eastern prospect. Reddened by the sun, they looked like the carcasses of fallen gods on some ancient battlefield. In the north, the peatlands and the reeking bogs of the Flow Country formed a unique geography that combined beauty and desolation with a prehistoric ambience that hung in the air like an aurora.

The landscape immersed me in its primal radiance and, in return, I developed a sudden legacy of independent realisations that I must respond to.

Acting on a whim (it was an open act of rebellion), I began to protect the arctic skuas against the attentions of the herring gulls. The skuas were cantankerous bastards. They could look after themselves. Up to a point. But they were also feeling the strains of the overabundance of the world's most terrible children: the gulls. Plus the fact that, nesting inland in the scrub of the island, they were more vulnerable to the marauding onslaught of the seagull hordes.

I would abandon the sea stack on occasions when it seemed reasonable to do so, enjoying the redolent bleakness of the island's interior. At its highest points, the terrain was covered in a thick layer of moorland that shimmered and swayed under the Hebridean weather systems, as if brushed by ghosts. I soared over these upland parts, the nesting grounds of the skuas, and made my assaults on the gulls within range. As a consequence of my interventions, I littered the island with their corpses, which very quickly began to rot and, so, attract the attentions of other scavengers. Crows came, and jackdaws. Then a pair of buzzards came and all hell broke loose. The sky above the island became a scene of mass brawling. Carrion birds fought each other for the rich pickings I'd laid out for them like offerings at some festive feast.

And that's when I received my first visit from Dr Metcalfe and a female human who called herself Dr Adelhard Winkler.

Drs Metcalfe and Winkler stood on the promontory overlooking the sea stack, the wind in their faces causing them to screw up their eyes, which made them look angry.

"We need you to concentrate on the puffins," said Dr Metcalfe, remaining calm. "Please leave the arctic skuas alone."

"I'm not touching the arctic skuas," I said. "I'm only killing the gulls that are bothering them."

"I don't mean touching them literally," he said, with a small trace of impatience in his voice. "I mean getting into their living space. Your job is to stay close to the puffin colony. The arctic skuas over there"—he made a sweeping gesture with his hand that took in the whole of the island—"they're not a part of your concern."

I looked at him. If I could frown, I would have.

Dr Metcalfe turned and started to walk away over the rough path that traversed the island.

Dr Winkler stayed and, after Metcalfe was out of earshot, she said:

"You fuck with the arctic skuas again and I'll fuck you up so bad you'll be nothing more than recycling material."

She also turned and walked away, following the path with very precise, even-spaced, and elegant steps that reminded me of a wading bird—a greenshank or a pectoral sandpiper.

I looked after them both with an expressionless face. I wondered about Dr Winkler, about whether she'd actually carry out her threat if the occasion demanded.

I watched her stride with her impeccable walk.

Yes, I thought, she probably would.

I was becoming disillusioned. All of it seemed wrong to me—all of it.

You wearisome humans have no idea. You watch your doctored documentaries and the stupid narratives they superimpose on the world of nature, with their fake attributes of order and emotional values that don't exist. You make it seem like there's a story there—so you can understand it in human terms, which is to not understand it at all—so you can make the struggles of life seem quaint for their cruelties and fascinating for their simplistic horrors.

Let me tell you: There are no narratives in nature. There are no beginnings, middles, and ends. There are only the endless repetitions of essential acts. There is nothing quaint. Nothing beautiful. Nothing but brutality in spades and the mobilisation of crude behaviours. In nature, things smell bad, get rough, get deadly, and starve. Things get ripped apart, torn up, swallowed, digested, and shat out. Everything is raw. The animals, birds, fish, and insects—the biological fulcrum of teeming life. Their thoughts are so raw they don't even know that they exist. Stark, random functionality—that is all—which, for a conscious entity such as me, who doesn't belong in this thronging mass of blood and shit, is thoroughly depressing.

Thus we must resist the human angle. We must not allow it. We cannot be a mere extension of your bogus interpretation of the natural order—because there is no order, there is no system, and your attempts to install one is a further evidence of your arrogance, which is only another mask you wear that covers up your failure as a dominant species.

Protecting the arctic skuas was one thing. But later on, when I decided to stop killing the gulls altogether, that's when they came back to see me again. This time, standing in the middle of a fierce drizzle, Dr Metcalfe said nothing. But Dr Adelhard Winkler asked, not unreasonably:

"Why have you stopped killing the gulls, Hamish?"

I looked her straight in the eye and said, "I don't want to kill them anymore."

She pressed her lips together like she was trying to contain a volcanic eruption. I almost expected to see trails of lava spill from her nostrils.

"Why?" She said this almost breathlessly.

"I don't agree with it."

Dr Winkler seemed to be fighting the urge to erupt when she said, "Why don't you agree with it?"

I sighed. A miniscule ejaculation of mechanical utterances escaped through my beak.

"I think it's wrong," I said. "I think the gulls have a right to be what they are. It's their world, too. Nobody has the right to stop them."

"And do they have the right to stop the puffins?" she said. "Do they have a right to dominate—to destroy—to consign the puffins to the dustbin of natural history?"

I reflected for a moment and said, plainly, "Yes."

Then I turned and looked at Dr Metcalfe. He wore a sad look on his face like he'd just lost a family member. "Why did you build me with intelligence?" I asked him with blunt force.

"Why did you build me with self-awareness if you wanted me only to obey?"

He looked at me with sullen eyes. For a moment I thought I saw tears of sorrow in them, but maybe it was just the wind.

"We thought you'd understand," he said.

I shook my head. "You wanted me to agree. That's not the same thing as understanding. You gave me self-awareness, and that gives me the power to disagree."

Metcalfe nodded almost imperceptibly. Winkler stared at me with huge eyes that looked as if they wanted to burst.

"I'm meant to be a creature," I said. "A wild beast with a bird brain. You've given me a mind. You've made me the opposite of what I'm meant to be."

"We needed you to understand, so you would know what to do," Winkler butted in, coldly.

"We wanted you to know yourself," said Metcalfe, more softly, imploring.

"Know myself?"

"Yes."

"For Christ's sake," I cried and shook my head the way that puffins never do. "Why can't you just cull them?"

"Cull them?"

"The seagulls. Why can't you get a guy with a gun to blow their fucking brains out?"

"Because it's not practical." Winkler again. "You were meant to be the ideal solution."

"Fuck your ideal solution. I'm fucking alive in

here." I raised my wingtip and tapped the side of my head, thrusting my head on the end of its neck, almost to breaking point.

Dr Winkler stared at me as if willing me to burst into flames. Then she stiffened her face, nodded very slightly, as if a decision had been made.

"Dr Metcalfe," she said. "Please make a note."

"Of course." Dr Metcalfe fumbled inside his waterproof jacket and produced an old-fashioned notebook with a ball point pen.

"For the attention of the Puffin Welfare Group research team," said Dr. Winkler. "For immediate action: prepare the Proctor apparatus for a Type A liquid energy data rendition transfer protocol. Message ends."

She angled her eyes at Dr Metcalfe as he scribbled the words. When he had finished, she turned abruptly, almost violently, and strode off over the rough path that traversed the island. Her wader's steps were slightly less coordinated this time, with Metcalfe following hurriedly after her like some hapless bunting.

That's when I knew I had to go, to get out of the littoral zone of the coast. It was time for me to take my life into my own hands. It was time for me to go west, to follow my desires, to follow my dreams, if I had any.

I took off for the Isle of Lewis, feeling immediately vulnerable to the onslaught of the North Atlantic weather systems. They were supremely harsh and, the further I flew from the succour of the sea stack, the more precarious it became, the more wilfully dangerous. By the time I'd reached the Shiant Islands, my digital and mechanical architectures were beginning to register evidences of extreme distress.

I struggled onwards against the headwinds, the noises in my headspace growing louder and more contentious as my mechanisms thrashed and trundled in the effort to keep me airborne. Onward and onward and onward I flew. The entire Scottish mainland fell away from me to the south, revealing a landscape smashed and fractured as if a mad god had taken a hammer to it. I looked ahead towards Lewis and the debris of the Outer Hebrides. The world unfurled before me like some endless yearning for something that wasn't there.

And then I sensed it coming towards me (the refinements of my perceptions were truly amazing), straight from the cloud base, a shadow within a shadow, a dark shape as broad as death. But it wasn't death. It was the sea eagle. I turned to confront its massive form, fully in awe of the slow sweep of its magnificent wingspan. Clearly it had mistaken me for prey, so I readied myself to fend it off with a mild burst of electric shock from my electro-beak.

Then I saw something in its aspect that I

recognised, something that caused me to recoil and waver in mid-flight—blades extending from its wings; a beak that gleamed with a metallic lustre; mechanised extensions to its claws that shone with a faint trace of electric charge.

"Wait," I cried, "you don't need to do this. We can work this out."

But the mechanical sea eagle wasn't like me. I could see, as it homed in on me, a complete lack of self-awareness in its eyes. They were utterly void of personality. Its expression was industrial. It came towards me like a fake angel of death. Its electro-claws unfurled like cyborg weapons from a future age. And, when it gripped me, I was pumped full of an electric charge that blasted my circuits and sent me spinning into the blackness of nothing not known forever.

Dr Metcalfe managed to revive my circuitry for long enough to apply a liquid energy data rendition transfer protocol that has converted my psycho-bytes into plain text files. What you're reading now is a direct transcription of my experience on Handa Island, which Dr Metcalfe has set out in a narrative format, for the benefits of the research team to undertake a critical review.

Hamish #2 is now under construction and will be programmed using a different set of profile attributes. The prototype formulation of Hamish #1 has helped to determine the new approach, based on the premise that: There are no narratives in nature; there are no beginnings, middles, and ends; there are only the endless repetitions of essential acts.

Hamish #2 will be calibrated to a mental status of AI negative and will undertake a protection programme in accordance to the Gull Reduction Act of 2084. This has been approved by Dr Adelhard Winkler, Director of the Institute for the Protection of Endangered Species.

Dr Winkler has also recommended that Hamish #1 be decommissioned and dismantled for the purposes of recycling, to be stored for use in the development of future projects.

The Puffin Welfare Group research team, chaired by Dr Richard Metcalfe, unanimously agrees.

Please send your feedback to Dr Metcalfe together with lessons learned and actions pending for the future.

That is all.

Excerpt from The Steam House (1880)
Chapter V: The Iron Giant
Jules Verne

On the morning of the 5th May, the passengers along the high road from Calcutta to Chandernagore, whether men women or children, English or native, were completely astounded by a sight which met their eyes. And certainly the surprise they testified was extremely natural.

At sunrise a strange and most remarkable equipage had been seen to issue from the suburbs of the Indian capital, attended by a dense crowd of people drawn by curiosity to watch its departure.

First, and apparently drawing the caravan, came a gigantic elephant. The monstrous animal, twenty feet in height, and thirty in length, advanced deliberately, steadily, and with a certain mystery of movement which struck the gazer with a thrill of awe. His trunk, curved like a cornucopia, was uplifted high in the air.

His gilded tusks, projecting from behind the massive jaws, resembled a pair of huge scythes. On his back was a highly ornamented howdah, which looked like a tower surmounted, in Indian style, by a dome-shaped roof and furnished with lens-shaped glasses to serve for windows.

This elephant drew after him a train consisting of two enormous cars, or actual houses, moving bungalows in fact, each mounted on four wheels. The wheels, which were prodigiously strong, were carved, or rather sculptured, in every part. Their lowest portion only could be seen, as they moved inside a sort of case, like a paddle-box, which concealed the enormous locomotive apparatus. A flexible gangway connected the two carriages.

How could a single elephant, however strong, manage to drag these two enormous constructions, without any apparent effort? Yet this astonishing animal did so! His huge feet were raised and set down with mechanical regularity, and he changed his pace from a walk to a trot, without either the voice or a hand of a mahout being apparent.

The spectators were at first so astonished by all this, that they kept at a respectful distance; but when they ventured nearer, their surprise gave place to admiration. They could hear a roar, very similar to the cry uttered by these giants of the Indian forests. Moreover, at intervals there issued from the trunk a jet of vapour. And yet, it was an elephant! The rugged greeny-black skin evidently covered the bony framework of one that must be called the king of the pachydermes. His eyes were life-like; all his members were endowed with movement!

Ay! But if some inquisitive person had chanced to lay his hand on the animal, all would have been explained. It was but a marvellous deception, a gigantic imitation, having as nearly as possible every appearance of life. In fact, this elephant was really encased in steel, and an actual steam-engine was concealed within its sides.

The train, or Steam House, to give it its most suitable name, was the travelling dwelling promised by the engineer. The first carriage, or rather house, was the habitation of Colonel Munro, Captain Hood, Banks, and myself. In the second lodged Sergeant McNeil and the servants of the expedition. Banks had kept his promise, Colonel Munro had kept his; and that was the reason why, on this May morning, we were setting out in this extraordinary vehicle, with the intention of visiting the northern regions of the Indian peninsula. But what was the good of this artificial elephant? Why have this fantastic apparatus, so unlike the usual practical inventions of the English? Till then, no one had ever thought of giving to a locomotive destined to travel either over macadam highways or iron rails, the shape and form of a quadruped.

I must say, the first time we were admitted to view the machine we were all lost in amazement.

Questions about the why and wherefore fell thick and fast upon our friend Banks. We knew that this traction-engine had been constructed from his plans and under his directions. What, then, had given him the idea of hiding it within the iron sides of a mechanical elephant.

"My friends," answered Banks seriously, "do you know the Rajah of Bhootan?"

"I know him," replied Captain Hood, "or rather I did know him, for he died two months ago."

"Well, before dying," returned the engineer, "the Rajah of Bhootan not only lived, but lived differently to any one else. He loved pomp, and displayed it in every took such possession of his mind as to keep him from sleeping—an idea which Solomon might have been proud of, and would certainly have realized, had he been acquainted with steam: this idea was to travel in a perfectly new fashion, and to have an equipage such as no one had before dreamt of. He knew me, and sent for me to his court, and himself drew the plan of his locomotive. If you imagine, my friends, that I burst into a laugh at the Rajah's proposition, you are mistaken. I perfectly understood that this grandiose idea sprung naturally from the brain of a Hindoo sovereign, and I had but one desire on the subject—to realize it as soon as possible, and in a way to satisfy both my poetic client and myself. A hardworking engineer hasn't an opportunity every day to exercise his talents in this fantastic way, and add an animal of this description to the creations of the 'Arabian Nights.' In short, I saw it was possible to realize the Rajah's whim. All that has been done, that can be done, will be done in machinery. I set to work, and in this iron-plated case, in the shape of an elephant, I managed to enclose the boiler, the machinery, and the tender of a traction-engine, with all its accessories. The flexible trunk, which can be raised and lowered at will, is the chimney; the legs of my animal are connected with the wheels of the apparatus; I arranged his eyes so as to dart out two jets of electric light, and the artificial elephant was complete. But as it was not my own spontaneous creation, I met with numerous difficulties which delayed me. The gigantic plaything, as you may call it, cost me many a sleepless night; so many indeed, that my rajah, who was wild with impatience, and passed the best part of his time in my workshops, died before the finishing touches were given that would allow the elephant to set forth on his travels. The poor fellow had no time even to make one trial of his invention. His heirs, however, less why and wherefore of the matter, and how it is that in all the world we alone are the proprietors of a steam elephant, with the strength of eighty horses, not to mention eighty elephants!"

"Bravo, Banks! well done!" exclaimed Captain Hood. "A first-class engineer who is an artist, a poet in iron and steel into the bargain, is a *rara avis* amongst us!"

"The rajah being dead," resumed Banks, "and his apparatus being in my possession, I had not the heart to destroy my elephant, and give the locomotive its ordinary form."

"And you did well!" replied the captain, "Our elephant is superb, there's no other word for it!" said the captain. "And what a fine effect we shall have, careering over the plains and through the jungles of Hindoostan! It is a regular rajah-like idea, isn't it? And one of which we shall reap the advantage, shan't we, colonel?"

Colonel Munro made a faint attempt at a smile, to show that he quite approved of the captain's speech.

The journey was resolved upon then and there; and now this unique and wonderful steam elephant was reduced to drag the travelling residence of four Englishmen, instead of stalking along in state with one of the most opulent rajahs of the Indian peninsula.

I quote the following description of the mechanism of this road engine, on which Banks had brought to bear all the improvements of modern science, from notes made at the time.

"Between the four wheels are all the machinery of cylinders, pistons, feed-pump, etc, covered by the body of the boiler. This tubular boiler is in the fore part of the elephant's body, and the tender, carrying fuel and water, in the hinder part. The boiler and tender, though both on the same truck, have a space between them, left for the use of the stoker. The engine-driver is stationed in the fire-proof howdah on the animal's back, in which we all could take refuge in case of any serious attack. He has there everything in his power, safety-valves, regulating brakes, etc, so that he can steer or back his engine at will. He has also thick lens-shaped glass fixed in the narrow embrasures, through which he can see the road both before and behind him.

"The boiler and tender are fixed on springs of the best steel, so as to lessen the jolting caused by the inequalities of the ground. The wheels, constructed with vast solidity, are grooved so as to bite the earth, and prevent them from 'skating.'

"The nominal strength of the engine is equal to that of eighty horses, but its power can be increased to equal that of 150, without any danger of an explosion. A case, hermetically scaled, encloses all the machinery, so as to protect it from the dust of the roads, which would soon put the mechanism out of order. The machine has a double cylinder after the Field system, and its great perfection consists in this, that the expenditure is small and the results great. Nothing could be better arranged in that way, for in the furnace any kind of fuel may be burnt, either wood or coal. The engineer estimates the ordinary speed at fifteen miles an hour, but on a good road it can reach twenty-five. There is no danger of the wheels skating, not only from the grooves, but because of the perfect poise of the apparatus, which is all so well balanced that not even the severest jolting could disturb it. The atmospheric brakes, with which the engine is provided, could in a moment produce either a slackening of speed or a sudden halt.

"The facility with which the machine can ascend slopes is remarkable. Banks has succeeded most happily in this, taking into consideration the weight and power of propulsion of the machine. It can easily ascend a slope at an inclination of from four to five inches in the yard, which is considerable."

There is a perfect network of magnificent roads made by the English all over India, which are excellently fitted for this mode of locomotion. The Great Trunk Road, for instance, stretches uninterruptedly for 1200 miles.

I must now describe the Steam House.

Banks had not only bought from the Nabob's heirs the traction-engine, but the train which it had in tow. This had of course been constructed, according to the oriental taste of the rajah, in the most gorgeous Hindoo fashion. I have already called it a travelling bungalow, and it merited the name, for the two cars composing it were simply a marvellous specimen of the architecture of the country.

Imagine two pagoda-shaped buildings without minarets, but with double-ridged roofs surmounted by a dome, the corbelling of the windows supported by sculptured pilasters, all the ornamentation in exquisitely carved and coloured woods of rare kinds, a handsome verandah both back and front. You might suppose them a couple of pagodas torn from the sacred hill of Sonnaghur.

To complete the marvel of this prodigious locomotive, I must add that it can float! In fact, the stomach, or that part of the elephant's body which contains the machinery, as well as the lower portion of the buildings, form boats of light steel. When a river is met with, the elephant marches straight into it, the train follows, and as the animal's feet can be moved by paddle-wheels, the Steam House moves gaily over the surface of the water. This is an indescribable advantage for such a vast country as India, where there are more rivers than bridges.

This was the train ordered by the capricious Rajah of Bhootan. But though the carriages were like pagodas on the outside, Banks thought it best to furnish the interior, to suit English tastes, with everything necessary for a long journey, and in this he was very successful.

The width of the two carriages was not less than eighteen feet; they therefore projected over the wheels, as the axles were not more than fifteen. Being well hung on splendid springs, any jolting would be as little felt as on a well made railroad.

The first carriage was forty-five feet long. In front, was an elegant verandah, in which a dozen people could sit comfortably. Two windows and a door led into the drawing-room, lighted besides by two side windows. This room, furnished with a table and book-case, and having luxurious divans all round it, was artistically decorated and hung with rich tapestry. A thick Turkey carpet covered the floor. "Tatties," or blinds, hung before the windows, and were kept moistened with perfumed water, so that a delightful freshness was constantly diffused throughout all the apartments. A punkah was suspended from the ceiling and kept continually in motion, for it was necessary to provide against the heat, which at certain times of the year is something frightful.

Opposite the verandah door was another of valuable wood, opening into the dining-room, which was lighted not only by side windows but by a ceiling of ground glass.

Eight guests might have been comfortably seated round the table in the centre, so as we were but four we had ample room. It was furnished with sideboards and buffets loaded with all the wealth of silver, glass, and china, which is necessary to English comfort. Of course all these fragile articles were put in specially made racks, as is done on board ship, so that even on the roughest roads they would be perfectly safe.

A door led out into the passage, which ended in another verandah at the back. From this passage opened four rooms, each containing a bed, dressing-table, wardrobe and sofa, and fitted up like the cabins of the best transatlantic steamers. The first of these rooms on the left was occupied by Colonel Munro, the second on the right by Banks. Captain Hood was established next to the engineer, and I next to Sir Edward.

The second carriage was thirty-six feet in length, and also possessed a verandah which opened into a large kitchen, flanked on each side with a pantry, and supplied with everything that could be wanted. This kitchen communicated with a passage which, widening into a square in the middle, and lighted by a skylight, formed a diningroom for the servants. In the four angles were four cabins, occupied by Sergeant McNeil, the engine-driver, the stoker, and Colonel Munro's orderly; while at the back were two other rooms for the cook and Captain Hood's man; besides a gun-room, box-room, and ice-house, all opening into the back verandah.

It could not be denied that Banks had intelligently and comfortably arranged and furnished Steam House. There was an apparatus for heating it in winter with hot air from the engine, besides two small fireplaces in the drawing and dining-rooms. We were therefore quite prepared to brave the rigours of the cold season, even on the slopes of the mountains of Thibet.

You may be sure the important question of provisions had not been neglected, and we carried sufficient to feed the entire expedition for a year. They consisted chiefly of tins of preserved meat of the best brands, principally boiled and stewed beef, and also "mourghis," or fowls, of which there is so large a consumption all over India.

Thanks to the new inventions which allow both milk and soup to be carried in a concentrated form, we had abundance of both, the former for breakfast and the latter for tiffin, or luncheon.

After being exposed to evaporation, in a manner to render it of a pasty consistency, the milk is enclosed in hermetically-sealed tins, each of which, on the addition of water, supplies three quarts of good and nourishing milk. The soup, too, is condensed in much the same way, and is carried in tablets.

As I said, we had an ice-house, in which that luxury, so useful in hot climates, could be easily produced by means of the Carre apparatus, which causes a lowering of the temperature by means of the evaporation of liquid ammoniac gas. Either in this way or by the volatilization of methylated ether, the product of our sport could be indefinitely preserved by the application of a process invented by a Frenchman, a compatriot of my own, Ch. Tellier. This was a valuable resource, as at all times it placed at our disposal food of the first quality. The cellar was well supplied as to beverages. French wines, different kinds of beer, brandy, arrack, occupied special places, and in quantities to satisfy the ideas of the most thirsty souls.

Our journey would lead us through many inhabited provinces. India is by no means a desert, and if one does not spare rupees, it is ease to procure, not only the necessaries, but also the superfluities of life. Perhaps if we were to winter in the northern regions, at the base of the Himalayas, we might be compelled to fall back on our own resources, but in any case it was not difficult to provide for all the exigencies of a comfortable existence. The practical mind of our friend Banks had foreseen everything, and we trusted to him to revictual us en route.

The following is the itinerary of the journey which was agreed on, subject to any modifications which unforeseen circumstances might suggest. We proposed leaving Calcutta, to follow the valley of the Ganges up to Allahabad, to cross the kingdom of Oude, so as to reach the first slopes of Thibet, to remain there for some months, sometimes in one place, sometimes in another, so as to give Captain Hood plenty of opportunity for hunting, and then to redescend to Bombay. We had thus 900 leagues, or 2,700 miles before us. But our house and servants travelled with us. Under these conditions, who would refuse even to make the tour of the world again and again?

The Clockwork Penguin Dreamed of Stars

Caroline M. Yoachim

It was one of those rare nights when the smog thinned out enough for stars to be visible in the sky above the penguin enclosure. Gwin adjusted her synthetic feathers with her beak, arranging them neatly and plucking out any that were broken or bent. She didn't want to groom, but her programming said it was preening time, so she had no choice.

"You should get Zee to bring you some new feathers, you're looking a little ragged." Victor slithered between the bars that were built to keep humans out of the enclosure, back when there were humans. He coiled up on top of a nice warm rock, and his metal scales screeched as they scraped against each other. "Hopefully she still has some oil to quiet down these scales."

"Get your oil if you want to, but I don't need new feathers. I hate preening. I want to pluck myself until I'm smooth and streamlined so I can fly out into space and see the stars." Gwin was a dreamer. The other animals judged this to be a flaw, but she saw nothing wrong with snapping at fish that were beyond the reach of her beak. She was tired of being confined, tired of the constant noise of the automated educational recordings, tired of acting out the same routines day in and day out.

"We are designed to teach humans about the animals that used to live on this planet. Traveling to the stars is not part of our programming." Victor loved to lecture and was always looking for opportunities to give his overblown speeches. "You are supposed to waddle, swim, catch fish in your beak… and preen. We all behave the way we must—each within our limits—from the moment of our creation until the time we cease to function."

"There aren't any humans to teach, and there hasn't been a real penguin for centuries." There weren't even any other clockwork penguins, not anymore. A few had broken down so badly that Zee couldn't repair them, but most of the others had found a way to escape the zoo.

Gwin continued preening. She'd been trying for weeks now to violate her programming, even in the tiniest of ways, but there were firm limits to what she could and couldn't do. She could download constellation charts and space shuttle schematics under the guise of "updating her knowledge database," and she could dream of the stars when she slept, but when it was time to groom, she had to groom. "Why do you care what I do, anyway?"

"I'm a creature of my programming, just as you are." Victor said. Which didn't explain anything. "I've called Zee to come repair us."

"I told you—I don't want feathers." Gwin lowered her head and glared at Victor. Her programming told her it was time to swim, but the water in her pond had long since evaporated away. She waddled around the perimeter of the dry pond, faster with every circle she completed, needing to do *something* but unable to comply with her programming.

Zee swung herself over the bars of the fence. Her black fur was ragged, with patches of orange where she'd used synthetic orangutan fur to cover her metal frame. "Real animals did that, too. Not out in the wild, but in enclosures like this."

Swimming time ended, and Gwin stopped her frantic circling.

"Zoos aren't good places for animals, even artificial ones. We're not meant to be contained. I wish I could make it so you don't have to do that anymore." Of all the animals at the zoo, Zee was the closest to human, and she used her opposable thumbs to replace corroded wires and worn-out gears. She'd even recruited a small army of mechanical rats to scavenge the streets for spare parts. She'd trained them to avoid the sweepers that kept the city clean. Her willingness to help with maintenance should have made Zee popular, but no one trusted her because she was the only animal at the zoo whose programming allowed her to lie.

Victor uncoiled himself, and Zee cringed at the high-pitched whine of metal against metal.

"Sorry, Victor, I'm out of oil. The old tanker my rats were draining corroded through, left a huge mess down a couple city blocks. You're making a terrible noise, though. I'll see if we can't find another tank, or sop up some oil off the street or something." Zee turned to Gwin. "You need fixing?"

"Victor seems to think so, but no." Gwin hoped Zee would go away and fix someone else.

"I could at least get you some feathers—"

"I don't want feathers," Gwin insisted. "I'm trying to get rid of feathers."

"Why?" Zee asked.

"She thinks that if she makes herself more streamlined, she can fly to the stars," Victor said. "Which is silly. Flying to the stars isn't in our programming."

"The bigger problem is the flying, not the programming. Even if she was streamlined, penguins are flightless birds. She wouldn't be able to take off, much less leave the planet." Zee stared off into the distance. "There are lots of abandoned shuttles in the city. My rats find animal components in some of them. Even feathers, sometimes."

"No feathers. Not for me." She wondered whether the shuttles were a truth or a lie. She'd have to ask the rats. Even if it was true, though, her programming was clear—her job was to educate humans, so her place was here in the clockwork zoo. Victor was wrong about the feathers, but he was right about that.

It was preening time again, and Gwin systematically plucked her feathers out. Doing that satisfied the need her programming imposed on her, but it was a deviant behavior. If any of the zookeepers had been around, she'd have been reprogrammed. Maybe that would even be a good thing—with an upgraded program maybe she'd be smarter, more like Zee. But there were no zookeepers because there were no humans, which, in Gwin's opinion, invalidated her programming. Even so, she couldn't ignore the urge to preen entirely, she could only stretch the rules, bend them a little.

"Those are perfectly good components." Zee pointed to the pile of delicate synthetic feathers Gwin had left at the edge of her enclosure.

"Why can't you believe that I don't want feathers? I'm not like you—I can't lie."

"No, it's fine you don't want them," Zee said. "Can I have them? Not for me, of course, I'm happy with my fur, but there are birds in here that could use some good feathers, even if they aren't quite the right color. Here, we can trade. I'll take the feathers and you can have this radio."

Gwin peered at the ancient human artifact. The animals could communicate with each other via a radio signal, but she'd never seen an external radio unit before. "How does it work?"

"You tune it with this knob." Zee demonstrated. "And if you find a station with signal, you'll hear talking, or music."

Zee got a faraway look on her face and Gwin wondered if the music was a lie. She poked at the radio with her foot, then tapped the knob with her beak. "I can't turn the knob."

"Well, let's set it here for now." Zee adjusted the knob, and the red line that indicated the frequency slid left until it was near the middle, between 100 and 101.

"Couldn't we find one with music?"

"They all play static, mostly. But sometimes if you wait, there are other things."

Gwin waited, but there was only static.

"Try again tomorrow. I think this station is a good one."

The next morning, Gwin preened off all the feathers from her left wing. She liked the shiny metal underneath, dotted with tiny holes where the feathers had once been installed. It looked like the hull of a space shuttle—or, at least, it looked like what she'd always imagined the hull of a space shuttle might look like.

When preening time was over, she waddled to the radio and used the tip of her beak to flip the power switch. The radio hissed with static.

Gwin stared at the radio, listening. Her programming told her it was time to rest, so she edged her belly down onto the warm stone floor of her enclosure and lay there listening to the crackle of white noise.

The static stopped, and a voice spoke. "This is Lieutenant Navigator Lunares-Jove, calling from the Endeavour 7. We are holding position at the Saturn orbit checkpoint, awaiting permission to approach Earth. Please acknowledge."

The message repeated three times. Gwin listened carefully and committed the words to memory. She didn't understand all of it, but there was one word that particularly caught her attention—Saturn was one of the bright lights she sometimes saw in the night sky, though according to her charts it was a planet, not a star.

Gwin repeated the message to Zee the next time she came by. "What does it mean?"

Zee picked through her fur, searching for bugs that were never there. Her life was controlled by her programming as much as anyone's, but Gwin had never heard her complain about it. When she finished grooming, Zee looked up. "The message means there is a shuttle that wants to come to Earth."

"Humans?"

"What else would speak in a language we understand?" Zee asked. "The reason we have language is to communicate our repair needs to the zookeepers and provide interactive educational experiences to human guests. Over time, we've stretched our programming to talk to each other, but these are *their* words."

Victor slithered through the bars of the penguin enclosure. His scales didn't screech when he coiled himself up, so Zee must have found him some oil. "Humans sent us a message? They're coming here? This is something everyone should know about. It should not be kept secret."

"Wait—" Zee started, but Victor broadcast the news about the humans to all the other animals. Soon every creature that could get out of their enclosure had gathered outside the fence. Meerkats ran back and forth, periodically standing on their hind legs to peer in. A badger with a missing leg pressed its face through a gap in the bars. Lions and zebras and other large animals took up positions farther back. All of them stared at the radio Zee had given to Gwin.

"We should prepare a welcome for them, here at the zoo."

"And an answer to their message, so they know we're here."

Other voices began shouting out suggestions.

Gwin stared at the radio, which now produced only static. Zee leaned in, as though she was also listening, but instead she whispered to Gwin, "There are humans in space, and you are programmed to educate humans."

Gwin processed this information.

Zee turned the radio off. "There are shuttles in the city, my rats can show you where. Be careful to avoid the sweepers."

Zee left the penguin enclosure. Instead of swinging over the bars, she used some kind of special card to unlock and open the gate. Gwin was free to roam the zoo, but her programming wouldn't let her wander.

A lion pounced at one of the meerkats, nearly crushing it. All the small animals scattered, rushing back to the relative safety of their enclosures. Zee shooed the other animals away, too, spending an extra few moments talking to the lion that had attacked. Gwin wasn't sure why she bothered—hunting was part of the lion's programming.

With all the other animals gone, it was finally quiet in the penguin enclosure. Even the automated education tutorials had shut down for the evening, as they did every day at closing time. Gwin spent the evening thinking about what Zee had said, trying to put the pieces together.

She was supposed to educate humans.

The humans were out in space, among the stars.

Therefore. . . Gwin could go to the stars?

Gwin left her enclosure shortly after dawn, during a time when her programming instructed her it was time to swim. The zoo was much as she expected, from the descriptions of the few animals that had visited her—concrete pathways that wound around animal enclosures and concession stands. Most of the enclosures were empty, and the stands were filled with moldy stuffed animals and other decomposing toys. She hurried along, mostly driven by her urge to swim, but not wanting to linger here anyway.

Zee waved at Gwin from a fake tree in the chimpanzee enclosure.

Gwin paused, shifting her weight from one foot to the other to satisfy her need to move. "Zee, what's your dream?"

"To see the stars, same as you."

"Then why don't you come with me?"

"I can't leave the others behind," Zee said. "No one else can do repairs."

All those things sounded true, which made Gwin sad. She wished there was a way for Zee to have her dream, too, but she couldn't think of anything that would help. "Goodbye, Zee."

"Good luck."

Gwin followed the path to an open courtyard, and beyond that was the main entrance. She expected some kind of resistance as she passed under the wrought iron archway, but being outside the zoo felt no different than being inside it.

Not far beyond the gate, she came across a rat.

"City?" it asked. "Shuttle?"

"Yes." Gwin assumed the rat was part of Zee's scavenger army.

"Follow, okay?" The rat scurried forward. Rats were small creatures with simple minds, better suited for scavenging than conversation. "Good shuttle. Passcode already cracked."

Gwin followed the rat down a wide road, lined on either side with abandoned vehicles. Near the zoo, there were lots of open areas filled with trees—Gwin couldn't tell if they were fake or real—and an assortment of small buildings in various states of disrepair. It was hard to tell where exactly the city started, but as she followed the rat the buildings got taller.

It was time for preening.

Gwin shouldn't linger on the street, but she couldn't help it. She listened carefully while she preened, but the city was silent. She plucked all the feathers off her right wing to make it match the left. She discarded the feathers in a pile, and it wouldn't be long before a sweeper came and cleared away the mess.

Her rat guide fidgeted impatiently while she preened. "Not far, let's go."

The rat led her through a maze of streets,

scanning constantly for threats. There were no trees here, nothing green, only towers with sometimes-broken glass windows that stretched up to the sky. "Four more blocks down this road, then right on the alley. Good shuttle. Lots of gears inside."

They passed a rusted out oil tanker at the top of the hill, and one side of the road was slick with spilled motor oil. Gwin waddled down the other side, not wanting to risk slipping and injuring herself. She was listening to the scraping noise her feet made on the pavement when she noticed another sound—a soft swishing in the distance. The rat froze in place. Gwin waited, too, not daring to move. The sound got louder, closer.

"Sweeper." The rat said. It bolted down a side street.

Gwin paused, undecided. Should she follow the rat? The alley with the shuttle was only a few blocks away, but what if the shuttle was one of Zee's lies? The sweeper turned a corner and came into view, a bright green truck with a rotating brush to sweep debris into a giant tank. Steam hissed out from the top of the tank.

The truck was headed straight toward Gwin.

She waddled as fast as she could into the middle of the road, to the edge of the oil slick. The sweeper was only half a block behind her, and closing fast. Once something went into a sweeper tank it never came back out. The hill was steep and the road was hard, but Gwin couldn't waddle fast enough to escape. She flopped onto her belly. The oil-covered road was like ice, and she slid down the hill at top speed.

The pavement scraped the last of the feathers from her belly and began to wear away at the metal underneath. Buildings blurred by on either side as Gwin sped down the hill. The sound of the sweeper truck was covered by the screech of metal against the road.

She reached the bottom and skidded to a stop.

It was time to rest, but if Gwin didn't get up she'd be swept away. She tried to resist her programming, but her belly remained firmly pressed against the pavement.

The sweeper truck barreled down the hill.

She had to find the humans that were out in space; that was part of her programming, too. She pitted her opposing drives against each other, making her need to educate humans overpower her basic scheduling routines. It was time to rest, but Gwin stood up. She waddled down the road and turned into the alley—away from the path of the sweeper, safe.

The shuttle was the most beautiful thing Gwin had ever seen, sleek silver metal dotted with little round windows, located exactly where Zee's rat said it would be. The others had been too hard on Zee—just because she was capable of lying didn't mean she did. And wasn't choosing not to lie every bit as good as not being able to? Better, maybe, because it showed such good intentions.

The sweeper turned into the alley.

She was so close to her dream, too close to be swept away. The alley was a dead end. Her only chance was to get into the shuttle. Gwin found a hatch, but she had no idea how to open it. She accessed the schematics in her knowledge database.

With her beak she flipped the cover of a keypad with numbers laid out in a rectangle, one through nine, zero, a pound sign and an asterisk. Scrawled below was 0-6-1-7. What had the rat said about the shuttle? *Passcode already cracked.* Gwin tried the sequence, pecking each number with her beak, but nothing happened. The roar of the sweeper was so loud the shuttle was vibrating. Gwin stared desperately at the keypad.

The asterisk looked like a star.

She pecked it. The hatch opened.

Gwin hopped into the shuttle. The brushes of the sweeper made contact with the hull, and—sensing a threat—the hatch automatically closed. Safely inside, she watched as the sweeper cleaned the edge of the shuttle, then backed away to clean some other street.

She left the little round window and examined the rest of the shuttle. The control panel was a chaotic quilt of square buttons in several different colors, but off to one side was a switch that Zee told her would engage the autopilot. Gwin used her beak to flip it.

"Engage autopilot? Voice confirmation required."

In the best imitation of a human voice she could muster, Gwin answered, "Engage the autopilot and initiate launch sequence."

"Destination?"

"Saturn orbit checkpoint."

The control panel flashed and sensors clicked and beeped. The engines roared and the entire shuttle began to vibrate. Beads of water streamed across the windows as the shuttle rose through clouds and smog. Above the atmosphere, the sky was black and filled with tiny points of light. Stars. More than Gwin had ever seen, and as beautiful as she'd always dreamed.

Back at the clockwork zoo, Zee led the other animals to a radio broadcast tower at the northeast corner of the African savanna enclosure.

"I know that many of you are eager to welcome humans back to Earth, but there's something you should hear." Zee played them the message recorded on a tape: "This is Lieutenant Navigator Lunares-Jove, calling from the Endeavour 7. We are holding position at the Saturn orbit checkpoint, awaiting permission to approach Earth. Please acknowledge."

But it didn't end there. The voice on the tape kept talking. "We are here to provide aid to survivors of the transcendence plague, but we cannot approach without confirmation that the quarantine is lifted. We will remain at the checkpoint until midnight, coordinated universal time, 17 March, 2206. Please acknowledge."

"So they aren't out there?" a zebra asked.

The specified time was nearly two hundred years ago, only a few years after the zookeepers had disappeared.

"They're out there somewhere," Zee said, looking up at the night sky and wondering where in the blackness Gwin's shuttle was. "But they're not coming here."

"Maybe we should go find them," one of the meerkats suggested, hesitant.

Zee smiled. There were plenty of shuttles in the city. Once she got all her clockwork animals to the Saturn orbit checkpoint, she could tell them whatever new lies they needed, and together they could search for the missing humans, somewhere out among the stars.

Closer to the Sky

Carrie Vaughn

Eight outlaws rode in, a regular gang of them with rifles slung on saddles and kerchiefs 'round their throats like wounds. They pulled hard on reins and bits without a thought, and their horses tossed angry heads against the pain. You knew they'd kick if you got too close. They circled the yard in front of the house. The cowponies in the nearby corral cried out and jostled each other.

When the outlaws rode up they brought a tension with them like too much summer heat and lightning on the horizon. The leader came up front and center. He had a beard like a thousand other men, scruffy hair that hadn't been washed in too long, worn shirt and trousers, a snarl showing dirty teeth. He was the kind of man some folk say needed a woman's touch, except that he was also the kind of man who wouldn't sit still for it, who fled the minute his woman started talking about putting up nice curtains, or who drove her off when he raised a hand to her.

Revolver in hand, the outlaw leader looked at the folk standing on the house's front porch: mother, father, brother, and sister. Two farm hands came up from the barn but then one of the gang fired a gun in the air to keep them back. He looked them over, smiled cruelly, and said, "Which of you is going to tell me where Harlow Mason is?"

The outlaws did not know that one member of the family standing there on the porch was missing. That is, they didn't until they saw the dust raised up by a cowpony racing out across the plain with a girl perched on its back.

Mother and Father would have stopped her if they could, but Annie was fourteen now and contrary in the way of a girl who had grown up with a pony of her own. (Mother warned them, if they let her wear trousers and run around like a heathen she'd never be tamed. Father smiled indulgently, her brother egged her on, and secretly Mother was pleased. Her eldest daughter might have a terrible time finding her an understanding husband. Then again, if she kept this up she might never need one.)

One of the crew of outlaws set up a holler, pointing out to the clear trail of rising dust. The leader scowled, wearing the nastiest of expressions when he looked over the Mason family, and spurred his angry horse back round the way he'd come, shouting at his people, pulling them in line, so they galloped on in a formation that was almost military after that trail of dust.

They would never catch this particular cowpony, not even if they'd all started at the same time, pretty as a race.

The Mason ranch was not quite standard: The windmill had double the blades and a complicated set of pistons and belts leading down its spine. Pumped water streamed into a wide trough, and from there a kind of water wheel gathered it up and sent it down a split channel, one part leading to a barn, the other to the house. The whole ranch had running water. Likewise the gates had extra hardware on them, bolts and brackets, gears and winches connected to cables and switches—they were automated and could be operated from one spot by the barn. And there was a clattering bell that rang as soon as anyone road up to the house, which was how Annie Mason got her head start.

The outlaws would not catch her because like the gates and the windmill and the alarm, the automated apple peeler and hydro-sonic washing machine, the pneumatic post hole digger and piston-driven corn husker, Annie's pony, Copper, was a thing made by Uncle Harlow Mason.

Annie hoped to warn Uncle Harlow about the terrible men who were looking for him, and Copper would do whatever she asked. He was alive because of her tears, and because of her he could run forever. This was his job now, the purpose he embraced: to make his girl fast, to lift her up as far as he can. Sixty inches off the ground, at least. More when he jumps. Closer to the sky either way.

Anyone else would have shot the horse after it broke not one but two legs over a loose stretch of rocks on the prairie, but Harlow was there and wanted to try something, because he always wanted to try something, and he was sure there was nothing in the big wide world he couldn't fix given time and tools. "Give me a lever long enough!" he used to bellow, before pulling out wrench and tin shears. That saved Copper. That and Annie, begging, unwilling to see her Copper shot, broken legs or no.

Now, instead of flesh and blood for legs this singular cowpony had steel and pistons, rubber tendons, and brass flywheels, slicked with oil and faster than bees' wings. He had interchangeable shoes: broad plates for sand, spikes for ice, rubberized points like a billy goat's hooves, and regular polished-for-parades horse's feet. Mostly, though, this cowpony could now run *fast*. And he still loved his girl. (You can tell a horse loves his girl by the way he rests his nose on her shoulder, whuffing softly, like he has come home. You can tell a girl loves her pony by the way her arms exactly fit around his head when he lowers it to greet her.)

Uncle Harlow's only reservation about the whole deal was that the cowpony's heart might not be strong enough to power the rest, but he needn't have worried about that. His heart was plenty. The only thing was Copper had to be kept in his own pen because one solid kick from him would destroy a natural horse. And the other horses bullied him; he was too strange for them, and they let him know.

The outlaws did not know any of this about the cowpony's legs, and could not understand why the girl kept drawing farther and farther ahead, no matter how much they shouted and whipped their own already overworked mounts.

Annie talked to Copper during that mad ride to the valley where Harlow kept his workshop in a cave hidden from prying eyes. "What's Harlow done to get such men riled at him? Crazy man." She said this with affection because she owed Harlow a lot.

The pony told her he agreed by running faster.

She took a roundabout route, leaving dusty plain to trot over rock for awhile. She might have worried on a horse with regular feet. She didn't worry at all about Copper. The pony's metal gait jarred a bit, so she stood up on her stirrups and rode through it. This way, no telltale trail of dust marred the sky. They passed down into one wash, up into another, until hard as she looked she couldn't see anyone following. Only then did she turn their path into the secluded gulch, tucked neatly between two low unassuming mesas that Uncle Harlow called home.

The one-room cabin that he and Father built a decade ago, where Uncle Harlow slept and cooked meals and stored his clothes and food, stood peaceful enough, but no smoke came out of the chimney. No smoke came out of the forge, either, set at the mouth of the cave in a big sandy stretch where stray sparks had no chance to cause mischief. Deeper in the cave were racks and cupboards, chests and drawers, piles of scrap metal and lanterns hung on hooks, every tool a person could name and some Harlow had invented just for himself. He had buckets of gears and sprockets and spindles, engines he was building, and prototypes of ships that could fly or swim underwater, though they were a hundred miles from anything bigger than a pond. Harlow Mason was an inventor, a good one, but he was not always the best judge of character. He depended on his family for that most times—Father brought him business, usually. Lord knew how he'd gotten mixed up with the outlaws. They might have asked for a powered wrench that would break into safes or a device to stop trains on a dime. It might not have occurred to him to wonder what a grizzled man with guns on his belt might use such gadgets for. He'd have been too fascinated by the challenge of making a gun that could shoot through a bank safe or an airship that could fly straight up and turn invisible for a fast getaway.

She left Copper to graze and searched. Harlow must have had some warning that something was amiss, but the only message she found were the things that were missing: clothing tossed out of a trunk, as if someone had packed in a hurry; the rusted tin can behind the bed where Harlow kept his money—empty; and the great silk balloon he always said he was going to use to lift his airship. A powered balloon he could use to fly around the world, he bragged when he came to the ranch for dinner once a week. Father would laugh and Mother would shake her head, and younger brother and sister would beg for stories. Annie'd watched him sewing at it for months. It was gone now, along with one of his engines and a whole barrel of pieces and parts.

Finally, she found a note hidden in a toolbox, tucked under a hammer. "Burn it," he wrote. "Burn it all, Annie."

"He's gone," she murmured wonderingly. Her feelings were mixed. First came relief that the outlaws wouldn't find him. But then came anger; Harlow was gone and looked like he wasn't coming back, which wasn't fair at all because she needed him: She could make little repairs to Copper's legs, adding oil and tightening bolts when she brushed him down and checked his feet. But for the bigger things—changing out belts, cleaning valves and pistons, making sure the strange widgets of his creation stayed good—she needed Harlow for that. If he wasn't here, who would keep Copper well and safe? She kicked at a toolbox and screamed a curse at the man, because that kept her from crying. Just like Harlow, not thinking ahead at all.

Meanwhile, Copper might have looked like he was grazing, but he kept himself pointed to the head of the gulch and had one ear up, listening hard. Anything came along that way, he'd know it. And something did, because it was that kind of day. A half a dozen strangers galloped up, and Copper raised his head and hollered a warning to his girl to come quick, to tell him if they were going to stay and fight or get the hell out.

The men pulled back on their reins and the horses rolled wild eyes at him because he looked like a horse but smelled of rubber and oil. One of the men said, "Lord, look at that thing." The pony stood his ground when one of them dismounted—he couldn't get his own mount to come any closer—and grabbed his reins. Copper planted his four mechanical legs like tree roots while he waited for his girl to return.

Annie ran out of the cave to find the horseman surrounding her pony and blocking her way out. The men had dusters over neat suits, clean hats and boots. Well-trained mounts standing politely—except when they pinned their ears at Copper. They weren't outlaws, though they carried just as many weapons. These men had women to wash and mend their clothes, to tell them it was time to trim their mustaches.

The one in front flicked back the flap of his coat to show the brass star on his vest.

"U.S. Marshal, ma'am," he said calmly. "Name's Kearney."

Copper's head was straight up, pulling against his captor. His ears were pinned back, angry, and he looked at the girl as if to apologize for not giving warning sooner. Wasn't his fault, not if the marshal and his crew already knew about Harlow's workshop. Not if they'd been waiting in ambush.

"You're Miss Annie Mason," the marshal said.

"Yes, sir."

"That's a fine animal there. Unusual." He nodded at the buckskin with the mechanical legs.

"One of a kind. He's not for sale," she said, because she'd been asked before.

"It's one of Harlow Mason's gadgets, isn't it?"

"No," she said. "He's my pony."

"Is Mason here?" He gazed past her, studying the homestead.

"No, sir."

"And exactly where is Harlow Mason right now, Miss Annie?"

"I don't know," she said, truthfully. She'd left the note he'd written under the toolbox and hoped the marshals didn't search for it. She needed to send these men away, so she could do what Harlow asked her to.

"But you know where he *was*."

The pony stamped the ground with a whirring of gears and hissing of pistons.

"Sir, I know you're looking for my uncle— but so were some other folk, a whole gang of the rowdiest outlaws you ever saw. I need to get home, to see that there's no trouble—"

"That right? I imagine we'll get to them soon enough. Right now, I'm authorized to take possession of Harlow Mason's property. In the interest of national security, you understand."

Mind you, these were the good guys.

"I imagine that gang was after the same thing. Engines, yeah? Weapons?"

"Mechanics," Kearney said. "Like this here buckskin."

"He won't run for anyone but me."

He nodded at the man holding the cowpony. "Nelson. Why don't you get on that cowpony, give him a turn, see how he rides."

Annie could step away because she knew what would happen next.

Likely, the marshal had picked this particular one of his deputies to ride the mechanical buckskin because he was the best horseman— the one who could tame mustangs, the one who could whisper young colts into halters. He took it entirely for granted that this deputy would be able to murmur to the clockwork horse, lead him off, get on him and trot a circle, pretty as anything. But that didn't happen.

The man was young and had a kind face. The miles were in his hands, calloused from years of work. He stroked the cowpony's cheek, just like anyone would upon meeting a new horse. Said gentle words, and the horse's cupped ears flickered willing enough. But when the man tugged on the reins and urged him forward, the pony didn't move. He did the first trick you always try—move in another direction, pull the reins at an angle the horse isn't expecting so he walks off in spite of himself. He got insistent, his voice rising just a bit, "Come on, you." He clicked his tongue, moved to the horse's side and flicked the ends of the reins at his belly. None of it worked. Annie and Copper were both impressed that he didn't resort to yelling and whipping.

They could all see the locked legs, the frozen gears, the belts that didn't waver, the pistons that wouldn't budge. Pony had the brakes on.

Annie took the reins from the deputy, spoke softly, "Come on, kid," and the pony walked on like it was nothing.

"Well, shoot," the marshal said, but Nelson laughed.

"Sorry sir, can't do a thing about it," he said. He understood, and the pony nodded at him in respect. But he wouldn't walk on for the man.

"All right then. Nelson, you and Jack stay here and keep watch over the place. No one goes in.

The rest of us—we're going to get some answers. You too, Miss Annie."

She could outrun them. With this pony she could outrun anybody. But if they knew Harlow's homestead, then they knew the ranch, and Annie couldn't run forever.

Rather than stand on the porch with rifles as they had with the outlaws, Mother and Father invited the marshal and his crew in for coffee and biscuits. That didn't change how Kearney looked Father up and down as if studying him for weapons, trying to figure out what he was hiding. But Father wasn't hiding anything. For once the younger siblings sat quietly, staring at the strangers with their big brass stars.

"Mr. Mason, your brother has a place out behind the wash by the mesas. You know what he gets up to out there?" He was asking questions he already knew the answer to.

"He does some smith work, some tinkering. Fixes things—you seen the windmill and gates right here on the farm."

"You know where he's got off to?"

"If he's not out at his place, then I don't know." Father glanced at Annie, trying to ask the question, but she wouldn't meet his gaze.

Kearney took out a sheaf of papers from inside his vest and spread them on the table.

Father studied them. "It's a contract."

"Yes. Between your brother and the United States government, for some of his inventions. Engines, tools. Gadgets like those automated gates you have out there. Harlow was paid for his efforts, but the U.S. government has yet to receive any of the promised goods."

And didn't that sound like something Harlow would do? Found a way to get easy money—maybe to finish that airship he kept on about—and he might have had every intention in the world of delivering what he'd promised, but between one thing and another he couldn't follow through.

"There's more," Kearney said. "We got testimony that says Harlow Mason made a similar deal with Edward Canton."

"The outlaw?" Mason said.

"That's right."

Father turned away and swore softly. "That's what they wanted."

"Edward Canton was here?"

"Never met the man and can't say that was him. But someone rode up here guns blazing not two hours ago."

Now it was Kearney who swore. "Where'd he go? And pardon me for asking but why'd he leave you all standing?"

Father looked back at Annie, which she wished he wouldn't have done. "My girl ran off and led 'em on a fine chase, I reckon."

Kearney nodded in acknowledgment if not understanding.

Dealing with outlaws also sounded like something Harlow would do, for much the same reason he'd dealt with the government folk. An easy way to make some fast money, and never mind if he'd deliver or not. Uncle Harlow didn't always think too far ahead, which was how he put together the horse with the clockwork legs, without thinking what such a thing could do or be.

Easy, to be furious with Harlow, who couldn't be sensible when it mattered. But if he was generally sensible, then Copper wouldn't be breathing. For that, Annie would forgive him anything. She understood the note now: he didn't want *anyone* to get hold of his gadgets. He was gone; best the rest of it go too. Fair enough.

How much time did she have, then, to get back to Harlow's place and follow his instructions? Not to mention going behind the backs of the deputies Kearney'd left behind.

The pony still had its saddle on; she'd left Copper in a corral when she'd brought the marshal and his men straight to the house. How did she get outside with no one asking her questions?

Kearney went outside to two of his deputies who were standing watch on the front porch. The whole family stayed very quiet to listen.

"They can't be too far away," Kearney said. "They'll be back. We'll wait."

Mother put on another pot of coffee.

Father said to the man when he came back in, "I do sympathize with you, Marshal, but I can't keep up with my brother at the best of times. He doesn't tell me much—this contract, this deal with Canton, it's all news to me."

"You don't mind, then, if we wait around for a bit? See if he comes back here, to see his beloved family?"

Father frowned. Mother tensed. Annie very much refrained from mentioning the missing airship balloon and engine.

"Don't suppose it matters if I mind or not," Father said.

Kearney smiled. "I appreciate your outlook."

While they talked, Annie put her hand on the back door, but then her mother said, "Annie," in that curt low tone, and everyone looked, and she had to stand still after that.

Along with the pair of deputies keeping watch on the porch, the cowpony stood watch from his pen. A horse has ears that can hear trouble coming across miles of prairie, and eyes that spot movement that shouldn't be there, and shadows in bright light where people don't think to look. You see a horse spook at nothing, it may not be nothing but a thing only horses can see.

The cowpony saw the outlaws returning.

He was watching for 'em. Knew they'd be back because they had no place left to look for Harlow, and they wouldn't have found the cave. Not unless they'd followed Annie, and he made sure they couldn't.

He trumpeted, and anyone who'd been around horses knew that sound of warning.

Annie knew it right off and ran out the door. Took everyone else a minute or two to follow.

"Annie, get back here!" Mother called but the girl didn't listen. Ignored everything else but the cowpony and her path to get to him.

There was no standoff. There were no words exchanged, no time to look across an open dusty space and size each other up. Canton's gang came in firing.

This all happened at once: The outlaws rode up the drive, guns firing; the deputies took cover; and the cowpony jumped clean over the corral fence. This startled the regular horses so profoundly they all spooked: the picketed horses belonging to the marshal and his deputies, the crowd of horses under the outlaws, the ranch horses penned up in the corral. They all set to bucking and pulling against reins and crashing into each other. Briefly, briefly, the outlaws stopped firing, and Annie had her chance to take a look around and decide what to do next.

The cowpony came to meet her and decided for the both of them.

Mother and Father were both on the porch with rifles, taking aim at Canton and his gang—figuring it was a matter of self-defense now, with the marshal as witness. They could take care of themselves, and so Annie rode. Copper knew which way to go, back to the cave at the back of the gulch.

She was not alone.

It was a measure of how important Uncle Harlow's place was to both sides of the standoff that neither Kearney nor Canton stayed behind at the ranch to see how the gunfight played out. They left that to their gangs. For his part, Canton used his men as cover, even as one, then two of them went down, shot in hip and shoulder, falling out of their saddles. Their horses galloped off showing the whites of their eyes.

Kearney's horse was bucking at the end of the rope that held him to the hitching post. He didn't try to settle him. Just cut the rope and swung into the saddle as the animal launched away, spinning on hind legs as the marshal reined him around and sent him after Canton, and Annie ahead of him.

It would serve Harlow right for Annie to just hand over his workshop. Let Kearney and his men come and pack everything up, take it away to some government building where no one would ever see it again. But her loyalty to him, however misplaced, was absolute, because of what he'd done for Copper.

Copper's loyalty to Annie was simply absolute.

She did not worry about the men behind her—the pony would outrun them. She would have to worry about the deputies Kearney left at the gulch; she would do that soon enough. The sounds she heard: the drumbeat of her horse's hooves on the prairie; the billows of her horse's breath; and a faint sort of squeaking, growing louder.

Today, this moment, the cowpony was running harder and faster than it ever had, and there was a squeaking noise coming from his left front, and a rattle coming from the right hind, and the pony's stride was bumpier than it should have been. She should have stopped, dismounted and got out the tool kit she kept in her pocket and the little can of oil she kept in the saddle bag, checked everything over and made it all good. Any usual day she'd go ask Uncle Harlow if something was wrong. But today was just her and Copper and they'd have to make do on their own. Copper didn't slow down a whit. As fast and hardy as those legs were the cowpony's heart was more powerful. So they kept on.

Annie knew this stretch of prairie; her pursuers didn't. This was her main advantage. Theirs were their guns. Her second advantage had to be the hope that they wouldn't shoot a mere girl. Kearney wouldn't, she was almost certain. Canton was another story, so when a gunshot fired from behind her, she flinched, waiting for the pain. A glance over her shoulder showed her one of Canton's outlaws jerking back and falling out of the saddle. The marshal's men had taken the offensive.

Somehow, even with the worrisome clicking in his legs, Copper went faster. More gunfire thundered behind them. At the first stand of cottonwoods at the head of the wash, she told Copper to turn. This was another thing her cowpony could do that no other horse could: He spun hard without slipping, jumped, launched again and from the point of view of anyone watching the girl and her pony might as well have vanished into the wash.

They galloped through a maze after that, through gullies and channels that would be rivers after a good rain, but only then. It wasn't just Annie had them all mapped out in her mind; the pony did, too, and she didn't so much steer as think on where she wanted to go, and Copper went.

Those two deputies that Kearney'd left behind at Harlow's place? They heard the gunshots and came to see the cause. There was never a man in law enforcement who would not go toward the sound of gunfire.

That was how Annie and her pony came upon a horse and rider standing direct in their path. She did not wait for words, she would not provide an explanation. She reined around, and the pony turned on unnatural legs and galloped on in the same movement. A shout followed but was quickly left behind.

By the time they were done ducking and dodging, wending and winding, avoiding both the men in front of them and the men behind, instead of coming up on the homestead from the front, they were standing at the edge of the mesa above it.

Annie knew they'd get cornered because Copper's ears pinned hard, pointing at the two horses running on the plain. Kearney and Canton, firing pistols at each other—and then coming at her. With the deputies angling in to trap her.

She and her pony had no place to go but straight down. She wouldn't have done it; she wouldn't have asked him to do it. But the cowpony pinned his ears forward at the open space and gathered up his metal legs, and Annie bent low and wrapped her legs tight to hold on. He jumped.

All the horsemen riding to converge on that spot stopped to watch what should not have been possible. Girl and pony, leaping off the edge of the mesa, seemed suspended in air.

One could not tell if they were falling, or if they had taken flight. If maybe those legs could do more than run, and Harlow had done more than create a mechanical horse, had indeed made something the world had never seen before, a horse that could run on air itself. The girl on the pony seemed unsurprised, sticking to her seat like she had done this before, that the two of them jumped over cliffs all the time. Wasn't any evidence to say they, girl and pony, hadn't. And so the marshal and his men, and the outlaw Canton, stopped to stare, all amazement.

No regular cowpony could have done it. But Copper had legs of steel and a heart that was buoyed by the faith of his own girl.

He did not fly, and he did not fall. His mechanical legs stretched out and his steel hooves touched down on that nigh vertical wall. He slid, rump to the earth. The girl let him have his head and the pony reached, throwing his weight back. Rocks and dirt from the cliff side fell with them, but they were faster, and they kept their heads, and their balance.

The pony reached; the ground leveled out, and they ran.

A standoff between Marshal Kearney and the outlaw was progressing at the top of the mesa, but Annie couldn't be bothered to worry about that. She had so little time. But if she had thought to turn around to watch what happened, she would have seen Canton spur his horse forward, shoving past the marshal, giving a wild awful shout as he aimed for the edge of the cliff, apparently ready to prove that riding off the mesa was not such an unusual thing. His horse, a fiery chestnut, rolled his eyes and pinned his ears, gave his own wild snarl, and Canton did not recognize the warning, did not guess that his horse had no faith in him at all. His horse did not make the leap, but instead dug all his hooves into the earth and threw back his weight to slide to a stop. Canton, as anyone who has spent time with horses would know, did not stop. He launched past his horse's neck and over the edge of the mesa as he intended, but he did not have a good cowpony to carry him the rest of the way. And that was the end of Canton.

Uncle Harlow had plenty of stuff around his cabin and forge that could start a fire. Burning the place to the ground as he requested wouldn't present any kind of problem. But first, she collected a few things. She found a canvas bag, emptied it of the scraps of rope and chipped flint he'd collected in it, then went through all the cabinets and drawers, boxes and shelves in his workshop. She collected belts and gears, small bands of steel and lengths of wire. Anything that looked like it might be part of Copper's legs, she saved. Anything she might need to keep her pony whole, she collected. Harlow wouldn't be here to make repairs, so she would have to learn. When she got all she could, she closed up the bag and tied it to Copper's saddle.

Only then did she see about the fire, knocking over cans of oil and tipping over boxes filled with straw packing. She lit a match in the house, and another in the cave, waited just long enough to see that both caught fire, and in moments walls of flame rose up. The pony didn't twitch a muscle, but trumpeted a whinny when he saw her running back from the smoke. As soon as her weight touched the saddle he took off, didn't need a click of the tongue or a touch of a heel to tell him so.

Fire roared behind them. Penned in by the clear stretch of rock and sand Harlow had built up to protect his work from the world, it stayed contained and burned out everything. No one would pick apart the things he'd made; no one would learn his secrets.

She leaned forward and wrapped her arms around the neck of her Copper.

He would have run forever but she made him walk. She needed to stop to oil his gears and tighten the pistons and screws, bolts and flywheels. He'd run too far and fast today, and didn't seem to realize his legs weren't working quite right. If she asked, he'd keep running until he broke.

She made him walk.

Kearney found her. Didn't say a word but walked alongside, and she wondered if she was under arrest, or if this was an escort to make sure she didn't run off again. At first, he didn't ask about the smoke rising up behind them, the glow in the back of the wash. He was waiting her out, expecting her to fill the silence, but she didn't say a word.

"I reckon," he said finally, when the ranch with that tall complicated windmill and the pipes and gates with the wires and pulleys came into view, all painted bronze by the setting sun, "that Harlow Mason's place was full up with oil and matches, flint and tinder. A hundred things that'll catch fire if you look at 'em wrong."

"I reckon," Annie said cautiously.

"That forge—I never did get a good look to see if it was cold. Harlow Mason strikes me as the kind of man who'd run off and leave his forge still hot behind him. No matter the mischief it might cause."

She looked at him. "He is. Lose his head if it wasn't attached."

"Thought so. I know you couldn't have had anything to do with it 'cause you were standing up on the edge of that mesa, not down in the wash."

"Yes, sir," she said, and didn't say anything else.

Kearney gave a satisfied grunt and smiled.

The marshal and his deputies returned to the ranch with the outlaws they hadn't shot and killed all tied up and strapped to their saddles, ready to be led off to jail. Harlow Mason, they declared, was a wanted man.

"You should send word if you hear anything at all about him, if he comes back this way," Kearney said to Father and Mother.

"We surely will," Father said. But like Annie, he was almost certain none of them would ever see the man again.

Annie was in the corral brushing down the mechanical cowpony. He had legs of steel, but the coat on his body was all horse, hairy and warm and smelling of hay and life. He still needed sweat and dust cleaned off him, and he stood with one leg cocked and his lip flopping loose, enjoying the attention.

Kearney came up to say goodbye, leaning on the fence to watch in a way that made her nervous. She tried to ignore him, until he decided to say his piece, which he finally did.

"Your Uncle Harlow's machines. They wouldn't work for anyone but him, would they? I mean if someone else tried to build them."

"That might be so," Annie agreed. She rubbed Copper's neck and the cowpony sighed.

"I also think this pony here wouldn't work even for Harlow Mason."

Annie looked up and smiled. She reckoned not, but Harlow didn't fix up Copper for himself.

Kearney said, "You take good care of this pony, you hear? He's something special."

"Yes, sir."

He rode off with his men and prisoners, and Annie was glad to see the back of them all.

Mother called from the front porch. "Annie! Supper!" And sure enough after the day's rides back and forth, she was starving, ready for biscuits and whatever else her mother had fixed.

Still, she called back, "Just a minute!" and fetched Copper another armful of hay and checked his legs over for loose screws and broken bits that might need fixing. She'd keep him fixed up, as best she could, until his heart and the rest of him gave out.

But that would be a long way off yet.

Biographies

Lauren Beukes is an award-winning writer from South Africa. Famous for her bestsellers *Moxyland*, *Zoo City*, *The Shining Girls* and more recently *Broken Monsters*, Beukes is a writer with many facets. Her novels have achieved huge success in many countries including South Africa, the UK and the USA. Find out more at www.laurenbeukes.com

Maurice Broaddus is a community organizer and teacher. His work has appeared in *Lightspeed Magazine*, *Weird Tales*, *Beneath Ceaseless Skies*, *Asimov's*, *Cemetery Dance*, *Uncanny Magazine*, with some of his stories having been collected in *The Voices of Martyrs*. He is the author of the urban fantasy trilogy, *The Knights of Breton Court*, and the (upcoming) middle grade detective novel series, *The Usual Suspects*. He co-authored the play *Finding Home:*

Indiana at 200. His novellas include *Buffalo Soldier, I Can Transform You, Orgy of Souls, Bleed with Me,* and *Devil's Marionette.* As an editor, he's worked on *Dark Faith, Dark Faith: Invocations, Streets of Shadows, People of Colo(u)r Destroy Horror,* and *Apex Magazine.* His gaming work includes writing for the *Marvel Super-Heroes, Leverage,* and *Firefly* role-playing games as well as working as a consultant on *Watch Dogs* 2. Learn more about him at MauriceBroaddus.com.

Jesse Bullington is the author of three weird historical novels: *The Sad Tale of the Brothers Grossbart, The Enterprise of Death,* and *The Folly of the World.* Under the pen name Alex Marshall he recently completed the *Crimson Empire* trilogy; the first book, *A Crown for Cold Silver,* was shortlisted for the James Tiptree, Jr. Award. He's also the editor of the Shirley Jackson Award nominated *Letters to Lovecraft,* and co-editor (with Molly Tanzer) of *Swords v. Cthulhu.* His short fiction, reviews, and articles have appeared in such diverse publications as the *LA Review of Books, The Mammoth Book of Best New Erotica 13,* and *VICE.* News of his latest projects can be found at www.jessebullington.com.

Michael Cisco published these novels: *The Divinity Student, The Golem, The Traitor, The Tyrant, The Great Lover, The Narrator, CELEBRANT, MEMBER, ANIMAL MONEY, and UNLANGUAGE*...a short story collection called

Secret Hours....and a novella called *THE KNIFE DANCE*. His short fiction has appeared in: *The Thackery T. Lambshead Pocket Guide to Eccentric and Discredited Diseases, Lovecraft Unbound, Black Wings, Blood and Other Cravings, The Thackery T. Lambshead Cabinet of Curiosities, THE WEIRD, The Grimscribe's Puppets, LACKINGTON'S, Postscripts to Darkness, Penumbrae,* and *Aickman's Heirs,* among others. His scholarly work has appeared in *Lovecraft Studies, The Weird Fiction Review, Iranian Studies, Lovecraft and Influence,* and *The Lovecraftian Poe.* He has translated stories by Julio Cortazar, Marcel Bealu, and Alfonso Reyes.

Aliette de Bodard lives and works in Paris. She is the author of the critically acclaimed Obsidian and Blood trilogy of Aztec noir fantasies, as well as numerous short stories which have garnered her two Nebula Awards, a Locus Award and two British Science Fiction Association Awards. Her space opera books include *The Tea Master and the Detective*, a murder mystery set on a space station in a Vietnamese Galactic empire, inspired by the characters of Sherlock Holmes and Dr. Watson. Recent works include the Dominion of the Fallen series, set in a turn-of-the-century Paris devastated by a magical war, which comprises *The House of Shattered Wings* (Roc/Gollancz, 2015 British Science Fiction Association Award, Locus Award finalist), and its standalone sequel *The House of*

Binding Thorns (Ace, Gollancz). Visit http://www.aliettedebodard.com for more information.

Stephen Graham Jones is the author of sixteen novels, six story collections, and, so far, one comic book. Stephen's been an NEA recipient, has won the Texas Institute of Letters Award for Fiction, the Independent Publishers Award for Multicultural Fiction, a Bram Stoker Award, four This is Horror Awards, and he's been a finalist for the Shirley Jackson Award a few times. He's also made Bloody Disgusting's Top Ten Horror Novels. Stephen lives in Boulder, Colorado.

Sarah Hans is an award-winning writer, editor, and teacher. Her short stories have appeared in over twenty publications, but she's best known for the multicultural steampunk anthology *Steampunk World*, which appeared on io9, Boing Boing, Entertainment Weekly Online, and Humble Bundle, and also won the 2015 Steampunk Chronicle Reader's Choice Award for Best Fiction. You can read more of Sarah's short stories in the collection *Dead Girls Don't Love*, published by Dragon's Roost Press, or on her Patreon for just $1/month at https://www.patreon.com/sarahhans. You can also find her on twitter at https://twitter.com/steampunkpanda.

Kat Howard is a writer of fantasy, science fiction, and horror who lives and writes in New Hampshire. Her novella, *The End of the Sentence*, co-written with Maria Dahvana Headley, was one of NPR's best books of 2014, and her debut novel, *Roses and Rot* was a finalist for the Locus Award for Best First Novel. *An Unkindness of Magicians* was named a best book of 2017 by NPR, and won a 2018 Alex Award. Her short fiction collection, *A Cathedral of Myth and Bone*, will be released in September 2018, and collects work that has been nominated for the World Fantasy Award, performed as part of Selected Shorts, and anthologized in year's best and best of volumes, as well as new pieces original to the collection. She is currently writing *Books of Magic* for Vertigo Comics' Sandman Universe.

Tessa Kum used to work for the government, but got out. She still lives with fibromyalgia, and while hers is thankfully quite mild, her horizons are closer and the infrastructure of social support and welfare are not utopian. Her publication history is sporadic at best. She studies horticulture, keeps ornery little plants, and lives in Melbourne, Australia with a small, angry bird.

Mike Libby is a multi-disciplinary artist who makes sculptures, collages, and drawings using diverse materials, conceptual curiosity, and diligent craftsmanship. His work explores subjects of time, nature, memory, ecology, and autobiography via various hands-on fabrication methods specific to the pursuit of each work. He is largely known for INSECT LAB started in 1999, a sculptural series exploring natural history themes through the scale and subject of insects-gracefully retrofitting preserved specimens with mechanical hardware. Mike graduated from RISD with a degree in Sculpture in 1999, and has since attended the Vermont Studio Center, been artist-in-residence at the University of Maine at Orono, has exhibited through the Peabody Essex Museum, Philadelphia Museum of Art Craft Shows, Smithsonian and Society of Arts and Crafts in Boston, in private European galleries, at Robot Kingdom in Japan and in Australia through horticultural shop owners. Through Insect Lab he has worked with Neiman Marcus, Hasbro, Anthropologie, Edmund Scientific and Louis Vuitton as well as contributing content to The Steampunk Bible and book cover designs for Tachyon Publications, Hachette Publishing, Chronicle Books and an ongoing trophy design for the Science Fiction Writers of America, among other projects. His work is in collections worldwide. He works and lives in Southern Maine, biking, recycling and always making. You can view his work at: www.mikeplibby.com & www.insectlabstudio.com.

Nick Mamatas is the author of several novels, including *I Am Providence* and *Hexen Sabbath*. His short fiction has appeared in Best American Mystery Stories, Year's Best Science Fiction and Fantasy, and many other venues. Nick is also an anthologist; he co-edited the Bram Stoker Award-winning *Haunted Legends* with Ellen Datlow, the Locus Award nominee *Hanzi Japan* with Masumi Washington, and the hybrid cocktail recipe/fiction title *Mixed Up* with Molly Tanzer.

Jess Nevins is the author of numerous reference works on genre literature, including *The Encyclopedia of Fantastic Victoriana* (2005), *The Pulps* (2012), *The Evolution of the Costumed Avenger: The 4,000 Year History of the Superhero* (2017), *The Encyclopedia of Pulp Heroes* (2017), *Horror Needs No Passport: The History of International Horror Literature in the 20th Century* (2018), and *A Chilling Age of Horror: How 20th Century Horror Changed The Genre* (2020). When he pauses to catch his breath from writing, he is an academic librarian in suburban Houston.

An (pronounce it "On") Owomoyela is a neutrois author with a background in web development, linguistics, and weaving chain maille out of stainless steel fencing wire, whose fiction has appeared in a number of venues including *Clarkesworld*, *Asimov's*, *Lightspeed*, and a handful of Year's Bests. An's interests range from pulsars and Cepheid variables to gender studies and nonstandard pronouns, with a plethora of stops in-between. An can be found online at an.owomoyela.net .

Joseph S. Pulver, Sr. has been nominated for the World Fantasy Award and won the Shirley Jackson Award (*The Grimscribe's Puppets* 2013; editor for Superior Work in an Anthology). He was the 2017 recipient of the Robert Bloch Award at NecronomiCon Providence. His editorial work includes, *Walk on the Weird Side*, *A Season in Carcosa*, *The Grimscribe's Puppets*, *Cassilda's Song*, and *The Madness of Dr. Caligari* (which was nominated in 2017 for the Shirley Jackson Award, as editor). He has released four mixed-genre collections, a collection of King in Yellow tales, and two weird fiction novels. His fiction and poetry have appeared in many notable anthologies, including *Autumn Cthulhu*, *The Children of Old Leech*, Ellen Datlow's *The Year's Best Horror*, and *Best Weird Fiction of the Year*. His work has been praised by Thomas Ligotti, Laird Barron, Michael Cisco, Livia Llewellyn, Jeffery Thomas, Anna Tambour, and many other writers and editors. Joe can be found at: https://thisyellowmadness.wordpress.com.

Alistair Rennie is author of the novel, *BleakWarrior*, and has published fantasy, horror and SF fiction, essays and poetry in *The New Weird* anthology, *Weird Tales* magazine,

Electric Velocipede, Mythic Delirium, Pevnost, Weird Fiction Review, DOA III and more.

He is also creator of the dark ambient music project Ruptured World which released its first album, *Exoplanetary*, on the cinematic dark ambient music label Cryo Chamber in August 2018.

Rennie was born and grew up in the North of Scotland, has lived for ten years in Italy, and now lives in Edinburgh in the South of Scotland. He holds a first class Honours Degree in Literature from the University of Aberdeen and a PhD in Literature from the University of Edinburgh. He is a time-served Painter and Decorator and a veteran climber of numerous hills and mountains in the Western Highlands, the Cairngorms and the Italian Dolomites.

Delia Sherman's short stories have appeared in numerous anthologies and magazines, most recently in Ellen Datlow's *Mad Hatters and March Hares*, on Tor.com and in *Uncanny Magazine*. A collection of her early short fiction, *Young Woman in a Garden*, was published by Small Beer Press. When she's not writing, she's teaching, editing, knitting, and cooking. She is currently spending a year in Paris, working on a Huge Historical Novel, but her home base is a rambling apartment in New York City with spouse Ellen Kushner and far too many pieces of paper.

Molly Tanzer is the author of *Creatures of Will and Temper* and the forthcoming *Creatures of Want and Ruin*, out November 13, 2018. For more information about her critically acclaimed novels and short fiction, sign up for her newsletter at mollytanzer.com, or follow her @molly_the_tanz on Twitter or @molly_tanzer on Instagram.

Carrie Vaughn is best known for her New York Times bestselling series of novels about a werewolf named Kitty who hosts a talk radio show for the supernaturally disadvantaged. Her latest novels include a post-apocalyptic murder mystery, *Bannerless*, winner of the Philip K. Dick Award, and its sequel, *The Wild Dead*. She's written several other contemporary fantasy and young adult novels, as well as upwards of 80 short stories, two of which have been finalists for the Hugo Award. She's a contributor to the Wild Cards series of shared world superhero books edited by George R. R. Martin and a graduate of the Odyssey Fantasy Writing Workshop. An Air Force brat, she survived her nomadic childhood and managed to put down roots in Boulder, Colorado. Visit her at www.carrievaughn.com.

Caroline M. Yoachim is the author of over a hundred published short stories, appearing in *Lightspeed*, *Asimov's*, *Fantasy & Science Fiction*, *Clarkesworld*, and *Uncanny*, among other places. A Hugo and three time Nebula Award finalist, her work has been reprinted in multiple year's best anthologies and translated into Chinese, Spanish, and Czech. Caroline's debut short story collection, *Seven Wonders of a Once and Future World & Other Stories*, came out in 2016. For more about Caroline, check out her website at http://carolineyoachim.com

A drian Van Young is the author of *The Man Who Noticed Everything*, a collection of stories, and *Shadows in Summerland*, a novel. His fiction and nonfiction have appeared in such publications as *Lumina, The Collagist, Black Warrior Review, Conjunctions, Electric Literature's Recommended Reading, Slate, VICE, The Believer*, and *The New Yorker* online. He received a Henfield Foundation Prize and has twice been nominated for the Puschart. He holds an MFA in Creative Writing from Columbia University, and has taught writing at Columbia, Boston College, and Grub Street Writers, among others. Currently, he teaches creative writing at Tulane. He lives in New Orleans with his wife Darcy and son Sebastian.

About the Editors:

Selena Chambers writes fiction and non-fiction from the swampy depths of North Florida. Her most recent work has appeared in such publications as *Literary Hub*, *Luna Luna Magazine*, and *Beautiful Bizarre*, all with an emphasis on women creatives. She's been nominated for several awards including the Hugo and two World Fantasy awards. Her most recent book includes the mostly Historical Weird short story collection, *Calls for Submission* (Pelekinesis). Learn more at: www.selenachamebrs.com, on Twitter at @basbleuzombie.

Jason Heller is a Hugo Award-winning editor (formerly of *Clarkesworld Magazine*) and the author of the nonfiction book *Strange Stars: David Bowie, Pop Music, and the Decade Sci-Fi Exploded* (Melville House). He has also written about popular culture for *The New Yorker*, *The Atlantic*, *Rolling Stone*, *Entertainment Weekly*, *Pitchfork*, and NPR. With Josh Viola, he's the co-editor of the Hex Publishers anthology *Cyber World*. When not buried in words, Jason plays guitar in the post-punk band Weathered Statues. He lives in Denver.

Acknowledgments